A NURSE'S DUTY

A NURSE'S DUTY

A NURSE'S DUTY

Maggie Hope

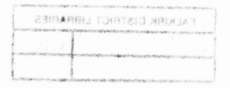
WINDSOR

PARAGON

First published as 'Under A Rowan
Tree' by Piatkus Books
This Large Print edition published 2012
by AudioGO Ltd
by arrangement with
Ebury Publishing

Hardcover   ISBN: 978 1 4713 1287 8
Softcover   ISBN: 978 1 4713 1288 5

British Library Cataloguing in Publication Data available

Printed and bound in Great Britain by
MPG Books Group Limited

Chapter One

'Now then, Rachel Knight,' said Gran, pushing open the bedroom door and striding into the room, 'what have you been up to?' She put her basket down on the highly polished mahogany table and removed her hat, sticking the enormous hatpin through the straw viciously before putting it beside the basket. 'By, I knew there was something the matter, I knew it in my bones this last few days but I couldn't get away any sooner. That daft lad I have on the farm is about as much use as a chap with no arms.'

'Hello, Gran,' said Karen, grinning with delight. She rushed up to the old lady and kissed the proffered cheek. She would have liked to give her gran a hug but knew that wasn't allowed.

'Oh, Mam,' said Rachel helplessly, and her voice was so small Karen gazed anxiously at the bed. Mam looked as though she was going to cry. Evidently Gran thought so too for she walked over to the bed and bent over her daughter, kissing her and patting her hand. When she sat down on the high bed her feet barely touched the mat, she was so tiny, but she wore a daunting air of authority.

'I knew there was something wrong,' she said again. 'Karen, go and put the kettle on, there's a good lass. I'm fair clemming for a cup of tea.'

Karen moved to the middle door which led to the kitchen but she hesitated to open it as she realized the doctor was still in the kitchen with Da. The doctor's voice rang out loud and clear and hateful.

1

'I'm afraid her heart's involved, Mr Knight,' he said. 'It's a flare up of rheumatic fever, of course. She must have had it as a child.'

Gran jumped off the bed and rushed to the door, flinging it wide.

'What did you say?' she demanded, her small, wiry body bristling. 'My Rachel certainly did *not* have a fever. She was never ill in her life—a few growing pains, that's all.'

Doctor Brown drew himself up in outrage and looked down his nose at the shabby woman who had interrupted him so rudely. He glanced at Da but he was looking stricken under the layer of coal dust which covered him all over for he had just come in from fore shift at the pit.

'Who is this person?' Doctor Brown asked at last, his plummy voice sounding strange, almost alien to Karen. Her ten-year-old heart swelled in resentment at this description of her lovely gran and she edged further into the kitchen so that she could stand beside her. But Gran needed no help in facing up to such a bit of a lad as this one, doctor though he may be.

'I'm the lass's mother, Mrs Jane Rain, that's who I am. And don't you talk as though I haven't a right to know what's wrong with my own bairn. I'm telling you, she never had a fever, not a bad one, not never.'

Doctor Brown pursed his lips. 'Well, Mrs Rain, as I was telling Mr Knight, your daughter most certainly has had rheumatic fever though it probably did seem as though she only had growing pains. To you, that is. A doctor would have diagnosed it differently.' With great deliberation, he turned his back on Jane.

2

'As I was saying, Mr Knight, her heart is involved. She will need plenty of rest and a good light diet. A month in bed for now, I'd say. I'll leave you a prescription for some tablets for her heart and a tonic.' He shook his head, frowning, as he pulled a prescription pad from his pocket and began to write. 'Poverty . . . poverty and ignorance. Bad feeding as a child, that's the usual cause. There's a lot of it around here. Lessons on nutrition are needed. Too much money is wasted, not enough spent on good wholesome food. One doesn't see half so much ill-health among the labouring poor of the south.'

'I fed my family right, as far as I was able,' snapped Gran. Standing beside her, Karen could feel her quivering with rage. She moved closer and took her hand but Gran shook her off. Clenching her fist, she stepped forward till she was almost under the doctor's nose.

'And what the hell do you know about it?' she demanded. 'You and your fancy airs. Who the hell are you?'

'Mother!'

Karen looked anxiously at her father. Gran had sworn, she had said the H-word, the word that was only ever said when it was being read out of the Bible. What would Da do to Gran for swearing?

'Well, I don't care, I don't give a d—' Gran faltered as she caught Da's eye and didn't quite finish the oath. She turned back to the doctor whose face had taken on an interesting mottled colour of red shading into white. 'You cannot be so fine and rich, else what would you be doing doctoring us poor mining folk? You're here for the fourpence a week we pay the panel. We're the

3

paymasters here, and don't you forget it.' She nodded her head vehemently and a stray wisp of hair fell from her topknot and across her eyes. Irritated, she pushed it back under a hairpin before opening her mouth to continue.

But Da had had enough. Grabbing her by the shoulders, he propelled her back into the front room and closed the door firmly, keeping his hand on the latch. Through the closed door, Karen could hear a foot being stamped and the muffled sound of Gran's voice.

'I'm sorry, Doctor,' he said. 'My wife's mother is a bit upset, like, she didn't mean to be rude. We are Christians in this house, we do not swear. Of course you must be right. You are the doctor after all. We'll do whatever you say.'

'Hmm!' said Doctor Brown, drawing on a pair of leather gloves with shaking hands and striding to the back door. Karen thought about reminding him that his pony and trap were standing in the front of the row but a look from Da silenced her as she opened her mouth. Likely he didn't want to go through the front room and face Gran again. Oh, well, he would only have to walk round the side of the Chapel to reach it, she thought.

'Will you be calling back, Doctor?' Da called after him as he went up the yard.

'I will,' he replied, and disappeared through the gate.

Da relaxed his grip on the latch of the middle door. He stood for a moment with his lips working and his eyes closed and Karen knew he was praying silently, or she thought he was praying though his fists were clenched at his sides. Then he opened his eyes and unlatched the door and

4

Karen's mouth dropped open once again for that was the first time she had ever seen him go into the front room black from the pit. She hesitated in the open doorway, not sure if she ought to follow him. In the end she stayed quietly where she was for she didn't want to be told to go out to play. If she did she would miss whatever Da was going to say to Gran and she didn't want to do that.

Gran was sitting by the bed looking almost as pale and wan as her daughter. Nevertheless, she glared defiantly at her son-in-law.

'Well, you didn't think I was going to let that mammy's boy talk like that to *me*, did you?' she asked.

Da glared back and Karen quailed for her. What would he do to punish Gran for swearing? she wondered. He couldn't make her go to every meeting at Chapel like he had done to Joe; Gran didn't go to their Chapel.

'I will not have swearing in my house,' Da said coldly. 'I know you are upset about Rachel but that is no excuse. The Lord dwells in this house.'

'Thomas,' said Mam, and her voice sounded so weak and thin that Karen could hardly hear it. Da changed his tone at once.

'I'm sorry, pet,' he said softly. 'An' I'm sorry if that fool of a doctor upset you an' all. But what's the good of arguing with them, they'll never understand anything, will they? You lie quiet and get some rest now.' He held his hand out to her and suddenly saw that it was still black and encrusted with coal dust. He looked quickly down to see if any had fallen on to the scrubbed floorboards or the clippie mat before retreating hurriedly to the kitchen.

'You shouldn't swear, Mam,' said Rachel.

'Nay, lass, I don't, you know that. I'm as good a Methodist as that man of yours anytime. But that pompous young ass got my goat, saying you weren't looked after properly when you was a bairn.'

'He didn't say that, not exactly,' said Rachel.

'Aye, well, he said something close to it,' Gran insisted. She looked up and noticed Karen standing by the door. 'Have you not put that kettle on yet, Karen?' she barked, and Karen darted into the kitchen where her sister Kezia was filling the zinc bath for Da to have his wash before the fire. The kettle was already on the fire and singing alongside a pan of broth.

'Gran wants a cup of tea,' said Karen.

Kezia nodded and paused in ladling hot water out of the boiler at the side of the fire to spoon tea into the pot and pour boiling water over it. Da stripped to the waist and knelt before the tub to wash while the girls carried two cups of tea into the front room. They were used to waiting in there while Da washed the lower half of his body. He would give them a shout when he was finished.

'It was necessary, Rachel, the men had to be fed first. It was them had to go out and find work when the lead mine closed, you know that. We would all have starved else.' She sighed. 'Eeh, but I was pleased when they got work in the pit here in Morton Main. Though I missed the dale, I did.'

'Here's your tea, Gran,' said Karen, holding out the cup, and Jane took it absently, her thoughts far away. Karen knew she was thinking of her lads, all gone now: one son taken in a fall of stone at the pit and the other with the lung rot. Gran had often

6

told her about them: the best workers in the county they had been, she often said.

Gran looked at her daughter, her eyes dark with pain. 'Maybe I could have done with less meself,' she murmured, 'though there was precious little for either of us.'

'Oh, Mam, it's not your fault. Don't start feeling guilty now,' said Rachel, moving her head restlessly on the pillow.

'I'm finished,' called Da from the kitchen and Gran jumped up, suddenly all brisk and businesslike. 'Now then, lasses, let's have our dinners. It seems like a week since I had me breakfast.'

After that, Gran started to come visiting more often, always landing on the doorstep unannounced, a basket in her hand with butter and eggs in it. She would fish her apron from the basket and tie it round her and by the time Karen and Joe came in from school at dinner time there would be a heavenly smell of meat pudding wafting down the yard and Gran would be standing at the table, thumping her fists into a batch of bread dough. Karen loved those days, for since the doctor had forbidden Mam to knead bread they had to make do with buying it from the store baker who came round with his cart every Tuesday and Thursday. And it just didn't taste like real bread.

There was the ordeal of having Gran wash her hair though, she thought ruefully. One Friday night the bath tin was out on the clippie mat before the fire and Gran was kneeling by it, rubbing soft soap into Joe's hair. He was twisting and turning, shrinking from the feel of her hard hands and fingers; his lips clamped tightly together

7

to stop himself from crying out loud for he was six now and a big boy.

'Sit still, will you?' said Gran, exasperated. 'I'll be finished in a minute. Fetch me a ladle of water to rinse it, Karen, and put a dash of vinegar in it.'

Karen rushed to do her bidding and Joe froze, his eyes tightly shut, while Gran poured the water over his head, catching his breath so that he stood up suddenly, coughing and spluttering.

'Your turn now, Karen,' said Gran, pulling a towel from the brass rail under the mantelpiece and wrapping it round Joe.

'I can do myself,' said Karen, but she didn't have much hope that she would be allowed to.

Why were Gran's hands so much harder than Mam's? she wondered, as tears were forced into her eyes under her grandmother's ministrations. Even on the occasions when Da had had to wash her hair it hadn't been quite so painful as this. And afterwards, when her hair was brushed and shining and Gran took the small-toothed nit comb down from the shelf and raked it through her hair over an old copy of the *Auckland Chronicle*, just in case she'd picked anything up from those mucky bairns down the row, Karen was sure the skin would be broken and bleeding. But the next minute it was all worth it for when they were all clean and in their nighties, sitting before the fire drinking cocoa, she heard Gran talking to Mam in the front room.

'I'll take the two little bairns up with me, while the school's out,' Gran said. 'Then it'll be easier for you. I'd take Kezia an' all but likely she's a good help to you here. Mind, if I was you I wouldn't let your Jemima get away with what she does. I mean, where is she the night? Out gallivanting, I bet. By, it's a good job your Thomas is on the night shift or he'd belt her for staying out so late. She's nigh on fifteen and it should have been her seeing to the bairns' bath night.'

Karen and Joe looked at each other, their eyes shining. They were going up to the farm, Gran's farm in Weardale, wasn't it grand?

'It's good of you, Mam,' they heard their mother say. 'If we have a bit of warm weather and there's not so much to do, likely I'll get my strength back. As to Jemima, you're right. I'll have to have a talk with her, that's all. But, you know, she's of an age when her friends are earning and she's tied to the house helping me. She's bound to feel a bit restless.'

Gran snorted but before she could retort the back door opened and Jemima rushed in, for once her face all radiant with eagerness.

'Mam!' she said, ignoring Karen and Joe and going straight into the front room. 'Mam, me and Kathy Taylor, we want to get a place. Look, there's an advertisement in the *Northern Echo*. Housemaids wanted in Manchester—£26 a year and all found.'

'Manchester? Don't be so daft, lass,' snapped Gran. 'What about your mam, the way she is? You're needed here, at home.'

'There's our Kezia,' said Jemima. 'She's big enough to help Mam. Why should it have to be me? Anyroad, it's for Mam to say, not you.'

'Don't you be cheeky to your gran!' said Mam, and Karen jumped in her chair, spilling a little cocoa down her nightie. For Mam's voice sounded louder and stronger than it had been for a long time.

9

'You've upset your mam now,' said Gran. 'Just you wait until your father gets in, he'll give you what for. Now leave your mother in peace while I get the bairns to bed. They have a long day tomorrow. They're coming up to the farm with me.'

'Please, Jesus,' breathed Karen as she knelt by the bed to say her prayers, 'make it so that Jemima can go away to place. And God bless Mam and make her better. And God bless Da and Gran and Kezia and Joe and me.'

She climbed into bed and lay waiting for Jemima to come. It was no use going to sleep now. Jemima would only pinch her awake to tell her all her complaints. When Jemima was in a bad mood she always did that.

'Are you asleep?' asked Joe from behind the blanket which was slung on a rope down the middle of the room to afford the girls some privacy.

'No, not yet,' answered Karen.

'It's going to be grand up on the fell, isn't it?'

'It is that.'

'I can't go to sleep, Karen, tell us a story.'

'All right.' Karen turned on her back and launched into the story of the Lambton Worm, a favourite of Joe's. 'Once upon a time, Lord Lambton's son caught a fish in the Wear. But it wasn't like any other fish he'd ever seen before . . .'

'No, it was great big long worm with goggly eyes an' great big teeth and so Lambton tossed it down a well,' said Joe.

'Well, if you want to tell me the story, you can,' said Karen.

'No, tell me. Tell me how he went to the foreign

10

war and while he was away it growed and growed and growed—'

'Will you two go to sleep?' demanded Gran from the bottom of the stairs. 'Mind, if I hear another peep out of you I won't take you back with me the morn.'

The threat was enough for both of them and they soon settled down to sleep and this time Karen's fears were unfounded for she didn't even wake when Jemima came to bed.

*   *   *

Karen's heart sang as she turned down the track to Low Rigg Farm and saw the rowan tree standing by the gate. It always came into view first and she watched out for it. She breathed deeply of the moorland air. It was so fresh and tangy, not like the air in Morton Main which was thick with the smell of the cokeworks, sulphurous and heavy and overlaid with the stink of the middens lining every back row. Even the muck heap by the barn smelled better than that, she decided.

'The rowan berries will soon be ready. You can help me make jelly,' said Gran. 'You can pick the wild raspberries in the ghyllie an' all. Oh, aye, you two are going to be a grand help to me.'

And they were. They picked pounds and pounds of the wild fruit and helped Albert, the orphan boy from Durham, look after Posy the cow and Daisy the Dales pony.

'Daisy's not a bit like a pit pony,' said Joe, searching in his pocket for the crust he had secreted from breakfast. He found it at last and held it out to her, and though there were bits of

11

fluff stuck to it she didn't turn her nose up at it but delicately took it from his fingers and munched contentedly.

'Well, she's too big for the pits anyroad, she's bred to work on the fell,' said Albert. He was a big-boned lad of about fifteen and already he was putting on the stature of a man. Joe idolized him and followed him about all day. 'I'm going up the high moor to check on the sheep later on,' Albert went on. 'Does you want to come?'

'Eeh, yes, Albert, that I do,' cried Joe, his eyes lighting up.

'Right then, better ask your gran.'

Joe raced into the kitchen where Karen was kneeling on a stool by the table helping Gran roll out suet pastry for the pot pie which they were going to have for dinner.

'Can I go up the high moor with Albert later on? Can I, Gran?' he asked, his brow knitted in anxiety in case she said no. But Gran nodded.

'You can both go, Karen an' all. It'll do you good, blow the cobwebs away. You can take some sandwiches and a bottle of water for a picnic tea.'

After dinner they set out, Karen carrying the basket and the two boys with crooks, Joe's almost twice his height. But he carefully watched Albert and tried to hold his crook just the same way though more than once he stumbled and almost tripped himself up with the unwieldy stick. But Karen was lost to everything but the moor stretching away above and below and all around them, for miles and miles. She watched the sheep skipping away at their approach, the lambs almost as big as the ewes now it was August. She laughed aloud at the cock pheasant which started up

12

almost under her feet with a flash of rainbow colours, and the hen birds, dowdy and fluttering, in the brilliant purple of the heather.

They reached a good spot for a picnic and Albert went off to check on the sheep which didn't take him long for Gran's stint on the moor didn't allow for many animals. And then they settled down to their picnic though it was little more than two hours since they had eaten the pot pie. Karen gazed about her, looking for the lone curlew which was calling out persistently but she didn't see it until Joe pointed it out. It must have some chicks close by, she thought. Its cry was so plaintive yet so throbbingly beautiful, it made her heart ache somehow.

'I wish we lived here all the time,' she sighed, and Joe looked surprised.

'But you'd want Mam and Da, wouldn't you?'

For a moment, Karen's happiness dimmed as she thought about her mother and father. 'Yes,' she admitted. 'But they could come and live here with us, couldn't they?' Yet she knew it was only a dream. There were no coal mines this high in Weardale so where would Da get work?

Chapter Two

'Jemima's gone away to work in Manchester,' said Kezia. 'I'm leaving school at Christmas anyroad. And mind, our Karen, you'll have to help me as much as you can till then, run the messages and such and do what I say.'

Karen and Joe were back in Morton Main for

13

the new school year. Karen gazed at her elder sister but she was too miserable at leaving Low Rigg Farm and her gran to bother complaining about Kezia's being so bossy.

'Now, Kezia,' laughed Mam, 'I think you'll both still be doing what I say. I'm still the gaffer here and I'm not completely useless yet.'

That was the nice thing about coming home though, thought Karen. Mam was looking and feeling better. She felt the lightness in the air. The house itself was brighter somehow, because Mam was better.

'Thank you God, for making Mam well again,' she whispered the next day, which happened to be a Sunday. She was sitting in Sunday School with the other girls in her class and Mr Dent, the Sunday School superintendent, was praying aloud in front of the crowded room and the children were sitting with their hands together and their eyes closed. Karen's thoughts began to wander as the prayers went on and she cautiously opened her eyes and squinted through her lashes at the boys' benches, across the aisle.

Robert Richardson was there, his head bowed in reverence. He was the son of the Minister and Karen supposed all his thoughts must be pious. Idly, she studied him. He sat next to Joe who was swinging his legs backwards and forwards impatiently though Robert seemed oblivious of it.

'In the name of our Lord, Jesus Christ,' said Mr Dent. 'Amen.' Everyone shuffled about and sat up and Mr Dent launched into the Old Testament reading and followed up with his sermon. He was talking about the trials of Job.

'Job was a just man and true yet many

14

misfortunes and calamities fell on him. But Job submitted himself to the Lord and God magnified and blessed Job. And we have to remember the story of Job when our way is hard and everything is going wrong, we have to trust in the Lord as he did and the Lord will help us in our troubles.' Mr Dent paused and turned the page of his Bible and began to read. Karen sat listening to the drone of his voice, waves of sleepiness threatening to overwhelm her. But she sat up, suddenly awake, as she heard the words of the text which hung on the wall at home.

'". . . He had also seven sons and three daughters. And he called the name of the first Jemima, and the name of the second Kezia, and the name of the third, Keren-happuch. And in all the land were no women found so fair . . ."'

Karen smiled, thinking of the many times Da had sat her on his knee and quoted the text. But when she looked up she saw Dave Mitchell and his friends nudging each other and grinning at her. She scowled fiercely at him. She didn't like Dave Mitchell, he was a big boy and a bully. And when Sunday School was over and she came out with the other girls, she wasn't surprised that Dave and his friends were waiting for her.

'Keren-happuch, Keren-happuch! Is that your proper name, then? Does your da think he's Job?'

'Leave me alone!' Karen shouted at them, her dark eyes snapping with anger. 'My name is Karen, you know it is.' Her father had changed the spelling of her name to the more usual Karen, but it was from the Book of Job that she'd got her name.

'Go on then, make us leave you alone,' said

15

Dave. 'Or mebbe you can get your seven brothers to chase us off, Keren-happuch.' The crowd of lads began to jeer and Karen bunched her fists in frustration.

'Leave our Karen alone!' cried Joe, running up and aiming a punch at Dave, but Dave easily held him off with one hand and slapped him with the other. He was at least a head taller than Joe and the younger boy was no match for him.

'Hey, there, stop that!'

Robert Richardson came out and strode up to the two boys, pulling Dave away from Joe and putting the younger boy behind him. Karen felt a surge of gratitude to him for sticking up for her and Joe.

'Aw, go on, what're you going to do about it?' asked Dave. 'You're a proper pansy. You won't fight on a Sunday, your da wouldn't like it.'

He planted his feet apart and grinned. 'Go on then, hit me, go on,' he jeered, and behind him his friends snickered. Karen's temper rose and spilled over. She rushed forward and kicked Dave hard on the shins, the steel toe protectors on her boots drawing blood so that he stepped back and shouted in surprise at the pain. Before he could recover himself, Kezia rushed up and grabbed Karen and Joe and darted into the yard of their house with them.

'It's lucky for you we live so close to the Chapel,' she said grimly to them. 'An' don't you let Da know you've been fighting on a Sunday or you'll get a belting. It would serve you both right, I reckon, but I won't have Mam upset, do you hear?'

Karen was still shaking with rage at the way Dave had held Joe and hit him and the way he had

16

spoken to Robert, but she saw the sense of what Kezia was saying. She closed her eyes tight and tried to force herself to calm down.

'Mind, hey, your sister has some spunk, hasn't she?' said Dave. His tone was admiring and Karen opened her eyes to see he was watching her and Joe over the yard gate.

'Go away!' she shouted at the top of her voice and marched into the house closely followed by Joe, who banged the door shut behind him. Only later, after they had eaten the dinner of roast beef and Yorkshire pudding and vegetables which Da had grown in the allotment down the road, did she remember Robert. Had he got away without having to fight? She felt a momentary pang of guilt at not checking he got home all right. Oh, well, she would thank him properly when she went to the evening service, she thought. But for some reason he wasn't at the service and eventually she forgot about the incident.

*   *   *

'Karen is a very bright girl,' said Miss Nelson, and Karen squirmed in her seat on the sofa. The horsehair cover was prickling through the thin cotton of her dress and petticoat but she daren't scratch the place, not when they had the headmistress visiting. It was the last week of the summer term and Miss Nelson was there to persuade her parents to allow her to stay on as a pupil teacher. The headmistress put her cup, a delicate, china cup with roses painted round the bowl which was one of the precious set Mam kept for important visitors, on its matching saucer and

17

placed them on the table. She looked earnestly at Thomas and Rachel Knight. 'It would be a shame if she had to leave school and go into domestic service. It would be an absolute waste of a good brain.'

Karen waited, holding her breath. Until now she hadn't let herself even consider the possibility of being allowed to stay on at school, though she had dreamed of being a teacher. She saw her father glance at Mam but she couldn't tell what they were thinking.

Oh, yes, please God, put it in Da's mind, let me be a teacher, she prayed, desperately trying to will him into agreeing. But her father still didn't say anything.

'Well,' Miss Nelson pulled on her gloves and rose to her feet, 'I'll leave you to discuss it. I'm sure you will do what is best for Karen.'

Karen jumped up and accompanied her to the door leading directly out to the front of the row. Miss Nelson paused in the doorway and looked round. 'Goodbye, then.'

'Goodbye, Miss Nelson,' echoed the family in unison, almost as Karen's class would do in school.

After she had gone, Karen looked anxiously round. Da was pursing his lips thoughtfully and Joe was grinning at her in delight.

'Clever clogs! Clever clogs!' he shouted, and Jemima, who was home for a week's holiday from her job in Manchester and looking very smart and grown-up, burst into angry speech.

'Why should she stay on at school? Me and our Kezia never had the chance. It's not fair.'

'Eeh, I don't mind,' said Kezia. She was eighteen now, courting Luke Nesbitt and saving hard for

18

her bottom drawer.

'I had to go away to Manchester when I was only fifteen,' said Jemima. 'And Kezia has had to work in the manager's house and help Mam. Why should our Karen have it easier?'

'Jemima, you wanted to go to place,' put in Mam gently.

'Only so that I could see a bit of life and not be tied in the house all day. And anyroad, I've been able to send a bit home, haven't I?' Once, and it was when Jemima got her first pay, Karen remembered, she had sent five shillings home.

'You're jealous, Jemima,' observed Joe. She rounded on him and clipped his ear with the back of her hand, her face suffused red with anger. Da stepped forward and towered over her, his hand raised.

'That's enough, Jemima! I'm ashamed of you. Now keep quiet or I swear I'll take the belt to you, big as you are. Sit down and keep quiet, do you hear?'

The whole family, including Jemima, sat still and gazed at him. Karen could only remember one or two occasions when Da had raised his voice in the house but when he did everyone sat quiet and listened to him. Once everyone was silent, Da sat back down in his chair and looked at Karen and she could tell by the pity in his eyes that any hope she had had of becoming a teacher was gone.

'You know how we are held, pet,' he said. 'You're old enough to know the pits aren't doing so well. You know we can't afford to keep you on at school, feeding and clothing you and buying books and things and you bringing nothing in. And though Jemima shouldn't have said what she did, it's true—she took her turn in helping your mother and so has Kezia. It's Kezia's time to do something different now, you know it is.'

'I'm all right, Da,' said Kezia, and he smiled at her.

'Aye, pet, I know you are, you're a good lass, a proper blessing from God. But you are courting Luke and you will be wanting to get married afore long. And why not? It's only natural.' He sat silent for a few minutes while he lifted a glowing coal from the fire with the steel fire tongs and lit his pipe. When he had the pipe going to his satisfaction he sat back in his chair. 'Well, Rachel, what do you have to say?'

'I'm sorry, lass, but your da's right,' she answered. 'I'm that proud of you doing so well though.'

Karen sat on the horsehair sofa, no longer feeling the hard prickle of the hair through her skirt. All she could think of was her crushing disappointment. Her eyes ached with unshed tears and there was a lump in her throat which felt as big as an apple.

'I do believe she's going to cry, the big babby,' remarked Jemima, and Karen's head jerked up.

'I'm not. I was only thinking,' she declared. 'I didn't want to be a teacher anyroad.'

Da looked keenly across the smoke billowing out of his pipe at her. 'Lies are an abomination before God,' he said. But he spoke gently, not exactly accusing her of lying.

'No, I mean it,' Karen said quickly. 'I'll leave school and see if I can get a morning job in Auckland. Then I can help Mam in the afternoons and study to better myself at night.'

20

'Mind,' said Jemima, smiling smugly now her views had prevailed, 'you're going to be the busy one, aren't you? And don't tell us you didn't want to be a teacher, 'cos it's a lie, all right.'

'I'm not lying,' said Karen, and even as she said it she realized it was true. 'I want to be a nurse.'

'A nurse? You mean you want to work in the workhouse hospital at Bishop Auckland?' asked Kezia, sounding very surprised.

'No, a proper trained nurse,' said Karen. 'We learned about it at school. All about Florence Nightingale and how she started training nurses and they went out to the war in Russia and that. And now all the big hospitals train nurses. Hospitals like the County Hospital at Durham and the Cameron at Hartlepool.'

Miss Nelson had told them the story of the Nightingale nurses only last week, but this was the first time Karen had even thought of trying to become one. But she wasn't going to let Jemima know how disappointed she was at not being able to be a teacher. No, she was not, she told herself. Mam interrupted her thoughts.

'Mind, Karen, nurses have to do some dirty jobs. Emptying chamber pots and the like. Are you sure you want to do that?'

Karen nodded her head with enthusiasm. The more she thought of it the more she wanted to do it. She felt like going after Miss Nelson that very minute to see if the teacher knew how she should go about being a nurse. 'I can do it, Mam,' she said.

Jemima laughed. 'Oh, aye? Well, we'll just see if you do,' she said, and Karen's resolve hardened further. She jumped to her feet.

21

'I'll go and see Miss Nelson now,' she said. 'She will tell me what to do.'

It was harder than she had thought it would be but she was determined to succeed and Miss Nelson helped her. For the County Hospital in Durham insisted that only girls with a matriculation certificate would be considered. Karen went to bed each evening with her head buzzing with French irregular verbs and in her nightmares she wandered through a maze of mathematics. Then there was the walk to the hospital in Bishop Auckland and a mountain of work awaiting her in the hospital kitchen where she had secured a part-time job.

Praise the Lord for Sundays, she thought to herself one Sunday afternoon. Da didn't allow studying of anything but the Bible on the Sabbath and no housework was done. And praise the Lord she was almost at the end of her studies. Soon she would be able to apply for a place as a probationer. She was sitting quietly, ignoring the whispers of the others, but all of a sudden she noticed that the noise had grown louder and they were looking over to the boys sitting on the opposite side. It was Robert Richardson they were all looking at, she saw. The Minister's son was just taking a seat beside Joe.

Karen watched him. He didn't usually attend the Chapel in Morton Main these days, but today his father was to preach. All the girls, apart from Kezia who was courting Luke Nesbitt, were watching Robert, and trying to attract his attention, he was so tall and good-looking and distinguished. And when he walked out to the lectern and read the lesson for his father, he looked so gravely handsome that there was not so much as the rustle of a sweetpaper from the girls and Karen watched him as hard as any of them. Why, she thought, he must be twenty years old by now. Hadn't Da said he was going for a doctor? Well, she wasn't going to be such a fool as to make sheep's eyes at him, she decided. She hadn't time for lads, not even those who were training to be doctors. Anyroad, doctors didn't go out with pit lasses, she knew that, even if she had been interested in him.

'By, that Robert Richardson is a bonny lad, isn't he?' Kezia's friend, May Thompson, was saying as the group of girls paused outside the Chapel after the meeting. The girls always stood for a few minutes by the Chapel railings, watching the boys who were standing across the road, laughing and talking together. Both groups were very busy pretending not to notice each other, laughing just a bit too loudly at their mates' jokes and glancing across the street and catching the eyes of the girls, quite accidentally of course.

Not Robert of course. He was in the vestry with his father and the Chapel steward. In any case, Robert, at twenty, was far too old to hang about outside the Chapel. Not that he ever had done, thought Karen, grinning to herself at the idea. Robert had been a serious boy, always by himself if his father wasn't around and always teased by the other boys.

'He is nice-looking,' Kezia said judiciously.

'But not as nice-looking as your Luke, eh?' laughed Karen as Luke detached himself from the boys and came over to claim Kezia for their regular walk. This was what usually happened; the courting couples gradually paired off for a walk and the unattached eyed each other surreptitiously before reluctantly walking home on their own.

'Not as nice-looking as me either, is he, Karen?'

She spun round in surprise. Dave Mitchell had crossed the road and was standing before her. Behind her she could hear the other girls tittering.

'Whoever said you were good-looking needs a pair of glasses, Dave Mitchell,' she retorted, drawing herself up and glaring disdainfully at him. Dave was not put off.

'Aw, go on, I know you like me really,' he said, grinning all over his freckled face. 'Howay, lass, come for a walk with me up the lane.'

Karen studied him haughtily. He didn't seem in the least put out by her remark. 'I'm walking up no lane with you,' she said at last, and set off for home. As that was the house next to the Chapel she had only a few steps to go but when she opened the gate and turned to fasten the latch after her, she found she was staring straight into his blue eyes.

'Dave Mitchell,' she snapped, 'will you leave me alone or have I to fetch my father?'

'You da's not in yet though, is he?' said Dave, grinning. 'And your Joe's gone down the dene with his mates. Come on, Karen. I crossed the road for you after Chapel, didn't I? You know that means I'm serious about you.'

'Maybe you are,' she said, 'but I'm not. I haven't got time to go out with lads, I'm going to be a nurse.' Without more ado, she walked off into the house without looking back.

'Who was that you were talking to?' her mother asked as she hung her hat up on the row of hooks under the stairs.

'Nobody special,' Karen answered, but Rachel noted the colour in her normally pale face and her curiosity deepened though she said no more.

Casually, Karen glanced out of the window before putting the kettle on for tea. No one was looking over the back gate, the row looked deserted. Maybe Dave Mitchell had at last got it into his thick head that she didn't want to go with him, she told herself, but strangely she felt a little flat as she got out the Sunday table cloth and set the table for tea.

*　　*　　*

It was May when Karen travelled to Durham to sit her matriculation examinations. She fingered the piece of coal in her skirt pocket. Joe had dug it up specially for her to bring her luck. Taking it out, she gazed at the outline of an oakleaf, miraculously preserved from eons ago in the black coalforest beneath their feet.

'A black diamond, it is,' Joe had said.

'Karen, you know what the good Book says about superstition,' Da had warned, frowning heavily. 'If it be the Lord's will that you should pass then you will, without the help of a dead lump of coal.'

'Yes, Da,' said Karen meekly. But all the same she wrapped the coal up carefully and put it in her skirt pocket. It might not bring her good luck but on the other hand it might and she didn't think that God was so mean-minded as to penalize her for thinking it.

The week of the examinations went off in a blur

25

of nervousness and work, so that she did not even notice that the other girls looked at her askance, so obviously a pitman's daughter in her black serge skirt and cheap shirtwaister and with her hands so red and roughened with the scrubbing in the workhouse kitchen for some extra pennies. But then came the weeks of waiting for the results, when, for the first time in years, Karen had a little spare time after the flurry of excitement caused by Kezia marrying her Luke.

'Why don't you go walking with Dave?' Kezia asked her one Sunday afternoon after Chapel. 'Goodness knows, he asks you often enough. You should get out more, Karen, and going for a walk with a chap doesn't mean you have to marry him.' Though in Kezia's case, it had meant that which made Karen smile. They were standing with Rachel by the back gate for a few moments, enjoying a chat in the summer sunshine before Kezia went on to her own house with Luke.

Karen went pink. 'Don't be daft, our Kezia,' she said, keeping her voice low, for Dave was still standing on the opposite side of the road with his friends. But she looked sideways at him as he laughed at something his friend said. He was so tall and handsome in his Sunday suit and highly polished boots and with his sandy hair glinting golden in the August sun. As she watched he detached himself from the group and came over to ask her to walk with him as he had done so many times before, or so she thought, as she got ready to say no yet again.

'Hello, Mrs Knight,' said Dave, nodding to the girls, and went whistling off down the row.

'He's fed up with asking, Karen,' said Kezia after

a moment.

'A good thing too,' she snapped, opening the gate and starting up the yard. 'I was sick of him asking an' all.' Rachel and Kezia looked at one another and smiled, both knowing that Dave was trying a new approach.

* * *

'Dave Mitchell was in the queue for the Eden Theatre with a lass,' commented Joe the following Saturday evening as he sat down to supper. He had just returned from Auckland where he had spent the afternoon and early evening. Karen didn't falter as she placed a plate of baked cow heel and onions before him and cut him a round of bread. Joe glanced up at her.

'I said—'

'I know what you said, Joe,' she said quickly. 'It matters nothing to me what Dave Mitchell does. Anyroad, what were you doing in the queue for the music hall? You'll catch it from Da if he finds out.'

'Aw, we didn't go in,' said Joe easily. 'We were just looking at the posters outside.'

Karen gave him a sceptical glance but she said no more. Instead she poured herself a cup of tea and sat down at the table beside her brother, sighing. For some reason she felt restless and dissatisfied with her life and she couldn't imagine why. Well, she thought wearily, tomorrow was her turn to work even though it was a Sunday and she had better go to bed or she would never get up in time for the walk in to Bishop Auckland. Saying goodnight, she went up the narrow, ladder-like stairs to bed. Only one more week before the

27

results came out.

But thoughts of her examination results were driven from her head as she walked back through the fields the following afternoon, for as she drew near to Morton Main she could hear the mournful sound of the colliery hooter. Karen broke into a run, her heart pounding and her throat dry. Oh, how she hated the sound, so different from the one which signalled the start of a new shift in the mine. This one was only blown when something had happened in the pit. Her steps slowed to a walk as she realized this was Sunday. How could there have been an accident when it was Sunday and the pit was idle? Only maintenance men went down the pit on Sundays.

As she rounded the corner of the row she saw that the usual knots of boys and girls loitering outside the Chapel were missing. Only a few housewives stood at their gates, talking quietly to each other.

'What's it? What's happened?' she asked breathlessly as she went in the house. There was only her mother there, sitting before the fire in spite of the heat of the day.

'I don't know what it is,' answered Rachel. 'Your father and Joe have gone to the pit yard to see if there's anything they can do. It has to be a maintenance man, there's nobody else in today.'

The women got the full story when the men returned. Both Da and Joe looked grim and tired. Michael Mitchell, a maintenance man and father of Dave, had been checking on reported movement in the rock strata above a thin coal seam when a wooden pit prop buckled and broke and a large stone fell on his head, killing him

28

instantly.

'Eeh, poor man,' sighed Rachel, shaking her head sorrowfully. 'I feel for Mrs Mitchell an' all. It's a good job she has Dave still at home.'

'Aye, well, I suppose it means she won't have to move out of the colliery house at least, not when Dave's a hewer,' Da agreed. 'Now, I think we'll say a prayer for the poor widow and the lad.'

Obediently the family fell to their knees and bowed their heads.

'Dear Father,' cried Da, lifting his head up to the white-washed ceiling as though he could see through his closed eyes and the ceiling and through the slate roof of the house to the heavens beyond, 'we ask you to give comfort to your servants, Millie Mitchell and her son, David. Be with them in their affliction, oh God, help them to know that their loved one has gone to a happier place where there is no pain or sorrow. We are assured that our brother Mitchell is with you now in glory, dear Lord, but we ask that you lay your hand on his family and give them peace. We ask it through Jesus Christ, our Lord and Saviour. Amen.'

Da got slowly to his feet and helped Mam up also. 'We brought him home on the flat cart, Rachel,' he said to his wife. 'No doubt you and Karen will be going to pay your respects after tea.'

Karen put the kettle on to boil and set the table. No one spoke. Even Joe was sitting grim-faced, staring at the fire. But when they sat down to tea, he broke his silence.

'We said that seam needed more supports, Da, the deputy told the under manager. Now there's a man dead.'

'Joe, we don't talk about work on a Sunday.' In spite of the tragedy which had happened that day, Thomas Knight was not about to relax his strict observance of the Sabbath any more than he had had to do already.

'But what if it had been tomorrow instead of today?' demanded Joe. 'That seam's nobbut two and a half feet high. That stone could have brought more down with it and blocked men behind it and then there would have been—'

'Joe! I said we won't talk about it today,' said Da, and he reached for the sugar bowl and spooned sugar into his pint pot of tea. 'I have a meeting to go to the night, over at Coundon. I would like some peace and quiet to think about it.'

Joe subsided into his seat and stared at his plate and Karen gazed at him with a new terror in her heart. Oh, she knew there was always danger in the pits but from the way Joe had shown he was familiar with the coal seam in question, she realized that he must work in it, or at least near it. She shivered at the thought that it might have been him or Da brought home on a cart and was flooded with a profound sympathy for Dave Mitchell and his mother. When she and her mother paid their sympathy visit that evening, she saw a different Dave altogether from the one she knew. His blue eyes were red and his shoulders bowed with emotion as he sat in a corner, taking little notice of anything. Karen went up to him and put her hand on his arm.

'I'm sorry, Dave,' she whispered. He looked down at her hand for a moment and covered it with his own but he did not speak and she could see he was too full of sorrow. Karen looked at his

30

mother who was sitting by the table, already dressed in black. She was dry-eyed and her face seemed more angry than sorrowful to Karen. Her lips were clamped tightly together and her pale eyes full of ire. Karen breathed a sigh of relief when her mother deemed they had been there long enough and they went out into the fresh air of the street.

The following week, Karen got her results and they were all she had hoped for. She had matriculated with credit in all subjects, even French. The first thing she did was to go into Bishop Auckland to Miss Nelson's house, for it was still the summer holidays and the school was closed.

'I did it! And all because of you. Oh, thank you, thank you,' she cried as the teacher opened the door to her. Miss Nelson's face creased into a wide smile of delight.

'I knew you would,' she said, though in truth she had been worrying about it all summer. They celebrated by going to the cafe in the Co-op store for tea and cream buns.

'My treat,' said Miss Nelson, 'you are going to need all the money you can save. Probationer nurses are not well paid, as I have told you before.'

'Do you think I will get into a training school now?' asked Karen, suddenly doubtful, and Miss Nelson smiled.

'I don't see why not. You've earned a place, I would say.'

Karen cut her cream bun in half and spread strawberry jam from a fancy glass dish on it. 'Jam and cream an' all,' she said softly.

'What?'

'Oh, nothing. It's just something my gran always says when we want something out of our reach. "You want your jam and cream an' all", she says.'

'Well, why not?' demanded Miss Nelson, and Karen went home light-hearted and full of anticipation of the future.

*   *   *

'It's because I come from a pit village,' she said dismally. The euphoria of her examination results had soon fallen flat when she began to receive rejections from one hospital after another. She was sitting at the kitchen table one Wednesday afternoon. All the way home from work her heart beat painfully in her chest for she was waiting for a letter from Newcastle Royal Victoria Infirmary saying whether she had been accepted for training. She had played the game she and Joe had played years ago, adding up the numbers on her horse bus ticket and dividing them by the lucky number, seven. If the result was nothing remaining, then her wish would come true but if there was only one left over then it would not. But the total had divided evenly and when she saw the letter propped up on the sewing machine cover under the window she had been so sure it was good news.

Da would think it served me right for being superstitious, she thought numbly, gazing at the curt message on the sheet of paper.

'Well, what does it say?' asked Mam eagerly, and Karen looked up.

'I didn't want to go as far as Newcastle anyroad,' she said, throwing the letter down on the table.

Karen had been trying for over a year to get into

32

a nursing school and was running out of hospitals to try.

'Look, pet,' said Rachel, 'I think you'll just have to settle for something a bit lower. You know Oaklands said they would take you on as an assistant nurse. Why don't you take that? You'd be able to get home, mebbe even live at home. I know we'll be all right with our Kezia living up the street but it would be nice if you were close by, wouldn't it?'

'I don't want to be an assistant nurse. That's not what I've worked for all these years, and certainly not in a workhouse hospital. I want to be in a *big* hospital,' Karen answered, close to tears. She clasped her hands tightly together, frustration and anger building up inside of her.

'I know you've worked hard, and you've done real well, you have, Karen,' said Rachel, her face twisting in sympathy with her daughter's pain.

'And I know why it is no one will take me,' said Karen savagely. 'It's always the same when I go for the interviews. "And what does your father do, Miss Knight?" And when I tell them he's a miner they look at me and down at my matriculation certificate as though they think it must be forged. They think pitmen are ignorant savages, that's what it is.'

Rachel was distressed. 'Nay, lass, you're wrong. I know some folk think like that but it's the twentieth century now, things are different from the way they used to be.' She clutched a hand to her chest and sat down quickly, a sweat breaking out on her pale face. Stricken, Karen rushed to her side, her own troubles forgotten.

'Oh, Mam, I'm sorry. I shouldn't upset you with

33

my problems, none of this is your fault. Are you feeling badly? Shall I get you your pills? A glass of water? Howay, now, come and have a lie-down on your bed for a while.' Karen put her arm round her mother's thin shoulders, ready to help her into the front room, but Rachel shook her head.

'No, I'll be fine here, pet. I just felt unwell for a minute, I'm all right now. Just get some water, eh?'

Karen ran into the pantry where the pail of water she had just brought in from the pump on the end of the row was kept. She poured a dipper of water into a glass and took it to her mother. While Rachel drank it, Karen watched her surreptitiously, alert to the danger of her mother slipping into a faint—something which happened too often lately. But no, Rachel's faint colour was returning to her cheeks, she was looking better already.

'Don't mention this little bad spell to your father,' she whispered urgently as they heard the click of the latch on the back yard gate. 'It's nothing, I'm feeling grand now.'

Da and Joe came in from the pit and then Karen was busy for a while, filling the zinc bath for them and setting out their meal. Afterwards, when she had a little time to herself, she put on her old shawl and told them she was going for a walk.

'Just to get a breath of air.'

'Well, don't be late, mind,' said Da. 'The nights are drawing in and I don't want you wandering about the fields in the dark.'

'I won't, Da.'

Karen walked to the end of the rows and on, past the colliery yard to the fields beyond, away from the stink of the coke works. Though it was a fine,

34

sunny evening, September was already half over and at this end of the country, autumn was beginning to turn the leaves and a sharp breeze was blowing from the north. Karen wrapped her woollen shawl closer round her shoulders and walked on as the road turned into a rutted country lane. Idly, she looked into a farmyard and saw the farmer herding the last of his cows into the byre. She paused for a moment, the smell reminding her of Weardale and her grandmother's small-holding on the moor. For a moment she felt a longing for the old place and Gran. But it was a working day tomorrow, she didn't have the time for a visit to Low Rigg Farm.

It was as she was walking back in the gathering twilight that she met David Mitchell just coming out of the corner shop with a packet of cigarettes in his hand.

'Hallo, Karen,' he said, falling into step with her. 'If I'd known you were out walking I would have come with you.'

She did not give him a tart reply as she might have done before the death of his father the year before, for she had seen him vulnerable and filled with a natural grief that day and it had softened her view of him. Still, she had refused to go out with him whenever he asked her for her mind was full of her ambitions and she couldn't think of anything else. Until now, that is. Today her ambitions had all come to nothing. She would never get a place on a training course at a big hospital; what was the use of trying any more? She felt worthless and humiliated and so Dave's attentions were balm to her soul.

'That would have been nice,' she said, and Dave

35

stopped walking in astonishment.

'Do you mean it?'

She turned to face him. Though now it was almost dark she could see little of his expression. But there was his outline against the darkening sky, large and strong-seeming, his cap pushed to the back of his head so that the brim made a kind of halo above him.

'I do,' she said, and moved out of the way for the lamp-lighter, plodding from lamp to lamp with his long pole. Dave bent his head to hers and she closed her eyes as he touched her closed mouth with his. Something trembled within her, disturbing her.

'I have to go now, Da doesn't like me to be out in the dark on my own,' she murmured. There was the hiss of gas as the lamp-lighter touched the end of his pole to the gas jet in the lamp and she saw Dave's face properly. He was gazing down at her, his expression triumphant.

'You're my girl now,' he said, and took her arm and held it over his. He walked with her to her gate and paused, his arm sliding round her. Karen glanced nervously at the uncurtained kitchen window where she could see Da sitting by the fire. Fortunately, his back was to them. Dave bent and kissed her, his kiss more insistent this time, pressing her lips on to her teeth so that she bent her head back as far as it would go.

'Karen! Come inside this instant, do you hear me?'

Both Dave and Karen jumped guiltily and she sprang back. 'I'll have to go,' she said hurriedly and ran up the yard to where her father stood towering in the doorway.

'What do you think you are doing, making a spectacle of yourself in the row? Showing yourself and your family up, you are, my lass. How could you?'

'I'm sorry, Da.'

'But it's not like you, lass, letting a lad kiss you and put his hands on you in the back street, and you not even courting! You must pray to God . . .'

'I am courting, Da,' said Karen quietly.

'What? You and Dave Mitchell?'

'We're walking out, Da.'

Thomas gazed down at his daughter, puzzlement plain on his face. 'But I thought . . . I thought you weren't interested in him? I thought you wanted to be a nurse, Karen?'

'Well, there's a big difference between wanting to and having the chance to, Da,' she said, unable to keep a bitter note from creeping into her voice as she walked to the row of hooks under the stairs and hung up her shawl. 'I'm sorry if I made a spectacle of myself,' she went on, 'I won't do it again.'

'All right, lass,' said Da. 'You know, Karen, sometimes we have to accept what God wants us to do, not yearn for what we can't have.'

'Yes, Da. Now I think I'll go to bed, I feel a bit tired. Goodnight.'

'Goodnight and God bless you, lass.'

Once in bed, Karen found herself unable to sleep, her thoughts were so mixed up. There was the insidious feeling of defeat underlying everything else. Dully she considered the options open to her. She could be an assistant nurse at the workhouse hospital and accept the fact that she would go no further. Or she could take a typing

37

course in Bishop Auckland; that and her Certificate of Secondary Education would get her an office job, she felt sure. But she didn't want to work in any office, that was something else she was sure of. She could carry on as she was doing now, working in the hospital kitchen and helping Mam in the house until such time as she should marry Dave. Dave . . . that was another disturbing thought. When he had touched her lips with his under the street lamp on the end of the rows she had felt something, an urge to hold him closer, to consider the strange trembling inside her, as though something long dormant was stirring at last. She touched her bottom lip which was still slightly sore from the way Dave had pressed it against her teeth out there by the back gate. And for the first time she wondered what it would be like to be married to him, to go to bed with him and have him take her in his arms.

Chapter Three

Karen heard the postman coming down the row, pausing every now and then as he delivered his letters. She cocked her head, listening. Not that they got many letters in their house, she thought, but there might be one from Gran. She wrote lovely, newsy letters. Anyway, Karen could do with some diversion.

The footsteps came nearer and stopped. She dropped the shift she had been mending on the bed and ran downstairs, getting to the door only a second after the postman knocked. But the letter which the postman was holding out to her was not from Gran, she saw. The buff-coloured envelope had a typewritten address and was stamped 'Royal Victoria Infirmary'.

*   *   *

'I've had an offer from the RVI,' Karen said baldly, the moment she walked into the Mitchells' sitting room where Dave sat, having just come off shift. The welcoming smile froze on his face and he jumped to his feet for he knew exactly what she meant.

'You'll have to tell them you can't go,' he said. 'We're getting wed on Saturday, how can you?' His voice was assertive enough but his eyes were anxious. Karen stared at him, unhappiness welling up in her. 'I wanted to go so badly, Dave,' she whispered. 'Oh, why can't women be like men? Why do they have to choose between getting wed and having a career?'

Dave shrugged. 'Don't be daft, Karen,' he snapped. 'Women are women, that's why.'

'But why shouldn't I go, Dave, if you agreed to it?' demanded Karen. 'We could put the wedding off—'

'No!'

He stepped forward and took hold of her by the shoulders. 'You'd rather go nursing than be wed to me, is that it?'

'No! No, I didn't mean that,' she said, but her tone was unconvincing even in her own ears. Dave stared down at her for a moment, his face under the layer of coal dust tense and angry. Then he relaxed as he thought of a solution.

39

'Don't tell them you're getting wed,' he said. 'Just go. They'll be none the wiser. Then, when you've finished your training, you'll get work nearer home. It's a champion idea, really.' He nodded his head and sat down in his chair again, resting his feet on the steel fender before the fire.

'I'll have to tell them, Dave,' she protested. 'And what about us, anyway? I'll have to live in, you know. What sort of a wife will I make then?'

'You'll have days off, won't you? I'll be all right. I'll be living here with me mam anyroad. I tell you, it'll be just fine. Think about it, Karen, man, we'll be a lot better off if you have a good job to look forward to in a year or two.'

She stared at him, sitting in his pit clothes before a blazing fire despite the fact that it was a warm day, one of the first warm days of the year. And one part of her mind noted that even in his pit clothes, Dave Mitchell was a fine-looking man; tall for a pitman and broad-shouldered. The red-gold of his hair glinted even through the coal dust plastered to it and his blue-green eyes sparkled too.

'I'd have to lie,' she said.

'No, no, lass, you won't. Just don't say anything.'

Dave got to his feet and lifted a work-calloused hand to the back of her neck, drawing her to him. His eyes darkened as he gazed at her mouth; he was determined he wasn't going to wait any longer for her. They were getting wed on Saturday even if it did mean he had to let her go off on this nursing thing she was so set on.

'I wouldn't worry about what kind of a wife you'll make, lass, you'll be the one I want,' he whispered.

'You'll get me all black,' Karen said weakly, but

40

already her lips were tingling in anticipation of his kiss. And when he kissed her she melted into his arms, and the tingle spread over her whole body.

'What's on here, like? You two are not wed yet, you know.'

The lovers sprang apart at the sound of Mrs Mitchell's voice. They hadn't heard her come in, they were so lost in each other. Karen's face flamed with embarrassment. She looked down at her cotton dress and brushed at the smudges of coal dust she saw there.

Mrs Mitchell stared at her with grim disapproval. 'I think you'd better wash your face an' all,' she snapped. 'This is a respectable house. I'll not have you going out of it with coal dust on your face like that. Not when you're not wed yet.'

'Oh, Mam, leave Karen alone, we've not done owt wrong,' said Dave roughly, and Mrs Mitchell softened immediately.

'Eeh, no, lad, I never said you'd done owt wrong. I'm just telling the lass for her own good.'

Over his mother's head, Dave pulled a wry face at Karen and shrugged his shoulders.

'I'll go then,' she said.

'Aye, that's right,' Mrs Mitchell answered, turning her back.

'An' don't forget what I said,' Dave called after her.

Walking back along the rows Karen felt the excitement rising in her. She could train as a nurse and still marry Dave. Why shouldn't she? If Dave didn't object to her being away in Newcastle for most of the time then that was the important thing. She would write a letter accepting the offer of a place as soon as she got home.

41

'It's not right, our Karen,' Da said sternly that evening. 'It's a lie and lies never do any good.'

She listened respectfully, just as the family always listened to Da, but she did not change her mind even though her father stated his views on the subject of lying every day during the following week.

*   *   *

'I've hardly had time to breathe,' commented Karen. It was her wedding day and she stood before the tiny mirror in the bedroom as Kezia combed her hair and pinned it on top of her head, curling strands round her finger and pulling them into place on Karen's brow.

'You'll be fine as soon as you get the ring on your finger,' Kezia reassured her. 'Why, I thought the time would never get around to three o'clock the day me and Luke got wed. Everyone feels like that.'

But I don't feel like that, Karen thought, though she didn't say it. What she felt was that time was galloping on and soon there would be no turning back for her.

'Are you sure you're doing the right thing, our Karen?'

Kezia's words made Karen give her a startled glance. It was as if her sister had read her thoughts.

'I mean, going off to Newcastle next month. I know you've got your heart set on nursing but—'

'I'm going,' said Karen.

Kezia took up the red roses she had picked that morning from Luke's garden to twine in Karen's

42

hair. She was silent for a few minutes, her mouth full of hairpins, but eventually the task was finished to her satisfaction and she stood back, taking the last pin from between her lips.

'There, what do you think of that?'

Karen gazed critically at her image in the glass. The roses did look nice, she decided, and at least they provided some colour. With her dark hair and eyes above the simple white linen dress, she needed colour. She'd lain awake for most of the night, that was the trouble; she had dark shadows under her eyes and her cheeks were paler than usual. She pinched them between her thumbs and forefingers, bringing a faint rosy glow to the white skin.

'Well,' she grinned and turned to her sister, 'at least the roses are bonny, that's something.'

'Oh, go on, our Karen,' retorted Kezia.

'Karen! It's ten to three, it's time we were going to Chapel.'

Unaccountably, she began to tremble and her eyes darkened as she stared at Kezia, unable to answer her father.

'We're coming now, Da,' Kezia called, and took a firm hold of Karen's arm. 'Howay, man,' she whispered urgently. 'You're not going to change your mind and show us all up now, are you?'

Taking hold of herself, Karen smiled at her sister and they walked down the stairs.

'You look grand, lass,' said Da, beaming at her, and Karen understood that for today at least nothing would be said about her insisting on going off to Newcastle to train as a nurse. Da was declaring a truce.

It was only a few steps to the Chapel and Karen

43

took her father's arm. They led the way, with her mother, grandmother, Kezia and her husband Luke following on. The row was quiet for most of the neighbours were already in their seats but the Minister, not Mr Richardson but a new Junior Minister, was waiting at the door to signal to Mrs Plews, the organist. There was a nerve-racking moment while the others of the family took their seats before 'Here Comes The Bride' rang out, embellished by only one or two wrong notes. Abstractedly Karen thought it was very good for Mrs Plews, whose fingers were becoming stiff with arthritis. Then they were walking down the aisle, Karen on Da's arm and Kezia, as matron of honour, behind them. And Karen forgot about the music as Da released her arm and stepped back and she was looking up into Dave's face.

Oh, dear, she thought, I'm not ready for this. She felt a great urge to turn tail and run. Dave looked like a stranger to her suddenly. What was she doing, putting her life in this man's hands? She glanced at the Minister and he smiled back—an understanding smile, but she knew he didn't understand. How could he? He was too young, he wasn't Mr Richardson. She had a sudden longing for the old Minister and his son; Robert would have helped her. She looked again at Dave and forced the panic down, deep into the pit of her stomach. She had to go on with it now, she had to make it the right thing.

The organ was playing the introduction and the music of Charles Wesley's lovely hymn of praise swelled up and filled the Chapel. Karen could hear her father's baritone booming out behind her:

Love divine, all loves excelling,
Joy of heaven to earth come down
Fix in us thy humble dwelling
All thy faithful mercies crown

She was overwhelmed by a sense of unreality, hardly hearing the Minister as he spoke to Dave. And then it was her turn.

'Karen, wilt thou take this man for thy lawful wedded husband?'

Dave nudged her and she looked up at the Minister, startled. What had he said? But of course there could only have been one thing.

'I will,' she mumbled, and beside her she felt Dave relax.

Afterwards, they went into the schoolroom for the wedding breakfast, Dave holding on to her arm. The feeling of unreality gradually faded and she took a sip of tea. It tasted funny. She didn't know what it tasted like, she couldn't think, it was all hot in her throat and made her cough. She turned to Mrs Mitchell who was sitting on her left to ask her about it but Dave caught hold of her arm and pulled her over to him.

'Ssh!'

'But the tea tastes funny,' protested Karen. 'I was just going to ask her what she thought of it.'

'Hers'll taste all right,' said Dave, and winked broadly. 'I didn't put anything in Mam's tea.'

'Dave!' Karen was horrified. She looked over to the Minister but thankfully he wasn't taking any notice, too deep in conversation with her father. Glancing round at the chattering guests, she lifted the cup as though she was going to take a sip and sniffed. Rum! That's what it was. She'd smelt it before, coming from the open door of the Vulcan Inn.

Karen looked at her new husband. She couldn't believe he had brought strong drink into the Chapel schoolroom.

'The Minister will smell it, Dave! And what about Da?' Dear Lord, Da would never be able to hold his head up in Chapel again if this came to light.

Dave grinned. 'They won't smell it, pet. Eat some ham and it will take the smell away. Aw, howay, lass, I just thought we'd liven things up a bit, what's a sip of rum?'

Karen was in a panic. Desperately she swallowed what was left in her cup to get rid of it and hastily ate up her ham and salad. Out of the corner of her eye she saw Dave put his hand in his pocket.

'I don't want any more, Dave,' she said urgently, 'nor you neither.'

He laughed and slipped the bottle back. 'All right, all right. But you'll have to make it up to me later on, mind. We'll see if we can get away early, eh?'

'If you like, Dave,' said Karen, who was willing to agree to anything if he drank no more rum, not in the schoolroom.

The rest of the reception was spoiled for her. She kept her head down all the time in case anyone smelled the rum on her breath and mumbled her thank yous through almost closed lips when the guests offered their good wishes. All she could think of was getting away into the fresh air. It was the first time she had tasted alcohol and she couldn't understand how anyone could drink it for pleasure. She felt sick and her head was

46

beginning to thump painfully.

At last the speeches were over and the last congratulations given. This being a Chapel wedding there was no dancing afterwards.

'You're going already?' asked a surprised Kezia when Karen and Dave stood up to go.

'I . . . I have a bit of a headache,' said Karen.

Kezia nodded. 'It's the strain of it, I should think,' she said. 'You'd best get along then.'

Karen and Dave were to stay in his mother's house on their own for the night. Mrs Mitchell, showing a rare flash of understanding, was staying with a friend of hers to allow them some privacy.

The young couple said their goodbyes and went out into the street to be surrounded by the children who had waited patiently for them.

'Shabby wedding! Shabby wedding!' cried the children. Dave flung the expected handful of halfpennies over their heads. They whooped and scrambled in the dirt and Dave and Karen were at long last free to walk up the rows and into the Mitchells' cottage. Karen was glad to hang on to Dave's arm for the fresh air made her feel worse, not better.

'You wanted to get away as much as I did,' he whispered. 'You want me, don't you?'

Karen nodded, though the only longing she really had was for a quiet lie-down. She stood quietly, leaning against the wall of the passage, and Dave pushed home the bolt of the door. Dimly, through her dizzyness, Karen was surprised. No one bolted the door in the rows or at least not often. And if they did, it wouldn't be at six o'clock on a warm summer's evening.

Dave turned to her and took her in his arms.

47

Limply she laid her head on his shoulder. They could sit down on the settle now, she thought, sit down quietly and have a cuddle. But suddenly pain shot through her as his hand closed on her breast, squeezing it hard in his strong fingers. At the same time he thrust his knee between her legs, scrabbling at her skirt, pulling it up over her thighs.

'Dave! Dave, I don't feel well,' she protested.

He laughed. 'Oh, no, you don't. I've heard about wives who have headaches every time their man fancies a bit but you're starting early, aren't you? Don't think you'll get away with that, me lass.' He pulled at the buttons of her dress. 'Howay, get this thing off,' he snapped impatiently, sounding like someone else altogether than the boy who had courted her for so long.

'Dave, at least wait until we get upstairs,' said Karen.

'What for? We're wed now, we'll do what I say. I'm the boss. And I say we'll do it where the hell I like!'

Karen's eyes opened wide. There was no swearing in her father's house and this was the first time she had heard Dave swear. She looked up at him to protest but when she saw his expression she thought better of it and began taking off her dress.

'And the shift an' all,' he commanded. Slowly she pulled off her shift and stood before him in her long cotton knickers. She stared at him, her face a blank. She wouldn't deign to let him see how shocked she was.

'Bye, you're a bonny lass,' he said huskily, and pulled the string of her knickers so that they fell to the ground. He lifted her up and laid her on the

48

stairs and took her there, with edge of the tread pressing so painfully into her back that the other pain, when it came, was a mere shadow of the one in her spine, the one which intensified with each thrust of his body. She was almost passing out when the weight on her eased and he got to his feet, grunting. Carefully, she sat forward and put her hands over her face.

'Howay, lass, get out a couple of me mam's glasses and we'll celebrate. We still have most of that rum.'

Karen looked at him, amazed at how normal his voice sounded. He was buttoning his flies. He hadn't even bothered to take off his trousers, she realized. Stiffly she got to her feet and picked up her shift and pulled it over her head, wincing as she felt the bruise on her back.

'Aw, come on, lass, there's nowt the matter wi' you. They say it's always hard for a lass the first time,' Dave said easily. He had noticed her wince. 'How about those glasses?' He turned his back on her and walked into the kitchen where he sat down before the fire. Whistling tunelessly between his teeth, he watched her go to the press and bring out a small glass.

'I won't have any, I don't think, Dave.'

'Suit yourself. All the more for me,' he answered indifferently, and poured out a brimming glass from the bottle he took from his pocket. The smell of rum filled the room and Karen had difficulty stopping herself from gagging. She felt tired to death. Though the pain in her back had settled down to a dull throbbing, her breasts felt tender and raw. She looked at the clock on the wall, thinking for a moment it had stopped. It couldn't possibly be just ten past six. But the clock ticked loudly and she sat down abruptly in the chair opposite her new husband and gazed into the fire.

*   *   *

Karen woke early the following morning feeling far too hot and uncomfortably sticky. She turned over on her back and flung off the bedclothes. The movement disturbed Dave and he grunted in his sleep but did not wake.

She turned her head and gazed at his face. Her husband, she thought. It felt strange. She moved her back slightly and felt a twinge from the bruise, but it wasn't so bad. She touched her breasts experimentally; they were tender and the nipples sore. She sighed. Maybe she would just have to get used to them being like that. Why had no one told her what to expect when she got married? She felt betrayed. Not even Kezia had breathed a word and even though it was a shameful, embarrassing thing to talk about, surely she could have at least hinted at it?

Dave had fallen asleep before the fire the night before and in the end Karen had gone up to bed on her own though she couldn't sleep. Sometime in the night Dave had come upstairs and climbed into bed and taken her into his arms. But it had been better that time, Dave had said it would be. He had been slower, more gentle, more like the Dave she knew now the rum had worn off. Karen frowned, remembering. He had withdrawn himself from her just as pleasurable sensations began to run through her, leaving her feeling flat and vaguely dissatisfied as she wiped her suddenly

50

damp belly with the hem of her nightie.

She was leaning on one elbow looking down at him when he opened his eyes and grinned at her.

'Can't stop mooning over me, can you, pet?' he joked, and pulled her down on top of him. 'Got a taste for it now, have you? Well, if you're ready I'm ready. Ever-ready Dave, that's my name.'

'Dave!' she protested, pulling away. 'It's morning already, time we were downstairs. Anyway, you know we have to be careful. We don't want to start a baby—not when I'm going to start training, do we?' For at least she knew it was this secret act between a man and his wife which gave them babies. That much she had learned from the whispering at school, even though she hadn't known what the act was.

Dave laughed. 'Eeh, Karen, for a lass that's going to be a nurse you know nowt, you don't. We won't start a bairn.'

She was puzzled. 'Why not?'

'Why, it's not how many times we do it, it's what goes in. And what doesn't go in cannot come out, can it?'

She was still puzzled, and her face showed it. He laughed again.

'But, Dave, it did go—'

And then she thought of the sticky stuff on her belly and something clicked in her mind and she collapsed on the bed, blushing furiously. Dave was so . . . so coarse. And as he talked about such private things he didn't sound loving, he sounded almost contemptuous. He took her again now, swiftly, without any regard for how she might be feeling, and a knot of resentment grew in her. She felt used, soiled. Was marriage always like this?

'It's not right. I never thought a lass of mine would want to live a lie like this.' Thomas Knight gazed sternly at Karen, his Bible held against the front of his black serge Sunday suit.

'I'm sorry, Da, but I wrote and said I would go and I'm going to,' said Karen. 'It's not a proper lie, I'm just not saying anything.'

'Lies are lies, Karen.' The wall clock struck the hour and Mr Knight moved to the door. 'I have no time to argue now. I'm on the Lord's work and I've never been late for a meeting yet. But I cannot ask God's blessing on your new life nor give you my own.' Without saying goodbye he strode off. Karen's lower lip trembled but her resolve was unshaken. She was going to go. She was a married woman now and her husband didn't mind her going, that was the important thing. Thinking of Dave, her depression deepened.

He seemed so different, so off-hand he could hardly be bothered to talk to her. She dreaded the times when they were in the house alone and he demanded sex, no matter if she was busy or what time of day it was. And all the time she would be listening for his mother's return, terrified she would find them half-dressed before the kitchen fire for that was his preferred place for 'making love'. Even in bed she was aware all the time of his mother being just the other side of the thin bedroom wall. Karen sighed as she walked back to the Mitchells' and opened the front door.

'A fine thing, an' all, going off to Newcastle when you should be here, seeing to my lad,' said Mrs

Mitchell as she walked in.

'Dave wants me to go, Mother,' said Karen, and the older woman sniffed. Karen pinned on her hat and picked up her luggage.

'It's not that I mind seeing to him—' Mrs Mitchell was saying when Joe knocked on the door.

'I have to go now, I'll miss my train else,' Karen said quickly, and escaped into the street.

'It's a wife's place—' Mrs Mitchell shouted after her but Karen hardly heard.

'Old witch,' said Joe as he took her luggage. Her spirits rose immediately and her excitement with it. She wanted to go and she wasn't hurting anyone else by doing it either, she told herself.

'It doesn't matter what anyone else thinks,' she said.

'That's right, pet,' said Joe, and nodded vigorously. She felt a surge of gratitude to him. He at least wanted to see her off and wish her well.

*   *   *

The first weeks in the hospital went by in a whirl of learning rules and scrubbing floors and making beds and taking them to bits again and re-doing them.

'As Miss Nightingale wrote' became a phrase that followed Karen all day and even into her dreams. Miss Nightingale had evidently given precise instructions on bed-making as well as every other possible aspect of a nurse's work.

'Miss Nightingale said that a good nurse can attend to a patient's needs without disturbing that patient.'

'Miss Nightingale said that a nurse who rustles is the bane of the patient. Unnecessary noise will do more harm to a patient than all the medicine in the world will do him good.'

'Miss Nightingale said that a good nurse will do . . .'

'Miss Nightingale said that a good nurse will be . . .'

Miss Nightingale was a paragon, all right, Karen thought grimly as she fell into bed utterly exhausted and with her hands red and chapped from scrubbing anything and everything with disinfectant. Why, they were in a worse condition than when she had worked in the kitchen at Oaklands. She rubbed glycerine and olive oil into them night after night, wincing as the glycerine bit into the cuts but persevering in an attempt to heal them. If I had been doing real nursing it wouldn't have mattered, she thought wearily, but so far all she was allowed to do was skivvy after the more senior probationers, not to mention Staff Nurse or Sister.

But at last she had a day off and was able to travel home to Morton Main. She rose at six o'clock as usual and took an early train for Dave would be at home this morning as he was on night shift. In any case, she had to be back at the hospital by eight-thirty in the evening and she wanted as much time as possible at home. She had written to Dave and told him when she would be coming and he was waiting for her outside the station, somewhat to her surprise.

'By, you look grand in that cloak and cap, pet, you really look like somebody,' he said admiringly as she came out. Of course he hadn't been waiting

54

on the platform. 'It's a waste of money buying a platform ticket just for the sake of a couple of minutes extra,' he explained as he gave her a quick peck on the cheek after first looking round to make sure no one who knew him was there.

She looked up at him, thinking he looked grand too, with his fair good looks. There was an air of suppressed excitement about him though. Surely it couldn't just be because she was home for the day?

'I'm going to emigrate, Karen,' he burst out without any preamble. 'Me and your Joe and some of the other lads . . . we're off to Australia next month.'

'Emigrate?' Karen stared up at him stupidly. She couldn't believe she had heard him aright. 'What do you mean, emigrate?'

'We're going to Australia, Karen.'

'Australia? I can't go to Australia, I've just started my training!'

There was a tiny silence as Dave looked down at her, his face curiously blank.

'No, I didn't mean . . . Aw, come on, Karen, let's get off home. Me mam's out visiting her sister up at Houghton, we have the house to ourselves.' Dave strode out of the station and on to the road leading to Morton Main so that Karen had to hurry to keep up with him.

'You were joking, weren't you? About Australia, I mean,' she panted as she caught up at last.

'Never mind now, we'll talk after,' said Dave, looking down at her, and she saw his eyes take on that curiously intent look and knew what it meant.

The minute they got inside the house Dave took her swiftly and, for Karen at least, with no joy at all, on the mat in the kitchen. It was over in two minutes and afterwards she raised herself painfully and rubbed her shoulder blade which had slipped off the mat and been in contact with the hard stone floor. Carefully, she pulled her drawers on and straightened her skirt and all the time she was weeping softly inside her head. Then she remembered what he had said and turned to face him.

'Now,' she said, 'tell me about Australia.'

Chapter Four

The train from Newcastle puffed to a halt in Durham Station and Karen climbed down on to the platform. Quietly she waited for the steam and smoke to clear, peering at the group of people clustered round a pile of obviously new basket-weave boxes, crammed full and tied round with an assortment of leather belts. No one had noticed her yet.

They were waiting for a train going down country, but not this one; this one only went as far as Darlington, and the journey these young men were embarking upon was much further than that, she thought bleakly. They were going to the other side of the world.

Content not to be noticed for a minute, she watched them. There were nine of them altogether, all from her home village, all dressed in their Sunday suits and with fresh-washed white shirts gleaming with starch and boots polished to such a shine they reflected the faces of their owners. And there was a cluster of mothers and

sisters and sweethearts with an air of brittle
cheerfulness about them. They smiled bravely and
chattered and took the least excuse to touch the
young men, hold their hands, pat their cheeks.

Some of the men were impatient, anxious to be
off, Karen noticed. They were casting glances at
the local train still standing on the platform,
wanting it to be away so that there would be
nothing to stop the Liverpool train from coming
into the station.

Karen stood apart. Now that the time had come
she found herself fighting to keep her composure.
Dave and Joe, she thought forlornly, feeling that
she was being deserted by both of them though she
knew it was silly to think like that. As she stood,
biting her cheek, the wind caught in her nurse's
cloak, billowing the material out in a bell and she
clutched it closer to her, shivering suddenly. She
wished that the Liverpool train would come in
quickly, that it was over. At least when they were
gone she would be free of this feeling of
desolation, this silly hope that it was all a mistake,
Dave and Joe were playing a joke on her. She
jumped when Joe looked straight at her over
Mam's head and spoke her name.

'Karen? What are you standing there for?
Howay, come and give us a hug. You're not letting
us go off to Australia without so much as a hug?'

Karen smiled quickly and moved forward to be
enveloped in a tight circle of her family. She kissed
her frail mother who was struggling to hold on to
her own composure. And then her father, tall and
stern, grey-haired and with a hectic colour in his
cheeks betraying the presence of the lung disease
which plagued so many of the men of Morton

57

Main. And Kezia, strong and practical, was there of course. There was no sign of Jemima though Karen had thought she would manage to get home to say goodbye to Joe.

'Wish me luck, Karen,' Joe said softly, and she gazed up into her brother's strong, intelligent face, a face so like her own with its dark eyes and frame of almost black hair.

'Oh, I do, I do, Joe,' she mumbled and looked away quickly so that he did not see the tears ready to brim. And there was Dave, just lifting his head from his mother's and staring straight at her so that she felt a tiny pang of guilt that she had not gone to him first.

'Dave,' she said, disengaging herself from her family and going to him. Dave, her husband of so short a time it still felt strange to think of him as such. Dave, who was going to Australia to make his fortune.

'So you came, then,' sniffed Mrs Mitchell. She glared at Karen, her expression mirroring her firmly held opinion that Dave was only going to Australia to get away from his wife and it was the wife's fault.

'Of course I came, Mrs Mitchell,' Karen replied. 'I got the afternoon off from the hospital specially.'

She spoke to the older woman but she was looking at her husband.

Dave stepped forward and took her hands in his and held them to him in that way he had, smiling down at her with his lop-sided grin, his head cocked on one side. And though she told herself he was emigrating for her sake as well as his own, she still felt a sense of betrayal.

58

'I must go straight back to Newcastle,' she said, looking down at his hands on hers, not wanting to lose hold of her resentment. Wasn't he going away for God knows how long? Hadn't he fooled her enough already?

'But not yet, not before we catch the train,' said Dave, drawing her away from his mother and the rest of the party from the village.

'Look at me, Karen,' he murmured, 'look at me.'

Reluctantly, she raised her gaze to his face. She looked at the light blue eyes and the fair, almost red hair; the freckled face. Dave was a handsome man, she thought with one part of her mind; with another she was thinking, Dave is my husband and he is leaving for the other side of the world. He didn't even consult me before he booked his passage on the emigrant ship. What will people think? The resentment welled up in her.

'I'll send for you, Karen, I promise I will,' he was saying. 'I'll find a house, you'll see, then as soon as you finish your training you can come out. Nurses are needed in Australia just as much as they are here.'

'Why do you keep on repeating that?' she asked. Surely he would send for her, couldn't she take that for granted?

'Well, I will,' he answered.

He'd been telling her he would send for her ever since the day he first told her he was going, she thought. Only now did Karen suspect he had been thinking of emigrating even before they were married, else why had he agreed to her going off to train?

'Leave your ring at home,' Dave had advised her when she had gone to Newcastle. 'Someone will

59

see it.' But she couldn't do that, it would be bad luck. Why, Gran thought that if you took your wedding ring off your finger something bad would happen to your marriage. And she'd been right, an' all, Karen thought miserably. For Dave had seen the notice pasted to a wall in Bishop Auckland and he was going to emigrate. Miners were wanted for the goldfields of Australia and her men were going. There would be only Da left.

'Gold must pay better than coal, eh?' Dave said to Karen, and she stared at him, disbelieving. But all he could think about was Australia. Even when she came home on her days off and he took her roughly, swiftly, he seemed far away from her. The distance was there in his eyes, it was a mechanical kind of loving only. And now the day had come, he was going. And not only Dave but Joe and most of the other boys she had grown up with. Oh, she thought desperately, she knew the wages had been cut at Morton Main Colliery and things were bad in the village, the future was bleak for the young lads. But Australia?

'Howay, lass, smile,' said Dave as he held her hands on the station platform as they waited for the train, 'I'll be gone in a minute.'

Karen smiled. The muscles of her face felt stiff and unyielding but Dave didn't notice. He grinned, excitement creeping back into his eyes. Once again his thoughts were in Australia.

'I don't know what you have to grin about,' Mrs Mitchell said in a voice rough with weeping.

'Nay, Mother,' he answered, 'don't be upset. You want me to get on, don't you?'

'There's nowt the matter with England. You can get on in England,' snapped Mrs Mitchell. 'There's

60

plenty of coal to dig here.'

Her mouth worked and her voice rose so that the other members of the group began to take notice. Both Joe and Da had turned to look, concerned, for if only one of the mothers broke down they all would.

They were saved by the whistle of the approaching train. There was a sudden flurry of activity as last hugs and kisses were given and boxes lifted on to shoulders strong from hewing coal underground.

'I'll send for you, Karen, I promise I will,' whispered Dave yet again. He was the first to jump on the train when the doors opened. There was a chorus of farewells and the doors were closed and the train was on its way, puffing out of Durham and taking away so many of the young men of Morton Main.

Karen waved until her arm ached, everyone left behind did. But it was Joe who stuck his head out of the window and waved back. There was no sign of Dave.

'Will you have time for a bite before you go back?'

Karen looked round at the sound of her sister's voice. Kezia was standing with Da and Mam, all three wearing that same look of anti-climax. There would only be Kezia left in the village to give an eye to Mam now, thought Karen with a pang of guilt, and glanced at her mother.

Rachel seemed weary, and was very pale. Now that Joe had gone she had dropped her brave front and looked as though she could do with a sit down and a cup of tea. Karen studied her, remembering the last time Mam had worn that exhausted look.

It had ended in her being confined to bed for a month on the orders of the panel doctor, the one Da paid fourpence a week for. Kezia and Karen noticed the look at the same time and moved forward together, both of them watching for signs of collapse in their mother.

'We'll go to the tea-room, it's not far, can you manage?' asked Karen as she took Mam's arm. 'I have a couple of hours before I have to be back on duty.'

They settled Mam on a seat in the tea-room and Karen brought her tea from the buffet and sat down herself before she remembered Mrs Mitchell. She would have to have a word with her mother-in-law, she realized, and hurried out on to the platform again. There were a few people from the village hanging about still but no sign of Mrs Mitchell. She must have gone straight home.

Well, there was nothing she could do about that, thought Karen. Dave's mother knew about her mam's poor heart, everyone in the village did; the damage done by the rheumatic fever had made her prone to fainting fits and collapsing at times of strain.

'I told you you shouldn't have come, Rachel,' Da was saying as Karen returned to her family. 'I told you it was too much for you.'

Da's hair was grizzled now and his breath short with the lung disease. Oh, he was an upright man, one who modelled himself on Job. But he was a quiet man at home and gentle with his women. It was in Chapel that he gave his impassioned sermons. There he was a 'blood and thunder' preacher. The pews were full when Thomas Knight was preaching, Karen thought proudly. He could hold a congregation enthralled for hours and never need to refer to a single note. All he needed was his Bible, his dog-eared copy of the King James Version which went with him everywhere except down the pit.

Karen rose abruptly to her feet. She had to get away. It was all right now she saw her mother was not going to have one of her turns. She bent over the table and kissed Rachel, anxiously noting the dry skin of her mother's cheek. Was it too hot? There were dark shadows under her eyes too; were they darker than usual?

'I have to go Mam, Da,' was all she said.

'I'll walk to the train with you,' said Kezia, quiet now, the acerbic note gone from her voice.

The sisters stood on the up platform waiting for the Newcastle train. The wind grew stronger now, blowing in gusts and lifting Kezia's shawl, showing the thickening of her waist, the start of a pregnancy.

'You're having a baby?' asked Karen, feeling another pang of conscience as Kezia nodded. With Jemima in Lancashire and herself in Newcastle, Kezia had a lot to cope with already.

Kezia correctly interpreted the look Karen gave her.

'Don't worry about me,' she said, 'I'm strong enough. I can manage fine.'

'Maybe I should have stayed in the village.'

'Why no, man,' Kezia said sharply. 'In spite of the fact that he didn't agree with you telling the lie about being married, Da's that proud of you getting on, he would hate it if you came home now. Anyroad, what's the difference? You'll be going off to Australia in a year or two, won't you?'

63

Karen glanced up the line, not knowing how to answer. The small local train chugged into the station and Karen kissed Kezia on the cheek, feeling the slight shrinking. Kezia was never one for displays of affection. The train came in and Karen climbed on and found a seat by the window where she could wave to her parents, now standing in the doorway of the tea-room watching her. Kezia had already crossed the bridge and was standing next to them, alternately glancing at the train as it pulled out of the station and keeping a watchful gaze on her mother. Karen settled down for the short journey to Newcastle, trying to quieten her mind for she had to be on duty in an hour or so and already she felt tired to death, strung out emotionally. She stared out of the soot-blackened window, not seeing the fields and trees and small groups of tiny houses clustered round towering winding wheels and colliery yards and tall chimneys belching smoke. Her thoughts were still with her family and the mining folk she grew up with. There would be a deal of sadness in Morton Main tonight.

*   *   *

'Stop fiddling, Nurse, and get on with your work,' Sister snapped.

Sister missed nothing, thought Karen as she dropped her fingers from her neck where she had been touching her wedding ring through the cloth of her uniform and returned to her work, terrified Sister would ask to see what was under her dress.

Sometimes it was hard to believe that she was really married, she mused, as she scrubbed the

64

sluice and bedpans until they shone before taking them out on a ward round and bringing them back to be scrubbed again. And the second-year nurse was waiting for her to help make the beds and Karen knew she wouldn't get her corners right first time and would have to face Sister's lashing scorn. Despairingly, she thought that the most important thing in the world to Sister was that the corners of the bedclothes should be just at the right angle and the wheels turned in precisely. Even the patients were expected to show just the right amount of arms and chest, covered of course in white linen, above the turned down sheets.

There were no letters from Dave or Joe either. She hated going back to Morton Main and facing people and telling them, no, she hadn't heard. They would look at her pityingly and she would know they thought she was a deserted wife.

Then one morning there was a lovely long chatty letter from Gran. Karen's heart lightened as she took it from Home Sister and slipped it into the bib of her apron to be read later during her ten-minute break for breakfast. She had recognized the copper-plate handwriting at once, the letters formed laboriously and painstakingly as Gran had been taught at the Wesleyan School in her youth. The beautiful letters contrasted oddly with the content for Gran wrote as she spoke, in the idiom of Weardale, words coming straight from the heart. She wrote of the doings in the dale and then continued to her main reason for writing:

Your mam told me that man of yours went off to Australia along of Joe. There'll be nowt good comes of it I doubt. It'll all end in tears, a

65

young couple separating like that. Maybe you should not have denied you were wed, our Karen, when you went to that grand hospital of yours. It was a lie and nowt good comes of a lie. Though I know how badly you wanted to better yourself, be a nurse. But why you had to go away and do this new-fangled training in Newcastle, I'll never know. You could just as well have learnt the trade from the lying-in nurse at Morton Main or gone as an assistant at the workhouse hospital in Auckland. Still, you know what you're doing no doubt.

Aye, well, I reckon your time there will pass. But I'm thinking of your mam. What's she going to do if you go gallivanting off to Australia after that man of yours? Kezia will likely have enough on her plate with the new babby coming and I fear for your mam.

Hoping you are keeping well as I am.

Your loving grandmother,

Jane Rain

Karen, sitting in a corner of the ward kitchen, reading the letter during her break, smiled wryly. She could almost hear Gran saying the words she had read. Gran's thoughts were always for her daughter, she worried incessantly about her.

Gran herself was wiry and strong and had never suffered a day's illness in her life. But her daughter Rachel had been at a vulnerable age when the hard times came to Weardale and they had left their mark. Thinking about her mother, Karen sat on longer than she should have done and was brought back to the present by the appearance of Sister in the kitchen doorway, the bow under her

66

chin quivering with indignation.

'Are you intending to sit there all day, Nurse?' she demanded. 'It's Matron's round this morning and the sluice is a pig-sty! Now, get in there at once.'

'Yes, Sister.'

Karen fairly scuttled past the bristling starch of Sister's apron, heading for the sluice. It was gleaming, not a thing out of place, just as Karen had left it before going on her break. Sighing, she picked up a cloth and the bottle of Eusol and began wiping everything once again. It was Thursday tomorrow and her day off. She would go and see Gran in Weardale. If she was up at dawn she might still have time to call at Morton Main on her way back. She could spend an hour or two with her family before reporting back to the hospital at eight o'clock.

*　　　*　　　*

'Eeh, our Karen, what are you doing here?'

The carrier's cart creaked to a halt and Karen climbed down before answering her grandmother who was walking along the path from Low Rigg Farm. Gran was dressed for a journey, she saw, her black, shiny straw hat clamped over her iron grey hair and a thick natural wool shawl tied round her shoulders. Karen's heart sank. Obviously Gran was going off somewhere.

'Whyever didn't you tell me you were coming?' the old lady demanded, placing her hands on her hips and surveying Karen.

'I . . . I thought I'd be a surprise,' she answered weakly.

67

'Aye. Well, you are that,' asserted Mrs Rain. 'I was just on my way to Stanhope, I was going to walk to the train. I've got a new lad now, he's not over bright but he's a good lad, he can look after the place for a couple of days. Aye, Alf's all right, not like the last 'un.'

Karen remembered the last young lad Gran had. He had been a disaster, always skulking in the barn.

'It's too far for you to walk, Gran,' she said now, bending down and kissing the old lady on the cheek. 'You should get the cart.'

'Hadaway wi' ye. It's nought but a stride or two. But you'd better come in now anyroad, I expect you're ready for a cup of tea.'

She turned to the carrier who was still standing, listening to the conversation with interest. It wasn't often Mrs Rain had visitors and he took his unofficial job as news gatherer seriously.

'You can call back for us on your way back from High Rigg, Amos,' she said. 'We'll be catching the Auckland train.'

'Aye, right you are, Jane.'

Amos touched his cap and clucked his horse into motion.

'Where are you off to?' asked Karen as she and her grandmother turned into the gate of Low Rigg, past the rowan tree which stood sentinel there. A carpet of leaves surrounded the trunk now that the summer was over, and the women crunched them beneath their feet.

Jane glanced quickly up at her granddaughter.

'How long is it since you were home, Karen?' she asked instead of answering.

'A fortnight. Why, is something wrong?'

'Well, I wondered.'

They had reached the kitchen door and Jane moved quickly to stir the fire together and put the iron kettle on the coals. Karen waited, knowing better than to question further.

'I had a funny night last night,' mused her grandmother, almost to herself. 'I was sure Rachel needed me. I kept waking up and going off again and there she was, time after time, holding out her hand to me.'

'Oh, Gran, it must have been something you had for supper,' said Karen, relieved that she had nothing really to go on.

'Aye, well.' Gran pursed her lips. 'I know the Minister says we shouldn't take any heed, it's only superstition, but I'm telling you . . . I have to go and find out for mesel'.'

'We can go together, Gran,' said Karen. 'I was going anyway.' A tiny throb of anxiety went through her. Gran's dreams had proved pretty reliable before now. She remembered the time she had come in from school to find Mam stretched out on the kitchen floor, the first time Karen had seen her collapse. Da had been down the pit and Kezia off to Auckland for the messages and Karen was panic-stricken, not knowing what to do. And then, miraculously, there was Gran coming in the door and taking off her shawl, her sharp eyes taking in what had happened as she moved to pick up her daughter. Small and slight though she was, she pushed Karen out of the way and lifted Rachel on to the settle, holding her against her thin chest, rocking her, talking to her. And Karen had watched, trembling, as Mam came to herself and cried softly and Gran carried on rocking her.

69

'Howay, my lass, your mam's here. You're fine now. I knew you needed me. I felt it when I was having me dinner, and I did no more than run for the train.'

Karen remembered, oh, she did. Was this another time like that or worse? The two women drank their tea quickly and were waiting at the gate when the carrier's cart came round the bend from High Rigg. The journey down, by cart and then by train, seemed twice as long as it usually did for both Karen and her grandmother were lost in their own anxieties.

*   *   *

'Mother! And our Karen an' all. Why didn't you let me know you were coming?'

Rachel Knight looked up in surprise as they walked in through the open front door of number two Chapel Row. Karen's heart lightened at the sight of her mother, obviously not having one of her turns. Rachel was standing by the table peeling vegetables and she looked fine. The dark shadows under her eyes had receded and her normally pale face was flushed. Whether it was from the heat of the fire or not, she looked well, better than the last time Karen saw her.

'You're not badly then? Do you mean to say I've come all this way and there's nowt the matter with you?' demanded Gran. Karen caught her mother's eye and had to smile.

'Oh, Gran, would you rather she was badly?'

'No, I never said that,' admitted Gran.

Rachel wiped her hands on her apron and turned to lift the kettle on to the fire. 'Have you

70

been having a dream again, Mam?' she asked.

'Aye, I did, an' it's not usually wrong neither,' snapped Jane, sitting down at the table and loosening her shawl.

'It's not wrong this time either, Mam, only it's not me for a change.' Rachel paused and sat down herself before continuing. 'It's our Kezia. She's lost the bairn.'

'Kezia? No!' exclaimed Karen, that it should be Kezia had not occurred to either her or Gran. Kezia never had an illness in her life, why on earth should she lose her first baby?

'I knew it. I knew there was something,' said Gran. 'Where is she then?'

'She's upstairs. She was here when it happened which is just as well, I could see to her. But sit down and have something to eat before you go up to see her. Kezia's all right now, she's got it over.'

Rachel poured out tea and buttered teacakes, working swiftly and surely as Karen remembered her doing in the days before her heart trouble became apparent. Karen got to her feet. 'I'll just go up, Mam, I'd rather go now.'

Opening the door of the bedroom she had shared with her brother and sisters—in those days there had been a rope slung across the room with blankets over it for a divider between the boy and the girls—Karen looked anxiously at the bed in the corner. 'Kezia?'

Lying in the middle of the bed, her sister turned to look at her. Her normally rosy face was pale and her eyes red with weeping. She looked strangely vulnerable as Karen walked hesitantly over to her.

'I lost the bairn,' Kezia said weakly, as though she was confessing to wrong-doing, and Karen

71

rushed the last few steps and took her hand. It felt cold and limp and not at all like Kezia's capable hand.

'I know, pet.'

There was a short silence. Karen stopped herself saying the obvious phrases like 'You've time yet' or 'You'll have another'. She was aware that for the moment Kezia couldn't think like that. She was in mourning for the child she had just lost.

'I'm that sorry.'

Kezia blew her nose on a man's handkerchief she drew from under the pillow. 'I know I'm a fool, making such a fuss. And it's too much for Mam to run up and down the stairs after me. I'm going to pull myself together and go back to my own house.'

'Gran's here,' said Karen, 'there's no need for you to do anything. And Mam looks well, doesn't she? Do you think she's beginning to improve?'

Kezia brightened for a minute. 'She does look well, doesn't she? She likes to be needed same as us all, I suppose. I just hope she doesn't try doing over much. You know what she's like, when she's well. She thinks she's better altogether, she thinks she's had a miracle cure.'

'Well, Gran's here. She'll keep us all straight.'

The sisters smiled at each other, remembering other times when Gran had come to the house and taken over, organizing the three girls and giving them their own lists of chores to do when they came in from school. Only Jemima had grumbled.

'Have you heard anything from Jemima?' asked Karen.

'A letter last week. It was the first since Christmas.'

The front door opened below and the sound of pit boots clumping through resounded up the stairs, ringing out as they did on the stone floor. Kezia's face crumpled.

'That'll be Luke, he's been on fore shift. He doesn't know about me losing the baby yet.'

Karen rose to her feet and patted Kezia's hand. She felt like weeping with her sister's pain.

'I'll go down now. I'm sure you want to see him on your own,' she said awkwardly.

In the kitchen Kezia's man was sitting on Da's chair by the fire and taking off his boots. Rachel and her mother were standing by the table setting out his food. Having told him the news they were giving him a few minutes, not looking at him, allowing him the only privacy these tiny cottages could afford.

Luke was a quiet man. He rarely had much to say at any time. He glanced up at Karen as she came into the room and nodded a greeting, his face a mask of sweat and coal dust yet strangely white above the line of his forehead where his pit helmet had come to. Stiffly, he stood up and took off his jacket, dropping it on to the newspaper in the corner which was there for the purpose of protecting the floor from the coal dust.

'Go on up now, Kezia wants to see you,' said Karen.

Luke looked down at his clothes, so permeated with the dirt from the pit that his body and clothes were the same uniform black.

'I thought mebbe I'd better have a bath first, like.'

'Nay, lad,' Gran interposed. 'Go on up. Your meal will keep till you come down and I'll have the

73

bath tin in an' all. But the lass'll be waiting for you, man.'

In his stockinged feet and pit dirt, Luke climbed the stairs.

In the kitchen below, the three women heard him groan and the thud as he fell to his knees by the bed and pulled Kezia into his arms.

'Nay, lass,' he cried, 'don't take on so. It's me that's sorry.'

Gran looked across the table at Karen, a look which she interpreted correctly for she took up Luke's meal which had been placed on the table and put it back in the oven to keep warm. Karen's heart ached for her sister's misery. It must be a terrible thing to lose a baby, she thought bleakly.

'There'll be coal dust on the sheets, it'll take a deal of getting out,' observed Mam in a detached kind of voice, but no one was worried about that. She coughed and changed the subject. 'There's a letter from Joe,' she said. 'It's on the mantelpiece if you want to read it, Karen.'

She felt a small thrill of excitement as she jumped up and stretched up to the high wooden shelf with the embroidered linen cover along it. A letter from Joe. He would probably say something about Dave. Maybe there was even a letter from Dave waiting for her in the office of the Nurses Home.

The letter had been posted in Sydney. They had got there all right then. She pulled out the three pages of Joe's neat, masculine script and read swiftly through them. They detailed all that had happened on the journey and told about the boarding house he was staying in for a few days before journeying up to the gold-fields.

74

The landlady is from Newcastle, Mam, and she cooks like it and all. So you see, I'm not like for starving, not yet at any rate. It feels really odd, the weather being so hot at this time of year, but you know me, I like it hot. My room has a balcony right along the length of it and the whole house is built out of wood. I suppose I must make the most of it for we'll be on our way up-country next week. I'll write again when I get settled . . .

Karen read the letter through, scanning it quickly. It was written in Joe's usual bright, optimistic tone. He wrote about Tot Wilson and Jos Smith, two others of the group which had emigrated from the village, but there was no mention of Dave. Had they had an argument, her brother and her husband? She sat back in her chair and looked up from the letter and saw Mam watching her closely.

'Have you had word from Dave, then?' asked Mam bluntly.

'Oh, I'm sure there'll be a letter waiting for me when I go back,' Karen answered rather too quickly.

Mam looked unhappy, her forehead creased in a frown.

'Well, I hope you're right. Anyway, why don't you go along to Mrs Mitchell's? She might have a letter.'

Karen looked at the envelope which had contained the letter. The postmark was weeks ago. But then, it wasn't surprising if there was some variation in how long it took for letters to arrive all the way from Australia. Dave could have written at the same time. She forebore to ask when this letter had arrived.

'I think I will, Mam,' she said, glancing at the oak-framed clock hanging on the wall. 'I have another two hours before I have to go for the train back to Newcastle.'

* * *

'Oh, it's you, is it?'

Mrs Mitchell stood back from her front door, grudgingly allowing Karen room to pass her and walk through to the kitchen.

'How are you, Mother Mitchell?'

'I'm all right. I'm managing fine on my widow's pension and I have a bit put by. The Union's good.' She closed the door and followed Karen through. 'I'll make some tea.'

'No thanks, Mother Mitchell, I've just had some. I haven't got much time, I have to be back at the hospital. I just came to see how you were and to ask if you'd heard from Dave.'

Mrs Mitchell sat down by the fire and motioned Karen to sit opposite. Her thin face broke into a smile as she delved inside her apron top and took out a letter, one with Australian stamps.

'Aye, I did. He's getting along fine. Reckons he might not go to the mines, he can find better chances in the city. He's got a good job, he says.' Mrs Mitchell held out the letter grudgingly. 'You can read it if you like.'

Karen felt cold. She forced her lips into a stiff smile.

'No, I expect my letter's coming. I haven't heard

76

from him yet. I expect there's a letter waiting for me back at the Home now, though. I'll get it when I go back.'

'Well, lass, I got this about ten days ago. I'm amazed he didn't write to you at the same time.' But Karen saw the little smile of satisfaction which the older woman couldn't quite hide as she pushed the letter back inside the top of her apron.

Karen got away as soon as she decently could, pleading the need to get back to Newcastle, but as she walked back along the rows to her parents' home she couldn't get out of her mind the look of triumph on her mother-in-law's face. Mrs Mitchell cherished the notion that Dave had written to her first. And why shouldn't she? Karen told herself. Dave was her only son, all the family she had left now, and he was on the other side of the world. But no matter how hard Karen tried to tell herself it didn't matter, she was humiliated.

She said her goodbyes to Kezia and the others and went off for the train to Newcastle with a feeling of anticipation. Today there would be a letter from Dave.

*   *   *

Back at the Nurses Home, Sister assured her there was no post for her. It will come tomorrow, Karen told herself firmly, and threw herself into work. She was on night duty now, the junior probationer on Men's Surgical.

The ward was full; thirty-three beds with only two nurses to see to their occupants. Night Sister popped in at odd intervals during the night to cast gimlet eyes over everything but things went

77

smoothly enough.

There were miners with broken limbs from pit accidents and men from the shipyards and docks. And one young lad in particular, Peter, small and vulnerable for his fourteen years for all his attempts to be a man among the men of the ward. He had lost a foot in a fall of stone, or rather it had had to be removed surgically after being squashed flat. The stump was healing nicely now but he whimpered in his drugged sleep and often woke up with a quickly stifled cry of distress.

Karen usually tried to give Peter a little extra attention when she could, though she had no real time to spare. But she would save him little treats: a jam tart from her own tea, a few sweets she had bought on her day off. She was well liked by the young boys on the ward, her air of practical sympathy attracting them to her.

Tonight, as Karen walked round the ward to the usual accompaniment of snores and groans, a beam of moonlight came in through the high window and illumined Peter's head, lighting it up where the night lamp failed. His eyes were open. He was following her movements, his head turning with her. She walked over to him.

'You can't sleep, Peter?'

He shook his head. 'I'm all right though, Nurse. I was just thinking, like.'

'Would you like a drink of cocoa?'

'Nay,' he whispered. 'I'm going home tomorrow, Nurse, the doctor says I'm better.'

'Going home?' Karen was surprised. It seemed such a short time since the surgeons had cut off his mangled foot. What would he do now? she wondered.

'Aye, I'm going to get a wooden foot, the doctor says. In a month or two, when it's healed, like, I'll be able to walk then.'

'By, that'll be grand, lad,' said Karen softly. 'It's not going to be so bad, then, is it?'

Peter shook his head, his eyes gleaming in the moonlight.

'Me da's going to ask the boss if I can get a job in the lamp cabin. I'll still be earning then.'

Peter's voice had grown louder, he was altogether more confident than he had been last time she saw him. The man in the next bed woke up and shushed him fiercely so that he subsided on to his pillows, chastened. But Karen saw him smile for the first time.

'Nurse!'

Karen jumped as she heard her senior's hiss from the desk in the middle of the ward. The door from the corridor had opened and Night Sister came striding in. Hurriedly, she straightened Peter's top sheet and carried on round the ward. It was almost dawn. Through the high windows she could see streaks of red in the sky. It was going to be a clear day.

There was no letter from Dave in that day's post, or the next, or on any of the days following. The year turned to spring and Karen was back on day duty and still no letter came. She immersed herself in her work and before she knew it the first-year examinations were looming. She didn't get home to Morton Main for a while; all her spare time was taken up in studying for she was determined to pass.

Some days Karen even forgot to look for a letter from Dave, sometimes she didn't think of him at

79

all. Inevitably, the image of her husband was fading from her mind. He had been gone almost a year.

But there were letters from Joe, short and scrappy, and the occasional picture postcard with views of Sydney and pictures of solemn-faced Aborigines.

Joe did not mention Dave. He talked about the heat and the dust, and how different gold mining was from coal mining, and how he was being promoted to foreman, and about Tot Wilson and Jos Smith, both of whom were working for the same company as Joe. Not a word about Dave.

Karen was too proud and embarrassed to ask Joe about him in her letters. She stopped going to see Mrs Mitchell when she was in the village but she knew Dave's mother had had another letter from him; Mrs Mitchell told everyone she saw. Karen couldn't bear to see the fresh triumph in her mother-in-law's eyes.

Chapter Five

One morning Karen picked up her post from the office in the Nurses Home and took it out into the garden to read as she still had fifteen minutes before she needed to report for duty. She was working in Outpatients and finding the work very different from ward work, but still, she was enjoying the change. And now the coveted Nursing Certificate was almost hers. Only a few weeks to go, she told herself happily as she waited for Home Sister to search through the post.

80

There were three letters, Karen saw with a tiny thrill of anticipation. She loved to get post. This time there was one in Gran's copper-plate hand and one in Kezia's. And the other bore an Australian stamp. It had been posted three months before. Karen gazed at it. She knew it wasn't from Dave. No, this one bore the unmistakable handwriting of her brother. It must be in answer to her request for news of Dave.

Karen's heart beat uncomfortably. She wasn't sure if she wanted to see what Joe had written. But time was getting on. If she didn't open the letter before starting the busy round on Outpatients it would have to wait until dinnertime and she wouldn't be able to get it off her mind all morning. With trembling fingers she slit the top of the envelope with the small scissors chained to her uniform pocket and drew out the single sheet, her pulse racing so that she could feel the beat of it in her throat above the stiff white collar of her uniform.

She stared at the page, her face flushed. She knew her brother, she could read between the stilted phrases he had written. Joe was embarrassed to have to tell her about losing touch with Dave, she could see that.

Why had Dave gone off from his friends? They had all been assured of work with the gold mining company. But then she remembered his mother saying Dave had got work in the city; it had slipped her mind before. Karen bit her lip. It was as though Dave had cut himself from his old life altogether. She didn't even know if he still wrote to his mother. Her family carefully avoided mentioning him on her visits home and Karen

81

herself had long since given up visiting Mrs Mitchell. She went on staring at the letter as though concentrating on it would give her the answer.

Dave loved me, she thought, he wanted me. Why did he change? Why did he marry me and then desert me like this? What did I do? A shadow fell across her bent head and she looked up quickly, forcing herself to smile and cover up her distress.

'Good morning, Nurse Knight, how nice to see you here. We can walk across to Outpatients together, can we not?'

Hastily pushing the letter under the bib of her apron, Karen rose to her feet. It was Robert Richardson, her childhood friend. She felt a surge of pleasure to see him. She had known he was a houseman now, working under the chief surgeon. It was a surgical clinic this morning, she remembered, orthopaedic cases, so Doctor Richardson would be working on it.

'Good morning, Doctor,' she said, smiling though her lips were stiff and she felt more ready to fall on his shoulder and howl than to smile and make polite conversation. They fell into step together along the path which skirted the side of the main building.

'Not bad news in your post, I hope?' said Robert, surprising Karen with his perception.

'No, not really,' she said, though in truth she didn't know whether it was or not, she was so confused. She would read the letter again when she had the time, she thought, and brightened her smile as she looked up at him. She remembered him so well from years ago when they were both children and his good looks had turned the heads of all the girls in the top class in the Sunday School. Robert was intending to become a medical missionary in Africa, she remembered his father saying.

Warming to her friendliness, he smiled back at her and as the smile softened his features he looked incredibly handsome though in a strange, detached way. He was tall and dark-haired with strong, even features. Karen moved her eyes away quickly in case he should think she was leading him on. She remembered him as a boy, coltish and gangling; pictured him sitting in the front pew at Chapel, his eyes tightly closed when they were supposed to be, his expression intense. Robert had been a lonely boy, always known by his full name whereas all the other Roberts were Bobs or Robbies.

'You weren't in Chapel on Sunday morning,' he commented, breaking into her thoughts.

'No,' answered Karen, feeling immediately guilty for she hadn't been on duty either and her companion knew it. And the Chapel was not far away from the hospital. But did it mean he had remembered she was at the hospital and had looked for her? The idea made her feel warm.

'You weren't feeling unwell?'

'No.'

Karen was saved the need for further explanation as they entered the Outpatients department. There was the usual crowd of people waiting to be seen, those on return visits and a sprinkling of new casualties. Karen murmured something and turned to go into the nurses' cloakroom to remove her cloak when Robert spoke to her again, surprising her.

83

'Can I see you as you come off duty this evening, Nurse?'

Karen gazed at him, startled. Any social encounter between medical and nursing staff was definitely frowned upon, surely he knew that? If she agreed and Matron ever found out about it, she would be thrown off the course.

But he saw her hesitation and was quick to offer a way. 'I meant, we could go to the Chapel fellowship together. It's Bible study tonight.'

'Well . . .'

'Nurse Knight?'

Karen was saved from making any decision by the entrance of Sister who frowned heavily when she saw her junior nurse apparently loitering with a doctor in full view of patients.

'Aren't you ready yet, Nurse?'

'Sorry, Sister.'

Karen hurried into the cloakroom and was out again in a trice. With her cloak and starched cuffs removed, she was ready for the day.

The morning was a busy one for her as she took off dressings or splints or both, ready for the doctor's inspection, and replaced them with clean ones afterwards. There was a steady flow of patients which only began to slow as it approached one o'clock. Karen was tidying the treatment room when a latecomer was ushered in to her, a young boy limping badly on a crutch. Automatically, Karen smiled at him and then realized it was Peter, the young amputee she had nursed during her spell on the surgical ward.

'Peter, how nice to see you, how are you getting along?'

'Hallo, Nurse,' he said shyly as she stretched out

84

a hand to lead him to the leather couch. Taking his crutch and leaning it against the wall, she looked down at his stump which was covered in a rather grubby bandage.

'I thought you had a wooden foot, Peter,' she said as she took off the bandage. The stump was angrily inflamed and suppurating.

'I 'ave,' said Peter, 'but me leg's too sore just now for it.'

Doctor Richardson came in and inspected the stump, lifting the lower leg with gentle hands.

'Well, young man,' he commented, 'I reckon you've been on this too much. When it gets even slightly sore you should keep off it, you know, unstrap the foot and give it a rest.'

'Yes, Doctor, I know,' mumbled Peter.

'Why don't you then?'

'It's when I'm working, Doctor. Sometimes I have to keep going,' answered the boy. 'I don't want to lose my job in the lamp cabin.'

Doctor Richardson nodded. He understood the boy's need to keep on working. 'Why don't you take your crutch to work with you, then you can use it if necessary?'

Peter looked down, flushing. 'I don't like to use the crutch if I can help it,' he muttered.

'Well, you're going to have to use it for a while now. There's no way you can put your artificial foot back on until you get that leg healed and hardened up again,' pointed out the doctor briskly, but his face softened into a smile as he looked down at the boy and he added, 'Never mind. If you're careful it won't take long—a week or two, that's all. You'll be walking almost like normal when you get used to it.'

'I won't be able to play football, though, will I?'

'No, you won't be a footballer, that's true. And I know you don't want to be told there are other things beside football but you'll find that there are—interesting things. You're a clever boy, Peter. You could study and get on. The Union would help you if you applied to them and showed you would work hard enough. Think about it.'

'Study? Me? Gan on, Doctor.'

'You could. If you need any advice, I'll help you. You can always get in touch with me here.' Peter looked surprised and thoughtful at the same time, forgetting about his foot for a moment, and the doctor turned to Karen. 'Clean it up, Nurse, and put a boracic ointment dressing on it and plenty of padding.'

As Karen moved to the shelves in the corner to take down the boracic ointment, Robert followed her. 'I'll see you tonight then,' he said, his voice lowered. 'I'll be on the corner at eight o'clock.'

'But—'

'Come back next week, Peter. And in the meantime, keep off that foot.' And he was gone before Karen could put him off.

'Is he your sweetheart, Nurse?' asked Peter, grinning widely. His sharp ears had caught what Doctor Richardson had said.

'No, of course not,' she replied, her face scarlet. 'Never mind him, hold your leg still while I see to it.' Obediently, the boy held out his leg and said no more, but she could see by the grin on his face that he thought he was right.

* * *

86

Karen walked to meet Robert that evening telling herself she was simply going to a Chapel meeting with a friend, there was nothing more to it. After all, Da would expect her to attend Chapel when she could. But she couldn't deny it was nice to have a good-looking man interested in her, no matter how innocent his intentions. She grinned ruefully to herself. The truth was Doctor Robert Richardson was good for her ego which had been bruised so badly after Dave's desertion. And she wasn't doing anything wrong in any case, not in going to a Chapel meeting, was she?

'Good evening, Nurse. You came then.'

His quiet voice broke into her thoughts as she turned the corner. He was waiting by the kerb, his Bible clasped under his arm. He took his hat in his hand as he greeted her and held her arm for the short walk to Chapel.

'Good evening, Doctor,' she answered him as formally, but felt the warmth of his arm through the good though well-worn cloth of his coat. It felt strange to be walking with a man like this, a man who was not Dave. She glanced up at the outline of his face against the light from a gas-lamp, fantasizing about what it would be like if she was free and he was really interested in her. What would it be like to be married to a man like Robert Richardson? But the short walk to the Chapel was over and they were turning in at the door. Soon they were studying the first chapter of St John's Gospel and when she glanced up at Robert she saw he was totally immersed in it.

What a fool she was, she told herself, he simply wanted to ensure that she did not stray from the fold, he wasn't interested in her. Why should he be? She had not enough about her even to hold the man she had married. She stared down at her Bible.

There was tea served in the schoolroom after the meeting, and a chance to socialize for a few minutes. Robert solemnly brought Karen her cup of tea and led her to a seat a little away from the others.

'Thank you, Doctor,' she murmured demurely.

'Do call me Robert,' he said. 'There's no need to be formal, is there?'

Karen smiled. She could hardly imagine him being anything but formal. 'And my name is Karen, you will recall,' she said, taking a sip of the hot sweet tea.

'Yes, I remember you so well, in Chapel at Morton Main. You and your sisters and brother. I used to envy you them, did you know that? Having brothers and sisters, I mean.'

Karen looked at him, seeing the lonely little boy he had been then still hidden in him.

'I didn't know that,' she said, warming to him. She would have liked to talk to him about those days but the schoolroom clock said a quarter to ten, it was time to go back to the Nurses Home if she didn't want to face Matron in the morning to explain why she was late in. 'I must go.'

He rose to his feet instantly. 'I'll walk you to the gate,' he said, and they said their goodnights to the others and went out into the lamp-lit streets with a few speculative glances following after them.

They parted at the gates and she hurried on to the Nurses Home, thinking what a strange man he was. Intelligent he must be to train as a doctor but so quiet and awkward with other people.

Except with patients, Karen mused as she got ready for bed. Robert could talk with sympathy and understanding to patients, look how he had been with young Peter. Careful, a small voice warned, don't get too friendly. Supposing Robert finds out about Dave and tells the hospital? She'd have to leave and with only a month or two before the finals.

Sighing, Karen lit a candle. It was 'lights out' in a couple of minutes. She picked up her unopened letters from Gran and Kezia and climbed into bed to read them in luxury for there had been no time during the day.

Gran's letter was short and scrappy, saying how she and Alf had managed the hay-making with Mr Bainbridge's help and she was well as she hoped Karen was. And wasn't it good that Kezia was having another baby? There was nowt like starting another bairn for making you forget about a miscarriage, she affirmed.

Karen was pleased, she hadn't known about it. She ripped open the second envelope and drew out the single sheet of ruled paper. This letter was short too, but Karen could feel the happiness bubbling in the news it contained.

. . . and the midwife says I'll carry this one all right, Karen. I'm already six months gone, I didn't want to say anything until I was sure it would go well. We're all fine here and the pit's going full-time so there's plenty of work, thank God. And Luke's earning good, just as well with the baby coming.

Hope this sees you well. It won't be long before you've finished training, will it? Mam

89

and Da send their love.
Your loving sister,

Kezia

Karen put down the letter and blew out the candle, feeling pleased for Kezia and Luke. It was lucky he'd drawn a good seam, she thought sleepily. She knew what it meant when the miners drew lots for the best part of the coal face to work. It was always nice to have good news, she thought drowsily, and turned over on her side and fell asleep.

*   *   *

I'm doing nothing wrong, Karen told herself one evening as she brushed her hair before the mirror in her poky little room. She gathered the dark mass up expertly with one hand and pinned it on top of her head before pausing and gazing at herself seriously. Her mother and father and gran would think it was wrong, she thought, and a small cloud overshadowed her pleasant anticipation at going to the meeting yet again with Robert. He liked her, she knew it, he liked her a lot, and she was flattered even though she was aware that she should do her best to put him off. But when she was honest with herself she knew she did not want to put him off altogether. It was pleasant to have a good-looking doctor interested in her, balm to her wounded pride.

We are just friends, she said defiantly, and took down the blue straw hat with white roses on the wide brim which she had bought last pay day. It was the first hat she had bought since she came to Newcastle and she loved the way the brim framed

90

her face, it was so becoming. 'What is wrong with going to a Bible class with a friend?' she demanded of the mirror. Standing up, she pulled her dress straight around her slim hips and went out.

Robert had not even tried to kiss her yet and if he did she was confident she would be able to handle it. Besides, she found herself liking him more as the weeks went by and she got to know him better. There was no harm in their friendship, none at all, she told herself, why shouldn't she have a man friend? She was happy for things to go on as they were with no complications and deluded herself into thinking this state of affairs could go on indefinitely.

When she saw Robert standing on the corner she went up to him happily and slipped her arm through his.

'I'm not late, am I?'

'No, not at all,' he answered gravely and led her into the Chapel. It was afterwards, after he had walked the few steps back to the hospital gate with her, that she realized she had been fooling herself for he drew her into the shadow of a beech tree which stood close by and gently pulled her to him.

'Karen,' he whispered, 'you know how I feel about you, don't you? And I think I am right in thinking you feel the same way about me?'

Karen stared up at him and found she had been wrong about this too, she hadn't the slightest idea how to handle it. He was bending his head towards her, gazing at her lips, and when his kiss came it was soft and sweet and his lips remained together. For a moment she closed her eyes and swayed towards him but only for a moment. Her head jerked back and she pulled herself from his arms.

'Robert!'

'Oh, I know, I should not kiss you in the street but I couldn't help myself, Karen. I'm sorry.'

'No, it was my fault,' she said breathlessly, and rushed away through the hospital gates and round to the Nurses Home, leaving Robert staring after her. She had been a fool, she told herself angrily. Robert was a man, wasn't he? Why should he be content with walking her to Chapel or meeting her supposedly by chance in the hospital gardens or in their work on Outpatients? She undressed and got ready for bed, knowing she would have to tell him the truth as soon as she possibly could. But as she slipped into bed, she felt restless and unhappy. Married yet not married, but she was a woman, wasn't she? With a woman's normal feelings. Not that she missed the intimate side of marriage one little bit, but it had been so nice having a man courting her again. And she admitted to herself now that Robert *had been* courting her. It was her own fault it had come to this, she should never have gone out with him. Tomorrow, the first time she saw him alone, she would tell him about Dave.

*　　　*　　　*

'I have something to ask you, Karen,' he said the following afternoon. There had not been any time to talk until then for the clinic had been a busy one and Sister particularly vigilant. Karen feared Sister was beginning to suspect them.

'Yes, Robert?' Karen was clearing up after the afternoon session and Outpatients was empty even of Sister, who was in her office, writing up the patients' notes. Karen didn't look up as she spoke,

92

trying to think of a way to tell Robert about Dave.

'Will you have dinner with me this evening?'

'Oh, Robert, you know I shouldn't. Suppose someone from the hospital saw us? It's not allowed.' Karen bit her lip for he had taken her by surprise and driven the half-formulated words of explanation from her mind.

'But you've almost finished your training. Once you have your certificate . . .' Robert paused as Sister came bustling by.

'Aren't you finished in there, Nurse?' she snapped, glowering at him. Doctors were not welcome in her department after hours and she made a point of making any lingerer aware of the fact.

'Eight o'clock,' he muttered to Karen and sauntered out of the room, giving Sister a happy grin as he did so, most unlike his usual expression. Sister's expression became more severe than ever. She glared at Karen.

'I hope you are not encouraging Doctor Richardson?' she said coldly.

Karen mumbled a disclaimer and hurried out of the treatment room into the nurses' cloakroom, her face red with embarrassment. Nevertheless, despite her guilty feelings, she thought how pleasant it would be to go out to dinner with him. She wanted to go to evening dinner, having never done such a thing in her life. In the world of Morton Main, dinner was at midday unless the man of the house was on shift when the meal would then be whenever he came up from the pit. Evening dinner sounded exciting and glamorous. There was no harm in going out to dinner, she told herself. They were just two friends going out for a meal, weren't they? And it would give her a good chance to tell him about Dave.

* * *

Of course, she should not have gone. She knew that as soon as they were seated at a corner table in a select little restaurant near the Haymarket. Robert was full of excitement, he could hardly wait until they sat down.

'You know what I have to ask you, don't you?' he said, reaching over the table and taking her hand.

'Oh, no, Robert. Please . . .' Karen flushed and looked down at the tablecloth.

'I want you to marry me, come with me to Africa.'

'Robert, you know I can't. The hospital—'

'You've almost finished your training, what does it matter if the hospital gets to know about us? If they object you can leave after you get your certificate. It's only a few short months before I will be finished too and we can be on our way. Oh, Karen my dear—'

Karen listened to him as he went on and on, endearments mixed with reassurances that it would work out all right. She had never heard Robert talk so much before, his words tumbling over each other. She looked up and saw his eyes shining with excitement and love. She knew she was going to hurt him terribly and was filled with remorse.

'Robert, I can't marry you,' she said quietly.

He went on talking, describing the life they would have together, how happy and fulfilled they would be working for God.

94

She tried again, a little louder this time so that the people at the next table looked up and then quickly back at their meal as though they had been caught out doing something terribly ill-bred.

'Robert, I can't marry you.'

He stopped in mid-sentence, the excitement dying from his face. He looked at her blankly for a moment before deciding he should humour her.

'Why not? Oh, Karen, we would be so good together. You're not afraid of marriage, are you? I wouldn't make you—'

Karen decided the only thing to do was to come right out with it. Taking a deep breath, she said it.

'I'm married already.'

Robert looked at her across the table, a half-smile of incredulity on his face. The waiter came to take their order and Robert waved him away.

'What did you say?'

Karen blinked rapidly. She wasn't hungry any more and the smell of food was making her feel sick. She couldn't look him in the eyes.

'I'm sorry, Robert, it's all my fault this, isn't it? You must think I led you on but I couldn't tell you, could I? Probationers have to be single women so I couldn't tell you, could I?' She was repeating herself in her guilty embarrassment.

Robert suddenly realized he was still holding her hand. He dropped it, visibly drawing away from her and clasping his hands together on his lap.

'You see—' Karen started again, but he interrupted her.

'Wait! Let me be sure I heard you aright. Did you say you were already married?'

'Yes.' She gave him a swift glance, her cheeks aflame. What she saw in his face made her feel even more uncomfortable. 'I . . . I didn't mean to lead you on, Robert.'

He grunted, showing what he thought of that line.

'And who is he, this husband of yours? And what's he doing letting you come away to train as a nurse?'

Karen cleared her throat. She glanced up over Robert's shoulder where the waiter was hovering. He followed her glance and with a muttered exclamation pushed back his chair and got to his feet.

'Come on, let's get out of here.'

Even in his emotional state he politely told the waiter they had changed their minds and gave him a tip before leading Karen out of the restaurant into the lamp-lit Haymarket. He hailed a cab. Telling the cabbie to drive around for a while, he handed Karen into it and climbed in beside her.

'Now,' he said, 'tell me all about it.' He was quiet and controlled again, his profile stern and dark, the happy excitement all gone from him.

'It's Dave. You remember Dave Mitchell from Morton Main, don't you?'

Robert nodded and gave a small bitter laugh. 'Oh, yes, I remember David Mitchell. How could I forget the boy who made my life a misery in the village? I might have known it would be David Mitchell.'

Karen bit her lip. It was true, Dave had been a one for tormenting boys who were different. And certainly Robert had been different from the other boys in the village. She remembered now that Dave had had a nick-name for him. What was it? Saint Bob, that was it. She remembered Dave and his cronies shouting it after Robert as he walked home from school, his shoulders hunched defensively. And she remembered how she had burned for him to retaliate. He was bigger and older than Dave. If he had turned on his persecutor, Dave would have left him alone.

'Well? Go on,' Robert prompted her.

Karen wasn't going to tell him of Dave's desertion. She had not even called it that to anyone as yet. But it was almost two years now and somehow when she started talking about him the whole story came out: how he had gone away to Australia and simply disappeared, shaking her off along with his old life.

'We were only married for a few weeks before he went and I was going to follow as soon as I finished my training. I never heard from him again. He wrote to his mother at first but even she hasn't heard from him for over a year.'

Robert said nothing. The only sound was the clip-clop of the horse's hooves on the cobblestones. Karen stared out of the window, unseeing.

'Well, we'd better get back to the hospital,' Robert said at last, his voice flat.

'You won't say anything to Matron, will you?' Karen asked tremulously. 'I only have a few weeks now. I'll go to another hospital when I have my certificate.'

'You're living a lie, Karen,' he said.

'Oh, please, Robert! Please don't give me away.'

The cab reached the hospital gates and he handed her down.

'Robert?'

'I won't give you away. As you say, it is only for a

97

few weeks,' he said and made to walk away before abruptly turning back to her.

'Oh, Karen, how could you? How could you marry a blackguard like David Mitchell?' he cried. Then, without waiting for an answer, he strode rapidly away from her.

She hurried up the drive with tears streaming down her face. Oh, she was a terrible, unfeeling woman to hurt such a good man as Robert Richardson. She had told herself it was all innocent but she knew in her heart she had been leading him on, she had. She had thought she could go out with him tonight and have a grand dinner and then tell him about Dave. And now look what she'd done. She was a terrible bad woman, she was, and Mam and Gran would be horrified if they knew of it. And Da . . . Karen didn't like to think what he would say.

Next day Robert was polite but distant when they met in the course of their work, his face closed up tight. Gradually, over the next few weeks, Karen stopped wanting to hide away whenever she saw him and they formed a polite, though constrained, working relationship.

She spent all of her spare time in her room, studying for her finals, and began to consider looking for work in another area, away from the North-East and Robert and her memories of Dave. She was not really needed by the family; Kezia coped wonderfully and even their mother seemed to be fairly fit and well. She was finished with men, Karen decided. From now on she would concentrate on her career. She was a good nurse with a lot to offer any hospital.

Kezia's baby was born at the end of October, a fine
boy. Karen went to see him on her day off, the first
time she had been home for some weeks thanks to
her studying. But now her finals were behind her
and she had her Certificate of Competence.

'He's grand, isn't he, Karen?' Kezia, sitting up in
bed with her baby in her arms, lifted him up so
that Karen could see him properly.

She looked at the tiny red bundle and agreed
with her sister. She took hold of the tiny fist and
wondered what it would have been like if Dave
had stayed, if it had been herself proudly holding
her first baby. But she pushed the thought away.
This was Kezia's day and she was very happy for
her sister.

'We want you to be godmother, don't we, Luke?'
said Kezia, and he nodded his head, beaming,
willing to agree to anything his wife suggested.

The baby was to be named Luke also and already
was being called Young Luke to distinguish him
from his father. It was a proud and happy day with
the family all gathered round, Gran too, down
from the dale for the day.

'I'll have to be getting back,' said Karen after a
while. 'I'm on duty tonight. But I'll get down more
often now that I've got my certificate. I won't be
studying so much.'

'I'll walk to the end of the street with you,' said
Mam, and Karen knew she wanted a quiet word.

'Your Da's that proud of you getting your
certificate, our Karen,' said Rachel as they walked
up the row, adding anxiously, 'You won't try going
off to Australia to look for Dave, now will you,

pet?'

'No, Mam, I won't. That's over. He must not want me or he would have written so I'm not going chasing after him. Anyway, I doubt I'd find him, it's a big country, you know. No, I'll stop in England, Mam, don't worry about that.' She hesitated for a moment before continuing, 'I might go down south, though. I saw an advertisement for a hospital in Essex in the *Newcastle Chronicle*. You won't mind that, will you? I will still be able to come home every year. I want to get away, Mam, what with Dave leaving me like that. I want to make a fresh start.'

'Eeh, Karen, I can't say we won't miss you, pet. But we understand how you feel. Mebbe it will be for the best.' Rachel kissed her and patted her on the shoulder. 'Now go on or you'll be late back at that hospital of yours,' she said firmly, and turned back down the row.

It was after Karen had said goodbye to her mother and was waiting for the horse bus to the station that she saw Mrs Mitchell. Dave's mother was walking along on her way back from the shops, basket in hand and an old woollen shawl clutched round her chest. She marched up to Karen and stood squarely in front of her. Karen smiled tentatively but this was ignored.

'I suppose you've been to see Kezia's new babby then?' Mrs Mitchell demanded. 'You weren't going to come and see me, I gather.'

'Hallo, Mrs Mitchell. No, I'm sorry, I haven't got much time. I have to get back,' Karen excused herself.

The older woman sniffed. 'It doesn't matter to you that it's your fault I'm left on my own, does it?

100

No, you don't give a tinker's cuss.'

'My fault? Why is it my fault?' Karen was stung into replying.

'It was your fault, all right. It was you drove my lad away, wasn't it? Leaving a poor widow woman all on her own like. You'd only been married a few weeks. What did you do to my lad to drive him to the other side of the world, that's what I want to know?'

'I didn't—it was Dave wanted to go, I wanted him to stay—'

But Mrs Mitchell wasn't listening to Karen. She went on and on, her voice getting louder and louder, until folk in the street began taking notice and Karen wished fervently that the bus would turn up and she could get away.

'By, if I'd known what would happen I'd have stopped my lad marrying a bitch like you! Turned him against his own mother, you did, not content with driving him away. I haven't had a letter from him for long enough, God knows what has happened to the poor lad. I can't sleep at nights thinking about him and worrying.'

'Mrs Mitchell, I can't help it if he's lost touch with you, can I?'

'No? He hasn't got in touch with you, has he? No, because he wanted rid of you, that's what. And I daresay he's stopped writing to me in case you find out where he is from me. Me, his own mother! And I was saving up to go out and see him, mebbe make a home for him like, poor lad.'

Mrs Mitchell folded her arms and glared, thrusting her face to within an inch of Karen's nose. 'You couldn't be a proper wife to my lad and now *I* have to suffer for it. Oh, it's all right for you,

101

away to your posh job in Newcastle, but what about me, eh?'

Karen was saved the necessity of replying as the horse bus drew up and she climbed aboard. A small crowd had gathered, mostly women with shopping baskets on their arms; they were drinking in every word avidly. This would provide plenty to talk about in the back rows for days and days. As the bus drew away Karen could hear her mother-in-law declaiming to the interested onlookers, nodding her head emphatically and shaking her fist after the bus.

I will get away, she vowed to herself as she stared straight ahead, ignoring the amused glances of her fellow passengers. I'll apply for the first post I see which is as far away from here as I can get.

When she returned to the village for young Luke's baptism on the Sunday before Christmas 1913 she had already left the Royal Victoria Infirmary and had secured a post as a staff nurse at Oldchurch Hospital in Romford in the county of Essex. Karen had never been in the South of England in her life and had only sketchy knowledge of Romford or Essex, but she didn't care. It was hundreds of miles from County Durham and that was all that mattered to her.

The day was sunny but crisp and cold and Young Luke was bundled up in two shawls over his christening gown so that only the lace hem peeped out. It was the robe which Gran had embroidered for her first-born. All the Knights had worn it in their turn and now Young Luke was the first of the new generation to be baptized in it. They set out for the church, Karen carrying the sleeping baby, watched anxiously by Kezia.

102

The proud father had his hands full too, for he was to offer the first person they met on the way to Chapel a piece of christening cake and a shiny new threepenny bit. The old custom was solemnly carried out to the delight of the young boy who was lucky enough to turn into the row at just the right moment.

'I asked if Mr Richardson would baptize the baby,' whispered Kezia. 'He's friendly with the new Minister, you know, and we all liked him when he was here.'

'Oh, yes,' Karen said absently as they took their seats at the front of the congregation. She was concentrating on holding the baby correctly and at the same time enjoying the sensation of having the tiny new life in her arms.

The service went well, Young Luke sleeping through the whole of it, and it wasn't until afterwards when friends were crowding round to coo over the baby that Karen looked up straight into the eyes of Robert.

'Hello, Karen,' he said softly.

'Oh—Robert,' she answered, his appearance taking her by surprise though it was perfectly natural for him to come with his father.

'I wanted to see you before you go away,' he said. She glanced up at him. He looked pale and unhappy. The chatter and laughter of the christening party seemed to recede into the background, leaving the two of them standing alone. Karen didn't know what to say; she had thought she had got over her feelings about him but here she was again, feeling like a guilty schoolgirl.

'Er—it was a nice service,' she said at last, a

remark he didn't seem to even hear. Bending his head to hers he spoke in a low, urgent tone of voice.

'Karen, I wanted to say I'm sorry if I made you unhappy. I thought about it afterwards and I realize you didn't mean me any harm.'

'Oh, no—' she began but he was rushing on. Taking her arm, he drew her slightly away from the company.

'Have you heard anything from Mitchell?'

Karen shook her head. 'No, and I don't think I will. I realize now he wanted to get away from me. He never wanted me.' She stared down at the ground. It was a hard thing for her to admit even now, her pride was so badly dented.

'Karen, I still care for you,' said Robert. 'I would wait for you. Do you know that in a few years, if you don't hear any more from him, you can have him declared dead? I would wait, my dear, no matter how long it takes.'

Karen looked at him helplessly. What could she say that wouldn't hurt him more? At that moment there was a buzz of voices. The christening party was breaking up and moving towards the door so she was saved the necessity of replying to Robert bar a quick noncommittal word.

'Howay, Karen, it's for you to carry the baby home,' cried Kezia, walking over to them and depositing Young Luke in Karen's arms before turning to Robert. 'You'll come back to the house with your father for a cup of tea, won't you?'

'It's good of you to ask me, but I have to get back to the hospital, I'm afraid,' he answered. 'I should have been on my way already.' He walked rapidly away up the row, leaving Kezia and Karen gazing

104

after him.

'A surgical registrar leads a busy life,' murmured Karen and Kezia nodded, forgetting about him. But Gran had noticed and as they were walking back down Chapel Row she fell into step alongside Karen. She gazed curiously at her granddaughter.

'You and Mr Richardson's son were thick enough there, weren't you? What were you talking about?' she asked baldly.

'Oh, it was about a patient,' Karen answered. 'Robert's at the RVI, you know. I nursed some of his patients.'

'Hmm,' said Gran. 'He looks as though a few home-cooked dinners would do him good, he's that thin and pale. Mebbe he's working too hard during the week and then having to rush back on a Sunday night, like.'

'You can't just leave patients because it's Sunday, Gran,' Karen pointed out.

'No, I know that.' She was quiet for a few moments before startling Karen with her next remark. 'Well, I don't think it's just overwork that's the matter with him. I think he looks like a lad who's in love—and not happily at that.'

Chapter Six

'Robert!' cried Karen. 'I thought you were in Africa!'

They stared at each other for a minute in the half-dark of the November afternoon, busy crowds of shoppers swirling round them. She was unable to take her eyes from him, he looked so ill, his skin

105

a parchment yellow and his eyes sunk into his head. But his smile was as warm and bright as it had ever been as he took her hand in his. His own hand felt hot and dry and bonier somehow, so that she felt a spasm of anxiety for him.

'I've been back for a few weeks now,' he said. 'Oh, Karen, it is good to see you. What a good thing I decided to come into Bishop Auckland this afternoon. But I understood you were having a great career in Essex? That's what Father said. And here you are, back again.'

'Robert, are you all right?' she couldn't help herself asking, hardly hearing what he was saying she was so disturbed by his appearance.

'Oh, yes, I am now. Take no notice of how I look. I know I'm enough to frighten the children at the moment but I'll improve now I'm back. I'm all the better for seeing you, Karen, it's as good as a tonic.'

'Robert?'

For the first time, Karen realized there was someone with him. Another man moved forward, smiling politely, and Karen noticed he wore a clerical collar. In the split second before Robert apologized and introduced them, Karen noticed that there was a similarity between the two men, though she couldn't put her finger on what it was. It certainly wasn't physical, for the stranger was shorter than Robert and fairly ordinary-looking. She dismissed the fancy from her mind as they shook hands.

'This is Father Donelly, Karen, a great friend of mine. We met in Africa. Sean, meet Sister Knight. Karen and I are old friends.'

Robert beamed at them both but Karen was still

106

watching him closely. Oh dear, he didn't look at all well.

'I didn't expect you to come home so soon, Robert,' she said, trying to cover up her worry at seeing him look so ill.

He pulled a wry face. 'No, I didn't expect to be back either. Look, let's go into the tea-room at the Co-op and talk over a cup of tea. We can tell each other everything that has happened since we saw each other.'

'Look, I'll be off now, you two don't want me with—'

'Nonsense,' Robert interrupted the priest. 'We'll all go in and have a cup of tea and a warm. I know you're not in a hurry, Sean, come on now.' He took Karen's arm in one hand and Sean's in the other and marched them into the tea-room.

They found a corner table and Karen watched Robert covertly. He had an air of bubbly cheerfulness very different from his usual quiet manner as he caught the eye of the waitress and ordered tea and toasted teacakes.

'Now,' he said when their order came and Karen had poured out the tea, 'you first. Tell me all about your work. I hear that everyone in the village is proud of the way you've got on. What are you doing in Auckland? You haven't got the sack, have you?'

Karen laughed. 'Not exactly. Just moving on— the war, you know. Next week I start a new post at a military hospital near Romford.'

'Oh, I say, that's good, isn't it? Don't you think so, Sean?'

Father Donelly nodded politely. He sat quietly, looking from Robert to herself, a slight curiosity in his eyes.

'Well, it's just a small hospital, converted from a manor house or some such—Greenfields is the name. I'll be in charge during the nights,' she said deprecatingly, though in fact she was quite proud of making such good progress in her career. After all, it was just about a year since she'd been promoted to Ward Sister.

'Small or not, I'm sure you've done very well,' declared Robert, and she smiled at him.

'Greenfields in Essex?' asked Father Donelly. 'Is that near Romford? Do you know, I have a friend there, from my seminary days—Murphy's his name. Isn't that a coincidence? Perhaps you'll meet him. If you do, mention my name.'

Robert suddenly put down his cup with a little clatter of china which made the other two glance quickly at him. He was white and trembling and a slight perspiration had broken out on his forehead.

'Oh, Robert, there *is* something wrong,' said Karen as he pulled out his handkerchief and wiped his face.

'It's this blessed malaria,' he muttered, and smiled weakly.

'I didn't last long in Africa, did I, Karen? I was only out there a year when I got it and had to come home to England.'

'Come on, I'll drive you home,' said Father Donelly, putting down his half eaten teacake and rising to his feet.

'No, I'm all right now, it was only for a moment.'

And indeed Karen was pleased to see Robert's hands had stopped trembling and a little colour was returning to his cheeks.

'All those years of work and preparation for

nothing,' he said with a trace of uncharacteristic bitterness. 'All my life I was going to be a missionary but when it came to it I was knocked out by malaria.'

'A particularly virulent strain of malaria, Robert,' Father Donelly pointed out gently. 'Perhaps God wanted you to work here, among your own folk, did you think of that? And if he did, who are you to go against him?'

Karen looked from one to the other. Now she knew what the similarity was between them: they were both dedicated men, dedicated to God, and it was a bond which made her feel oddly left out.

'I must go,' she said. 'I have shopping to do and I must get back.'

The two men got to their feet. 'Will I see you again?' asked Robert.

'I go back to Essex tomorrow.'

All three walked to the door and Karen waited with Father Donelly as Robert paid the bill.

'Don't forget, if you see Father Murphy, tell him he owes me a letter,' said Sean.

'Yes, of course,' answered Karen. 'But I won't be going into Romford much when I start my new job.' They looked at Robert as he spoke to the cashier. 'He's been very ill, hasn't he?' she went on and Father Donelly nodded.

'Yes, he has. But he will be better now he's come home. Of course, he can't go back to Africa. He will have to settle for a life here.'

Robert finished paying the bill and they went out into the darkening street. The gas lamps were lit and shedding pools of light on the pavement and a raw wind was blowing down from Cockton Hill.

'Will you write to me when you get settled?'

asked Robert. Karen nodded.

'I will, I'll write next week. Care of the Manse, is it?'

'Yes.'

He took her hand and she could feel him shivering in the wind.

'You must go, Robert, it's bad for you to be out in this weather.'

'Yes. Come on, old man,' said Sean firmly. 'I'll drive you home.'

Karen was thankful to see that the priest's car was parked just across the street. It was an Austin 15 with a hood so Robert would be out of the wind on his ride home. She looked after them as they started down the street towards the marketplace. Poor Robert, she thought, I hope things go right for him soon, he deserves it. Sighing, she turned back to the shops. She wanted to buy Christmas presents for Kezia's boys; it would be a good idea to leave them with her mother to save posting from Essex. Then all she had to do was pack her small bag ready for the journey south. The train she wanted to catch left very early in the morning but she had to settle into her new home ready for work the following day.

'I saw Robert in Newgate Street,' she remarked to her mother as she unloaded her basket on the kitchen table.

'Oh, yes, I heard he had had to come home, poor lad,' said Mrs Knight. 'He caught some foreign disease, didn't he?'

'Malaria. He looks as though he's had a bad time with it too.'

Rachel gazed at her daughter shrewdly, noting her concern for the Minister's son. 'I used to think he was fond of you, Karen,' she said. 'A bit smitten, like. Pity is you didn't marry him instead of that—'

'Mam! Don't talk daft,' Karen said sharply.

'I was only saying,' shrugged her mother.

'Sorry. I didn't mean to snap. Well, I'd better get on with my packing, I have an early start tomorrow.'

'Righto, pet.'

*   *   *

Greenfields Military Convalescent Home was too small to accommodate the nursing staff so Karen had arranged for lodgings in the village. It was already growing dark on the day following her encounter with Robert when she set out to walk from the station. She pulled her cloak around her, shivering slightly. There might not be the cold north-easters like there were at home, she mused, but the air was still damp and chill and there were wisps of fog rising in the hollows.

The walk took longer than she had remembered from the one time she had tackled it before so that when she finally arrived at the cottage she was cold and hungry and tired and her bag felt as though it weighed twice what it had that morning when she set out from Morton Main.

Mrs Blakey, Karen's new landlady, flung open the door even before Karen had time to lift her hand to the knocker. Her plump face wore a smile of welcome which shone out from the gloom of the unlit passage.

'Come away in, ducky,' she cried, 'and welcome. My neighbour said he would look out for you at the station but he must have missed you—he's been back for half an hour now. I was quite worried. Never mind now, sit down by the fire and thaw yourself out. I've got a nice chicken in the oven all ready for our first meal together. I'm sure you could do with a good meal, coming all that way?'

All the time Mrs Blakey was talking, scarcely giving Karen time to answer, she was bustling about, taking her cloak and bag and dumping them on the hall stand then leading her into a large kitchen at the back of the house, hung with brasses which gleamed in the light from the blazing fire in the grate. Karen relaxed as the heat from the fire hit her. This kitchen might be very different from the one in Chapel Street but it had the same warm, welcoming atmosphere. She could be happy here, she thought.

'You're very kind, Mrs Blakey.'

'No, no, you must call me Annie,' she cried as she lifted from the oven a golden chicken surrounded by roast potatoes.

'Oh, it smells gorgeous,' gasped Karen. 'We only have chicken at Christmas at home, though my gran has a small-holding on the moor and sometimes she brings us a boiling fowl. Do you know, you remind me of my gran somehow, even though she's small and thin.'

'I'll take that as a compliment,' beamed Annie, and the tone was set for their relationship. By the end of the evening the two women were calling each other by their first names. Annie told Karen how she was running the farm on her own while her two sons were away at the war, and Karen told Annie all about her brother Joe who was in the army too.

'Though he's in the Australian Army,' she explained. 'He emigrated in 1910 and now he's back in Europe with the ANZACs.'

Annie was such a friendly body, Karen thought happily as she took her candle up the stairs to the tiny bedroom which was to be hers for the foreseeable future. She could make a friend of Annie, the first real friend she would have made since coming to Essex.

Sinking into the soft feather bed, she was soon happily anticipating her new job. Previous spells of night duty had taught her to adapt to working at night and sleeping during the day, and she felt she would settle to it in no time. As Greenfields was just opening as a convalescent home, all the staff were in the same position as she was. It would be an interesting experience, starting from scratch.

*   *   *

Karen found herself furiously busy in the next few weeks as wounded and maimed men arrived at the hospital after being patched up elsewhere and pronounced on the mend. The battles were intensifying every day and more and more wounded were coming home, till the hospitals were overflowing.

'The poor lads are coming here earlier and earlier,' Karen confided to Annie. 'I mean, earlier in their treatment than they did at the beginning. We could do with a few more nurses. We're stretched to our limit.'

Annie sighed sympathetically. 'I don't know how you do it,' she said. 'It would tear me to bits, young boys hurt badly like that.'

'You would manage it if you had to,' Karen replied as she pulled on her cloak for yet another night at Greenfields—one which was to have been her free night.

All the nurses were working longer and longer hours and Karen was no exception, often not leaving the hospital until nine or ten in the morning.

*   *   *

It was almost ten o'clock the following morning and she was giving the night report to Matron when there was a knock at the door. Matron sighed and glanced wryly at Karen. This was the third attempt they had had at getting through the report and each time they had been interrupted by some emergency or other.

'Come!' she called, and the door opened to admit Doctor Clarke and another man, a priest or minister of some sort, judging by his collar.

Doctor Clarke, a young houseman seconded from Romford, had been up since two o'clock. He wore an unbuttoned and crumpled white coat and a slightly dishevelled air. Matron stared at him in disapproval.

'We may be busy, Doctor, but I don't think that's a good enough reason to let our standards slip,' she reprimanded.

He glanced down at his coat and buttoned it hastily.

'Oh, sorry, Matron. I was just leaving when I met Father Murphy on Ward 2 and thought I'd bring him in to meet you as he's new to the place.'

The priest stepped forward as Doctor Clarke

114

introduced him to Matron and she bowed her head in stately acknowledgement, a gesture Karen knew to be copied from the Matron of Oldchurch Hospital. The thought made her twinkle with suppressed mirth as she too was introduced to Father Murphy.

'Father Murphy has recently come to St Michael's. And this is Sister Knight, our Night Sister, Father.'

'Hallo. How are you, Sister?'

His accent was musical and touched with a West of Ireland brogue, his handshake firm and cool. His calm grey eyes looked steadily into her brown ones.

Karen was answering him politely when she remembered Robert's friend whom she had met in Bishop Auckland.

'Oh,' she exclaimed, 'I believe I met a friend of yours last time I was home—a Father Donelly?'

Father Murphy was breaking into a smile and nodding when Matron's icy tones interrupted them.

'Sister, this is neither the time nor the place for social chit-chat. I have a busy morning ahead.'

The priest, who fortunately had his back to Matron, pulled a wry face and Karen smiled, looking anything but sorry as she made her apologies to Matron and left the room. As she walked to the front door of the old house Father Murphy was close behind her so that they happened to set off down the drive together.

'That lady reminds me of Mother Superior at my infants' school,' he remarked and laughed, an infectious sound with which Karen found herself joining in.

115

'Hospital matrons can be like that,' she answered.

'You're going into the village?' he asked as they came to the gates.

'Yes, I'm lodging with Mrs Blakey.'

'Oh, yes, I know the lady.'

They turned on to the road to the village and walked a little while in silence, but an easy silence, Karen realized with surprise. It was as though they knew each other well. She was still pondering why this was when he spoke again.

'You were saying you had met my friend Sean— Father Donelly?'

'Oh, yes, I met him in Auckland, he was with a doctor friend of mine. He mentioned you to me when I told him where I was going to work.'

'But Auckland? Surely not.'

'Yes, Bishop Auckland.' She nodded her head then laughed. 'Oh, I see, you thought I meant New Zealand. No, County Durham.'

'Oh, yes, Sean is in Durham. It's a while since I heard from him though. Not since he was out in Africa last year.'

'Well, he says you owe him a letter, I was to tell you if I met you.'

'And here you are, it's a small world, as they say.'

He laughed aloud and his laugh was deep and musical. As they reached Annie's garden gate Karen stopped and looked up at him. His grey eyes were fringed with long, black lashes. Striking eyes, she thought dreamily. He was slim and tall and the black of his clerical garb suited him.

Karen blinked. What on earth was she doing standing here talking to a priest? And worse, allowing herself to feel attracted to him? By, Da

116

would have forty fits if knew about it.

'And how is Father Donelly?' the priest was saying but the smile faded from his eyes as he sensed her withdrawal. Karen was opening the gate and backing up the garden path.

'He's fine. Well, goodbye, Father.'

The sentence came out in a rush and Karen fairly ran round the side of the house to the kitchen door.

'Is that you, Karen?'

Annie was bending over a frying pan on the open fire of the range and the room was filled with a strong smell of bacon. She straightened up and looked round, her brow knitting as she saw Karen's flushed face.

'Oh, dear, you look a bit tired and upset. Is something wrong?'

Karen shook her head and smiled reassuringly at her. 'Nothing a good day's sleep won't cure, Annie,' she declared. 'I'm tired and hungry that's all. Mind, that bacon smells grand, it does.'

'Best come and eat it while it's hot, then,' advised Annie as she emptied the pan on to a plate and set it on the table. 'Then up to bed with you. I put a hot bottle in so it'll be nice and warm.'

Chapter Seven

There was a letter from France. It had to be from Joe. Joe, who had travelled halfway across the world with the ANZACs, and escaped unscathed from Gallipoli, thank God.

'There's a surprise for you.' Annie was beaming

117

with pleasure as she saw the effect the letter had on Karen. 'Oh, aren't you going to open it?' she added in surprise as Karen put it by her plate.

'Later,' she said and Annie had to be content with that.

Karen ate her pie and drank the hot sweet tea as she listened to the inconsequential chatter of her landlady. Annie was inclined to be garrulous but then, reflected Karen, she had been on her own for a year or so now. The letter was propped before Karen's plate, a treat to be enjoyed later in the privacy of her room.

The anticipated pleasure of reading the letter kept a half-smile playing around her mouth while the blazing fire in the grate lent colour to her cheeks and glinting highlights to her dark, waving hair, for once hanging loosely on her shoulders without the restrictions of her cap.

Annie had been a little disappointed when she took the letter up to her room in the afternoon and Karen was aware of it but she really wanted to read it in private. She would tell Annie anything interesting in it later. She heard the back door close after the landlady as she went about her evening chores. There were the hens to lock up in case a fox got in and one or two other things to do before she could settle down before the fire for the evening.

Karen flung herself on the bed and slit open the envelope. Eagerly she began reading, then with a muffled exclamation pulled the candle on her bedside table closer to make sure she had read aright.

'Dear Kerry,' Joe began, and Karen knew straight away that he had good news for her. He

118

was the only one who ever called her Kerry, and then only when he had something good to tell her. Da frowned on the use of pet names. Karen grinned to herself and turned over on to her stomach, propping herself up on her elbows with the letter on the pillow.

I am coming back to England for a spot of leave so by the time you get this I'll probably already be in London. If you can manage to get the time off to meet me I will be in Liverpool Street Station at six o'clock Saturday the twelth. I *have* to see you. If you can't make it I will travel down to Greenfields on Sunday morning.
I have very important news!
Don't be alarmed. I won't tell you now, though. It will be better when I see you.

What news could be so urgent and yet not urgent enough to tell her in a letter? The question teased her mind all the time she was completing her preparations for going on duty. Donning a clean apron and 'Sister Dora' cap, she thought about it. After all, it couldn't be bad news. Joe was in England and apparently uninjured. He must be all right, else why would he say he was here for a spot of leave? And hadn't he said it was good news?

Disappointing Annie even more, Karen called goodbye and slipped out of the house. Wrapping her cloak closely around her, she walked briskly up the lane. Roll on Saturday and the prospect of a lovely reunion with her brother. Tomorrow it was, only one more night to work. It was her night off anyway, she didn't have to ask for it off. She

119

wondered if she should ask for Sunday, though. It might be possible.

The night air was damp and cold and creeping wisps of fog began to obscure the old house even as she walked up the drive to the front door. She could hear the muffled roar of the river as it flowed by the edge of the steeply sloping lawns in its rush to the sea. It was swollen with recent rain as was often the case.

Thankfully, Karen let herself into the hall which was warmed by a smouldering log fire. Shedding her cloak at the hall stand, she glanced briefly in the mirror hanging over the great stone mantel before going to Matron's office to take the report.

Matron was sitting at her desk and Karen saw with a sinking heart that she was juggling with the names on the off-duty list. She sat straight in her chair and favoured Karen with a slight smile of greeting.

'Oh, there you are, Sister. I trust you slept well?'

'Yes, thank you, Matron,' Karen replied, deciding to get her request in quickly while her superior was in a good mood. 'Er . . . I was wondering, would it be possible for me to have Sunday off besides Saturday? My brother is home from France and—'

'Impossible, Sister.'

Karen's hopes of a weekend with her brother were dashed immediately. What was more, the affability with which Matron had greeted her was completely gone. Her tone was frigid now.

'As it happens, I was going to ask you if you wouldn't mind working tomorrow night, Sister? You know we are woefully short of staff.'

Karen's heart dropped even further but she

wasn't going to give in on this, not when Joe was coming to London.

'I'm afraid I can't, Matron. I have arranged to meet my brother. After all, I worked through my last off-duty night.'

'There's no such word as can't for a nurse . . .' Matron was beginning, but stopped as she looked at Karen's flushed but determined face and sighed heavily.

'Oh, very well, Sister, you have the right to take your off duty of course.' Pushing the off-duty list aside she picked up the report book and went through the list of patients with Karen, her voice icily formal.

*　　　*　　　*

Later in the evening, Karen was just emerging from Ward 1, the former drawing room of the house, when she met Father Murphy again.

'Good evening, Sister,' he said, and again she felt that little spark of attraction. She couldn't understand it, she thought, as she answered his greeting.

'I hope you don't mind, Sister? I mean, my disturbing you at half-past nine at night. But I did promise I would come back to see Private Buckley. Poor man, he's lost his younger brother. He got the news today.'

'Of course. But it's lights out at ten, you understand? I'm sorry, but I have the other men in the ward to consider. Though I was really sorry to hear about Private Buckley's brother, it was in his report.'

He went into the ward and Karen sat down at

121

the table in the hall and took out the medicine list. Calling Nurse Ellis from the ward to double check the drugs with her, she opened the dangerous drugs cupboard with the key fastened on a chain to her dress pocket.

*   *   *

Karen sat on the train going up to town. She felt rested and happy and was eagerly looking forward to seeing Joe. Gazing at her reflection in the carriage window she saw that excitement had brought roses to her cheeks. She moved closer to the window and realized the dark smudges under her eyes were much fainter than they had been lately. Short tendrils of hair had escaped from under her cap and she put up a hand to anchor them into place before leaning back in the seat and closing her eyes, letting her mind wander.

The night before had been fairly quiet, giving her time to chat a little with the wakeful ones. And there were always wakeful patients, no matter how many sleeping draughts she gave out on orders from the doctor. Father Murphy was good with them, she mused, he didn't seem to mind how long he sat patiently listening to a wounded soldier. A nice man he was.

After the priest had gone she had sat a short while with Private Buckley, just listening to him, letting him talk about his brother.

'Tom and me, we had a vegetable barrow before the war,' he had said. 'There were just the two of us, you know. Our dad was killed when he was thrown from his cart when the axle broke. And Mum, well, she died in '07. She had the consumption.'

Private Buckley had smiled, and Karen knew he was remembering his mother. 'She was a good 'un, my mum. A fighter. She came over from Ireland to be a housemaid when she was only twelve. And then she met our dad and they got married. I was only four when he was killed and our Tom only two.'

Private Buckley had gone quiet and Karen knew he was thinking of his brother. After a while he started again.

'Our Tom was only seventeen, you know. He shouldn't have been there but he would go. He couldn't stand being left on his own, see.'

Karen thought he had talked enough for the time being.

'You should try to sleep, Private. I'll bring you some cocoa. That will help,' she'd said. The soldier had looked at her blankly.

'Thank you, Sister, but I don't really want to sleep. It's the dreams and that. You dream everything's all right again and then when you wake up . . . Anyway, I'm off home tomorrow for a week, then it's back to France for me.'

Karen shook her head slightly and sat up straight as the train drew into Liverpool Street Station. Forget about the hospital and Private Buckley, she told herself. You're going to meet Joe and you'll have a lovely time. Tomorrow you can think about the war and the hospital but tonight is for Joe and a lovely time with him. 'Sufficient unto the day is the evil thereof,' as Da would quote.

*   *   *

A wave of love washed over her as she saw Joe waiting at the barrier. An older, graver Joe than she remembered, she had time to note, though he still had a ready smile and wave when he caught sight of her. She ran the last few yards and flung her arms around his neck and she was laughing and crying together.

'Why on earth are you crying, lass?' he chuckled after he'd lifted her up and swung her round in the air and put her down again.

Joe laughed and hugged her again but there was something lurking in his eyes which belied his laughter and brought a faint foreboding to her. She chided herself for being fanciful as she took his arm and they walked out of the station.

'Where shall we go, Joe?'

As if it mattered where they went so long as they were together and could talk like old times.

'We'll go in here, why not?'

Joe steered her towards a little teashop and opened the door, ushering her in before him. The bell tinkled and people sitting at the tables looked up at him, at his Australian sergeant's uniform and his bronzed face under the bush hat with the brim turned up at one side. He easily attracted the attention of the waitress though the teashop was full and somehow she found them a table in a corner, away from the door.

They ordered tea and scrambled eggs on toast, and when the waitress had gone Karen sat back and happily gazed at him.

'You look different, Joe.'

'Well, I am a few years older, pet. Mind, you don't look any older. Still the bonny lass you were when I went off to Australia, you are.'

'No, you're different, not just older,' she insisted.

Joe laughed again, a deep laugh which had heads turning in their direction once again. 'I'm a sergeant now,' he pointed out. 'It's the air of authority. I have to keep my dignity now or I'll lose my stripes again.'

'Again? You lost them? How did that happen?'

Joe glanced away for a moment before he answered. 'Oh, just a little misunderstanding. I was having a joke with one of the lads,' he said easily, and Karen relaxed. He was still the same Joe who had taken a toad into Chapel and let it loose among the pews, causing the girls to scream and stand on the seats in the middle of the reading from the Gospel. The same Joe who had tickled her side while they sat together during those interminable sermons, trying to get her to laugh. The same Joe who had been ordered to bed so often without any supper for his behaviour in Chapel, and the same Joe for whom she had smuggled food under her pinny.

'What are you thinking?' His eyes crinkled in amusement. 'You look so far away. You always were a dreamer. Penny for them?'

'I was thinking of the old days,' she confessed. 'Sitting in Chapel with Kezia and Jemima and you. Mam and Da sitting in front, and Da turning round to hush you and threaten you with dire punishment when you got home. How many Sunday teas and suppers did you go without, do you think?'

'Don't remind me. All that baking Mam would do for Sunday tea and the only cakes I got were the ones you smuggled up to me. Aiding and abetting a criminal, that was. And Jemima and

125

Kezia so prim and proper.'

'There's only Kezia at home now,' said Karen. 'Jemima doesn't go home very often and I don't get many holidays. If it wasn't for Kezia, I don't think Mam could manage.'

'No.'

They fell silent, thinking of Kezia. When they were younger they had not realized what a hard time she had had of it, leaving school and skivvying at the manager's house up on the hillside above Morton Main, close to the older agricultural village of Morton. Then spending the whole of her day off working in her mother's house, cooking and cleaning. Kezia lived for her family and Karen felt a pang of guilt as always when she thought of her.

'I have to talk to you, Karen. I have news of Dave.'

Joe's voice brought her back to the present and she stared at him. Having dropped his bombshell, Joe was sitting back and watching his sister anxiously.

'News of Dave?'

Karen was suddenly shaking, her heart beating so loudly she thought Joe must surely hear it from across the table.

'He's dead, Karen.'

The statement was blurted out baldly. Joe was full of concern as he saw her fluttering hand begin to fiddle with the cutlery. He leaned forward and laid his hand over hers, stilling it.

'Don't, Karen, don't be upset. He wasn't worth it, really he wasn't.'

'No. I know. I'm not upset,' she murmured, struggling to keep her voice steady. 'How do you

126

know he's dead?'

'I went to Australia House to look at the casualty lists. I was looking to see if any of my old mates were on them. And there it was: David Mitchell, Sydney. But I was on my way to France and I had no time to come to see you and didn't want to put it in a letter.' He paused before adding, 'Gallipoli. It was at Gallipoli.'

'Gallipoli?' repeated Karen, wonderingly. How could he have been killed at Gallipoli? He was in Australia, wasn't he? No, Joe must have got it wrong. David would never have volunteered for any war, he wouldn't have been at Gallipoli.

'Yes, that's right. I had heard he had joined the army at the beginning of the war.'

Karen sat quietly thinking it over. Numb, that was mainly how she felt. For one wild moment, when Joe had mentioned Dave, she had thought he was coming back into her life and panic had seized her. Not again, she had thought. I couldn't go through that again. I don't want him back. I don't love him. I don't think I ever did. She raised her head to Joe who was still gazing anxiously at her over the table. And she thought, the main thing I feel is relief. I'm relieved it is over.

'It's all right, Joe,' she said calmly. 'Perhaps I should be heartbroken but I'm not. I don't know, maybe I am for the wasted life, but there are so many wasted lives, aren't there? But for myself, no, I can't pretend to feel something I don't. It was all over so long ago, for me he was already dead.'

'Well, I thought I'd better tell you straight away, Karen. I wrote to Mrs Mitchell too, it was only fair.'

'Oh, yes.' Karen thought about Dave's mother,

she would be grief-stricken. Karen was sorry for that.

'We won't talk about it any more, eh?' said Joe. 'Let's just enjoy our tea and then we'll go out somewhere after, what do you say? We could go to a music hall if you like.'

Karen opened her eyes wide and held up her hands in mock horror.

'A music hall? Joe Knight, how can you suggest such a thing? I'll tell Da on you, I will.' She grinned wickedly. 'Which music hall do you fancy then?'

They went to the Alhambra and saw Vesta Tilley impersonating a sergeant major. And they giggled and laughed and sang along with everyone else in the crowded theatre. Forgetting Dave and the war and the hospital for a whole two hours, they had a roaring good time.

Afterwards, still chuckling, they came out on to the dark street and Joe went with her back to the station. They waited in a companionable silence for the train to Romford where Karen would get her connection to Littlemarsh, the small market town near Greenfields village.

At the last minute Karen was overwhelmed with sadness and anxiety for her brother; he had not mentioned the Front but she could imagine what it was like for him there by the things she had heard from her patients.

'Where are you staying, Joe, is it a good place?' She could ask him about that even if she couldn't ask him about France.

'Oh, yes, not far away either. The local Wesleyan Minister arranged it for me.'

Karen nodded, that was all right then. She

128

sought for something else to say. Goodness, they had been chattering all evening, why was it so hard now?

The train came in and the precious evening was over.

'See you soon,' Joe called as she leaned out of the window. 'Keep your pecker up!' And as an afterthought, 'God bless and keep you, lass.'

And you, thought Karen as she took her seat. And you, Joe, God keep you safe. Then she was on her way back to Essex.

*   *   *

Patrick Murphy was sitting with Father Brown, the parish priest, enjoying a bed-time chat over a glass of whiskey. He stretched his legs out to catch some slight warmth from the desultory, smoking fire and wished for his bed. But the old man sitting opposite him was looking expectantly at him, wanting to be told of Patrick's afternoon at the hospital. Until recently, Father Brown had performed the hospital visiting but he was getting older and his legs gave him trouble so Patrick had been sent to take over the most arduous of his duties.

'How is that young man, Father, the one who had both his legs amputated? Private Lynch, is it? He's on Ward 2 as I remember.'

'He went home at last, Father. No more fighting for him,' answered Patrick. There was no way they could patch up amputees and send them back to fight, thank God, he thought, thinking of another boy who had been pronounced fit to return to France only that morning. Patrick was a troubled

129

man, more troubled every day. How did one counsel boys, tell them that the Lord was watching over them, and then watch them go back to the battlefields of France?

'Have another, Father?'

Father Brown was holding out the whiskey decanter and as Patrick assented he splashed a generous amount of liquid into his glass.

'You look tired tonight, my boy,' he commented, and Patrick seized the opportunity to make his excuses and go to bed.

'I am, Father, I am. If you don't mind, I think I will have an early—'

The sound of the telephone bell coming from the hall made him pause and both of them listened to the footsteps of Mrs Best the housekeeper as she went to answer it. A telephone call at this time of night could only mean a call from the hospital. Not many people in the village apart from the doctor owned a telephone. Urgent calls for the priest usually came by messenger.

Mrs Best, her plump form wrapped in a woollen robe and her hair hanging in a thick plait over one shoulder, opened the door.

'It's Greenfields, Father Murphy,' she announced.

'Thank you, Mrs Best.'

Patrick got to his feet, went out into the hall and picked up the telephone.

'Hallo, Father Murphy here.'

'I'm sorry to bring you out on a cold night, Father, but it's Private Buckley. He is so very low, almost suicidal, Father.'

'I'll come straight away,' said Patrick and put the phone back on its hook. Calling an explanation to

130

Father Brown, he picked up his bag and went out to the stable. Patrick had recently acquired a pony and trap, for the house he shared with Father Brown was one-and-a-half miles from the hospital.

As he harnessed the pony a feeling of sadness came over him in connection with Private Buckley. The soldier had been doing so well until he got the news of his brother's death, but now the heart seemed to have gone from him.

Patrick sighed, feeling inadequate. Here he was, going to offer the comforts of his faith to yet another eighteen year old who should have been at home with his family, not lying broken on a hospital bed. Except that this particular eighteen year old didn't have a family anyway, he reminded himself dismally.

Sister Knight, the young Night Sister, popped into his mind as he led the pony out into the road. Now she was good with the men: not only at relieving their bodily discomforts but seeming to know exactly what to say to comfort their minds too. He climbed into the trap and flicked the reins, setting the pony into motion, still thinking about Sister Knight. He often found himself thinking of her lately. Too often, he knew.

*   *   *

Karen was only half a mile down the road from the station when she heard the sound of a pony trotting behind her, its hooves ringing out smartly on the metalled road. She moved over to the side and looked back, hoping it was someone from the village who would give her a lift. She was deathly tired now and emotionally wrung out after taking leave of her brother once more without knowing when she would see him again.

As Karen turned to face the driver of the trap a shaft of moonlight appeared through a gap in the darkly scudding clouds and illuminated her face, making it glow strangely white against the dark background of the hedge. The pony shied, neighing in fright until soothed by soft tones which Karen recognized with a tiny lift of her spirits. Father Murphy. He must be out on a call.

'Hallo there, are you after a ride to the village?'

'Oh, yes, Father Murphy, please.'

His lilting brogue was a delight to her and she smiled as he got down from the trap and handed her up. He was silent as he resumed his seat and took up the reins, encouraging the pony to a fast trot, all his attention on the animal.

'I'm very grateful for the lift.' Karen peeped at him but all she could see was his dark profile against the sky.

'Sure now, it's a pleasure, Sister,' he replied, and fell silent once again.

Karen felt she ought to make some small-talk, but what could she say to a priest? He was a great mystery to her. She knew nothing much about Catholicism or priests, coming as she did from a strict, Non-Conformist background. She had met priests often in the hospital, of course, but it was different here without her stiffly starched apron and cap . . .

'Going to the hospital, are you?'

They were rolling along nicely now with the lantern on the front bobbing merrily. The priest relaxed and turned his attention to Karen.

'No, not tonight, Father.' The title sounded

132

strange in her ears, she had used it so rarely before. But why should she call this man Father? she wondered abstractedly. She called her priest Mister . . .

'Been up to London, have you, Sister?' he asked.

'Yes, that's right. I've been up to see my brother, he's home on leave from France. Well, not home, exactly, I mean he's in England. He's with the ANZACs.'

'Oh?'

'Yes, he emigrated to Australia before the war. It's the first time I've seen him since then. Oh, I've had a grand time this evening, it was lovely to see him again.'

'I'm pleased for you,' he said.

They were entering the village now and Karen realized she had been chattering about herself without asking him what he was doing out so late.

'Are you going to the hospital now?' she asked, thinking it was not a good time of night to be called out.

'Yes. I'm often needed in the small hours, as you know. That's usually where I see you.'

There was no need to amplify this to Karen, she nodded simply. They both knew why he was called out during the night. The small hours, she thought, when despair pounced.

Father Murphy drew the pony to a halt by the gate of the cottage and jumped lightly down to assist Karen's descent.

'Thank you.'

Her voice was almost inaudible for as she felt his hands on her, a sudden tingling shot through her body. It made her feel awkward, gauche even; she didn't know how she felt. He stood in silence,

133

looking down at her, a strange expression on his face, lit now by the moon which had come fully out. For one magical moment she thought he was going to bend down and kiss her; unconsciously she lifted her face nearer. But abruptly he dropped his hands and turned back to the trap.

'Well . . .' said Karen. 'Goodnight, and thank you for the lift.'

'Goodnight.'

The spell was broken. He gave a stiff wave as he drove off without even looking at her and she felt bereft. She stood for a short while, gazing after him, before letting herself into the cottage.

'I was getting a bit anxious about you,' said Annie. She was waiting up and Karen felt a pang of guilt.

'I'm sorry I'm so late, Annie.'

'Never mind. Praise God, you're here now. You never know though, it's not safe up in London with those Zeppelins flying about.'

'Oh, Annie, there weren't any Zeppelins,' Karen chuckled. Annie was a right worrit, as Gran would say. 'I met Father Murphy on the road,' she continued, sitting down in the chair opposite Annie's. 'He gave me a lift, he was on his way up to the hospital. Oh, Annie, I've had a grand time, I have, but it's lovely to be back here in the warm. It is a very cold night, I think there'll be a storm.'

'Father Murphy, eh? Isn't he the one who took over from Father Brown? Is he nice? As good as the rector with those poor boys?'

'Oh, yes, a nice man.'

Yes, a nice man, thought Karen dreamily as she sat before the fire letting the warmth seep into her while Annie bustled about making cocoa.

Once in bed, Karen's mind ranged over the evening, remembering the show and Vesta Tilley and the laughter shared with Joe. And she had been so proud of her bronzed, handsome brother as they had walked down the street arm in arm. Joe was—well, Joe was Joe and she loved him.

Even though she was tired, she was still too excited to sleep, her mind still active. She turned over on to her back and put her hands under her head. Joe had reminded her of so many good times at home and for the first time in ages Karen was homesick for the North-East and her family. It was a pity Joe hadn't time to go home before he went to France this time. By, Da would be like a dog with two tails if he saw Joe, and Mam would be too.

Through the curtains, Karen heard the patter of rain on the window and the howling of the wind as it rose. The threatened storm had arrived then.

At last, she allowed herself to think of Dave, feeling a twinge of sadness for what might have been. But it was only a twinge. She had done her mourning with a bitter yearning long ago, when he had deserted her. Now it felt as though her short marriage had happened to someone else.

Chapter Eight

'Help! He . . .'

The cry was cut short as Karen pushed open the front door of the old house. She sighed. Oh dear, she thought, not another night like last night. She hung her cloak on the hall stand and glanced into the mirror to check her cap was on straight, smiling wryly at her reflection. This wasn't the attitude she should start the night with, she told herself. She really must be ready for a night off. Shrugging, she headed for Ward 1, the ward the cry had come from.

Opening the door of the ward, she ducked with practised ease as she saw the missile flung from the soldier's hand and fast coming her way. She managed to evade the urine bottle; it went whizzing past her ear to crash against the end wall. Obviously a near miss for the young VAD too, she saw. The nurse was trembling with shock as she stood in the doorway of the makeshift sluice.

'Oh, Sister!'

The relief on Nurse Jennings's face was heartfelt as she rushed into explanations of what was happening. 'It's the new one in the end bed, Private Harvey. He ... he ...' Her voice was rising and she stuttered in her urgency to tell Night Sister and be relieved of the responsibility.

'Pull yourself together, Nurse,' snapped Karen in her best imitation of Matron. 'Do you want the whole ward disturbed? Come with me, this instant.'

Karen strode into the ward, the converted drawing room of the old house, Nurse Jennings at her heels.

'Keep away! I'm telling you, I'm not going back, I'm not! I'm going home. I'm English, not bloody French. I'm not going back to France, I tell you.'

The young soldier, hardly old enough to be in the army by the look of him, crouched high on his pillow at the head of the bed, glaring at the two nurses. His hazel eyes were dark with

136

determination, his light brown hair sticking to his forehead with sweat. Undeterred, Karen strode towards him.

'Now, lad,' she began, but halted in her tracks as he grabbed a bottle of lemonade from his locker top with his one good hand and raised it threateningly. Yet she could see he was trembling and unsure of himself, and his wide eyes reflected the horror of some awful nightmare.

She held up a warning hand to Nurse Jennings to stop her also.

'Hush, now, lad,' she said softly. The boy in the bed stopped shouting and looked warily at her. Pushing Nurse Jennings back towards the door of the ward, she spoke quietly to her, trying to instill calm and convey urgency at the same time.

'Go to the supper room, find a doctor and a porter and bring them back. Your senior nurse, too.'

Nurse Jennings was still trembling with fright but nevertheless was unwilling to leave the slightly built sister with a 'loony', as she privately thought of the soldiers suffering from shell-shock. She looked dubiously at Karen.

'Go on now!'

The VAD flushed and rushed off to the annexe in the grounds where the supper room was located. Karen heard the ward door swing closed and the bang of the front door a few seconds later without taking her eyes off the soldier. Experience had taught her never to do that. Quickly she went over in her mind which of the staff might be available to help. If Doctor Clarke was in the supper room and they could get hold of the night porter . . . Why, oh why, did this sort of thing always happen when

137

staff levels were at their lowest?

None of this showed on her face. She smiled sunnily at the boy crouched on the bed. Private Harvey, the girl had said, hadn't she? This was Karen's late starting night, she had had an extra couple of hours off, coming on duty at ten instead of eight, and she hadn't yet had time to read the report, let alone the notes on the new patients. And now that would have to wait until this one was settled down.

'Howay, lad,' she coaxed, for she had recognized his accent as soon as he had spoken. He had to be from the North-East, somewhere close to her own home, though maybe a little further north. Deliberately she thickened her accent, allowing it to turn into a pronounced Northumbrian burr. Smiling steadily, she walked slowly up to him and held out her hand for the bottle of lemonade.

'Why, hinny, what're you going to do wi' that? You're surely not going to hit a little body like me? Let me have it now.' The soldier didn't move though he lowered the bottle slightly.

'You'll never get better if you don't sleep, you know, now will you? Eeh, lad, you've been dreaming that's all, you've had a nightmare. Howay man, you're all right now, you're fine you are. You're back in England now, no fighting allowed here, eh? You got a "Blighty" one, they can't send you back. It's home for you, lad, just as soon as you're well enough to travel, so the more sleep you get the sooner that will be. Where is it now, Hexham mebbe?'

Karen let the sing-song cadences of the North-East soothe the agitated boy. He stared at her suspiciously without answering at first, but allowed

138

her to take the lemonade bottle from him and help him back under the blankets. Quiet now, he lay back, watching her steadily.

'I'll tuck you up nice and cosy, shall I?' Karen deftly adjusted his pillows and straightened his sheets, all the while talking to him softly. 'You're not from Newcastle, are you? I can tell that, like. Where did you say you were from?'

'Tynedale,' he said at last.

'What's your name, lad? Your first name, I mean?'

'Nick.'

'Good God! Are we ever going to get any peace this night?'

The voice was an irritated whine and Karen knew it immediately.

'Go back to sleep, Corporal, everything's fine now.'

She glanced over at the man who had complained. Why do some patients get irritable the moment they begin to get better? she wondered. They could be more trouble than when they were seriously ill, and this particular corporal had been complaining for days now. It was high time he went on his way. He stared back at her before grunting and turning over on to his other side so that his back was to her.

Karen forgot him and gave all her attention to Private Harvey. Feeling his brow, she judged it was only slightly hotter than normal. Surreptitiously she looked at the bandaged stump where his right forearm and hand should have been. No seepage there. So far so good. She studied his face. His eyes were closing now as he drifted off to sleep. Oh, well, she needn't have sent for any help. He

139

looked so young, lying there, so vulnerable, almost like a child. How old was he? Seventeen? Or even younger? No doubt a volunteer for the army, she thought wearily.

His breathing became regular and Karen moved off to do a ward round, noiseless in her rubber-soled shoes. Most of the men in the ward were well on the way to recovery, thank goodness. Private Harvey was the only new patient.

The opening of the ward door brought her swiftly back down the ward. Nurse Jennings was back with Doctor Clarke and someone else, not a porter though. She peered round the doctor to see who it was. They certainly could do without a visitor at this time of the night, or was it morning? Time was getting on. But no, it was Father Murphy. Nurse Jennings must have asked for his help when she couldn't find the night porter.

'I'm sorry we disturbed you, Doctor,' Karen apologized to the duty houseman. 'I thought we would need assistance with Private Harvey. He was very distraught—a nightmare, I think.'

'No trouble, Sister,' Doctor Clarke replied. 'I was still up as it happens. Father Murphy and I were with Private O'Donnel on Ward 3. He kindly offered any assistance he could give.'

Karen looked past him at the priest. 'Hallo, Father Murphy,' she said as though she had only just noticed him.

'Evening, Sister,' he answered, and their eyes met for a moment before she turned back to Doctor Clarke.

'Is something wrong with Private O'Donnel?' she asked. 'I haven't had time to read the report yet, I was busy with Private Harvey from the minute I

140

came on duty.'

In her thoughts she hurriedly reviewed Private O'Donnel's case. Oh, yes, he was one of a batch of men from last month's intake, all of them blinded at Ypres.

'Nothing physical, Sister, apart from his eyes, of course.' The doctor sighed.

All three of them moved aside for Nurse Jennings who eased herself past the group. She was calmer now that she had the reassurance of having her seniors with her. Someone had called out softly at the end of the ward and Nurse Jennings hurried to answer.

Disaster struck as she passed the dressings trolley, already laid for the morning's dressing round and covered in a sterile dressing towel. Her apron brushed against the covering cloth, bringing it off the trolley, and with it an enamel kidney dish, filled with instruments. The clatter reverberated in the ward as the dish bounced and forceps and probes skidded across the floor, waking up all the men and Private Harvey especially.

'Help me! Help me! She's brought them in, the bitch! They'll force me . . .'

Private Harvey screamed with rage as he saw the two men in the doorway with Karen in his first hunted glance and came to his own conclusions.

'Quiet there! Quiet, I say,' bellowed the corporal, sitting up in bed and glaring at Private Harvey. But he was not to be intimidated, he was past that. In a single movement he was out of his bed and shaking awake the man on his other side.

'What? What?' The poor man shaken awake so rudely tried to free himself from the boy's demented grasp but Harvey hung on in

141

desperation.

'Help me, man. Howay, they'll take us all back over there. We have to fight now, we have to stop them,' Harvey cried. He cast a fearful glance at the men in the doorway who were mixing with his dreams and lending them a horrible reality.

The doctor and Karen took less than a second to spring into action but they were closely followed by the priest who had evidently summed up the situation and moved in to help. Karen and Doctor Clarke each took one side of Nick Harvey and pulled him off the other patient. He struggled all the while but somehow they managed, with Father Murphy's help, to get him back into his own bed. Karen murmured soothingly all the while, hardly knowing what she was saying. At last they had him there, sitting on the edge, quiet for the moment and unsure of himself. Blinking rapidly, he looked from one to the other of them making no effort to lie down or fight to get away again.

Karen looked for the VAD to help her get him comfortably back under the bed clothes but Nurse Jennings was standing well out of range of Nick Harvey, wringing her hands, shocked to the core by his violence.

'Come along now, old chap,' Father Murphy said softly, his voice calm and reassuring. He bent over Nick and put a hand on his shoulder 'I'll help you into bed, shall I? No one's going to send you back, you know. You'll make yourself worse if you don't get some rest.'

Karen looked up at him. She had almost forgotten the Father's presence. He appeared so calm and understanding, she thought to herself, almost as though this was an everyday experience

142

for him. Nick Harvey looked at him too, staring at the pleasant handsome face above the clerical collar.

The private relaxed visibly, his shoulders sagging, and allowed himself to be tucked up in bed once more—only to spring up again as he heard Doctor Clarke speak. 'The sedative, Sister.'

Grabbing the bottle which Karen had put down in the melee, Nick Harvey raised it in self-protection. But the priest stood his ground, talking softly and persuasively, and Karen slipped away to fill the hypodermic syringe with a bromide.

'No!'

He had seen the syringe and tried to rise, dropping the bottle as he did so. But he was caught on either side by the two men, who forced him back on the bed and tried to hold him steady.

'I'll hold his legs. You lie on top of him, Father. Then we should be able to hold him still long enough for Sister to administer the sedative. Quickly now, Sister, in the thigh.'

Father Murphy did not hesitate but it took all his strength to hold down the patient without hurting him, even though the doctor was hanging on to his legs. Karen's cap came off in the process but the combined expertise of the doctor and nurse told and eventually she was able to administer the drug. After a few minutes, his eyelids drooped and cautiously they all relaxed, breathing sighs of relief.

Mentally, Karen scolded herself for not putting the bottle well out of the boy's range in the first place. That only showed how ready she was for her night off. Ruefully, she picked up her cap and smiled at the men, chuckling as she saw the priest's

143

hair over his eyes and Doctor Clarke's tie all askew.

'You two look as dishevelled as I must be,' she said as they moved away from the bed. 'How about a cup of tea? Nurse Jennings will see to it.' The young VAD certainly looked as though she could do with something to take her mind off what had happened. Karen regarded her critically.

'By the way, what happened to your senior nurse? I thought I asked you to get her?'

Karen spoke to the nurse but it was Doctor Clarke who answered.

'Oh, we were closer than the annexe, Sister. We brought Nurse Jennings back with us. I thought it best,' he said smoothly, giving the young girl a sympathetic glance. 'But I will have a cup of tea. I'll have to wait around a while in any case, just to make sure he is really out for the rest of the night. Ten minutes or so at least.'

Nurse Jennings blushed and scuttled off to the kitchen. Karen sighed. That one would never make a nurse, no matter how hard she tried, but in this war it was difficult to get the right sort of girl. Most of the trained staff were in France or working in the big hospitals. And with the present flow of casualties, few women were turned away.

She led the way to the desk in the hall which served as her office. There were two comfortable chairs beside it and the men sat down as they waited for their tea while Karen took her place at the desk.

It was Nurse Ellis, the senior nurse from Ward 1, who returned with the tea tray.

'I'm sorry, Sister,' she apologized. Evidently she had been briefed by Nurse Jennings concerning the trouble in the ward. 'Private Harvey was asleep when I went to supper.'

'Not your fault, Nurse,' Karen replied, and she smiled gratefully as she put the tray down on the desk and slipped quickly into the ward to check on the patients. She was a solid, dependable type and Karen felt that with her back in the ward she could relax for a few minutes before doing her rounds again. She picked up the teapot and poured the tea.

'Biscuit?' Smiling at Father Murphy, she offered the plate of biscuits. If this was going to be one of those nights she might as well make the most of the break, she felt. As he took the tea her attention was caught by his hands. They were strong-looking and well cared for, with oval nails cut short and straight. They reminded her of a surgeon's hands, she reflected as she sipped her tea.

Doctor Clarke began a conversation with Father Murphy and Karen turned to the neglected day report. Why on earth she was thinking so much about the priest she didn't know, it wouldn't be long before she had to write the night report for Matron, she thought wryly. Just as well to read the day report first. The old house creaked a little and the occasional snore or grunt came from the wards, but apart from that there was only the murmur of voices from the priest and Doctor Clarke. Perhaps it was going to be a quiet night after all.

'Well, I'm going to get some sleep while I can,' said the doctor finally. Standing up, he drained his cup and went out. Father Murphy sat on a while, taking his time over the tea. Karen finished

145

reading the report and sat back for a moment or two.

'What is it, Sister?'

Karen started, realizing she had been staring at him. Hurriedly she got to her feet, feeling flustered.

'Oh, nothing. I'm sorry if I seemed to be staring—I'm tired, I think. It's a good thing it's my night off tomorrow. I must get on with my rounds now.'

He also rose to his feet. 'Your night off, is it? You'll be going up to London, perhaps, are you?'

'Oh, no. I'll just be pottering about, helping Annie my landlady, maybe taking a walk if it's a fine day.'

He looked thoughtful. 'I will be visiting in the village tomorrow. Perhaps I'll see you.'

Karen nodded, thinking he was only being polite. 'Well, goodnight, Father Murphy.'

She went into Ward 1 to check with Nurse Ellis, who was sitting in the pool of light by the centre desk.

'Everything quiet, Sister,' the nurse reported. Private Harvey was sleeping, looking even younger than when he was awake.

'With a bit of hick everything should be quiet until "lights on" at five o'clock,' said Karen.

'Yes, Sister.'

*　　　*　　　*

Karen left the ward, noticing that the priest had gone from the hall, presumably home to bed. Well, she thought, she still had to check the smaller wards upstairs before getting on with the office

146

work.

Upstairs it was quiet too. The nurses were folding gauze and lint squares and packing them in steel drums, ready for the steam sterilizer. They worked in the dim light of a lamp placed at the end of the ward where they were least likely to disturb the patients but could still keep an eye on them.

'Good work,' Karen whispered. 'Don't bother coming round with me, not when you're busy.' Sometimes there was so little time for this work that the supply of dressings and swabs needed during the day could run out. She went silently round, pausing at each bed, noting one patient, Private O'Donnel, who was restless in his drugged sleep, muttering to himself and moving his bandaged head from side to side. She watched him for a moment but he showed no signs of waking properly so she went on her way down to the desk in the hall.

The whole house was quiet as the dawn light began to filter in through the high windows. Karen hardly noticed as she worked busily on, writing her report and checking the early-morning treatment sheets.

When at last she could relax, it was Father Murphy's face which came into her mind. She couldn't think why she found him so intriguing, she was no longer interested in men and certainly not in a priest, be he never so attractive. But he was attractive . . . . too attractive altogether for her peace of mind. There, she'd finally admitted it to herself.

She wondered what his Christian name was as she gathered her notes together and placed the tidy piles in their folders. But the day was almost here, she had other things to think about. She could hear voices coming from the wards, the deep tones of the soldiers mingling with the lighter ones of the nurses. Getting to her feet, she smoothed her apron and straightened her cap. It was time for her to help with the difficult dressings, not to indulge in romantic fantasies.

Chapter Nine

Patrick drove away from Greenfields Hospital filled with a sense of utter inadequacy. The bitter words of Private O'Donnel went round and round in his head, questions he had answered with platitudes and statements he had been unable to refute convincingly. The pony clopped his way along the country lane, the reins slack as he relived the scene as he'd sat by the soldier's bed only an hour ago.

'Don't talk to me about God, Father,' the soldier had protested. 'I've heard enough, so I have.' He sat up in bed with his back straight as a poker and his bandaged eyes staring straight ahead sightlessly, his lips compressed into a thin, hard line.

'Don't be saying that,' said Patrick. 'You know you will be sorry for it when you feel better and go home to Ireland. Just now you feel low because of what's happened. But you must hold on to your faith for God in his mercy—'

'Mercy? God's mercy, is it, Father? And where was his mercy when my mate was blown up in front of me? Blown to bits with not a decent piece of

148

him to bury even? Not that we have time to bury any of the poor devils. No, it's over the top we have to go, climb over the bodies, be they dead or dying, over the top into—'

'Hush now, hush, my son, this does you no good,' said Patrick. He got out of his chair and took the soldier's hands in his, trying to instill some calm into the boy. Private O'Donnel's voice was rising hysterically and his head began to move from side to side in agitated, jerky movements, but as Patrick held on to his hand he collapsed back on to his pillows and was quiet. After a moment, Patrick tried again.

'God—'

Private O'Donnel interrupted savagely. 'There is no God,' he stated.

Patrick marshalled his thoughts.

'You're overwrought, my son. You must hang on to your faith, you are saying things you don't mean. What will your poor mother think? You will break her heart.'

Private O'Donnel smiled without mirth. 'My mother is dead, Father. She died of a fever after we were evicted from our home. I was four years old. Now, Father, where do you think your God was when that happened?'

But Patrick had no ready answer—at least, not one which did not sound like yet another platitude. Nurse Ellis came and gave the soldier a sleeping draught and as he fell into a troubled sleep, Patrick crept away.

As he drove home he felt restless, unsettled in himself. He almost went into the church but changed his mind and headed off down the road in the direction of a patch of woodland. The wind

149

blew coldly off the Essex marshes but he hardly felt it. His thoughts were melancholy. He was homesick, not so much for Ireland as it was now but for the Ireland of his childhood. He felt isolated somehow, cut off from his own kind in spite of the presence of so many Irish soldiers in the convalescent hospital.

Or maybe it was because of them, he admitted to himself. Especially the very young ones, some of them barely eighteen, the boys who looked up at him from their narrow beds with such trusting eyes despite their experiences in the trenches. They reminded him of himself as a young boy, full of hope for the future. Of the first time he had dared to think that he himself might be a priest, if he worked hard enough and prayed hard enough.

The day Father Brannigan had said to him, 'Do you ever think of becoming a priest, Patrick?'

Himself a priest? Oh, he remembered well the wonder of it. The revelation it had been to him to think that he could do it. He could, he could. To be a priest and bend over the Host and say, *'Hoc est Corpus Meum'*, This is My Body. Patrick sighed, deliberately breaking off that particular memory. It had been a long hard road since that day and perhaps he would have fallen by the wayside were it not for his mother; she had been so filled with ambition for him he thought it would have killed her if he had failed.

How ecstatic she had been when he had won the scholarship and gone to the school run by the Brothers. He remembered only the contempt and hatred he had had to face there. How his bowels would turn liquid when he had to enter the classroom presided over by Brother Jamieson so that he had to race for the lavatories in the yard, the water closets which should have been so much cleaner than the earth closet at home on the farm but smelled so much worse, so that he often vomited as well and was even later getting to the classroom. And how Brother Jamieson would run the leather strap across his own palm once or twice with an anticipatory gleam in his eye and the other boys would titter nervously.

'Hold out your hand,' Brother Jamieson would say, and it was a point of honour not to flinch or pull back even though your palm stung and burned with a fire which surely must be as hot as the flames of Hell.

Patrick rubbed the palm of his right hand with the thumb of his left, feeling the heat of that old pain despite the cold of the December day. Then he put the hand up to the side of his face, feeling the blow which had so often followed the leathering.

'Impertinent boy!' Brother Jamieson would hiss, his light blue eyes half closed in menace. 'What do you mean by looking at me like that?' And the blow would knock Patrick off his feet so that he fell against the legs of the desk, his head flung back to crack against the hard wood. And when he could stand he would stumble to his seat, not looking at his classmates in case he should catch a gleam of sympathy and break down crying.

Dear God! What in heaven's name was making him so maudlin? Patrick shook his head and thrust his hands deep inside his pockets. Those days were long gone and there was no sense in dwelling on them. It had been so different when he had entered the seminary. He had met Sean Donelly

151

there, the clever, saintly Sean who had befriended him and never minded that he was just a country boy from County Clare. He relaxed as he thought of Sean. It was good to think that he was in England too, after his year in Africa. What would Sean think of him now if he knew where his mind was going?

Patrick got down from the trap as the pony had reached the presbytery. He took the horse from between the shafts and led it into the stable to settle it down for the night. As he worked he struggled to free his mind from the depression which had settled on him. How was he to comfort the boys in that hospital when his mind was full of doubts? He had prayed and prayed and fasted and done penance but to no effect; there was no answer to his doubts. When he faced the wounded soldiers, the devout, the ones who believed unquestioningly in God and his Holy Church, whose faith was their very lifeline at this terrible time, he felt no empathy. He was a sham, no good to them at all.

'I want to get away,' he said aloud in the dark stable lit only by a candle lamp. 'I want to live a normal life, be like any man, marry, have children.'

'Is that you, Patrick?'

He jumped and looked across to the house where Father Brown was standing in a pool of light by the back door. Had the old priest heard what he was saying? Patrick felt like a guilty schoolboy. Quickly, he closed the stable door and walked the few intervening yards to the house.

'It's me, Father,' he said.

'Come in now, and close the door,' said Father Brown. 'Is it not a terrible cold night to be out and about? Did I hear you talking to someone just now?'

'Just the horse, Father. I was talking to Daisy, settling her down.'

'Well now, come away in and we'll have a nightcap together.' Father Brown turned and led the way into the sitting room where a fire still burned in the grate. He sounded cheery and glad that Patrick had returned and given him someone to talk to. Not at all as though he had heard anything to disturb him, thought Patrick, glad that at least he did not have to explain anything to the old priest, not tonight. He accepted a glass of Powers whiskey and sat down in an armchair. Perhaps a chat to Father Brown about parish doings was just the thing to take his mind off his doubts. The older man chatted on and Patrick answered him, smiling and asking questions of his own, trying to keep a look of interest. He watched Father Brown's face in the flickering light from the fire, animated as he discussed the work he loved. Just like Father Brannigan had been, at home in County Clare.

'It is a noble calling, Patrick, there is none more noble than to be a priest of the Catholic Church. I hope when the time comes you will hear the call and answer it, my boy. To be privileged to serve God in such a way. And after that, to serve Ireland, to help free her from the yoke of the English,' Father Brannigan had said to him, his voice full of emotion. Patrick remembered how his heart had swelled with pride at the idea that he could do either of those things. He smiled gently now and Father Brown looked strangely at him for he had been telling Patrick of how he had been out

153

that very afternoon to comfort a poor mother who had lost her son in the war.

'Ah,' he said, 'you're tired, Patrick, of course you are, and ready for your bed.'

'I am, Father,' he admitted. He drained his glass and rose to his feet. Everything looks black in the night time, he reflected. A good night's sleep was what he needed all right, and then tomorrow he would be more cheerful.

*   *   *

'Hallo there, Sister. You look very busy. Would you like a hand?'

Karen, who was on her hands and knees by the flowerbed outside Annie's parlour window, grubbing up dead leaves and flowers with a trowel, hurriedly got to her feet and looked towards the gate which Patrick was just opening.

'Father Murphy, how nice,' she said, automatically putting a hand up to push back a stray lock of hair and smearing earth across her cheek in the process. In spite of the cold wind she felt hot and bothered and thoroughly at a disadvantage. Self-consciously she began to untie the sacking apron which she was wearing to protect her dress. 'I didn't expect to see you, Father.'

'Oh? I thought I said I would be in the village today, Sister?'

Patrick walked up the garden path just as Annie appeared round the corner of the cottage with a basket of eggs in her hand.

'Oh, a visitor,' she said.

'It's Father Murphy, Annie. You know, I've told

154

you he visits at the hospital. Father, this is Mrs Blakey, my landlady and good friend.'

'Pleased to meet you, Father, I'm sure,' said Annie, holding out her hand and shaking Patrick's enthusiastically. 'Won't you come in and have some tea?'

He glanced at Karen, looking a little unsure of himself. What he had really wanted to do was invite her to go for a walk with him.

'Well, I don't know—' he began.

'Oh, come on, Father, it gives us an excuse to have a break too. I've new-baked scones and strawberry jam. You'll like my scones, I'm sure. Will you take the Father into the parlour, Karen? I'll soon put these away and put the kettle on.'

The parlour, she thought, suppressing a smile. Annie had a nice sense of what was right and for her that meant the vicar and the doctor were shown into the parlour, along with only a few select others. The Minister of Karen's Chapel did not rate the parlour but evidently Father Murphy, as a priest, did.

'It will be warmer in the kitchen,' suggested Karen.

'No, no, the parlour, Karen,' Annie insisted as she led the way indoors. 'The fire is laid just to put a lucifer to.'

The air in the parlour was distinctly chilly as Karen opened the door and went in. She shivered as she motioned Patrick to a horsehair armchair. She found the box of matches on the ornate marble mantelshelf and lit the fire, standing back to watch as smoke curled round the kindling until at last a tiny flame appeared. She lit the gas mantle on the wall to make the gloomy room look a little more cheery and then picked up the bellows and blew on the smoking fire. All the time she felt strangely shy, which was quite ridiculous, she told herself.

'Karen,' said Father Murphy, and she put the bellows down and moved over to the opposite armchair.

'Yes, Father?'

'Nothing. I mean . . . I hadn't heard your Christian name before.'

'It's from the Bible. You know, "Job had three daughters, Jemima, Kezia and Keren-happuch",' said Karen, speaking quickly and nervously. She put her hands down on the edge of the chair, feeling the pricking of the horse hair on her skin. 'My father is a lay preacher, he named his daughters after the daughters of Job. Though he changed the spelling of my name a little—a not e. Not his son though, he only has one son, and he's called Joe. Joseph. We're Methodists, you see.'

'Yes, I believe you have said before,' he said. Karen realized she had been babbling and fell silent, wishing Annie would hurry up with the tea.

'The daughters of Job were beautiful too,' the priest said softly, so softly that Karen thought she must have misheard him. She looked up and saw he was watching her steadily. Blushing, she jumped up and went to open the door for Annie whom she could hear coming down the passage from the kitchen.

Annie brought a touch of normality into the room as she bustled about, pouring tea and handing out plates, chattering cheerfully as she did so.

'Please excuse me, I won't be a minute,' said

156

Karen and escaped up the stairs to her room, where she was mortified to see in her mirror that she had a streak of dirt across her cheek and that most of her hair was falling down from the pins which had secured it on top of her head. He must have been hard put to it not to laugh at the sight of me, she told herself as she rubbed furiously at her face with a flannel dipped in cold water from the jug, and redid her hair. She would have liked to have changed her dress but felt she had already been long enough away, so with a last look at her reflection she went downstairs again.

In the tiny parlour the air was already warmer and Annie had drawn the curtains against the darkening day so the scene was quite cosy.

'Come and have your tea, Karen, or it will be cold,' she said. 'I was just saying to Father Murphy, I don't know how you manage to do what you do for those poor boys up at Greenfields House. I know I couldn't do it, not in a month of Sundays, I couldn't.'

'Sister Knight is a very good nurse,' said Father Murphy, and Annie smiled with gratified pride as though the compliment reflected on her somehow.

'Just ordinary, I'm afraid,' said Karen, sitting down and accepting the cup of tea handed to her by Annie. She looked at the priest and somehow caught his eye and held it for a moment. Something, she wasn't sure what, passed between them, something which excluded Annie, albeit unconsciously. There was a silence for a minute or two and Annie looked at them both before putting down her cup and getting to her feet.

'Well, if I can leave you two on your own. I hope you don't mind, Father? There is the stock to see to.'

'Oh, I'll go—' he said, rising to his feet.

'Nonsense, you stay and have a chat with Karen,' said Annie. 'After all, it's her you came to "see".' She left the room looking perplexed and concerned but Karen and Father Murphy didn't appear to notice. They sat quietly for a while, the only sound the crackling of the fire in the grate.

'Tell me more about your home and family,' he said. 'Your father's a preacher, you said?'

Karen nodded. 'Yes, a lay preacher. But he's a miner really. All the men in our village are with the pit, one way or another.'

'Is Karen a common name for a girl in your part of the world, then?'

'Not really. Biblical names are common, though.'

She gazed into the fire, remembering home, and almost without knowing it she was telling him all about the village, the closed community it was with the Wesleyan Chapel as its focal point, about her mother's weak heart and her father who carried his Bible everywhere.

'Even down the mine?' asked Patrick.

'No. Everywhere else, though.'

And she told him of her sister Jemima who had gone away to Lancashire, and Joe who had gone away to Australia, and how now there was only Kezia left at home to help her mother. But she did not tell him about Dave. He was not only gone from her life now, he was dead, she need not think of him any more.

At last she roused herself and looked up. He was relaxed in his chair, his legs stretched out in front of him towards the fire and his hands clasped in his lap.

158

'Now it's your turn,' she said. 'Tell me about you. I don't even know your christian name?' Karen blushed, realising it might not be appropriate to ask. 'What was it that decided you to become a priest?'

'It's Patrick . . .' he began but his smile faded and he looked away quickly as though she had said something embarrassing to him.

'Is something wrong?' asked Karen.

'No, nothing,' he assured her.

'It makes you sad to think of home.'

'Yes.' He jumped at the excuse. 'Well, now, what can I tell you? I come from a small farm in Killinaboy, County Clare. There is my mother and father and Daniel, my eldest brother. And James, of course. He's in the army and married now with a family in London. I am the youngest. It was the dearest wish of my mother that I should be a priest. She worked all the days God sent for it, she did. She would take eggs and butter into Corofin to the market and even walk to Ennis sometimes, saving every penny so I could stay at school and go on with my schooling. It was the proudest day of her life when I entered the seminary at Maynooth.'

Father Murphy—Patrick—fell silent and after a moment, Karen prompted him.

'Corofin, did you say? Where is that?'

'A mile down the road from home. And Ennis is the county town.'

The sound of Annie's footsteps as she came in the back door of the cottage made Patrick glance at the clock on the mantelpiece.

'Half-past five!' he exclaimed, getting to his feet.

'Oh, you're still here,' said Annie as she popped her head around the parlour door. 'Would you like

159

to stay for supper, Father? We have plenty.'

'No, no, I must be on my way, though it's good of you to ask me. Father Brown will be wondering where I've got to, though.'

Karen walked with Patrick to the gate. 'I'll see you at the hospital then, Father,' she said. The evening was black dark, the only illumination that which came from the open cottage door.

'No doubt, Sister, no doubt.'

To Karen he sounded cold and formal, not at all the man she had glimpsed beneath the priest's garb as they sat and talked in the parlour. He said his goodbyes and went away without even taking her hand and Karen felt sad and lonely as he disappeared into the night.

*   *   *

Patrick lay in bed, tired but wakeful. He had eaten supper with Father Brown then gone up to his bedroom and stayed on his knees by the side of the bed much longer than he usually did. Afterwards he had got into bed, only to lie awake.

He thought of Karen, of the way the firelight had played on her face as she talked of her family, the special look of tenderness which she wore as she spoke of her parents. He was wondering how it would feel for her to look at him in that way when he caught himself up and tried to put her out of his mind.

Deliberately, he made himself think of his childhood, of when he was a small boy and carrying his sod of turf to school with him as his contribution to the heating, for the National Board provided none. He thought of the cold, stone floors of the school and the labourers' children who would be barefoot and sometimes crying on a bad winter's day as they had to walk over the stone flags or sit with their feet lifted uncomfortably so that they did not rest on the floor. He himself had boots but many did not. Was it any wonder that some of them learned little?

Patrick's thoughts shifted to his old home. It too had a stone-flagged floor and white-washed walls with a picture of the Holy Family on one wall and the Irish nationalist Robert Emmet on the other. And the black-bellied pot hanging over the turf fire and the two wooden chairs standing before the fire and the bench along the wall by the door. The dresser on the other wall with its rows of many-coloured Delft, his mother's prize possessions, and the high bed in the corner—too high to sit upon during the day. And he thought of his mother, sitting there knitting by the light of the fire, her old-fashioned red petticoat tucked round her legs for warmth. But not his father. He would be down at Delaney's bar with his cronies and Daniel too; Daniel was getting more like their father every day that came.

Restlessly, Patrick turned over in bed. He did not want to think about his mother or her piety and unshakeable faith in God.

'There is no God,' he said softly to himself.

Is there not? something within him answered ironically. 'Then why were you down on your knees so long tonight?'

He remembered the words of Private O'Donnel. The soldier was so bitter, and with reason some would think. Patrick turned on his back, feeling detached from the argument raging in his head.

161

'What was it decided you to become a priest?' Karen had asked.

My mother, he should have replied. But that was not fair and not even true. He had believed, had wanted to be a priest, had wanted to minister to the people. He was the clever one in the family and worked hard to get to the seminary, eager to give his life to Christ and the Holy Catholic Church.

I was fooled into believing, the voice inside him said. Just like the soldiers. I didn't know God didn't exist. There is nothing so bad as the desertion of a Being which was not there in the first place.

Suddenly, Patrick jumped out of bed and fell to his knees. He was shocked to the core by what he had been thinking. Surely the devil was working in him tonight? He would pray for forgiveness for the rest of the night.

Chapter Ten

Karen and Nick Harvey stood by the door of the ward where Father Murphy was celebrating Mass. They had helped some of the patients to get there and now Karen was standing by in case she was needed. At least, that was the reason she gave herself. The door was ajar and she could see Patrick in his robes, as remote and mysterious to her as the Latin of the Mass. Yet on the wards he was so human, so sensitive to the feelings of the men, especially those whose minds were affected by shell-shock.

162

She watched Patrick as he offered the sacraments, heard him murmuring something and the answering 'Amen'. He was so absorbed in it, she thought, struck by the resemblance of the service to the one she was used to in her own church. She stood watching and trying to listen, making no effort to analyse her feelings.

'It's ending now,' said Nick. He stood quietly by her side, waiting to be told what to do next.

Patrick came to the door and saw them there. For a brief second, he looked disturbed, vulnerable in some way, but then his calm mask came down.

'Morning, Sister,' he said as he reached the doorway. 'Morning, Nick, how are you today?'

'I'm grand, Father,' answered Nick. 'Merry Christmas.'

'A happy Christmas to you too. And you, Sister. I thought you would be at your own church?'

Karen blushed, feeling something of an intruder, remembering how strange Patrick had seemed to her during the service.

'I'll be there this evening, Father. Six o'clock.'

She had a sudden vision of other Christmases and going to Chapel with Da and the others. Da, the local preacher, so different from Patrick and yet in some ways so like. What would her father think of her if he knew how she was feeling right now? She took a step backwards, distancing herself.

Patrick's grey eyes were puzzled as he sensed her change of mood but men from the other wards were coming out now and he moved to help get the wheelchairs through the door. There was a buzz of conversation and he joined in, chatting with the men, asking after their families or when they were

163

going home. But his conversation was slightly mechanical, his thoughts still with Karen. The soldiers sensed it and soon moved on.

Looking back, he saw her still standing there, watching him. She blushed like a child caught doing something naughty and rushed into busyness, talking brightly to the men as she seized hold of a wheelchair.

'I can take one, Sister, I can. I'm fine, man, I can do it,' insisted Nick, eager to help.

'Oh, thank you, Private.' Karen gave him a brilliant smile, glad that he should claim her attention. Anyway, she told herself, she had to be careful not to put him off; Nick was so easily snubbed. And when he was snubbed his nervous twitch would reappear. His attachment to her seemed to help his fragile mental stability.

'Careful now, you go first,' she said to him, and he negotiated the first wheelchair into the lift which the military authorities had had installed by the side of the staircase. She did not look back so did not see the yearning in Patrick's eyes as his priestly mask slipped momentarily.

* * *

When Karen left the hospital at twelve o'clock, the atmosphere she left behind her was bright for a change. The men were laughing and whistling carol tunes and singing popular songs. They were completely different from her usual view of them. Because it was daylight, she supposed; nighttime was depressing for both patients and staff.

Walking the short distance to the cottage the magic was still with her. The day was cold but

164

sunny and she felt quite light-hearted in spite of her lack of sleep. She was humming the tune of 'Oh, come, all ye faithful' as she let herself in the door of the cottage. There was a lot of post on the hall table, she saw with happy anticipation. A letter and parcel from home, and a card from Joe.

'That you, Karen?' called Annie from the kitchen.

'No, it's Father Christmas.'

Karen smiled at her friend as Annie came into the hall. There was plenty to smile about, she thought. Warmth permeated the house and a delicious smell wafted in from the kitchen. Annie had made a special Christmas lunch, sacrificing a goose.

'Happy Christmas, Karen,' she cried as she handed over a loosely wrapped parcel and kissed Karen heartily on the cheek.

'There. I suppose you know what it is? I've been on with it for weeks.'

'No, I can't think what it can be,' said Karen with a grin, for it had to be the dusty pink jumper which Annie had been knitting and which was whisked out of sight whenever she came in. 'Thanks, Annie. Wait a minute and I'll get you your present, it's upstairs.'

Karen ran upstairs and retrieved the leatherbound writing case with its lavender-scented paper and envelopes which she had bought for Annie the last time she was in Littlemarsh. Quickly, she changed into a plain skirt and top and put the pink jumper on top.

'It's lovely, Annie, a perfect fit, isn't it? It must have taken you ages to do,' she enthused. 'And here you are, here's your Christmas present. Now

165

you can write to the boys as often as you want and the smell of lavender will remind them of home.'

'Oh, isn't it grand!' Annie beamed. 'Won't they think I've gone all posh? They're used to getting letters on that cheap paper I buy from the village shop.'

'I don't suppose they care, so long as they get a letter,' said Karen.

Their lunch was happily festive and crowned with the glory of Annie's plum pudding and brandy sauce. The kitchen was warm from the oven and Karen began to feel pleasantly full and sleepy.

'I'll go up now, Annie,' she yawned. 'Thanks for a lovely meal. You've made Christmas a happy time for me even though I'm away from home.'

'I'd have been on my own if it wasn't for you,' Annie pointed out. 'It's no good being on your own at Christmas time, is it? But you go up, lovey. I've put an extra hot brick in the bed. I won't call you till six, then? Give you a little extra time?'

'Oh, yes, thanks.' Karen looked at the marble clock on the dresser. Two o'clock already. Well, she'd leave her post until the evening and Annie could share in the excitement of opening the parcel.

As she laid her head on the pillow, Karen fell asleep immediately, a deep, dreamless sleep, waking more refreshed than she had been for quite a time even though she'd only had four hours in bed. She lay for a few minutes, revelling in the cosy warmth before she remembered her letters and parcel and jumped out of bed.

It was a damp, dark evening when Karen went back downstairs but in the kitchen the lamp was alight and the fire bright and hot. Annie was sitting

166

at the table, re-reading the embroidered cards from her boys in France.

'Oh, they are lovely,' said Karen. 'Such delicate work too, especially that one with the French flag entwined with the Union Jack.'

'Yes.' Annie got to her feet and replaced the cards in their place of honour on the mantelpiece. 'I'll get the tea now, shall I?'

'Please,' Karen answered absently. She was eagerly trying to open her parcel, obviously the work of Kezia, it was tied up so thoroughly. At last she undid the last knot to reveal a thick, soft shawl. It was just like the one Kezia crocheted every year for the Chapel sale of work, always the same pattern and always the same shade of serviceable grey. But it was soft and warm and typically useful. Wrapped in the shawl was an embroidered text framed in oak.

'Oh, that's pretty,' exclaimed Annie. It was the painstaking work of Karen's mother, 'God is Love' with entwined forget-me-nots.

'To hang over your bed,' Mam had written on the note.

There was a letter from Da, too, in the copperplate hand he had learned at the Wesleyan School.

'He has a lovely hand,' commented Annie, who was still watching over Karen's shoulder.

'Yes. He left school when he was nine, too, that was when he went down the pit. The boys had to in those days, the family needed the money. But he went to the Sunday School at Chapel, of course, and tried to carry on with ordinary schooling besides the religious teaching.'

'It must have been hard.' Annie filled the teapot

and placed it on the table before bringing a plate of buttered scones from the larder.

'I'll pour the tea, shall I?'

Karen nodded absently as she opened Da's letter.

Dear Karen,

Your mother and I keep fairly well, thanks be to God. I hope you are well too, working hard for those poor lads and going to Chapel regular. We trust this evil war will be over soon and then maybe you will come home to us. May the Lord bless you and keep you safe until we meet again.

Your loving father,

Thomas Knight

'All well at home, I trust?' Annie leaned over the table to offer the plate of buttered scones to Karen who looked up, half smiling.

'What? Oh, yes, everything's fine.' Dear Da, she mused, so brief and to the point yet somehow the letter was satisfying in the way it showed his love for her. She took a buttered scone and bit into it as she picked up Joe's card which had a picture of a group of soldiers before the ruin of a bombed-out building.

'How'd you like to live here? Merry Christmas and God bless you, Joe.'

Well, like father like son, she thought.

Turning over the other letter, she frowned. Gran's handwriting looked shaky somehow, not her usual firm hand. Karen opened it and saw a single sheet. The letter was skimpy, not like one of Gran's usual rambling, unpunctuated missives.

168

Karen searched for a clue as to what was wrong but Gran simply wished her a happy Christmas and gave a few items of news concerning friends and neighbours. But then, Gran wouldn't give any bad news in a letter.

'Something wrong?' asked Annie.

'No, I don't think so. It's just that Gran doesn't sound quite herself, somehow.'

'Well, she is getting on,' said Annie. She knew all about Karen's family, taking as she did a keen interest in all their doings.

'She usually writes such long letters though.'

'Maybe she was busy,' suggested Annie.

'I suppose so.' Karen gathered up her post. 'I have to be on my way now or I'll be late.'

Sighing, she dressed for work and let herself out of the front door, calling a soft 'goodnight' to Annie as she went. Gran was very much on her mind as she walked up the lane to Greenfields.

Gran was running the small-holding on her own now apart from some help from the neighbours. Alf had long since joined the army, Karen remembered. Gran didn't keep many animals, but she had a stint on the moor which allowed her to run a few sheep. The living was meagre but it was a living, and of course she would have her pension.

She must be seventy, Karen thought with mild surprise. Gran was strong and hardy, a capable woman. Karen had always had the notion that she would go on for ever. She thought of the times Gran had come down to Morton Main when Mam was ill, shedding her shawl and bonnet as she came in and rolling up her sleeves at once. And the huge dinners she would make out of a scrag end of mutton, or sometimes a meat pudding boiled in the iron pan for hours, ready for when Da came in from the pit.

'It's probably nothing,' Karen said aloud as she turned into the drive of the hospital. Gran could just have been tired when she wrote the letter. Or maybe it was just Karen herself, reading too much into things. She forgot her grandmother as she let herself into the hall and saw Patrick standing before the fire.

'Good evening, Father,' she said, suddenly aware that her nose and cheeks were red with the cold and tendrils of hair had escaped from her cap yet again and were dangling over her face. She went to the mirror and pinned them back with nervous, darting movements. Once again she felt that strange twist of emotion which he inspired in her, and it made her feel awkward and clumsy.

'Have you been here all day, Father? I mean, you were here most of last night . . .'

Her voice trailed off as she saw his unsmiling face through the mirror.

'Good evening, Sister,' he said formally, and she thought how distant he looked and tired, too. His grey eyes were sunk in dark shadows. 'No,' he continued, 'I came in about half an hour ago to see Private O'Donnel. Poor man, he likes to hear a voice from home.'

Just like Nick, thought Karen as Private Harvey came out of the ward as he always did when he heard her voice.

'Hello, Sister. Can I help you with anything?' he asked eagerly.

'Thanks, Nick. I'll be in in a little while, after I've taken the report. You go in now.'

'How did you find Private O'Donnel?' she asked

170

Patrick after Nick had disappeared back into the ward. Perhaps Private O'Donnel was the reason for Patrick's unsmiling face. Why should she think it had anything to do with her?

'Fair enough, Sister, fair enough. He will be going home soon, so Doctor Clarke tells me. He is more settled now, more resigned to his blindness. He was talking quite happily tonight.'

'Oh, good. That is good.'

Karen waited for a moment before turning her attention to Day Sister who had appeared from the wards and was opening the report book ready to give the report. Matron had had a free afternoon today, Karen remembered.

*   *   *

Patrick watched her as she bent her head over the book. She was so slight, like a girl, though she must be about twenty-eight, he judged. When she came in from the cold this evening she had such a glowing look to her eyes, such a bloom to her cheeks. She had made him want to forget the sadness of the day, the strains and worries. He thought of how sweet it had been to be alone with her in the cottage parlour that afternoon a few days ago. She aroused feelings in him which he knew were forbidden to him yet he could hardly stop himself from giving in to the impulse to touch her, take off that silly cap and let down her shining hair and thread his fingers through it. He wanted . . . Well, it didn't matter what he wanted. He could imagine what her reaction would be if he should do such a thing. Shocked horror, he had no doubt.

He moved abruptly to the door and the women

171

looked up from their contemplation of the day report.

'Goodnight, Father.'

The title echoed mockingly in his ears as he strode round the house to where his pony and trap were waiting faithfully. He drove down the drive and along the lane to the village, unhappy and confused. He thought of having a word with Father Brown, but the old man was not the right person, he knew. He ought to talk to his bishop, he thought, but didn't want to do that either. Sean, that was the man he would like to unburden himself to. But Sean was so far away, somewhere in the North, where Karen came from.

Karen, he mused, Karen-happuch, daughter of Job. And hardly knowing what he was doing, he turned the trap round and headed back to Greenfields Hospital.

*   *   *

There was still a little magic in the air as Karen made her rounds of the wards. Most of the men had been resident for a week or two and were truly convalescent, not just judged to be so by field hospital doctors desperate to make room for fresh casualties. Consequently, everyone seemed in a happier mood apart from the ward full of blinded men upstairs. The men on Ward 1 were chatting amiably, Karen found when she made her round, Nick following faithfully on behind.

'Evening, Sister, come to tuck us in, have you?' called one. The man in the next bed went further.

'If you get tired during the night, Sister, there's room for you in here,' he said, holding back his

172

blankets and leering. But it was a joke which went sour for the rest of the men turned on him angrily.

'Less of that, you.'

'Keep your dirty mouth shut, Private.'

The calls were coming from all sides and the offending soldier turned bright red and huddled down in his bed.

'I meant no harm,' he muttered. 'No offence meant, Sister.'

He looked so crestfallen that Karen felt sorry for him; he was obviously ignorant of the strict code of morality which existed between the men and their nurses. He was just a boy pretending to be a man, she reckoned.

'That's enough, boys,' she said firmly to the rest of the men. 'Time to settle down now.'

She had a word with the senior ward nurse and continued on her rounds.

'Well, if there are no nightmares we might have a quiet night,' she remarked to Nurse Ellis who was on duty on the first floor.

'We can only hope,' she answered with a wry smile. 'Will you check the medicine list now, Sister? If they have their sleeping pills in good time that could help our prospects for a peaceful night.'

On her return to the hall, Karen was surprised to see Patrick back in his position before the fire and her pulse jumped as it always did when she saw him. He was watching her come down the stairs, and as she glanced up and caught his unguarded expression she was startled almost to the point of halting in her tracks.

Gone was the mask of seeming indifference which he had worn so often lately and in its place

173

there was a yearning vulnerability, naked in its longing. For an eternal second they gazed at each other with the bond of mutual attraction freely admitted and shining from their eyes. A surge of joy ran through Karen. He saw it and an answering brightness came over him.

The moment was brief, shocking in its abrupt end. He began to tremble. Dragging his coat from the hall stand, he once more strode off into the night.

Karen stood quite still, waves of crimson firing her neck and thundering in her ears. She hung on to the banister with both hands and closed her eyes.

'You all right, Sister?'

The voice, sharp with concern, penetrated Karen's consciousness and she opened her eyes. Nurse Jackson, recently seconded from Oldchurch Hospital, was standing in the doorway of Ward 1.

'Yes, I'm fine,' Karen said shakily. 'Just a slight headache, that's all, I've taken an aspirin.' She forced herself to speak normally, smiling at the nurse who was regarding her with undisguised curiosity. Briskly, she went over to her desk and sat down. Picking up the report book she opened it and gazed at it unseeingly, fighting to gain control of her emotions, to silence the clamour of her body.

'Why did Father Murphy come back? Did he forget something?' asked Nurse Jackson.

'He must have done, I think, there were no calls for him that I know of,' said Karen.

Nurse Jackson brought the drugs list over to her for her perusal and signature and Karen went with

174

her to the drugs cupboard to count out the tablets and measure out sleeping draughts.

Christmas night passed peacefully which was just as well, considering Karen's abstracted thoughts. Her mind see-sawed from elation as she remembered Patrick's expression when he saw her on the stairs to depression when she remembered his headlong rush to get away from her.

She went home to bed next morning, still unsure of herself, but by the next evening her confusion had subsided, leaving only a happy glow inspired by a hope she refused to admit existed.

Chapter Eleven

Karen was humming softly to herself as she walked up to Greenfields on the evening of Boxing Day. There was a muted roar from the river which ran below the lawns at the back of the house and the wind moaned high in the elm trees lining the drive. Rain spattered on her umbrella; it had started just as she was leaving the cottage. No wonder the river sounded so loud, she thought as she let herself into the hall. It had rained so often lately, though it had been fine for most of today.

There was a policeman standing by the desk with Matron, Constable Jones from the village. They glanced up as Karen entered and she was struck by their grave expressions.

'Is something wrong?' she asked as she stood on the doormat, her folded umbrella in her hand, dripping water on to the mat.

'Indeed there is, Sister,' Matron answered

tersely. 'There's been a tragedy, less than an hour ago. It was Private O'Donnel. He went into the river. Intentionally, I'm afraid.'

'Oh! But he seemed so much better last night, Matron, almost cheerful. I thought he was over the worst.' Karen looked stricken.

The policeman cleared his throat and Matron glanced at him.

'Oh, I'm sorry. You know Constable Jones, don't you, Sister? This is Sister Knight, Constable.'

'Yes, we've met,' he said, nodding gravely to Karen. 'About Private O'Donnel, Sister, you didn't notice anything unusual about him last night, did you? Nothing which could lead you to think this might happen?'

'No, as I told Matron he seemed to be so much brighter than usual, that's all. But how did it happen?'

'If Sister had noticed anything last night she would have put it in the report, Constable,' Matron interjected, then turned back to Karen. 'They often are more cheerful once they've made their minds up to it, Sister, haven't you seen it before? How to know what's on their minds is difficult though. Most often recovery of spirits is a sign of general improvement but it can mean a patient has made up his mind about something. And he *was* so much better today that the VAD took him out into the garden for a breath of fresh air. It was so nice in the sun this afternoon. She left him sitting on a bench, wrapped in a blanket when the rain threatened, while she got the wheelchairs inside.'

Matron looked grim. 'Of course, with hindsight, she should not have left him alone but the rain

176

came on so fast and we are so short of staff. Well, O'Donnel followed the roar of the water and threw himself into the river at the bottom of the garden. As you know, it is swollen with all the rain we've had recently.'

'But did they get him out, Matron?' Karen was horrified. That poor boy, she thought, hardly believing it.

'Doctor Clarke and the porter got him out, he was caught in a tree branch so he wasn't swept away. But it was too late, I'm afraid, he was dead.'

Her heart plummeted and Karen felt a despair which was physical in its intensity. Yet she knew she had to control it, cover up her feelings. There was still the routine work on the wards to do and she and her night nurses would have to get on with it while Matron and the day staff saw to all the dismal details of the death. They could not lay out Private O'Donnel as they normally would in the case of death, for suicide was a crime and the body would be taken away by the police for an official autopsy. But there were still questions to answer; every one of the day staff had to account for their movements at the time of the death as also had the ambulant men, just to rule out any suspicion of foul play.

Of course, when Karen did get on to the wards, she found that the news had run through the small hospital immediately. All the patients were aware of the death of Private O'Donnel; they always did know when something like this happened.

'Sister! Sister!'

As Karen entered Ward 1, Nick called to her. For once he was sitting on his bed, making no move to get up to greet her. His eyes were anxious and disturbed and a tic had appeared at the corner of his mouth.

'Hallo, Nick. Look, don't worry, everything's all right.' She tried to speak with reassurance but it was difficult and she found herself with nothing more to say. Instead she patted his hand and busied herself in tidying his bed and getting him to lie down properly in it, before progressing round the ward. But every time she glanced back at him she saw he was watching her anxiously.

There was a restlessness and tension in the air; the men were slow to settle to sleep. Private O'Donnel was not mentioned but he was on all their minds, she could see that plainly, so she lingered longer than usual by each bed, trying to calm their uneasiness. Consequently it was very late by the time she took her rest hour, almost two o'clock.

She was not hungry, the thought of food making her feel ill. All she wanted to do was go off by herself somewhere and sort out her bitter thoughts and mixed up emotions. Even the smell of food from the supper room made her nauseous as she neared the annexe so, remembering the empty wards upstairs, Karen decided she would go into one of them. Just until she could pull herself together, she told herself.

Quietly, she let herself back into the main house and climbed the stairs, heading for a small, two-bedded ward. She closed the door softly behind her and walked over to the window. The curtains were open and she stood, gazing out over the lawns to the river beyond, though in the dark of the night she could see very little. But she could hear the muffled roar of the water, just as Private

O'Donnel must have heard it, and she shivered slightly, trying to make sense of it all. Why did such things have to happen? Why, oh why was there so much suffering in the world? The age-old questions went round and round in her head.

The ward she was in had been part of one of the main bedrooms of the house which had been partitioned into two. The partition wall was very close to the window where she stood and she leaned against it and put her hand up to the windowframe. She rested her head on it, at last allowing the tears to fall unheeded, a safety valve for her pent-up emotions. After a moment she took out her handkerchief and dried her eyes and as she did so heard a muffled sound from the ward on the other side of the partition. Someone spoke, she could hear clearly through the thin wooden wall.

'Dear God, is there no end to this?'

It was Father Murphy. No, she wouldn't think of him as Father Murphy, it was Patrick, and she loved him. A yearning for him filled her mind. She needed him desperately, and why not? He was a man like any other, wasn't he? And he was suffering himself in that room by himself, she could hear he was. She would comfort him. She put her handkerchief away in her uniform pocket and walked out into the darkness of the upstairs hall before entering the room next-door.

'Patrick?'

She had been right, it was him. As she went into the room and closed the door behind her, he rose from where he had been sitting on a bed and took an involuntary step towards her. A warning voice inside her made her hesitate but it only lasted a

179

second. His being a priest didn't matter to her. He needed her, she knew he needed her. Letting her emotions take over, she moved swiftly to him and took him in her arms, holding him, putting an arm around his neck and pulling his head down to hers.

Gently, she kissed his lips and then cradled his head on her breast, murmuring her love and compassion, rocking him slightly like a hurt child. She had an overwhelming urge to assuage his grief and by so doing find comfort herself.

'Karen,' he whispered, but she closed his mouth with her lips and pulled him down on to the bed. It was the most natural thing in the world to her when he gave an inarticulate groan and his arms tightened around her waist. He was no longer a man in need of her comfort, he had become the urgent lover.

Patrick enfolded her in his arms and kissed her eyes, her neck, the hollow in her throat; his kisses hesitant at first but becoming more frantic every moment till she could feel his need of her mounting and her own desire rising in response. She looked into his eyes and lost herself in them, though they were half-closed and darkened, the tears still beading his lashes sparkling strangely. Suddenly his eyelids flew open and he lifted his head and gazed at her. Karen lay quiescent, letting his gaze range over her, waiting for him.

'Sweet Jesus, help me!' he cried. 'I love you . . .'

But Karen did not hear what he was saying. Her emotions, so long denied, were boiling over, drowning every conscious thought. All her inhibitions were swept away as though they had never been. His touch was creating a fever in her blood which mounted and threatened to envelop them both.

Patrick's hands were on her body, trying to free it from the constrictions of the stiffly starched uniform. With trembling hands she helped him, stripping off her clothes quickly and dropping them on the floor. One button proved obstinate and he tugged at it impatiently until it came free and flew across the room, bouncing off the washhand stand with a reverberating 'ping'. In the end she brushed aside his inexpert hands impatiently and loosened the ribbons of her camisole herself, pulling it over her head and flinging it down.

And then they were lost, quite lost in the urgent, sexual need they had both ignored for so long, in the strong and passionate longing they had for each other. And the clamour in their blood rose like a spring tide which finally submerges a rocky shore.

His hands were on her breasts, touching the suddenly upright nipples, caressing, his touch tentative at first but becoming hard and demanding, cupping her breasts and holding them as he bent to take a dark-ringed nipple in his mouth. The ache in her rose to fever pitch and she strained towards him, desperate to ease the shafts of exquisite feeling running through her. And at last he found the damp mound between her thighs and her senses sang in exultation as he entered her and the world faded away as she climaxed for the first time in her life. Nothing was real, nothing but this, this moment, this supreme moment.

When at last they collapsed on the bed together, exhausted, Karen's first conscious feeling was one of elated happiness, exultant and triumphant. She

181

held him, caressing him and murmuring endearments.

'My lovely man, my precious love,' she whispered, kissing his eyes, his throat, his lips. And he stroked her back slowly, contentedly, the euphoria following their love-making enveloping them both until he was sleeping peacefully in her arms. This was what it was all about, she thought, this was what love really was meant to be. Briefly, she remembered Dave in absolute wonderment that she should have thought she cared for him. Why, she had been playing at love; she had been like a little girl pretending to love. Her feelings for him had been a pale imitation, a shadow of the real thing. What a fool she had been, she thought, before dismissing even the memory of Dave from her mind. Then she too dropped into a deep sleep.

*   *   *

When she awoke, the dark was absolute, a pitch black darkness. She felt warm and contented though for a moment she couldn't think where she was or why she had such a feeling of well-being. Yet she could feel Patrick's body, warm and long and lean, pressed up against her. And she smiled and turned to him, nuzzling into his neck and his arm tightened around her.

'Karen,' he murmured, and she leaned her head back and looked up into his face. He was still asleep, he had said her name in his sleep. He loves me, she thought with a rush of tenderness, and the thought flooded her with deep happiness.

But then the events of the night came back to her, and she remembered where she was in a rush

182

of alarm. She was supposed to be on duty, she might be needed on the wards, there were wounded soldiers to attend to.

Raising herself carefully from under Patrick's arm, she slipped out of bed and hurriedly dressed. But she found time to drop a kiss on his cheek and cover him lovingly with a blanket. He murmured in his sleep and turned over on to his side but did not wake. Smiling tenderly to herself, she let herself out of the room and went downstairs. Going over to the mirror above the mantle, she tidied her hair and pinned her cap straight. She was supremely happy, an emotion which seemed rock solid, unassailable.

Glancing at the watch pinned to her apron, she was surprised to see she was not as late as she had thought. Smiling at her reflection, Karen went to check with the nurses on the wards. She had not been missed, there had been no emergencies or disturbances, the hospital slumbered as deeply as Patrick, her lovely man. It was almost as though God had allowed them time out to confirm and consummate their love.

She forced herself to think of her work and the duties yet to be done as she came back into the hall and sat down at her desk to begin her report, though the words danced before her eyes and she found it impossible to stop her thoughts from straying to the small ward upstairs.

'I'll take my rest hour now, Sister, if I may?' said Nurse Ellis as she came into the hall. 'This must be one of the quietest nights we've had in an age. Apart from . . .' She blushed painfully, remembering the tragedy of Private O'Donnel.

Karen knew what Nurse Ellis meant and a tinge

of sadness went through her again for the waste of a young life. But it was not enough to dispel her euphoria. She smiled sympathetically at the nurse.

'It is, Nurse,' she said. 'Well, go on then, enjoy your meal.'

Nurse Ellis put on her cloak against the bitter night wind and made her way over to the annexe. As she walked over the gravel path towards the lighted window of the nurses' dining-room, she puzzled over the change in her superior. Sister had not taken her to task for her lack of respect for the death of Private O'Donnel; rather she had sympathized with her. And what on earth had brought such a glow to her face and brightness to her eyes? Shrugging, the nurse went into the rest room and washed her hands. Oh, well, it was none of her business in any case.

In the hall, Karen glanced up from the case-notes as she heard someone coming down the stairs. She knew it was Patrick even before he came into view. She half rose and smiled as she saw it was indeed her love. But as he came nearer the smile disappeared as she saw his face was set and white, eyes dark and haunted and jaw clenched.

'Patrick . . .' she said uncertainly, suddenly afraid, dreadfully afraid, so that her heart began to beat painfully.

'Goodnight, Sister.'

His eyes were chips of flint, his voice like ice. He looked at her as though she were evil incarnate as, without another word, he rushed out of the hospital, wrenching open the front door and hurrying away, leaving it ajar.

Karen stared at the door, paralysed in a long

184

moment of fear. But at last she got to her feet and walked to the door, her legs wobbly and unsure. She stared after him but he had already disappeared and after a moment, through the drumming of her heartbeat, she could just hear the clop of the pony's hooves fading into the distance. A cold wind blew into the hall and the papers on her desk rustled, a couple of them falling to the floor. She folded her arms across her breasts, wincing a little at the slight soreness left where his fingers had touched her. The pain brought her back to an awareness of herself and where she was. Slowly, Karen closed the door and walked back to her desk.

She shivered though she was not really aware of the cold air which had come into the hall. Mainly, she realized, she felt dirty, soiled. Her vision blurred, the room swam about her and she had to grasp the desk with both hands to lower herself into the chair. She sat perfectly still as she fought her encroaching faintness and struggled to regain her composure. Picking up her pen she forced herself to go on with the report. One by one she brought to mind the names of the soldiers asleep in the wards and wrote a few words by each name. And eventually, her long years of training came to her aid and she was able to complete her night of duty, though there were intervals when she had to struggle to hold on to her composure.

At last it was morning, a dark and dank morning. Karen's mind and body relaxed in spite of herself as her spell of duty came to an end. As she did so she found she was beginning to feel the aches and bruising left by their violent love-making, and total exhaustion threatened. But at long last she was

185

handing over the report to the day staff and was free to stumble down the drive and along the lane to the cottage.

Mumbling something about a headache and only wanting her bed, she ran past a concerned Annie to the haven of her room. Here for the first time she turned the key in the lock of the bedroom door. Flinging off her clothes, she scrubbed herself all over in the cold water from the ewer until her skin was red raw. Then she dried herself sketchily and, getting quickly into her all-enveloping nightgown, crawled under the covers.

Unbidden, her thoughts ran chaotically over the night. Her own shamelessness. How could she have done it? What did he think of her? Wanton? An evil Jezebel? Her knowledge of Catholicism was scanty, she had not even considered it in the euphoria following the discovery that she loved and was loved in return.

Painfully aware that what had happened was wrong in her own world, deeply wrong by the standards of her own family and the mining community in which she had spent her childhood, Karen's thoughts ran on as she moved restlessly in the bed. Sex before marriage was not unknown in Morton Main but it was frowned upon heavily. And if it happened then the man was expected to marry the girl or be drummed out of the village, whether there were any consequences or not.

Consequences! A baby! Dear God, no. What would she do if she was to have a baby? Karen sat up in bed as the thought came to haunt her. She would be an unmarried mother, an outcast, she knew she would, for hadn't Patrick shown by his precipitate rush from her that he wanted nothing

186

more to do with her?

Roman Catholic priests do not marry. Oh, yes, she knew this. But in her ignorance she had thought that now he loved her, he would leave the priesthood and everything would come right.

How naive this idea had been was slowly dawning on her. How could she have imagined that she meant more to him than his church? They hardly knew each other! After her years in hospitals, why was she so ignorant of the world? The despairing questions went round and round in her mind. How could she possibly know if she was pregnant or not after only a few hours? Fallen wrong, the folk at home would say. Fallen wrong. Fallen wrong, fallen . . .

There was a soft knock at the door which startled Karen out of her frenzied thoughts.

'Are you all right, Karen?' came Annie's whisper.

She didn't answer, pretending to be asleep. She heard Annie try the door, then, finding it locked, she sighed heavily and went downstairs and Karen relaxed. She could not have faced her friend, not yet; everything was too new and raw, she would not have been able to conceal how she felt and thought. Restlessly, she turned over on to her stomach and pressed her face into the pillow.

Total exhaustion finally overtook her and she slept, a heavy, dreamless sleep which lasted until the banging of Annie's fist on the door and her friend's anxious calls woke her.

'Karen, is there something wrong? It's past six o'clock.'

Making a supreme effort to rouse herself, Karen called back:

'Righto. I won't be a minute, Annie.'

She was heavy-eyed and the headache she had pretended in the morning was painfully real now; her temples throbbed with it.

She had come to a decision, though. If Patrick made it plain at their next encounter that he wanted her out of his life she would apply for a transfer back north, the Cameron at Hartlepool perhaps. Or, no, she probably could obtain a post in Bishop Auckland itself; there was the cottage hospital or the workhouse hospital. In any case, she would go back. It was the only thing she could do. Like a wounded animal, she would bolt for home.

Mechanically she began her preparations to go on duty. As she pinned her hair up before the tiny mirror her brown eyes looked back at her from great, dark circles set in a white face. Even her lips were pale and colourless. Resorting to an old childhood trick, she wet her little finger and rubbed it on the red cover of her hymn book, transferring the colour to her bottom lip. Rubbing her cheeks to give them some colour too before she went down to the kitchen to face Annie's concern, she braced herself for the ordeal of the night. She had to work at Greenfields and Patrick, as a priest, had to minister to the Roman Catholics among the wounded soldiers. She would have to meet him, she thought dismally, they would probably meet quite often. And she had to be prepared for that, she had to be in control of herself, she could not break down.

Chapter Twelve

'Are you sure you're not coming down with something?' asked Annie. 'You're so pale, Karen. It worries me to see you looking so tired all the time.'

'No, I'm fine, Annie,' she answered. 'It's just the wrong time of the month, that's all.'

Thank God, she thought, at least that particular worry had been dispelled when she woke a few days ago with the familiar ache in the small of her back. It was such a relief to have to get out of bed for a sanitary cloth from the clean-washed pile in the bottom drawer.

Five nights had gone by and Karen hadn't seen Patrick. If he had been in the hospital it wasn't during her spells of duty. The nights had dragged for there were still a number of empty beds in the old house. A lull in the fighting at the Front, she supposed dully, though she couldn't think about the war, her mind was so filled with Patrick. Every time the front door opened, her heart leaped in case it was him. The ache for him was ever-present, all-consuming.

'It's a good thing it's your night off the night after tomorrow,' declared Annie. 'It's not natural for folk to work all night and sleep during the day. It'll make a nice change for you to be free on a Saturday. It's better than your usual Friday at least.'

It was the time of day Annie enjoyed the most, the half-hour before Karen had to go on duty. It was a chance to talk except that lately Karen had

had much less to say for herself. She seemed to have something on her mind.

'There's nothing bothering you, is there, Karen?'

The question made her glance up, startled. She had been staring at her teacup thinking of Patrick. Why had he acted as he had? He loved her, she was sure of that, he couldn't have made it any more plain. And yet he had acted as though he hated her afterwards. She could not rid herself of the memory of him as he came down the stairs that night; he had acted as though he couldn't bear even to look at her. She went over and over the scene in her mind. Feeling wretched, she forced herself to reply to Annie.

'No, don't worry so much about me,' she said, making a deliberate effort to lighten her mood. 'As you say, I'm ready for my night off. And the weather has been so wet and dreary. I think we are all waiting for the spring.' The phrase sounded trite in her ears.

'Look, I'm going into Romford on Saturday, why don't you come with me? We can look round the market and have a spot of lunch, what do you say? If I feed the animals before we go, they'll be all right until tea-time. What do you think?'

'Oh, I think I'd rather just spend a lazy day at home, Annie. You don't mind, do you? I've letters to write and I want to sort out my wardrobe. But you stay as long as you like. I tell you what, I can lock up the hens and feed the pigs then you could go to the moving pictures, what about that?'

Annie was disappointed and it showed on her face. 'Well, if you don't want to go with me . . .' she muttered, and disappeared into the scullery.

Karen gazed after, knowing she was upset. But

190

her own misery was so intense it excluded other feelings. All she wanted to do was hide away at home, she felt so depressed and tired. Sighing, she went back up to her room to prepare for work. Only one more night after this one. With any luck she would get through to Saturday without encountering Patrick, she told herself, yet she longed to see him.

The unusually long-lasting lull between batches of new patients was over, she discovered, as she entered the old house. There was an air of bustling activity about the place though the hall was deserted. Karen climbed the stairs to Matron's office to take the day report.

'Good evening, Sister. Fifteen new patients today, amputees mostly. I've put them in the small wards so they can have some peace and quiet.'

The small two-bedded wards, thought Karen numbly. If they had only arrived five days earlier, then there would have been no place in the hospital for her to come together with Patrick and she wouldn't be carrying this great lump of misery around with her now. But even as she walked over to the desk and took the book from Matron, she was berating herself for thinking such a thing. What were her troubles compared to those of the wounded?

'They are a little later than usual coming to us, casualties from the November campaign at Cambrai,' Matron was saying. 'All of them are recovering nicely, so you shouldn't have much trouble with them.'

As Karen entered the first of the two-bedded wards with her medicine tray, she was struck by the cheerfulness of the two soldiers lying there, even

191

though one had only one arm and the other's leg had been amputated below the knee. Nick was sitting on a hard chair between the two beds but he sprang to his feet when he saw Karen.

'Hello, Sister,' he said, sounding quite animated, the depression following the death of Private O'Donnel lifted now. 'I didn't know you were back. We've been talking. John here says that now the Americans are coming over, none of us will have to go back, not never. There's thousands and thousands of Yanks, you know, millions. The war will be over before we know it.'

'Well, I daresay John knows what he is talking about,' she answered him as she put the tray down on an elegant inlaid occasional table, probably dating from the Regency period and left here by the owners of Greenfields. 'Now . . . Private Jenkins. That's you, John, I take it?'

He nodded and pulled a wry face as she measured out a dose of Syrup of Ferrum, and handed it to him. 'Do I have to, Sister? I feel fine, really I do.'

'You've lost a lot of blood. Now don't be such a baby,' she said severely.

'Well, can I have a black bullet for after?'

Karen cast him an exasperated glance and saw he was grinning impishly, obviously ragging her.

'Just take your medicine, Private Jenkins,' she said, trying to sound like Matron.

'Well, orders is orders,' he replied dolefully and downed the thick treacly stuff. Groaning, he clutched his stomach theatrically with his one hand.

'I'll fetch you your cocoa, that'll take away the taste,' said Nick sympathetically and hurried from the room.

'I won't have him running about after you two always, mind,' declared Karen as she handed the other soldier his dose, 'tomorrow you will wait for the trolley coming round like everyone else.'

Private Jenkins grinned at her as she left the room but his grin faded as he glanced over at his companion. 'A nice little billet we've landed in, mate,' he said. 'Nothing like a pretty nurse or two about the place, is there, Tommy? A better tonic than that bloody awful syrup.'

'You're right there,' Tommy nodded. 'But then, any billet's better than the one we had in Cambrai. It's almost worth having to learn to walk with a peg leg to get away from that hell-hole.'

In the next ward, Karen heard the conversation through the thin wood of the partition as she measured out a dose of the medicine for the occupant of the bed where she and Patrick . . . No, she wasn't going to think about that, not now. She deliberately began to consider the progress of the war. Was it true that the arrival of the Americans would be enough to tip the balance in favour of the allies? Fervently, she hoped so. The fact that Joe was still over there, in 'that hell-hole' as Tommy described it so graphically, was a constant worry in the back of her mind.

*   *   *

Karen was lying on the sofa before the fire in Annie's cosy parlour. The house was quiet. It was Saturday and Annie had gone to Romford so Karen had the house to herself. She couldn't even hear the ticking of the kitchen clock from where

193

she lay. She felt warm and content as she drifted off to sleep. Her agony over Patrick was less dominant in her thoughts though still there, hovering in the background.

Her dreams were of home. She was sitting in the front room of the house in Morton Main with Dave. They were on the horsehair settee and Dave had his arm around her waist and was whispering in her ear.

'I'll send for you, Karen. I will, I promise I will,' he was whispering, and she was nodding her head. 'I won't desert you, Karen,' he went on, 'I swear I won't.' But now it wasn't Dave, it was Patrick.

She was abruptly anxious and tried to look up at his face but he held her head against his shoulder so she couldn't move. She struggled to pull away from him but his arms tightened round her and she couldn't move. Panic rose in her so that in the end she was fighting to get away and he let her go. She jumped up and ran to the door where she turned to see him sitting with his legs crossed and his arms resting along the wooden frame of the back of Mam's settee, tapping on the wood with his fingertips, tap, tap, tap, tap.

'You're a frigid bitch,' he said pleasantly, as though he was complimenting her. 'No wonder you can't keep a man once he finds out you're no good in bed.' And his fingers tapped, maddeningly, on and on.

Karen sat up with a start, disorientated until she realized she was in the front room all right, but this was Annie's front room, the parlour, two hundred and more miles from Morton, and someone was knocking at the door.

'Karen? I'm sorry if I startled you. I knocked but

194

there was no answer and the door was open—'

'Patrick!'

She started up to go to him as he stood uncertainly in the doorway, love and hope leaping within her and shining from her eyes. But he didn't hold out his arms to her, just stood woodenly in the doorway, and she stopped, elation fading a little though not altogether. For surely he had come to her because he loved her? He had been wanting her as much as she had been needing him, else why had he come? She gazed into his eyes, trying to read the emotions she saw there. His grey eyes were deepened now almost to blue. There was such an appeal in their depths, she knew it. He did love her, he did!

'Karen, I . . . we have to talk about this,' he said at last, his voice husky.

'Yes.'

She put out her hands to him and drew him into the room. Closing the door behind him, she moved closer to him, holding up her face for his kiss. And he stepped back.

'Karen, I have to explain to you, show you how impossible this is. I'm sorry, Karen. Oh, so sorry. My dear, it should not have happened, I should not have let it happen, it was all my fault. My life is dedicated to—' But she put her fingers to his lips and hushed him before he could say any more. She wasn't going to listen to him.

Karen held on to his hand and pulled him further into the parlour. She heard what he was saying but refused to acknowledge it. He was making a mistake but she wouldn't let him reject her. He would regret it all his life and she wouldn't let him make such a grievous error. For he loved

195

her, she was certain of it, she had seen it in his eyes. He couldn't hide it. He was a man before he was a priest. A man in love with her as she was in love with him. She wasn't going to give him up to anyone or anything, she would not. She felt strong and filled with the power her love gave her and she would win him, she surely would.

'Whisht, whisht,' she murmured, and somehow they were standing before the settee and one of her hands slid up around the nape of his neck to the crisp, short hairs there and her body was close against his as she drew him down with her. Her lips were clinging to his and she was guiding his fingers into her hidden places and somehow they had left the settee and were lying on the soft rug before the fire and then there was nothing and no one in the world but the two of them.

They were lost in a whirl of sensation, deliriously heady. The excitement was mounting, thrilling every nerve in her body, and she knew it was the same for him for they were one now, joined forever. Exultant release washed over them like a spring tide and they sank into it, pillowed by it. Then a languor overtook the wave, a sweet, heavy, slumbrous languor, and then they were still.

It was the kitchen clock chiming four which woke Karen. Patrick's head was on her shoulder and the floor was hard through the thin covering of the rug so that her hand and arm were pricking with pins and needles. But that was nothing, she wouldn't have moved to ease her position for anything. The fire had burned low but there was still sufficient life in it to bathe them in a warm glow. Or was it all coming from within her? she wondered lazily. She was filled with a triumphal contentment. She had won, she was sure she had won, Patrick was hers.

He turned on to his back, easing the pressure on her shoulder, and a shaft of pain shot up her arm, making her wince. Patrick stirred and opened his eyes and she smiled at him, full of her love.

'Hallo,' she said.

'Hallo, my love,' he answered, and bent his head the small distance it needed to be able to kiss her on the nose. 'I never thought it would be like this,' he went on softly, 'so beautiful. I love you, Karen. God help me, I do.'

'And I love you. Oh, Patrick, we'll be so happy together, you'll see, how could it be wrong? We were meant to be together. It's the most natural thing in the world, can't you just feel it? Oh, Patrick, I'm so happy.'

A shadow crossed his face and he raised himself on his elbow and leaned over her. He gazed at her as though imprinting her image on his brain.

'What is it?' she asked.

He shook his head. 'Oh, Karen,' he began, but stopped when he heard the squeak of the front gate opening. 'Someone is coming,' he went on, his tone changing completely. Rising to his feet, he adjusted his clothing, for in their haste to come together they hadn't taken the time to undress fully. Karen too was on her feet, smoothing down her dress, tying the tapes of her drawers. But she was smiling indulgently.

'It's only Annie,' she said softly. 'She's been to Romford for the day. It'll be all right, you'll see. She will understand when we tell her about us.'

'No! No, we can't tell her. Don't you see, we can't?'

197

Karen was startled out of the haze of happiness which had enveloped her and stared at him, seeking an explanation for his vehemence.

'But why? I thought—'

'Sit down, Karen, for goodness' sake. Sit down, please. We must pretend nothing has happened. Please, for my sake, Karen. I can't have any of this getting back to the presbytery.'

Dimly, she heard the back door of the cottage open and Annie's cheerful voice.

'Karen? Where are you, love? I've had a lovely time. I bought a dress length of artificial silk on the market, a proper snip it was.'

Karen and Patrick stood facing each other. She could hear Annie perfectly well, a part of her mind could even respond to her friend. She opened her mouth to answer and Patrick's eyes widened in entreaty. Karen sat down abruptly and smoothed her hair back from her face with quick, nervous fingers. Patrick sat too, in the chair furthest away from her, sitting back and folding his hands in his lap, crossing his legs away from her. In the second before Annie opened the door Karen darted a glance at him and quickly away for she couldn't bear to see his face so set and white, almost like a stranger's.

'Karen? Why didn't you call? Were you asleep?' Annie came into the room but stopped as she saw Patrick. 'Oh, I didn't realize you had a visitor. I'm sorry, Karen. How are you, Father Murphy? Those poor boys up at Greenfields still keeping you busy, I suppose?'

Patrick rose perfunctorily to his feet and murmured something inarticulate but Annie didn't seem to notice anything.

'Haven't you offered Father Murphy any tea, Karen? Oh, and look at the fire, it's almost out. What have you been doing?'

They gazed at her in silence, the question hanging in the air. But Annie was on her knees, picking up the tongs and lifting lumps of coal on to the fire, quite unaware of the consternation in the minds of Patrick and Karen. She rose to her feet and dusted her hands together as a small plume of blue smoke rose from the mended fire.

'There, that's better. Now, I'll make a cup of tea, and we can drink it cosily in here. I'm sure I could do with a cup. I bought a packet of fancy biscuits on the market, we'll have them with it.'

Patrick got to his feet and cleared his throat. 'Not for me, Mrs Blakey,' he said, not looking at Karen. 'I have to get back. Father Brown will be wondering where I am. Good afternoon to you both.'

'Oh, are you sure?' asked Annie, but Patrick was already at the door.

'Yes, I must go, but thank you for the offer,' he answered, his voice tight. 'If you'll excuse me?'

Karen couldn't bear to let him go like that without another word and she too was on her feet and following him.

'I'll see you out,' she said, more for Annie's benefit than anything. She didn't even notice that her friend was suddenly watching them intently, though with some bewilderment.

'Patrick?' She hurried after him to the gate, willing him to turn round and speak to her. But when he did stop it was with his back to her and his hand on the latch as though he was ready to take off again any second.

'Please, Karen, let me go now. It's over. I'm sorry, I should not have done it, I had no right. God knows how sorry I am.'

'Sorry? But you love me, Patrick, how can you be sorry? We belong together. We do, we do!' she cried, forgetting the need to keep her voice low, and he looked anxiously up and down the lane. Luckily it was deserted. No one could have heard her. He turned to face her at last.

'It's over, Karen, it should never have happened,' he repeated tersely, his voice shot through with pain. 'I am a priest, for God's sake.'

'But I love you and you love me. You can't deny it, Patrick, not now.' She caught hold of his coat as though she would hold him to her physically but he disengaged her fingers.

'No, Karen. If you love me you must forget it.'

Karen watched as he strode off down the road. She struggled to regain her composure, refusing to cry, refusing even to give in. Surely he would realize what a mistake he was making? He needed her, she was certain he needed her. All she had to do, she told herself, was hang on, wait for him to realize he needed her. Stubbornly, she refused to think about his church, her rival, so cruel and uncompromising. It was wrong, so wrong. Hadn't she been brought up to believe in the priesthood of all believers? Priests were not a race set apart, they were not. She would win in the end, oh, she would, she vowed to herself. Taking her handkerchief from her dress pocket, she blew her nose. Patrick's figure disappeared round the bend in the lane and Karen turned back to the house.

She would see him at the hospital, she told

herself. She would work something out so that they could have a quiet talk together. She was not giving up, no, she wasn't, all she had to do was have a proper talk with him.

'Tea's made, Karen,' called Annie from the front door and the prosaic quality of the words amazed Karen. How could she drink tea with Annie when her world was ending?

'Coming,' she answered, and went in.

'What brought Father Murphy here again?' asked Annie curiously as they drank their tea before the fire.

'Oh, he was just passing,' said Karen. (Just passing!) Annie glanced at her and bit her lip but forebore to ask any more. As soon as she decently could, Karen excused herself and went to her room. She lay on her bed with her arms folded across her breast, hugging to herself the memory of him as they had lain on the hearthrug, his head on her shoulder and the whole lean length of him against her. 'It's not over,' she whispered to herself. 'Oh, no, it's not over.' She refused to acknowledge the dark doubts in the back of her mind. She would wait and eventually she would meet him at the hospital. It would be worth the waiting.

Chapter Thirteen

Karen did not see Patrick for more than a fortnight. She even considered going to the presbytery to seek him, she felt so desperate. But what if she summoned up the courage to walk past

201

the statue of Mary and the Baby Jesus to the front door, and then had it slammed in her face?

She tried to put him out of her mind and even succeeded for short intervals; she was not even thinking of Patrick as she walked up to the hospital one evening, she was thinking of Nick Harvey, feeling a little worried about him. He was still so attached to her and she hoped the military authorities wouldn't send him home, not for a while at least. She saw the boy every time she went on duty and knew he was not ready to fend for himself. He probably never would be, she thought, sighing.

Patrick was standing in the hall with Doctor Clarke when she opened the front door and both men looked across at her as she entered. Karen was taken completely unawares, the hope and the dread rising instantly within her. Now it had actually happened, it felt almost unreal.

'Good evening, Sister,' said Doctor Clarke, and she mumbled a reply. Her composure had deserted her and her face burned so that she turned quickly away from them, using the excuse of hanging up her cloak. Her hands shook and she fumbled with the loop of material which for some reason refused to go over the hook on the hall stand. In her confusion she dropped the cloak and Doctor Clarke looked at her in surprise as she bent to retrieve it.

'Something's making you clumsy tonight, Sister,' he remarked with a smile. 'Haven't you been to bed today?'

He glanced at Patrick and his smile faded as he saw the priest was acting strangely too. Without a word of farewell, he was heading for the door.

202

'Goodnight, Father,' the doctor called after him, looking bewildered. They had been in the middle of a very interesting discussion of the Royal Flying Corps, so why was Father Murphy cutting it short?

Karen stood up with the errant cloak in her hands and saw the door closing behind Patrick. If anything, her confusion increased and her cheeks burned more fiercely. Carefully, she hung up the cloak and, without raising her eyes to the doctor, sat down at her desk and gazed sightlessly at the report.

'Well, I'm going off now, Sister,' said Doctor Clarke uncomfortably.

'Yes. Goodnight, Doctor.'

Gradually Karen's pulse steadied. Nothing had happened that she had not expected. The thing was, she had to keep her head, she had to act normally. Day Sister appeared and they discussed the report. When Day Sister went off duty, Karen did a round of the wards, helping with patients where the ward nurse needed help, checking sleeping draughts and pills, ready for the medicine round. At last it was time for supper.

In the dining room she took a cup of tea but refused any food. She sat alone and allowed herself to think about Patrick. This time, perhaps because it was the middle of the night when spirits are low, she was ready to face the fact that he didn't want to speak to her.

He wanted nothing to do with her, she could tell that. He was avoiding her, he must be. Before Christmas she had met him two or three times every week as they both went about their work at the hospital. Now she hardly saw him at all.

'I must get away,' she whispered desperately.

203

Like an injured animal, she longed for home. She would see Matron in the morning and give in her notice, say that she must go home.

* * *

Matron was not pleased. She wore that particularly forbidding expression used by all the hospital matrons Karen had known when they wanted to convey their displeasure to a junior nurse. Karen was standing before the desk in Matron's small sanctum at eight o'clock on a dark, grey morning after a particularly dark, black night and had just tendered her resignation.

'What do you mean, you wish to resign? Do you not know there's a war on?'

Matron's chipped ice eyes stared sternly at the slightly built sister. Karen looked at the iron grey hair pulled back in a bun under her cap, the strings of which were tied in a stiffly starched bow under her chin, the badge of her rank.

'Do stop fiddling, Sister.'

Karen hastily put her hands behind her back. 'Please, Matron, it's my mother, you see. I must go home, she's ill.'

A sudden inspiration, that, and surely only a small white lie.

'Well now, Sister, so are all of our patients ill, have you thought of them?'

'Yes, Matron, of course. But my mother's heart—'

It was true, Karen told herself, Mam did have heart trouble. Aortic stenosis, a legacy of rheumatic fever. She pushed aside the uncomfortable thought that she hadn't let her

204

mother's heart trouble stop her from coming down to Essex to work in the first place.

'I'll be able to work in the local hospital, Matron, I just need to be near, to help when I can . . .' Her words died away under Matron's stare.

'You do seem to be upset and worried. I suppose it's only natural,' she allowed. 'Well, it's no good trying to keep you here against your will, though you will be missed here. You have proved to be a capable nurse.'

'Thank you, Matron,' said Karen, looking humbly down at her shoes.

'You know the difficulties we have in getting decent staff, even for a small place like Greenfields,' Matron went on. She sat back in her chair and sighed. 'Oh, very well, Sister. I'll just have to try to replace you. I suppose you will be willing to work the usual month's notice?'

'Oh, yes, Matron, of course, Matron. Thank you very much for being so understanding.'

Karen backed out of the room, hearing herself gabbling. But now she had given in her notice she felt calmer as she walked down the drive and out on to the lane which led to the village.

Oh, she wanted to go home, she did, she burned to go home. No, you don't, one part of her mind put in. If you leave you might never see Patrick again. The thought was unbearable. Beneath her cloak she fumbled in her dress pocket for her handkerchief as the tears sprang to her eyes.

Patrick is married to his church, he doesn't want me, she told herself. The very best thing she could do for him would be to get away from him as quickly as possible. Blowing her nose, she decided to put all thoughts of him out of her mind and

205

concentrate on her work. Surely, if she threw herself into it, she would get through the month somehow? Pulling her cloak closely around her against the bitter wind from the coastal marshes, she hurried on down the lane to Annie's cottage.

*　　　　*　　　　*

'Morning, dearie,' Annie greeted her, in her usual bright and cheery manner. 'You're a little late this morning, aren't you? Never mind, I've kept your breakfast hot by the fire. I'm sure you must be ready for it in this nasty weather. The wind is enough to cut you in two.'

'Oh, yes, I am late. Sorry, Annie. I went to see Matron this morning.'

'Nothing wrong, is there?'

'No, nothing wrong.'

Karen picked up her knife and fork and contemplated the food on her plate. She felt slightly nauseous, a feeling which the bright yellow of the egg yolk seemed to accentuate. Carefully, she put her cutlery down again and looked up at Annie. She had to tell her she was leaving.

'I have to go home, Annie,' she said, without any preamble. 'I gave in my notice this morning.'

Annie sat down at the table with a thump, dismay showing on her face.

'But why, Karen? Is there something the matter? At home, I mean? Oh, dear, I will be sorry to see you go. We've been such good friends, haven't we?'

'I know, Annie, I know. But I must go home, please understand.' She gazed at Annie, dark eyes beseeching her to understand.

'I must go home.' She repeated it almost to herself. It was true, she had to go. She felt an almost physical need.

Annie watched her, a question in her eyes.

'Karen, what has happened? Is it a man? One of the doctors maybe, has he let you down? I know you haven't mentioned anyone and you're not a secretive person, but there must be something.'

Karen reddened and looked away and Annie was contrite. She put an arm round her lodger's shoulders.

'I'm sorry, Karen, I should mind my own business. You don't have to tell me anything. Anyway, I know what it's like to long for your own family about you.' She glanced briefly at the silver-framed photograph of the two soldiers which stood on the mantelpiece and sighed.

'Come on, Karen, what you need is a good sleep. Eat your breakfast, do, and then you go on up to bed. But remember, if ever you need a friend to talk to . . .'

Wildly, her thoughts touched on what Annie might think if she knew the truth. Would she despise her, throw her out? But maybe not. Annie was a moral woman but she was also very human.

'Thanks, Annie. I'm not hungry, I'm afraid. I think I'll just go up now.'

Karen smiled wanly and rose to her feet. 'As you say, a good sleep is what I need.'

The wintry sunshine was filtering through the bedroom windows as she readied herself for bed. She drew the curtains against it and climbed under the blankets, closing her eyes tightly, willing herself to sleep.

During the next couple of days, Karen threw herself tirelessly into her work. Feeling guilty about her imminent departure on top of everything else, she tried to be available whenever the wakeful needed comforting during the long nights. She helped out on the wards, often forgoing her rest periods to instruct the VADs.

'I'm glad it's you tonight, Sister,' one man said as she pushed the dressing trolley up to his bed. 'A nice, cool touch you've got with dressings. Better than that Nurse Jennings, I can tell you.' The men in the neighbouring beds murmured their agreement.

'Now then, you mustn't say that,' Karen reproved him. 'I'm sure she does her best.' She turned to Nick who, as usual, was following her around, anxious to help. 'Draw the screens, will you?'

Nick hurried to do her bidding and the men teased him gently.

'You like Sister, don't you, Nick? Her boyfriend, are you?' said one and the others chuckled.

'Don't tease him,' said Karen, but Nick was not offended. He was smiling broadly, delighted with the idea. Since Karen had told them that she was leaving to go back North, he had been despondent. He did not want to stay in Essex without her. It made him anxious to go home himself, at least he would be closer to her there. Before that he had been dreading his discharge from the hospital.

*   *   *

Next morning, as Karen let herself out of the front door of Greenfields, she saw a priest walking up the drive. A priest who, as he drew nearer, looked strangely familiar.

'It's Father Donelly, isn't it?' she asked as he walked up to her as though he intended to speak to her. 'Are you here instead of Father Murphy?' Had Patrick decided it was best for him not to risk meeting her? Karen wondered, her hurt feelings surfacing.

'Good morning, Sister,' said Sean Donelly, his face unsmiling. 'No, I'm not here to replace Father Murphy, I'm here to see you. Do you mind if I walk with you to the village?'

'No, of course not,' said Karen, her brow wrinkling in mystification. They fell into step, Karen peeping up at Sean's forbidding expression as they walked.

'It's not Doctor Richardson, is it?' she said at last. 'Is Robert all right?'

'He was when I left Durham,' said Sean. 'In fact his health has improved greatly. No, it's nothing to do with Robert.' He paused before turning to face her. 'I had a letter from Patrick,' he said. 'I came down to Essex to see him, to persuade him to give you up.'

'Oh.'

Karen was white-faced. She walked over to the hedge and stared over it to the river, its brown water turbulent in its rush to the sea.

'Did he ask you to talk to me?' she said after a moment.

'No, he did not. I have not seen him. Evidently he has gone up to London to visit his brother. Father Brown said Patrick has not been himself

209

these last few weeks, so he told him to take a week off as his brother was home.'

Karen turned to face Sean, looking up into his face. He returned her gaze unblinkingly, his condemnation of her plain to see. She bit her lip.

'Patrick told me about you, though. He wrote to me. That's why I came down to see him. I have to stop him, make him see what a terrible sin it will be if he doesn't give you up. And you—you must go away, leave him. Don't you know you are endangering his mortal soul? And you yourself will be damned as an instrument of the devil.'

'No! It's not like that. I love Patrick. In my church we could marry, we could be happy.'

'Your church? What are you talking about, woman? He is a *Catholic* priest.'

Sean took hold of her by the arm and swung her round to face him, bending his head to her, his eyes glittering.

'But you are married already, aren't you? Oh, yes, I know about you. I made it my business to find out about you. Your husband deserted you, and went to Australia. But you are still married to him.'

'I'm not. I'm a widow. He was killed . . .'

'A widow, are you? But you weren't a widow when you used your wiles to entangle Robert Richardson, were you? Oh, yes, he told me about you. Do you realize you ruined his life too?'

'No, I didn't. It wasn't my fault if Robert fell in love with me. I told him about Dave.'

'And did you tell Patrick about your husband?'

Karen suddenly slumped. No, she hadn't told him about Dave, she thought dully.

'Oh, what does it matter now anyway? You've

210

wasted your time coming here, Father Donelly. I'm going home, I leave at the end of the month. I gave Matron my notice this morning. Now let me go home, I'm tired. I've been working all night.'

'I'll let you go in a minute. First I want your promise that you won't get in touch with Father Murphy again.'

'I'll have to see him in the hospital, I have the rest of the month to work,' she pointed out.

'Then go now, make some excuse. Go before Patrick comes back.' Sean was uncompromising.

'Leave me be!'

Karen had had as much as she could take. Wrenching her arm from the priest's grasp, she ran off down the lane to the safety of Annie's cottage.

*   *   *

'Lies breed lies,' Gran used to say, and Karen could almost hear her saying it when she stood before Matron yet again and said she had to leave immediately.

'My mother is worse,' she said, 'I have to go.'

'Well,' said Matron, not without sympathy for she could see that her Night Sister was distraught, 'if you must, you must. At least it would have been your free night tonight, so I have a little time to rearrange the staffing. I would advise you to have a good night's sleep and travel tomorrow, though. You'll be no use to your family if you collapse on them too.'

Nick was waiting for Karen outside the office. 'I'm going home too, Sister,' he said, full of excitement. 'Saturday, I'm going.'

'Good for you, Nick,' Karen answered, managing

211

a smile. 'I hope you have somewhere to stay?'

'Yes, Sister. I have the address of a boarding house in Durham. Will I be able to come to see you, Sister?'

'Why, yes, you can.' Karen forced herself to think of him, of how he had stayed at the hospital longer than usual because his disturbed nightmares were still recurring. 'I am glad you're going home, Nick,' she added warmly. 'That means you're getting better, doesn't it?'

'Yes, I'm better,' he answered. 'If I write to you, Sister, will you write to me?' Nick sounded diffident. Perhaps she didn't care whether she saw him again or not, perhaps she was only being polite. He had had too many rebuffs in his life to suppose anyone could like him for himself.

'Of course, Nick.' Karen's smile widened into a grin. 'Don't you think I'll miss your cheeky face?'

He beamed, his cheeks flushed with happiness. All he needed was her approval.

Karen picked up a notepad and wrote down the address of her parents. 'I can always be reached there,' she said, 'even if I'm working away.'

Nick put the slip of paper in his pocket as Karen pulled on her cloak for the last time.

'Goodbye, Nick, look after yourself.'

' 'Bye, Sister, I'll see you soon,' he answered. She glanced around the hall, feeling a sense of finality and regret. Then she began walking down the drive of the old house.

It was a fine, bright morning for a change, with a promising hint of spring in the air and snowdrops in full bloom under the hedgerow. Jewel-like crocuses peeped from beneath the beech trees which lined the drive and daffodil leaves were

212

thrusting up towards the sun.

Looking back from the gate, an unexpectedly piercing shaft of pain shot through her for what might have been, together with a terrible longing to see Patrick, just once more. But she knew she could not. Sadly she walked on down the lane to the cottage.

* * *

Next morning, Karen was up early but not before Annie. She could hear her landlady moving about in the kitchen. This was the day, thought Karen, she was going and she would never see Patrick again. Drearily, she washed and dressed and finished packing her boxes before going downstairs.

'Now, Karen,' Annie greeted her as she came downstairs, 'I want you to eat a proper breakfast today. You've that long journey ahead of you after all.' She was using her firm, no-nonsense tone of voice.

'There's porridge and bacon and eggs. I've waited for you, too. I thought we might eat breakfast together as it's your last day.' She looked Karen up and down. 'You're so thin, I'm sure your mother will think I haven't been feeding you properly.'

Karen smiled and followed her into the kitchen, sitting down at the table obediently though she didn't feel the least bit hungry. She watched Annie bustling about with plates of food, thinking how fond she had grown of the older woman.

'I'll miss you,' she said.

Annie paused, looking at the plate of porridge

213

she was about to put down in front of Karen.

'Me too,' she said softly. 'It'll be lonely here without you.' She soon cheered up though. 'Well, my menfolk will be back soon. This war can't go on much longer, can it?'

Karen managed to eat the porridge before Annie took away the plates and brought on the fried food, talking cheerfully as she did so.

'Now, I've put you up a nice lunch, some cold chicken and a pasty. And there's some of my . . .' She broke off in dismay as Karen rose to her feet abruptly, upsetting her tea cup, and rushed out into the yard to the drain where she was promptly very sick. Bent double, she retched miserably, over and over. Then, leaning against the stone wall of the cottage, she struggled to regain her composure. Slowly, she managed to still her pounding heart and fight back the waves of nausea.

'Come on now, come to your bed. I don't think you should go all that way today. You're not well enough, you need a rest. Leave it until tomorrow.'

Annie was beside her, putting a comforting arm around her shoulders and leading her back indoors to the warmth of the fire. A quick suspicion had entered her mind as to the real reason for Karen's precipitate flight home.

'Are you sure you haven't got something to tell me?' she asked as Karen relaxed in the armchair. 'Is this because some man has let you down? I only want to help you, Karen.'

Blankly, she stared at Annie's worried face. What did she mean, what was she talking about now? Had she guessed about Patrick? Karen's face flooded with colour but then she chided herself.

214

Annie couldn't possibly know about Patrick. Oh, no! The realization hit her. Annie thought she was pregnant.

'I'm all right, really I am. I must have eaten something which disagreed with me, that's all. I'm not in any trouble, really I'm not.' How could she be? This time, the thought hadn't even occurred to her. In any case, it was too early for symptoms, much too early, she told herself.

Earnestly, she gazed at Annie who gazed steadily back, saying nothing. Her suspicions were growing stronger by the minute. Karen sat down at the table, willing herself to act normally. She surveyed the congealing food in front of her and had a hard job not to rush out into the back yard again. Carefully, she held her head up and looked out of the window at the variegated ivy on the barn wall. After a short while, the nausea receded and she felt able to talk.

'I will still go today, Annie. I'm perfectly well and can get a lift to the station with the carrier. I've asked him to stop for me.'

'Well, I can't stop you, Karen,' said Annie, 'but I still think you would do better to wait until tomorrow.'

'No, I've made up my mind,' Karen said. 'I'll go today.'

Annie recognized the determination in her voice and said no more.

At ten o'clock, Karen duly climbed aboard the carrier's cart, bound for Littlemarsh. He slung her boxes in the back and they were ready to go.

'Goodbye, Annie, thanks for everything you've done for me. I'll write and let you know how I'm getting on.'

Karen waved to Annie, standing forlorn at the cottage gate, until a bend in the road hid her from sight. She felt like weeping herself. Annie had been a good friend to her during her stay in Essex. For a moment she almost asked the carrier to stop, to let her off. Panic swept over her. She was going home, she wanted to, but never to see Patrick again . . . was she being too hasty? Might he have come round if she had stayed?

Sweet Lord, she prayed, closing her eyes, please let me see him again, please. I couldn't bear not seeing him again.

'Are you all right, Sister?' asked the carrier. Karen opened her eyes and looked into his concerned face.

'Just tired, thank you,' she answered. And she was, she thought, tired to death.

Chapter Fourteen

The basket weave boxes were heavy on Karen's arms as she struggled out of Morton station, named for the village half a mile away, the original settlement, not the cramped rows of the mining community. Somehow she had to make it to old Morton village and out the other side to the unmade road which led to the colliery village.

The wind was, if anything, more biting than it had been in Durham City, sweeping over the hills and small valleys. Putting down her boxes, she pinned on her hat more securely and wrapped her scarf around it for good measure. Taking a firmer grip on her luggage, she set off.

216

Her heart leapt with love and delight as a man came round a bend in the road pulling a bogey behind him. His cap was pulled down tightly over his ears and his white muffler crossed over his chest as, with one hand in his pocket and the other pulling the home-made cart, he strode up to his daughter and planted a warm, whiskery kiss on her cheek.

'Da! You got my letter then?' Karen flung her arms around him with an exuberance which made him back off uncertainly. Such a show of emotion!

'You all right, lass?' His gruff, well-remembered voice almost made her break down and sob out her story there and then, but she controlled herself firmly.

'I'm fine, Da, just fine. And you? And Mam?'

'We're in grand fettle. Your mam hasn't been bad for weeks. I thought I'd bring the bogey, likely your boxes are heavy.' He busied himself stacking the boxes on the cart. 'I'm in fore shift so I don't have to go down till twelve. I reckoned I'd just see you home first.'

'Oh, Da,' cried Karen, 'all this way and you have to go to work. You shouldn't have come, I could have managed.'

He regarded her solemnly. 'I think not. No lass of mine is going to wander the roads at this time of night on her own.' He stopped and looked sternly at her. 'That's not what you got up to in London, is it?'

Karen laughed helplessly, reminded of the times he had stood on the corner of the street waiting for her when she was courting Dave, to make sure she was in the house by nine.

'Well, then.' Taking hold of the rope and pulling

217

the bogey round, he set off in the direction of Morton Main, Karen trotting beside him. They spoke little. He was a naturally silent man unless he was in the pulpit, but the silence was companionable.

At last the familiar view of the towering pit-head winding wheel and the giant slagheap could be seen outlined against the sky. Four rows of houses were strung out from the pit yard while on a slight prominence a more imposing house set in a large garden stood in splendid isolation—the manager's house. At the opposite end of the village the Chapel stood foursquare, watching over the rows which were lit by gas from the colliery. In another few minutes, Da was leading the way into Chapel Row and Karen was home at last.

'Come away in to the fire, you must be starved,' Mam cried from her position in the open door of the house next to the Chapel. She must have been on the lookout for them, thought Karen, and loving tears threatened to overwhelm her. Mam led the way in from the door which opened directly into the front room. Her still young-looking face was wreathed in smiles, animation and excitement overcoming her fatigue. But reaching down to kiss her, Karen was struck by the frailty of the slight form, even smaller than her own. A pang of guilt shot through her. She saw that Mam was worse than she had been when Karen went away, her breathing shallower, her skin almost translucent. And here was she, Karen Knight, preparing to bring disgrace on the family. Oh, God help me, she thought. Deliberately, she pushed the agony to the back of her mind and spoke warmly.

'Oh, Mam, it's so good to see you. It seems like

218

ages. And you look so well,' she fibbed as she walked with her arm around the frail shoulders. They went into the kitchen and Karen looked around, puzzled for a minute.

This main room of the house seemed strangely different, smaller than she remembered. The walls were papered but the pattern had faded over the years to an even light brown, almost coffee-coloured. There was a scrubbed wooden table in the centre of the room covered in a cotton cloth already laid out with bowls to take the barley broth which was bubbling on the fire in a large iron pan.

A new—made of red rags—clippie mat covered the flagged floor in front of the fire with a rocking chair on one side and a hard-bottomed chair on the other, Da's chair. A mahogany press and a few varnished kitchen chairs completed the furnishings.

Yet the room was warm and welcoming. Brass rails twinkled from the tidy-betty which screened the ash box under the fire, as did the one suspended from the mantel shelf. A pendulum clock ticked calmly on the wall.

'I'll do that.' Karen brought her attention back from her contemplation of the black-leaded range and hurried to take the pan from Mam who had begun stirring the broth. Placing it on the steel fender she brought the bowls and ladled out the broth, which was giving off a delicious smell.

Her parents sat back and watched her with love and pride shining in their eyes. She knew what they were thinking: this was the daughter who had made good, succeeded in her ambition to become a nurse and was now a nursing sister. Even though they had not agreed with her telling a lie about her

219

married state to the hospital authorities, they were well pleased with the result. For the moment they were content to have her home again. What would they say when they knew about Patrick and the child? It was the first time Karen had actually thought of her pregnancy as being real, that there would be a child, and she was shaken by the realization.

'Come on, Da,' she said abruptly, 'eat up, you have a long night ahead of you.' She sat down at the table and picked up her spoon.

'We thank you, Father, for all your blessings . . .' Da's voice intoning the Grace made her put it quickly down again. How could she have forgotten? But they hadn't noticed. Now they were tucking in to supper. Da had only a few moments before he had to go.

'You can tell us all about what you've been doing in the morning, Karen.' He smiled as he kissed her on the cheek and then went round the table to do the same to Mam. 'We want to know all about how things are in London and what it's been like in that place in Essex.'

He picked up his bait tin of sandwiches and a bottle of water, and went into the tiny back kitchen to change into his pit clothes. Letting himself out of the back door, he went whistling up the yard.

'Maybe we should just go to bed now, Karen,' suggested Mam. 'There'll be plenty of time tomorrow. The oven shelf is in your bed so you'll be nice and warm. By, but you look peaky. Why, you've great shadows under your eyes. Are you sure you're not sickening for something?' Karen looked up and caught her concerned expression.

'Oh, Mam, I'm all right, it's just that I've had no

220

sleep. You're right though, I think we both need a good night's rest.'

Mam pursed her lips but said no more.

Karen collected the soup bowls and took them into the scullery to rinse. Her mother was busy lighting a candle which she took from the mantel. Karen banked up the fire with fresh coal, turned back the clippie mat in case of a spark, then put out the paraffin lamp.

'Goodnight, God bless.' The familiar words came naturally to her lips as they parted at the head of the stairs.

'You take the candle, pet, I can see all I need to.' Mam left her, for the big brass and iron bedstead in the back room.

Karen slept so soundly in her own little black iron bed with its patchwork quilt and feather pillow that she did not wake up until the sound of Da's voice penetrated her consciousness.

Goodness! It must be late if he was back from the pit already. She jumped out of bed and dressed quickly, shivering in the icy air. Pulling on her grey shawl, the Christmas present from Kezia, she tied it across her breast and behind at her back. Her teeth were chattering and she could hardly tie the knot, her fingers were so numb. She had forgotten how cold this room could be. It was over the front room which did not often have a fire lit except on high days and holidays. Her parents' bedroom was over the kitchen and some warmth seeped up from there.

'Morning, Karen.' Da looked up from his breakfast egg as she came into the kitchen. The heat from the fire came in welcoming waves and she went over to it, standing with her back to it and

221

letting it seep into her chilled body.

'Morning, Da. By, it is cold.' She laughed ruefully. 'I'd forgotten how cold it can be.'

'Healthy weather.' Father sat back in his chair and hooked his thumbs in his braces, grinning. Mam came in from the back kitchen, a tiny room, little more than a store room and pantry. Dishcloth in hand, she stood smiling fondly at her younger daughter. 'I thought I'd let you have a lie in, pet,' she said. 'You looked so tired last night.'

'Thanks, Mam, I'm fine now.' Karen smiled at the worn face. 'You sit down now. I'm here and you can take it easy for a while. It'll be a nice change for me to look after the place and see to the meals.'

She led her mother to the rocking chair by the fire and, pouring her a cup of tea, set about making toast for her own breakfast.

The door opening made her look up from the toasting fork held against the bars of the grate to see her sister Kezia coming in.

'Kezia! How lovely to see you. And you look so well.'

'I thought I'd pop in to see you on my way to the shop. I usually do to see Mam, anyroad.'

Kezia was strangely shy as she crossed over to Karen and gave her a peck on the cheek. She was awkward in her embrace and turned quickly away to ask her mother how she was. Kezia had put on weight since Karen had last seen her. Somehow Karen hadn't thought she would turn into a buxom, almost middle-aged housewife quite so soon. Karen noted the red cheeks and the faded fair hair drawn back in a bun at the nape of her neck. Kezia was dressed drably too, a large

222

enveloping apron covering a plain brown dress which reached to her ankles.

'Why have you come back then, Karen?'

Her shyness made her abruptly direct but three pairs of eyes turned to Karen and she realized all the family must have been wondering.

'I don't know.' She gave a little laugh. 'It's ages since I was here and I thought I'd get some fresh northern air and stay home for a while. I needed a holiday and I'll be able to get work here eventually. If not in Auckland, then Durham or Hartlepool.'

'I thought something must be wrong for you to come home before the end of the war. I mean, I thought you were so busy, nursing the wounded,' said Kezia.

'What matters is that you're home now, lass, and we're glad to have you,' said Da, jumping in to relieve the momentary silence.

'Cup of tea, Kezia?' Karen paused, pot poised.

'Well, I think I will have a cup before I get on.' Kezia sat at the table, folding her arms comfortably across her chest, and proceeded to bring her sister up to date on the latest happenings in the rows.

'A fair number of people went away at the beginning of the war,' commented Da. 'A lot of pitmen joined up. In the end, the government had to stop them, there weren't enough to man the pits.'

'Aye. But then, there were those called up last year. They went off happily enough. Well, it was an escape from the mine, wasn't it? But they found themselves still tunnelling underground in an attempt to reach German lines. Some grand plan

223

of the generals, likely.'

Karen listened to the tragedy of the young girl whose sweetheart was killed in one of the tunnels, and the scandal when she found herself in the family way. She felt a lurch in her stomach at this and hurriedly launched into the story of Nick and his disturbed mind, and how so many boys were returning from France in a similar state. The family clucked sadly, shaking their heads.

Grandparents and aunt laughed indulgently as Kezia recounted the latest mischief of her younger boy and showed suitable pride that young Luke had been top of the class at arithmetic.

Then Karen told of her meeting with Joe.

'What a good time we had on that night out in London,' she said, smiling as she thought of it. 'Oh, Mam, he looks so fit and well and brown and handsome in his Australian uniform. All the girls were looking at him. You would have been proud.'

'I am proud of him,' Mam interposed quietly. Karen laughed. Of course they all were. But then she had to tell them about Dave.

'I wasn't sure if you'd heard but Dave's dead. He was killed at Gallipoli.' The plain statement was delivered unembellished. They gazed at her in silence, trying to gauge her feelings on this. But Karen showed no distress and after a short pause the chat went on in a more cheerful vein.

At last Da stood up. 'This won't buy the bairn a new bonnet. If I don't get to bed, I won't get to work tonight.' And away he went up the stairs, leaving the women to get on with the day's work.

'I'll pop in and see you when you come back, eh?' Karen called after Kezia.

'Make it teatime, then you can have tea with the bairns.'

Karen began clearing the breakfast dishes then emptied the tin bath, left by the side of the fire after Da's bath. She dashed the pit clothes against the yard wall to rid them of coal dust. For the moment she could lose herself in hard physical labour and forget the nagging doubt in her mind. But she knew the respite was only temporary.

Next day, Karen was in the Co-op store getting in the groceries for her mother.

'Well now, will you look who has deigned to come home?'

Heads turned as the thin but penetrating voice rang out and Karen shrank inside. The last thing she wanted was a confrontation with her mother-in-law. But there was nothing else for it.

'Hello, Mrs Mitchell,' she said, forcing a smile. 'How are you?'

'Will you listen to her. The proper madam she is, isn't she?' Mrs Mitchell demanded of the surrounding shoppers, most of whom had perked up with curiosity. There was nothing like a good row to liven up a slow-moving queue.

'Please, Mrs Mitchell, I have done nothing wrong,' said Karen wearily.

'Nothing wrong? Nothing bloody wrong? You call making my lad go to the other side of the world and leave his own mother to fend for herself "nothing wrong"? And you gallivant off to London to enjoy yourself! You care nothing about your own family, let alone me!'

Mrs Mitchell folded her arms and sniffed tearfully. 'My bonny lad, my poor Dave,' she said.

'I'm sorry he was killed, Mrs Mitchell, really

225

sorry,' said Karen. With a suddenness which made her step back involuntarily, Mrs Mitchell burst out in fury.

'He's not dead! He's not! If he was dead they would have sent me an official letter, a telegram or something. I don't believe that lying brother of yours, he always was a sly sod. He never liked my Dave.'

'Mrs Mitchell, come on now, don't upset yourself,' one of the women said. 'You're not doing yourself any good at all.'

'Nay, I know I'm not,' Mrs Mitchell answered, her face crumbling in self-pity. 'But, you know, it's more than a body can stand to have to come face to face with the hussy what ruined my lad.'

Karen turned her back. It was her turn to be served in any case. She bought her groceries and walked out of the shop, looking straight ahead, ignoring both Mrs Mitchell and the other women.

'See that?' she heard her mother-in-law say as she opened the door. 'Cannot even give me the time of day, can she?'

The door closed after Karen. She walked down the street and turned the corner to the pit rows. She held her head high, her face blank though two flags of bright colour lit her cheeks. It was natural, she supposed. The woman was Dave's mother after all. She had to blame someone for the loss of her son.

It wasn't until she was almost to the door in Chapel Row that she thought about what Mrs Mitchell had said about not receiving official notification. Surely, next-of-kin would have received a letter or something? But then, Dave may not have told them about his wife and mother in England. The tiny doubt dissolved. Of course he was dead, hadn't Joe said he was killed at Gallipoli?

A couple of weeks later, on a balmy spring day, Karen was scouring the front step with sandstone to obtain the pristine cleanliness demanded by her mother. Scrubbing away until her back ached, she was overtaken by a bout of vertigo. Black patches appeared before her eyes. She would have fallen had she not grabbed the door post and hung on. Closing her eyes, she kept still for a second or two until the pounding of her pulse steadied.

She was fairly sure now, all the signs indicated a baby was on the way. Once more Patrick came unbidden to her mind. His face was visible before her closed eyes. She could almost feel his strong body with his arms around her. Her sense of loss became unbearable then. She was desolate. Tears oozed from under her closed eyelids and ran down her cheeks unheeded.

'Karen!'

Kezia's shocked voice brought her back to reality. Hurriedly she wiped her eyes on a corner of her apron, sniffing rapidly and fighting to regain her composure, muttering something about a cold.

Kezia looked shrewdly at her, not deceived at all.

'Now come on, down to our house, I think. We don't want to upset Mam, do we? There's no one else in, Luke is on back shift.'

Without more ado, Kezia grabbed Karen's arm and whisked her down the row to her own front door. Bustling around, she seated Karen by the fire and stirred the coals until they burst into life.

'Now, I want to know what this is all about. And don't try to tell me it's nothing, because I know it

227

isn't.' Kezia folded her arms with uncompromising determination. 'Come on, I want the truth. I can't help if I don't know what it is, now can I?'

'Oh, Kezia!' The despairing cry reminded her of the times when Joe and Karen were small and came to her to get them out of some childish trouble.

'Come on now, out with it,' she encouraged.

'I'm pregnant.'

The shock of the bald statement, without the use of any euphemism, took Kezia completely by surprise.

'What? You mean you've fallen wrong?'

'Yes, I'm expecting a baby. About nine or ten weeks gone, I reckon. Oh, Kezia, what am I going to do?'

'Who was it? You never told us you were courting.' Suspicion crossed Kezia's mind. 'He's not married, is he? Or in France? Or dead? Tell me right now, Karen, I have to know. For the love of God, man, think about Mam, it will kill her! And Da, what about Father?'

The apprehension showed in Kezia's anxious eyes and she sat down abruptly.

'It's not this sick boy you've been telling us about, is it?'

'No!' Karen was so shocked at the thought that for a moment it lifted her out of her dumb misery.

'No, Kezia. It was a married man.' The lie slipped out so easily, too easily. She was getting good at it, she thought.

'I didn't know, Kezia. It was such a bad time with all the wounded and everything, and I loved him, Kezia, oh, I did. I do.'

'You can't.' Kezia's voice was harsh. Karen had

228

never known it so harsh. 'If he's married then I don't want to know, you simply can't love him. Oh, Karen, did he tell you he was single? The dirty blaggard.' Her harshness melted and her voice broke.

'Yes. No. Oh, I don't know, Kezia. All I know is that I love him and I'm going to have his baby and I will never see him again. What can I do?'

There was no ready answer from her. Both women sat and stared at the scrubbed table as though the answer was to be found written on it. The wall clock ticked louder and louder until Karen felt herself deafened.

'I think you must go to Gran.'

The remark fell like a stone into the pool of silence. Karen was bewildered for a moment. Gran? The farm in Weardale?

'Gran?'

'Yes, Gran. That's what I said. You will have to tell her, of course. She will shout and carry on, but she will take you in and you can make yourself useful. That way the village won't know and we can break it gently to Da and Mam later. You can use a married name up the dale and people will think you're just another war widow. That's right, that's the best thing.'

'But what about my work? I have to earn a living, Kezia.'

'Don't be so gormless! Sometimes I lose patience with you altogether. How can you work in the hospital when you're having a baby? Goodness, Karen, you can be such a loony sometimes.'

Karen sobbed quietly as Kezia folded her arms and reflected. 'Now, how are we going to get you up there without letting it out to Mam?'

Karen wiped her eyes and blew her nose She was being a weak fool, sitting crying and letting Kezia do all the worrying. 'I could say I'm not too fit and need some fresh air up in Weardale before I go back to work. Mam was saying I looked peaky.'

Warming to the plan, she smiled tentatively at Kezia, mutely asking her forgiveness for bringing this trouble to the family. Kezia smiled back absently. Now the first shock was over her mind was engaged with the practicalities of the situation; Karen could see she was busily working it out. Kezia was always like that: her love for her family and need to protect them were the mainsprings of her life. And now Karen had landed her sister with this and Kezia would feel she had to protect them from this terrible scandal.

'It would kill Da if it came out and everyone was talking about it,' she said.

Guilt flooded over Karen. She hung her head and closed her eyes tightly. Dear God, she thought, I'm sorry, I'm sorry. I don't want to hurt them, of course I don't. But what can I do?

Chapter Fifteen

The following Sunday, Karen went with her family to the morning service in Chapel. There were quite a few heads turned their way as they walked down the aisle but most of them were smiling and there were some whispered greetings for her. It wasn't until she was seated beside Kezia and the service began that Karen realized that the preacher was Dr Robert Richardson. The Minister was taking the service in the main chapel of the circuit, she had expected that, but when Robert climbed into the pulpit Karen whispered to Kezia: 'I didn't know Robert was a lay preacher.'

'Yes, he's been doing it for a year or two now. A good one an' all,' Kezia answered.

Robert was announcing the hymn, a Charles Wesley one: 'And can it be that I should gain an interest in the Saviour's Blood?'

The congregation stood to sing and Karen gazed at Robert as he stood, hymn book firmly in his hand even though he had no reason to look down at it, he knew the words so well. They all did. His voice rang out in a clear baritone, strong and true. He looked fit and well; he must be over the trouble he had had which had brought him back from Africa, she mused.

The hymn came to a close and there was a rustling as they all sat down. Robert waited until it was absolutely quiet before commencing to pray. It was when he finished the prayer and opened his eyes to look out over the congregation that he saw Karen. He stared at her, his face full of surprise. She smiled slightly. He faltered in his announcement of the next hymn, mixing up the numbers, but the next minute he had corrected himself and apologized, carrying on with reading out the first lines of the hymn.

Robert barely glanced at her as he read the notices and the stewards took up the collection. Later on he gave a well thought out sermon which had Kezia and Luke nodding their heads in approval. As the service ended and they all filed out to shake hands with the preacher, Karen hung behind so that she would be the last one out and able to have a few words with him. Robert kept glancing at the door. As she came near he stepped forward and took her hand. He held it, smiling down at her gently.

'Hallo, Karen,' he said. 'I'm so glad to see you.'

'I'm glad to see you, Robert,' she said. 'Especially as you seem so much better than the last time I saw you.'

'Yes, I am,' he answered. 'Are you home for long?'

'For good. At least, I'm not going back to Essex. On Monday I'm going up into Weardale to stay with my grandmother.'

'Would you like to come back with us for a bite of dinner, Doctor?' Mam interposed. 'We've plenty and to spare and you'd be very welcome.'

'Thank you very much, Mrs Knight, I'd be pleased to,' said Robert, and they all walked the few steps to the house next-door.

The back door was handier for anyone coming from the Chapel and a mouth-watering smell of roast beef emanated from the oven as they went into the kitchen. Robert sniffed appreciatively.

'Smells good, Mrs Knight,' he commented. 'Do you mind if I sit in here? I'll keep out of your way. I'm not really a front room sort of person.'

Mam smiled at him. 'I know, lad. You're welcome to sit wherever you like.'

After a while, Da came in from his service in a neighbouring Chapel and he and Robert began an animated conversation about an article in that week's *Methodist Recorder.* Karen tied an apron over her Sunday dress and mixed up a large bowl of Yorkshire pudding to go with the meat.

Robert kept glancing up at her as she moved to

and fro from the table to the oven, and once or twice she caught his eye and smiled at him. For all his well-cut suit and fine linen, she thought he looked at ease, almost at home in the shabby living-room cum kitchen. She wondered if he was still friendly with Sean, Father Donelly. Had they discussed her when Sean came back from Essex? The thought made her feel uncomfortable and she looked over at Robert again and saw he was watching her, though bending his head courteously to listen to her father. No, she decided, he would not discuss her with anyone, he was an honourable man.

After lunch, Robert suggested that they take a walk together.

'To catch up on things,' he said.

'Aye, go on, Karen,' said Mam approvingly. 'It'll do you good. You look as though you could do with a mite of fresh air.'

Karen was glad to get outside. The smell of the meal had become oppressive to her and she was feeling slightly queasy. They walked along the top of the rows and took the path across the fields which led to Old Morton village. The day was fine but there was a bracing wind blowing down from the dale and Karen buttoned up the serge collar of her coat, thinking longingly of her nurse's cloak, so warm and all-enveloping. They walked in silence for a while.

'Why did you really come home, Karen?'

The question sounded abrupt in the silence and she looked up, startled and blushing furiously. *Had* Father Donelly spoken to him?

'What do you mean?' she asked. But Robert had stopped walking. Taking her hand, he gazed

233

earnestly at her.

'Karen, perhaps this is not the time, you've only just come back, but I know your husband was killed, your father told me. You are a widow now, free to marry again. You know how I feel about you.'

'But Robert, you don't know me, not as I am now. It's years since we saw each other. How can you possibly still love me?'

'I do,' he asserted. 'I've never loved anyone else. I always thought you would come back one day. I thought you would have Mitchell declared dead after the decreed time had elapsed and I was willing to wait, but now there's no need, is there? You are free.'

Karen gently pulled her arm out of his grasp and walked on up the path towards a stand of ash trees, their limbs still bare and brown with only the faintest hint of buds to come. Marry Robert? How could she marry him? How could she marry anyone, feeling as she did about Patrick? And Robert especially, he was almost a stranger to her after all this time. Besides, once he found out about the baby he would change his mind, of course he would. No man wanted to bring up another man's child.

'Karen?' Robert was close behind her. 'Karen, it's too soon isn't it? I should have had more sense than ask you when you've only just come back. It was . . . well, when I saw you in Chapel this morning, looking up at me as you did, I thought—I hoped you had come back to see me. Daft, I know, but Karen, I do love you. I've never looked at another girl. If I can't have you, I'll have no one.'

'Oh, Robert,' she said helplessly. 'You don't

234

know anything about me, the woman I am now.'

'I know I shouldn't have spoken so soon, I was too precipitate. I'll wait a while. We'll get to know each other again. Karen, we could have a fine life together, I know we could.'

'I'm going to stay with Gran in Weardale,' she pointed out. 'I won't be here, you won't see me.'

'It doesn't matter. I have the car, I'll come up and see you sometimes. Won't you say I can do that?'

'Well—'

He was quick to catch the note of hesitation. 'I'll do that then, I'll visit you when I can. I promise I won't try to pressure you any more—not for a while at least.'

Karen gazed at his earnest, handsome face, his broad, well-developed shoulders. Broad enough to shelter any girl, she thought dumbly. Oh, why could it not have been Robert? Deliberately, she looked away, over the fields to the minehead and chimney stack, smokeless today as it was Sunday. The sky was darkening and there was a hint of rain in the freshening wind. She shivered.

'Come now, we'll go back,' said Robert, seeing the shiver. He took her hand and held it firmly over his arm. As they walked she could feel the warmth of him through the broad cloth of his coat. He was turned slightly towards her, shielding her from the biting wind.

Robert, she thought, and for a moment she was tempted to agree to marry him. He would be the answer to all her troubles. But she knew it was only a fancy; she could not bear to have anyone but Patrick. And then there was the baby growing inside her. They parted at the end of the row and she watched as his tall figure disappeared in the direction of Old Morton. Drearily, she went back inside.

*   *   *

Next morning, in the cold little bedroom in Chapel Row, Karen was packing her boxes once again in readiness for the train to Bishop Auckland where she could catch a connection to Stanhope in Weardale, the nearest town to her grandmother's isolated moorland farm.

'You're sure there's nothing the matter, Karen?'

Mam was standing by the kitchen table looking worried as she came down with her boxes. Karen tried to reassure her.

'Oh, Mam, I'm all right.' She smiled brightly as she put the boxes down by the front door. 'I just want to go up and see Gran for a while before I start work.'

'But can you afford it? I mean, taking a holiday and you not working all these weeks. I'm sure I don't know how you manage.'

'I'm all right, I've told you, Mam. I've a bit saved and I'll earn my keep on the farm. And Gran will be pleased to have me. I sent her a post card yesterday so she knows I'm coming.'

'Why, yes, I know she'll be pleased to have you.'

Mrs Knight forebore to ask more searching questions. After all, Karen was a widow and in charge of her own life.

'Oh, I forgot, this came for you when you were upstairs. A letter from Essex by the postmark.' She smiled at Karen. 'A letter from a friend might cheer you up a bit. We had a card from Joe too.

236

Just to say he's all right, but it's lovely to hear from him, isn't it?'

Looking at Joe's card, Mam hadn't noticed Karen sit down quickly at the table, her colour going from white to rosy red in a second. Trembling, she looked at the envelope then felt a sick reaction when she recognized Annie's handwriting. Closing her eyes momentarily, she berated herself. There was no reason at all to think it might have been from Patrick.

'Karen, hinny, whatever is it? Oh, it's because of Joe. You two were always close. Did you think he was hurt? He's fine, see for yourself,' cried Mam as she glanced up from Joe's card.

Blindly, Karen took it, fighting hard for control. 'Yes, Mam, it's grand to hear from him, isn't it?'

She turned over the card with its red 'Passed by the censor' stamp, to the picture of the ferocious Turk on the front, and giggled helplessly in spite of her emotional state. How like Joe! Turning back to the message she read: 'Got yours on Friday. Glad everybody well. How would you like to meet this fellow in the street? I'm in the pink, love, Joe.' Dear Joe.

'Well, you'd better hurry, pet, if you want to catch that train. Now you've got everything, haven't you? Drop us a line and let us know how Gran is. I'm sure the farm's getting too much for her but she does want to keep the tenancy. Don't forget.'

'I won't. And mind you look after yourself.' Karen hugged her mother. 'Don't be lifting anything too heavy or anything like that now.' She pushed the letter from Annie into her bag. She would read it on the train, it would pass the time

237

nicely. Fixing her hat firmly on to her head and pinning it to her unruly curls, she picked up her boxes and went out.

Passing Kezia's door which was standing open she called her goodbyes and her sister came hurrying out, her hands floury from bread-making so that she had to hold them away from her clothes. Leaning forward, she kissed Karen on the cheek and whispered softly to her.

'Now don't worry, I'll find a way somehow. I know I'll have to tell Da and Mam sometime, but I want to pick my time. After all, there's a few months left. And Gran will be all right about it, you'll see.'

'Thanks for putting up with me, Kezia. I'll send you a card. I'd better go now.' With a last look at the row of cottages which was her childhood home, Karen thought desperately that she would never have the courage to come back. And even if she did, how could she shame her parents?

*   *   *

It was not until Karen was on the train to Stanhope that she remembered Annie's letter. She had taken control of herself again and was determined to try to forget the past and look only to what was to come. She loved the journey which she knew well from the times she had stayed with Gran for her holidays as a child. In spite of her heartache she found herself looking out for landmarks and noting them with satisfaction. Now she sat back in her seat and took out the letter. There was plenty of time to read it before she reached Stanhope. But the first two lines made her

238

sit up with a muffled exclamation.

Dear Karen

The reason I am writing to you now is that I have had a visitor. It was that Catholic priest, you know, Father Murphy, the one who visits up at the Hall, and he was in a proper taking with himself. Evidently he had not realized you were going home and he wanted your address, but I didn't like to give him it without you knowing. It should be all right with him being a priest but I wonder? Him being in a state, not at all like a priest, if you know what I mean. Karen, I knew something was wrong and made you fly home. Was it him? There were those times he called to see you at the house and we never knew why, or at least I didn't. He has been back twice but I told him I couldn't give him your address. Please tell me what you want me to do?

I hope you are feeling better now you are back with your family. Things go on the same here, as you can imagine. There's a lot of new wounded up at the Hall, poor beggars.

Always your loving friend,

Annie

Karen's first reaction was one of panic. Then she realized Annie had not given Patrick her address. For a moment she had wanted to run and hide, anywhere, in case he found her. Then she felt a crushing disappointment as she saw there was little likelihood of that; Annie hadn't given him her address.

Laughing shakily, she visualized the family's

239

astounded reaction if a Catholic priest turned up on the doorstep in Morton Main asking for her. Not to mention the neighbours. She couldn't think what they would say but tongues would certainly wag. She folded the letter and put it in her pocket.

The train whistled and slowed as it steamed into Stanhope in Weardale. Hastily she gathered her crazy thoughts, straightened her hat and stepped out on to the platform as the train ground to a halt. She was going to begin a new life here in the dales, the past behind her. But first she would write to Annie and tell her on no account to give Patrick her address.

Chapter Sixteen

'Father Murphy! You're back then. Did you have a nice time in London?'

Patrick was brought up short as he saw Nurse Ellis standing by the desk in the hall, taking the report from Day Sister. Somehow he had been expecting Karen to be there on her own.

'Yes, thank you, Nurse. I was visiting my brother, he's been home on leave,' he answered. 'Er, is Sister Knight in one of the wards? I wanted to see her about something.'

'Sister Knight has left the hospital,' said Day Sister, her tone disapproving.

'Left the hospital? You mean she's ill?'

'No, I do not, Father. She's left the hospital for good, gone back to her home somewhere up North. Left us very short-handed, she has. A very unprofessional thing to do, rushing off like that.'

240

Patrick turned on his heel and went back out. Too late, he thought numbly, too late. But Karen would not have left without leaving him a message, surely? What had he done to her? He had to find her, he had to. Annie would know where she was, surely she would? He would find out her address from Annie. Perhaps she was still with Annie. The hope this thought offered fired him. He set off for the village almost at a run and as he went he berated himself for taking so much time to make up his mind.

He remembered wandering round the village and out on to the high road that night he last saw her; he had been disturbed and unable to settle to sleep and thought a walk would help. At least it might quiet his tumultuous thoughts a little.

He came to a lonely inn about a mile outside the village and on impulse went in and ordered a whisky. There were few men in the bar and after greeting him respectfully they left him alone; there was that about him which discouraged company.

Patrick was every bit as hurt and confused as Karen. He thought of the shock on her face as she had come into the hall earlier on and seen him. It had been as deep as his own. She looked smaller somehow, thinner, her face pinched and white. And he was the cause of it. He had hurt her badly when all he wanted to do was gather her up and cherish her, protect her from the world. But that was forbidden him. He had no right to feel for a woman the way other men had, no right at all. It was a sin, a carnal sin. The words went round and round in his head but they were only words, they meant nothing to him, not compared with his feelings.

241

Patrick sipped the last of his whisky and ordered another.

Why should I not love a woman? he asked himself. I do love her, I'm not ashamed of loving her. What sort of a God could let a man feel like this if it was forbidden him? Is there a God? Are we all deluding ourselves, the whole elaborate edifice of the Church, is it a sham? If there is a God and he doesn't care about the war and the suffering and death wars bring, why should he care about me and my troubles? Better to think there is no God.

Taking out the letter which had come for him in the morning's post, the letter from Sean which was in answer to his, he read it through yet again. Sean, his friend from seminary days. But he had not written what Patrick wanted to hear. Sean was firm in his demands that Patrick should forget his doubts and turn back in true penitence to the Faith.

. . . you must put this woman behind you, Patrick, you must give her up, repent. Go to see the bishop, you need spiritual counselling. Loss of faith can be a temporary thing. You must carry on. You must pray to God and in time your prayers will be answered . . .

And in a postscript, Sean had said he was coming down to Essex to see him, to make him see sense, and to speak to the woman if need be.

'I have met her, Patrick,' he concluded. 'You are not the first man to be entangled with her, she is a . . .'

Patrick's mind cut off the word Sean had called

242

her there. It wasn't true, he knew it couldn't be. Sean was simply trying to make him put her out of his life. But Patrick couldn't. Rising abruptly, he went back to the bar and ordered another drink and when it came he resumed his seat in the corner. He sipped the whisky and a picture of Karen as she entered the hall of the hospital an hour or so before came into his mind. His thoughts swung away from the guilt he should be feeling to the love he had for her. Repent? Why should he? He loved her, why should he give her up? Surely a love like this could not be wrong, it was as natural as breathing air. And whatever, Karen was not the reason for his lost faith. His eyes had been opened as he worked with the broken minds and bodies of the young soldiers at Greenfields.

He had already kept an appointment with his bishop. Sean was quite wrong in thinking he could help.

'I am living a lie, my life is a sham,' Patrick had said. And he had listened dumbly to phrases which were supposed to help. Phrases which meant nothing at all to him, they were only words and hadn't he mouthed similar phrases himself, to the young men on the wards? 'Is there something you are not telling me, my son, something, someone, involved in this, drawing you away?' asked the bishop. Was he used to young priests coming to him like this, ordinary men who had thought they were above ordinary human love and had discovered they were wrong? Or did a priest sometimes panic when he realized that he was human after all and fallible, he could not be Christ, he could not even be Christ-like?

Patrick had not told the bishop about Karen, he

could not. He shook his head. 'You must pray, get down on your knees.' 'God knows, I have prayed . . .'

'You would not use such a term if you did not believe, deep in your heart. You are risking your immortal soul here, man.' The bishop had sounded irritated, impatient. 'You must pray, pray unceasingly that God will forgive you.'

Patrick had left unmoved in his resolution. When he entered the priesthood he had been following a path which was mapped out for him since he was a child. Then he had thought what a grand thing it would be to be a priest. He had listened to his mother and shared in her fervour. Oh, how she had worked and longed for him to become a priest, how she boasted about him to anyone who would listen.

'Patrick is to go to Maynooth,' she'd said, bringing it into every conversation she had with anybody. And Patrick had listened and desperately wanted it. He worked and prayed that he would succeed. He had a true vocation, he was sure of it. It had been the happiest day of his young life when he entered the seminary. His faith was absolute, his love of God the greatest thing in his life. The beauty of the Mass, the sublime beauty of the Catholic Faith itself . . . there had been no doubts then, none at all.

But the war had changed everything. He felt his eyes were well and truly opened now. He drained his glass and rose to his feet. He had come to a decision. In these last weeks he had avoided Karen as he struggled to make up his mind. But tomorrow he would go to her and tell her, ask her to forgive him for the way he had treated her. It was not his love for Karen which had forced his decision, he told himself. It was the senseless suffering and slaughter of this war, the wasted lives such as Private O'Donnel's, the misery of war. It was a world revealed without God. Patrick bade the barman a short 'Goodnight' and left the inn.

*　　　*　　　*

Next morning, though his resolve remained firm, Patrick had to change his plans. In the post there was a letter from Betty, his sister-in-law. His brother James was home from France, having sustained an injury to his left arm in the battle for Passchendaele and he was home on leave recuperating.

'. . . it's not serious,' Betty had written. 'He would have written himself except that he is left-handed, as you know. Still, we would be pleased to see you if you could manage to get up to London for a few days.'

'Of course you must go, Patrick,' said Father Brown when told of the letter. 'You've been looking strained yourself these last weeks. A spell away at your brother's will do you good. Don't worry about the boys at Greenfields, I'll see to them. After all, it's only for a few days. Or perhaps a week. Take a week, Patrick.'

Nothing could change much in a week, he told himself. He thought of leaving a note for Karen, but how could he express in a note what he felt? He could go to see her at Mrs Blakey's cottage but he knew she would be going to bed for the day just about this time. She might already have gone. And Mrs Blakey might ask awkward questions if he insisted on seeing Karen. Annie had looked sideways at him the last time she had seen him with Karen. In the end, he went off to Hackney, which was where his brother lived, without doing anything to get in touch with Karen at all. She would still be at the hospital when he got back, he reasoned, and in the meanwhile he had more time to consider his best course of action.

*   *   *

James, Patrick's brother, was sitting in a comfortable armchair before the fire with his youngest child Alice, who was three years old, on his knee, sleeping. He was a tall, strong man with a red face sporting a thick moustache and a close-cropped head which only showed the black of his hair by the line of slightly longer hair at the top of his brow. He looked to be in the rudest of health were it not for the fact that his left arm was in a sling.

'Ah, it's you, Patrick,' he bellowed, whereupon the child in his arms woke up and started to grizzle. 'Betty! Come and see to Alice, will you? She wants her bed, I'm thinking.'

'I don't want to go to bed, Daddy,' cried Alice, her grizzles turning to wails so that Patrick had to raise his voice to be heard over the din.

'Hallo, James. You look well enough I must say. Betty said you had been hurt but there's not much sign of any injury from here. Are you sure you haven't been having us on?'

'Shame on you, and you a priest. It's hard as nails you are,' said James cheerfully.

'What's all this racket? For God's sake, give me

246

little Alice, Jimmy. She may be our third but you haven't an idea in your head about children. Why you want to go shouting on as though you were on the parade ground, I don't . . . Oh, hallo, Patrick. How good of you to come. Take a seat while I see to Alice, I'll not be long.'

Betty took the protesting Alice away and Patrick took off his coat and hung it over a chair before sitting down in what was obviously Betty's chair, an American rocker upholstered in a peculiar shade of lime green. Sitting back and stretching his long legs out to the warmth of the fire, he nodded towards the sling on his brother's arm.

'How bad is it then?' he asked. 'It has to be fairly bad for them to send you home like this.'

'Not so bad, not so bad. I was due some leave soon, it just meant I got back a bit early. It's just a flesh wound, healing already. Right through my sergeant's stripes it went, though, and me just having sewn them on. Still, at least it meant I could get Betty to sew them on the new jacket.'

'Sergeant, eh? When did this happen?'

'Ah, well, promotion comes quickly in this war.'

James's face saddened for a brief second but then he smiled across at Patrick.

'And how are you getting along now? How do you like it in Essex? Keep you busy do they, the English?'

'Irish, a lot of them,' said Patrick. He gazed into his brother's kindly face and was tempted to tell him all his troubles. But this was not the time. Betty would be coming back into the room and no doubt his young nephew and niece would be turning up soon.

'Irish?'

247

'At Greenfields, it's a military hospital, a convalescent home really. We get quite a few Irish.'

A tinge of sadness ran through him as he thought of Private O'Donnel.

'Injured fighting an English war,' said James, startling Patrick for the same thought was running through his own head.

'It's terrible times just now,' James continued.

Just then the back door opened and Jimmy and Mary, the older two children, came in. Betty came down from putting Alice to bed and set about preparing a meal. Patrick sat back in his chair and watched his brother's family, the two children squabbling one minute and laughing together the next, their mother bustling about and every now and then, when the squabbling threatened to turn into an out and out boxing match, scolding them absentmindedly. And James, the father, sitting back in his chair, contentedly puffing on an old briar pipe and letting it all flow over his head. And even though James would inevitably have to go back to France in a week or two, Patrick envied him. Oh, how he envied him. The feeling was a hard, poisonous ball in the pit of his stomach with tentacles reaching into his brain. He smiled at the two children who were sitting under the table out of the way of their mother's feet, playing a game of five stones and arguing about it.

'They remind me of when we were their age,' he said to James. 'Didn't you always cheat, just like that one?' He indicated the little girl, Mary, who was blatant in her determination to win the game. James grinned and sucked on his pipe contentedly.

After supper, the two men decided to go to the

Lion, the pub on the corner.

'Go on, out of my way,' said Betty. 'It'll give me a chance to get these two off to bed and put my feet up for an hour.'

James had obviously been waiting for this for he rose to his feet with alacrity, tapping out his pipe on the bar of the fire and putting it into his pocket.

'Get me the can and I'll bring you back a pint of stout,' he said. 'Coming, Patrick?'

Once the brothers were settled at a table in the pub with pint pots of porter before them, James took a long swallow of his drink before gazing across at Patrick.

'Now then, out with it. Tell me what it is that's ailing you.'

'There's nothing—' Patrick began a half-hearted denial but James interrupted him.

'Don't be trying to cod me. I know there's something and by the look of you it's something serious. So out with it now.'

Once Patrick began, he found it hard to stop before he had told James the whole story. He sat gazing at the pot of untouched porter and said it all; his doubts about God, his loss of faith, a loss which was deepened by his feeling of helplessness when he saw the broken minds and bodies of the young boys who came to Greenfields. He even told James of Private O'Donnel, the boy who was blinded in the war and had come to Greenfields to convalesce. He told his brother of how he had tried to comfort Private O'Donnel, the hours he had spent with him, talking to him about God. And how he had failed the young soldier in the end for Private O'Donnel had killed himself. James listened, saying nothing, waiting until

249

Patrick had finished.

'So you see, I failed him,' Patrick said at last. 'How could I not fail him when my own faith had gone? I should never have been a priest, James. I'm a sham, pretending to something I have not got. The war just made me realize it sooner than I might have done. I am an ordinary man, I want to have an ordinary life—a life like yours. A wife and a family.'

He thought about Karen, picturing her doing the things which Betty had done earlier in the evening, making a meal and seeing to children with himself there, looking on. And the thought was unbearably sweet to him.

James sat silently for a short while. He took a drink of his porter and replaced the pot on the table, his brow creased in thought. Absently, he rubbed the elbow of his injured arm with his good hand.

'I worried about you even before you entered the seminary,' he said eventually. 'It was Mam, wasn't it? She was desperate to have a son a priest. She pushed you too much.'

'It wasn't all Mam,' Patrick demurred. 'I was dazzled by the idea too. I was sure I had a true vocation, persuaded myself into it. But what if I left the priesthood now, James? The shame would kill her.'

'No, no, she would survive, she's a strong woman. We all have to live our own lives, Patrick, do what we think is the best for ourselves. Can't you remember how she went on when I told her I wanted to marry Betty, a Protestant and an English woman at that? I would be cast out from the family, she said, she would never speak to me

250

again. Yet once Betty and I were married, she came round. Such a fuss she made over Jimmy and Mary when we took them over to Clare.'

Patrick smiled, remembering the day in 1914 when James had brought his family over from England to see them. He had been home himself for the weekend and he would never forget his mother's face as she saw her grandchildren for the first time. Her natural hospitality had forced her to welcome her son's wife and the only question she had asked was whether the children were being brought up in the true religion, were they baptized Catholics?

'They are indeed, Mother, what else would they be?' James had answered.

Patrick's smile faded as he remembered he had not yet told James about Karen. He hesitated, not at all sure how to bring up the subject.

'You are very happy with Betty,' he said at last.

James snorted. 'I would be, were it not for this blessed war. I'll be going back to that hell-hole next week, not even knowing if I'll see her or the children again before the next world. For the love of God, man, how happy can we be under such conditions?'

Patrick was contrite. 'I'm sorry, James,' he hastened to say. 'Here am I going on about my troubles when you have such terrible ones of your own.'

'Everyone has troubles, especially in wartime. I'm sorry too, sorry I let loose like that. Come on, drink your porter and I'll get another in before we go back.'

When James came back from the bar with the pots in his hand, he had obviously been mulling

251

over what had been said for he glanced shrewdly at his brother.

'What made you ask if Betty and I were happy just now?'

Patrick shrugged. 'Oh, I don't know.'

'Come on now, there's something else, some girl, is it?' James nodded as Patrick looked up in surprise. 'I thought so. Well, tell me about her then.'

Patrick began, slowly at first, but then his voice took on the unmistakable tone of love and enthusiasm as he talked to his brother about Karen, how lovely she was, what a good nurse, how good and sympathetic with the young men at Greenfields. He told James of how he talked to her during the small hours, how good she was to talk to, how she seemed to understand him.

'I love her, James. I want to marry her and settle down and have a family by her.'

James pursed his lips and Patrick watched him anxiously, waiting for the words of condemnation he was sure would come. But when James spoke he simply asked about Karen's name.

'Karen? That's a funny name, isn't it?'

'From the Bible—Karen-happuch, daughter of Job,' said Patrick. 'Her father is a Methodist local preacher.'

James whistled between his teeth. 'Is he, by God? Well, would you think of that now?' He looked up at the clock above the bar which showed ten o'clock. 'We'd best be getting back now, I'll just get Betty her stout,' he said, picking up the can he'd brought with him and going to the bar.

Patrick stared at his back, his feelings in turmoil. It had felt good telling his story to James; his brother had listened so sympathetically to it all. Yet his attitude seemed to change when Patrick told him about Karen. Had James turned against him?

In this Patrick was mistaken. As they went out into the dark, foggy night, Patrick carrying the can of stout for Betty, James turned to his brother.

'Listen, Patrick. If there is one thing I have learned in this blasted war it is that you have to seize every chance of happiness you can get so long as you're not causing harm to anyone else by doing so. You have your own life to live and you must live it. If you want this girl, if you love her, then you must leave the church and marry her, and to hell with everything else.'

*   *   *

It was a week later when Patrick took the train down to Littlemarsh. Though he had been anxious to get back to Karen, he knew James was enjoying his company. In any case, he himself was enjoying being in the centre of a family again, could feel his spirits lightening as the week went by.

He walked briskly out of the station and turned on to the road which led to Greenfields village. His mind was made up. He would drop his bag off at the presbytery, get Daisy and the trap, and go straight on to the hospital to see Karen.

Father Brown came out of the study as he entered the hallway.

'You're back then, Father. How did you find your brother?'

'Yes, I'm back.' Patrick paused, anxious to be off again. 'James is fine, Father. It was a minor wound

253

in his arm, it's almost healed.' He hesitated. 'Look, Father, I must go now, I have an urgent appointment. I'll see you when I get back and we'll have a long talk.'

Father Brown sounded huffy. 'Very well, very well, if you must go, you must. Though where you have to go in such a rush is a mystery to me, you haven't even read your messages yet. You had a visitor, too.'

But Patrick had gone. He was racing round to the stable behind the house and didn't hear the last few words. Soon he was driving through the village and on up the lane to Greenfields Hospital. Arriving at last at the front door of the old house, he jumped down from the trap and hurried into the hall, only to be told Karen had left the hospital.

And now he was opening the gate of Annie's cottage and knocking at her door. Please still be here, Karen, he murmured as the front door opened and Annie stood there, a lamp held high in her hand.

'Father Murphy!' she exclaimed. 'What on earth are you doing here at this time of night? Come in, come in, do. Is there something wrong?'

Chapter Seventeen

'I'm sorry, you'll just have to find somewhere else to live. I simply can't do with it, man. There's all that racket during the night disturbing my lodgers an' all, not to mention the washing.'

The landlady gave Nick an uncompromising

stare and he dropped his eyes in embarrassment and looked unhappily at the worn brown linoleum on the floor of the passage outside his room. He had had another bad night, the third since he came to this lodging house in Claypath, Durham City.

'But where can I go? What can I do? The doctor said I must . . .'

'This isn't a bloody hospital, man! It doesn't matter to me what the doctor said.' The landlady put her hands on her hips and became even more strident. 'That's my last word on't. Out. By twelve o'clock, mind.' Turning on her heel, she descended the narrow staircase on her way back to the kitchen.

Nick watched her descent hopelessly. Sighing he went back into his room and began to gather together his few personal belongings. The twitch under his right eye was working furiously and his hands were trembling. Where could he go? There weren't many places in Durham left to try.

It was all the fault of these nightmares, he thought. Last night had been a bad one though. He shuddered as he remembered it. Vividly he had relived all the terrors of the trenches in the time before the shell burst so close to him. How everything had gone into slow motion. The horror of seeing his friend disappear into a thousand pieces beside him before the splinter which took his arm brought him merciful oblivion. But the nightmares were almost worse. These nights he went through it all again but didn't wake up in a field hospital. No, he woke up in this small, smelly room in a cheap lodging house.

Last night he had wet the bed. The cold, clammy sheets had made his dream even more hideously

255

real, so like the cold wet mud of the trenches. He had screamed aloud, over and over again, bringing the whole household awake and into his room before turning away in disgust at the smell.

'Bloody hell, man,' one of the lodgers had shouted as he stood at the door wearing only his shirt. 'Aa thowt the Huns were 'ere! Why, man, pull theesel' together. What a bloody stink!' Holding his nose ostentatiously he had stamped back to his own room, muttering about snivelling bairns under his breath. And Nick had seen the disgust on the faces of the other men before they too turned away.

He was left with his shrinking shame. Now, as he packed his old kit bag, he wondered wildly what he was going to do. Then the memory came like a sudden shaft of light through clouds. Karen. He would go to see Sister Knight and she would tell him what to do. Sister Knight always knew what he should do. She would help him. Shouldering his kit bag, he straightened his back and marched down the stairs. Now at least he had a plan.

'Right, you off then?' The landlady was waiting for him at the foot of the staircase. She held out her hand. 'That will be ten shillings rent you owe me. There's the washing and the cleaning and the week's rent.'

She favoured Nick with a belligerent stare, as though she was expecting an argument. But he simply put down his bag and reached into the pocket of his worn overcoat, a relic from pre-war days for he hated to wear his uniform greatcoat. He pulled out a handful of coins and one or two crumpled notes and handed her the money. Grabbing it from him as if she felt he might change his mind, she opened the door to the street.

'Right then, away wi' ye. And good riddance! Ye aughta be in Sedgefield loony bin, man!'

Her parting shot struck straight through Nick but he did not look back or try to retort. Head held high, he carried on down the street until he turned the corner.

Sedgefield, he thought bitterly. Maybe she was right and he did belong in a mental hospital. Putting it out of his mind, he considered his diminishing store of money and decided to walk to Morton Main. After all, it was only a few miles and there was the incentive of seeing his beloved Sister Knight when he got there. She was his lifeline, she would understand.

Nick was very tired, the lack of sleep of the night before combined with a still poor physical condition making him ache all over with the effort needed to cover the stretch of road between Old Morton and Morton Main. His head was aching and his kit bag weighed a ton.

He was thankful when he reached the house of Karen's parents and put his bag down on the step while he knocked on the door. It was a warm day and he was feeling very hot and bothered so he searched in his pocket for his grimy handkerchief and wiped his face. He could feel the stubble on his chin, uncomfortable against the cloth, and he felt dirty and disreputable. For the first time he began to doubt his reception.

'Yes?'

The door had opened and a strange woman stood there, a woman a few years older than Karen, thicker set, yet bearing a strong family likeness. She was looking at him with a frown and

257

he was intimidated.

'Er . . . does Sister Knight live here?'

His voice squeaked as he stood up straight, instinctively turning slightly so that his missing limb was not noticeable.

'She's not here. What do you want?'

Kezia stared at the slightly smelly, scruffy young man. What could he want with their Karen? And hadn't she herself enough on her plate with Mam upset and Da's dinner to get, then there was Luke and the bairns to see to.

'What is it, Kezia? What's the matter?'

Now Mam had come to the front door and was peering over her shoulder. Kezia was doubly vexed. She hadn't wanted Mam to be disturbed.

'Just a tramp, Mam.' In her vexation she spoke with little regard for Nick's feelings. 'He says he knows our Karen. It's all right now, you go back and sit down. We don't want to have to get the doctor, do we?'

Her voice was tender as she took her mother's arm and tried to lead her back into the kitchen where a fire was burning even on this warm day.

However, Mrs Knight would have none of it. 'Kezia, how can you? Where's your Christian spirit? You must give the young man some food and see what he wants with Karen.' As sometimes happens with frail women, she was becoming a little shrill in her animation.

'I just want to know where she is . . .' Nick interjected diffidently. He knew he was shabby and needed a shave but was still shaken at being taken for a tramp.

'But what do you want with her?' Kezia was not going to give him information about her sister's

258

whereabouts without knowing more about him.

'Well, she gave me this address and said that I . . .' Nick faltered.

'Karen's gone away. She's gone up the dales. Come in, young man, and we'll give you some food and a couple of bob. Not that we have much ourselves but we can spare you that,' Mam said kindly.

'Mam!' Kezia, who did not believe in encouraging layabouts, looked horrified. 'Food, yes, but not money.' She looked at her mother, whose colour was a little too high and eyes a little too bright. She knew the warning signs.

'All right, Mam, all right. Now you come and sit by the fire in the kitchen, I'll see to it.'

Unprotesting, her brief show of strength over, the mother did what she was bid by the capable daughter. It was true, she felt a bit off-colour today, what with Karen going just when she had got used to having her back. For something told her that she wasn't going to have her youngest daughter living at home any more. Then there was Joe living in Australia. Though he was in Europe now there was no guarantee he would even see them before he went back to his adopted country. But there was still Kezia and the bairns, she thought. That was a comfort.

Kezia saw her settled and went back to the tramp at the door, but he was gone. Strange! She stepped into the street and looked up and down but there was no sign of him. Shrugging, she closed the door and took a quick inventory of the front room to make sure nothing was missing before going through to the kitchen again.

'He's gone, Mam. Some of these tramps are

funny folk. I suppose they have to be, to be tramps in the first place. They don't like other people, that's what it is. Now forget about him. We were willing to feed him, it's not our fault he took off. I'll make a nice cup of tea, eh? Before I start the dinner.'

She bustled around the kitchen, filling the big, iron kettle and putting it on the fire, settling it down safely on the steel bars. Surely she had enough on her mind without worrying about strange tramps!

*   *   *

Nick had taken advantage of the women being occupied with each other to slip away down the street. He was shaken by the offer of charity. He still had some money left from the army and anyway he had worked for his own living ever since he left the Home when he was fourteen.

This had been a flaming, rotten, bloody day. Why couldn't he just start again now he was out of that devil of a war? He pondered it as he left the long, straggling streets behind and struck out on the road back out of the village, the road he had come in by earlier. A cart trundled past him on its way to Durham but Nick ignored the driver's offer of a lift. He wasn't in the mood to mix with people. He would just walk along till he came to a haystack or barn where he could spend the night.

Maybe it was true, he wasn't fit to live with, he thought bitterly. The doctors hadn't helped him much, too busy and too impatient like everybody else. Except for Sister Knight. She was never impatient with him. She was good and kind and

260

always had time for him.

Where was she? He thought about it as he kicked up dust in the road. Maybe he would never find her, maybe she didn't care. The humiliation of his encounter with the woman who resembled a fairer and plumper Karen seared his mind. Tramp! He was no tramp. Kezia's words came back to him. What was it she had said? 'Up the dales', that was it. That was where Karen was. He could go up the dales. He knew where that was, hadn't he worked in Tynedale? Why, he knew the way there from Durham. He could go to Tynedale and someone there would tell him where Karen was.

Lifting his head resolutely, he stepped out more firmly. He would find somewhere to sleep and tomorrow he would buy a train ticket to Hexham from his dwindling store of money. Coming into Morton village he bought a steak and kidney pie and a bottle of ginger beer for his supper. He took the road back to Durham and, coming upon a stone barn which he had noticed earlier in the day, settled himself in a corner hidden from the road. There were still the remains of a hay crop in it and he made a nice bed from it, pulling the loose hay around him.

Taking out his ginger beer and pie he began his supper, feeling easier in his mind now he had a plan. From Hexham he could explore the dales and the weather was nice and clement so he could sleep rough. Content, he finished his simple meal and taking his boots off lay down to sleep.

Nick woke in the grey dawn to the busy chirping of the sparrows nesting in the roof of the barn and the cold morning mist prevalent in the North-East. He had slept soundly with no nightmares to trouble him, for a change. Shivering he tried to pull more hay around him in his corner but it was no use, he couldn't get back to sleep. He was too uncomfortable altogether.

Reluctantly he got up and brushed the hay from his clothes, putting his boots on with his one arm and tying the laces as he had been taught, using his teeth to help. Going out to the farmyard only a short distance away, he stealthily drank from the pump by the horse trough. It was ice-cold, but welcome. A cow lowed in the shed and he looked up quickly at the blank windows but the house remained quiet. Not even a dog barked. Wiping his mouth with the back of his hand, he picked up his kit bag and set off on his quest once again.

Chapter Eighteen

As Karen stepped out of the station at Stanhope in Weardale, the sun was warming the old stone-built town with its late-afternoon glow. Her heart lifted to the remembered beauty of the scene. The station was in a hollow and she looked up to the main part of the town on top of the bank opposite, surrounded by green hills.

Karen had picked a Monday to come because it was Gran's shopping day and she could have a ride up to the farm without causing Gran the inconvenience of turning out specially. Even as she looked up the road she saw the old trap with the farm pony, Polly, in the traces, coming down the incline. But Gran was not holding the reins, it was a middle-aged man whom Karen recognized as

Gran's nearest neighbour, Fred Bainbridge.

'Hallo there, lass, I've come to pick you up. I was coming into Stanhope for the messages anyroad, and your gran isn't so well today.'

'Hallo, Mr Bainbridge, how are you? It's good of you to come for me. What's wrong with Gran, do you know?' Karen said as he jumped from the trap and lifted her boxes into the back, swinging them up easily.

'She's all right, you know,' he continued as he saw Karen's look of concern, 'just a bit of a cold. She's not getting any younger, like. I've been helping her out a bit lately, what with all the lads off to that dratted war.'

Karen's face cleared with relief. 'Well, so long as it isn't anything serious. Oh, Mr Bainbridge, I haven't seen you for years but you look just the same as you did then. And Mrs Bainbridge and the family? Are they well?' Karen climbed into the seat beside him as she spoke.

'Aye, fine.'

Wasting no time, he clucked at Polly and they were away up to the town, past the imposing avenue of lime trees along the broad main street. Karen had a brief glimpse of the medieval church on the right and the castle and market place on the left before they were leaving the town and turning to climb the moorland road leading higher up the fell.

They both got down from the trap to ease the load on old Polly as they came to the steepest part of the road, walking along in quiet companionship. Mr Bainbridge was kindly but taciturn as were so many of the hill farmers and Karen knew better than to chatter needlessly.

263

She was worried about Gran despite his assurances. Gran loved her outing to Stanhope and the Co-op store. There was a bus service now, to and from Wolsingham, and there was the railway, so the town could get quite busy. After the quiet of the hills, Gran enjoyed a bit of life. I'll soon see how she is for myself, Karen thought, and turned her attention to the countryside around.

The heather was just coming into leaf, giving a slight greenish tinge to the brown of the moor. Close at hand small patches of brighter green showed where new grass was pushing up in the warmer weather. Once out of the valley there were few trees except for the clumps planted round the farms as windbreaks.

'Oh, I'd forgotten how empty the moor seems,' said Karen. 'The farms seem to be planted in the middle of nowhere, don't they? No roads to be seen, just the empty land.'

'Hmm,' said Mr Bainbridge, looking slightly surprised.

She turned back to her contemplation of the fell. At the wayside there were wild flowers, violets and celandines beginning to peep out at the world from little hollows in the stony ground. By, it's grand, she thought, her spirits lifting in tune with the spring.

'Nearly there now, lass.'

Karen jumped as Fred's quiet tones broke into her thoughts, making her sit up in eager anticipation. Sure enough, there was the track leading to Low Rigg, the little farm which had been tenanted by Gran's family for so long. Oh, how she had always loved coming here.

And there was the rowan tree, planted by her

264

grandfather, or maybe it was her grandmother's father, to ward off the devil and bring good luck. It stood only a few yards from the gate of the yard, rooted firmly in the rocky soil against the sweeping winds which came over the top of the moor from Westmoreland. It was sturdy and strong with its feathery green leaves so fresh and lovely, the white of the flowers to come just bursting from the bud. The rowan tree. For Karen it was always the symbol of the old place, reminding her of childhood days on the farm with Joe and Kezia. The few green fields clustered around the old stone buildings, the spring grass bright in the sun, were like an oasis on the fell, she thought.

'You're here then.'

Gran was standing in the scullery doorway wiping her hands on a sacking apron. She looked somewhat diminished from Karen's memory of her, slighter, older. Of course she's older, Karen chided herself. But her smile was the same as it had always been and Karen climbed down from the trap and ran to kiss her cheek, rough and reddened by a lifetime of working out of doors.

'Coming in for a cup of tea, Fred?' Gran called over her shoulder to Mr Bainbridge, who was lifting supplies out of the trap before taking Polly out of the traces and leading her to the low fell.

'I don't think so, Jane, if you don't mind.' Fred put the box of groceries on the scullery table. 'I'll have to get back for the milking. John is over at Rookhope working and May finds it hard now on her own. So I'll likely see you next week, eh?'

With a nod and a smile for Karen, he mounted his motor bike which he had left in the yard while he took the trap to Stanhope, and rode further

265

down the track to his own place.

Karen and Gran moved into the farmhouse kitchen where the shadows were already gathering and a warm fire was lit against the chill of the evening. Karen relaxed visibly and took off her hat, refusing to think about the letter in her pocket.

'Now then, lass, tell me what has happened to you since I saw you last. How did you like working in Essex? Are you glad to be back up here?'

'Oh, yes, Gran, I am glad to be back, and especially glad to be back in Weardale. I'm so glad to see you.' She gave the old lady an impulsive hug which was returned with interest. Brown eyes smiled into brown eyes with loving accord.

'We'll have our tea then,' was all Gran said. Nothing else was needed. She bustled around laying the table with ham and pease pudding, sour milk scones and bramble jam. An iron kettle was bubbling on the fire and she pulled it forward, steadying it on the brass rail before mashing the tea. She covered the brown teapot with a patchwork tea cosy and together they pulled up the bare kitchen chairs to the table.

'Eeh, I am glad to see you lass, I am. We'll have a good crack when we've had our tea, eh?'

'Aye, Gran.' Karen slipped easily into the local way of talking. She sat down at the table and Gran poured the tea. They both had healthy appetites, even Karen who had been off her food lately, and made short work of the meal. Afterwards Karen sat back with a sigh of repletion and looked at Gran.

'Mr Bainbridge said you weren't very well?' she said. Gran was never ill, the idea was strange to her. Karen had always thought she would go on forever.

'It's nothing, just a cold, it's about better. Really what I wanted to do was tidy up for you.'

Karen laughed as she glanced round the spotless kitchen. Tidy up, indeed. But she was relieved all the same, though not quite sure Gran was telling the truth.

'Aye, well,' she said, 'we'd best get the stock fed and locked up for the night. Are you going to give us a hand? We can have a long talk after, eh?'

At a quarter to eight, all chores finished, the two women got down the mat frame which stood by the kitchen wall and started work together on the intricate pattern which Gran had chalked on the harn. The bright strips of cloth were sorted into heaps and they set about working the strips into the fabric with sharp pointed prodders.

It was steady repetitive work, needing little thought, so the women could chat away without wasting time. Karen could remember many an evening when she and Kezia had sat on either side of the frame, prodding away and being watched critically by Gran. And she would tell stories. She always had a great fund of stories about the lead-mining days when the valley was full of men and their families.

After some small talk, news of the dale being exchanged for news of the colliery village, Gran brought the conversation round to what was on her mind, what had been bothering her since she first got the letter from Karen to say she was coming up to stay with her for a while and which had bothered her even more when she saw her granddaughter's pale face and the dark circles under her eyes.

'Now then, lass, you might as well tell me. It's as plain as a pikestaff to me that you are expecting. And not too happy about it either, I see. Has Dave been home and gone off again? By, I could kill that man with my bare hands.'

She bent her head and prodded away furiously. Karen's hands stilled over the mat, a piece of cloth, scarlet in her hand. The pause lasted for a couple of minutes before she spoke.

'Oh, Gran, Dave's dead. He was killed in the war. It's not his fault, any of this. It's not his baby. I'm sorry to bring this trouble to you. I didn't know what to do and Kezia said . . .'

'An' who else would you bring it to?' Gran broke in as Karen's eyes brimmed with tears. 'Don't tell me it's not Dave's fault. If he hadn't gone off like that, this wouldn't have happened. I don't believe for a minute you would have gone with anybody else if you'd still been married. Proper, I mean.' Gran prodded on furiously, stabbing at the harn backing viciously, and Karen couldn't help wondering if she could see Dave's face in it.

'Who is this man, anyroad? He got you into trouble and left you, did he? Lord's sake, Karen, you're no blooming good at picking a man and that's a fact. How you can be so barmy I don't know, you being the clever one in the family too, or supposed to be. You certainly don't get such bad judgement from our side of the family, I can tell you. And you with such a good job and your mam so proud of you. And what about your mam, anyroad? You've not mentioned her yet. Does she know about this? It's not going to do her any good, held how she is, now is it?'

Karen could not find the words for an answer, though in truth Gran didn't seem to be looking for one. She jabbed away, the prod-der going in and out like a piston, never pausing in her work. Her tongue kept pace with her hands, her tirade went on, and Karen saw she was getting through a prodigious amount of cloth. But now her voice rose as she thought of the trouble ahead, not least for her frail daughter. 'Then there's our own neighbours. I know we're sparse on the ground here but we're all friends and they go to the same Chapel as us. It's not just on Sundays neither. What would we do without our social evenings and Bible classes and such? We'd have no life at all.'

It was true, thought Karen miserably as she bent her head over the mat frame. Though the landlords were the Church Commissioners as might be expected of this County Palatinate, it was Wesley who had taken the trouble to evangelize the dale with its wild, rough lead miners and limestone quarriers, and most of the folk left in the dale now were Methodists.

After a while, Gran laid down her prodder and gave her granddaughter a stern look. She had come to some decision, Karen saw.

'Well, Karen, listen to me, this is what we'll do. You're a widow. So are a lot of poor women these benighted days. Nobody's to know the bairn's not entitled to a name unless we tell them. I know it's not right but it cannot be helped. It's not hurting anybody else. But just for myself, I want to know, was the man married? Is that the reason? Did he trick you, Karen?'

She sighed. 'No, Gran. He didn't trick me. And

he's not married except maybe to his church. Oh, Gran, he's a priest.'

'A priest?'

Gran looked puzzled, not understanding what Karen meant at first.

'A Roman Catholic priest.'

Karen had finally managed to tell someone the truth but hearing herself blurting it out like that she could hardly believe it herself. Gran was stunned for a while, speechless. When she did find her tongue, her words were bitter.

'A priest, eh? A blooming priest. No doubt smarming his way into your life when he knew all along it was bound to end badly. A sin for him and a sin for you but he gets away Scot free and you are left the scarlet woman.'

'Oh, no, it wasn't like that. It wasn't,' Karen was moved to protest. 'It just sort of happened. We were both upset, a poor boy killed himself and it just happened. It was only the once. Well twice. It wasn't Patrick's fault.'

'Only the once, eh? Well, they say that them that gets all the gravy don't always get the pudding. And an Irish priest too, be blowed, judging by his name. Well, I've seen them, over at Wolsingham, and the nuns too. There's a convent there.' Gran bowed her head over the mat again, stabbing at the harn. 'It's him being a Roman Catholic though that's the hardest to stomach. Eeh, Karen, what will your da say when he finds out? He'll be proper mortified, he will that.'

Karen could think of nothing to say to that, it was the plain truth.

'Anyroad,' Gran went on, 'it doesn't make a ha'pennyworth of difference now whose fault it

270

was or even who it was. We must just get on with it.' She put down her prodder and began sorting through the strips of cloth for the colour she wanted. 'You did wrong, lass, there's no denying it. But I know you, you must have had some feeling for him or you would never have done it.'

'I did, Gran. I still do. I can't help it.'

'Well, that's the cross you'll have to bear, isn't it?' Gran's voice was sharp. Her hands trembled as she began to clear away the work and Karen felt like crawling under the stone flags of the floor to see her gran so upset through her. Gran saw Karen's downcast face with the tears brimming and she softened.

'Well, we'll say no more about it now. Howay, lass, we'll have a bite of supper. There's one thing sure, you're not the only one this has happened to, not by a long chalk.'

Karen helped roll up the strips of cloth and put them in the bag, putting it away in the corner cupboard. The mat frame went back against the wall and the kitchen was tidied once again.

'I'll fill the kettle.' She went out into the scullery to the bucket of fresh spring water brought in earlier. Well, at least everything was out in the open at last, she told herself, but the thought didn't bring her any consolation.

*   *   *

Sitting on the broad window-seat of the little bedroom overlooking the farmyard, with the rise of the moor beyond, Karen opened Annie's letter again. Tucking her feet up inside her long flannel nightgown, she read it once more by the

271

light of the candle she had placed on the ledge beside her.

There was a scrap of comfort, a tiny warm glow, in knowing Patrick had sought her out. He must not be completely uncaring. But why had it taken him so long? She pondered the question. All these weeks. If he had really cared he would have been in touch sooner, before she left Essex. Perhaps he simply felt guilty? Then there was the question, should she tell Annie to give him her address or not? Not, she thought, not if he was only motivated by guilt.

Karen's doubts and fears seemed to solidify into a great aching lump in her chest, a lump she was beginning to know well. She stared out at the rowan tree, standing there so tall with a halo of silver where the moon was coming up behind it. Solitary, it stood guard over the small-holding and there was a sort of comfort in it. Karen's thoughts wandered back to her childhood, how she and Joe and Kezia had made necklaces from the berries. They had used the trunk to hide behind in games of hide and seek. The flowers had been just the thing for garlands when they had played at being fairies. Deliberately, Karen kept her mind on those days. She felt she couldn't bear to think of Patrick any more, not that night.

A shadow flitted from the back door and across to the field gate and Karen leaned forward to peer through the darkness. It was Gran, checking on the animals, she supposed. She leaned back and sighed. The night was peaceful. Only the whinny of one of the Galloways, Polly or Jess, sounded in the quiet. Karen stood up slowly in the darkened room and the peace of the place seeped into her. She would have her baby here and work on the farm, she decided. If money was short she would get work at the cottage hospital. She and the baby would be fine, they would survive.

For the first time she began to look forward to the baby's coming. It would be a part of Patrick which would be hers and so doubly precious. Gran came through the gate, and seeing the light from Karen's candle, waved. She opened the window and leaned out.

'Everything all right, Gran?' she called softly, afraid to disturb the magic of the night.

'Grand, lass,' came the reply. 'Jess foaled all by herself, quite easily, a filly.'

'That's lovely, Gran. And a filly. That's good, isn't it?'

'Aye. She'll fetch a fair price at the auction mart next year if we decide not to keep her. Well, get away in to your bed, the night air's not good for you nor the bairn.'

'Goodnight then, Gran.'

Karen half-closed the window as Gran let herself into the house. Blowing out the candle, she climbed into bed. She pulled the blankets up to her chin, feeling a sudden chill as a breeze sprang up from nowhere. Sleepily, she thought about what she would do tomorrow. First she would write and tell Annie not to let Patrick have her address. He was better off forgetting all about her. What good would it do anyway? He could not marry her and she knew she could not continue their relationship without marriage. Tomorrow she would write to Annie. She could send a card to Kezia and Mam and Da while she was about it. An owl hooted softly and its shadow swooped down into the

273

farmyard. After a mouse, she supposed. Yawning, she turned over on to her side. Her long, exhausting day finally took its toll and Karen fell into a deep and restful sleep.

*   *   *

Coming out of the cow shed with a pail of milk in her hand, Karen paused to take a deep breath of air. Idly, her thoughts ran back over the last few days since she had come to the farm. They had flown by, she realized. It must be the rhythm of farming life. She hadn't been sick that morning, nor the day before either, and her vertigo was disappearing, thank goodness. Taking the milk into the small scullery which did duty as a dairy, she poured some into the jug and the rest into a bowl to settle. Glancing up at the speckled mirror above the stone sink, she was pleased to see how fit she looked. The clean moorland air and outdoor life had brought a bloom to her cheeks and shine to her hair. She was finding the physical work pleasant too. She had been taught to milk at ten years old and found she hadn't forgotten how.

Scrubbing out the milking pail, she looked out of the window at the gander. He and his two geese had come to recognize her and he stopped his menacing display every time he saw her. Dreamily, she scrubbed at the pail. She liked the animals; she had almost forgotten how she had loved them when she was small.

Some of the hens had hatched chicks and a number of lambs had been born to the ewes brought down from the fell in expectation. There

274

was also Jess's foal, so that altogether there was an air of new beginnings on the place which entirely matched Karen's mood.

The baby moved within her, a tiny fluttering but stronger than usual, and Karen held her breath. That was the fifth time, she thought. Somehow it made him feel so much more real. For it was a he, she was sure. She smiled, feeling deeply at one with the natural world around her.

'I think that's the postman coming down the lane,' observed Gran, coming in to put on the kettle for their morning break.

Something overshadowed Karen's feeling of content. Annie had not replied to her letter as yet. Karen presumed she was too busy to write for a while; she would, no doubt, when she could. There might even be a letter from her in this morning's post. Patrick was still much on her mind, she was unable to forget him yet content somehow if not happy exactly.

There was a letter from Kezia, that was all. Karen swallowed her disappointment as they sat down to their tea.

'Well, has Kezia told your mam yet?' Gran asked after a moment.

'Not yet.' Karen lifted her eyes from her letter and looked at Gran, her face troubled. 'Mam's had another bad turn, though Kezia says here that she is getting over it. I wonder if I should go home to see her? Do you think I should?'

'Don't be a fathead, Karen. Wouldn't that give everything away? Anyroad, Kezia says she's getting over it. We'll just wait and see.' Gran's tone was impatient but she too was looking thoughtful and sad. She pulled a wry face and stood up from the

275

table, gathering the pots together.

They carried the dishes into the scullery and began the washing up. Water had to be carried from the spring up the field behind the house and heated up on the range but at least there was a brownstone sink in the scullery with a drain to the gulley outside. In her nursing life, Karen had got used to having both hot and cold water on tap. She had almost forgotten how much extra work was caused by the necessity to carry it from a distance and heat it over the fire. She wondered for a moment how much it would cost to bring a proper water supply to the house, a fortune, probably. Looking out of the window as she slowly dried a cup, she was thinking that the view beyond the farmyard was idyllic. The war was a faraway dream to her as she idly watched the animals.

She listened to the drone of a bee busily searching in a bed of 'snow in summer' under the window. People said the war would end soon, the postman had told them. Karen wondered if Joe would come to see them before he went back to Australia. Her heart lightened at the thought, then came a quick niggling doubt. What would he think about the baby?

Her attention was brought back to the present by a sudden exclamation from Gran. 'Just look at the gander! He's walking up and down like a guardsman on parade.'

Karen had placed a clutch of goose eggs in a nest in the old dog kennel in full view of the window and the broody goose had been sitting on them since breakfast. The gander was taking his responsibilities seriously and was walking up and down before the kennel, filled with his own

276

importance. He looked so proud it was a shame to laugh at him. Around him the hens were scratching in the dirt and a couple of young pigs were rutting in search of tasty morsels. There was the occasional honk from the gander and the grunting of the pigs. Karen and her grandmother smiled at each other in mutual amusement.

Suddenly the yard erupted with noise, startling both women into rushing for the door. With a loud honking from the gander and even louder squealing from the pigs, one porker came flying past the window, literally flying, and firmly attached to his tail was the gander, flapping his wings and flying low off the ground. The pig had gone too near the kennel and at last the gander had the chance to show his mettle. The porker squealed and the hens flapped madly. Karen grabbed a broom and rushed out to try to separate the warring animals.

At last the bold defender released his grip, honour satisfied, and stalked back to his post. The pig, Karen and Gran collapsed in a heap, the two women unable to speak for laughing.

'Come on, Karen, get up,' Gran said at last. 'You're getting too big for these carry-ons and I'm getting too old.'

They climbed to their feet, smoothing down their aprons. Karen tucked a wisp of stray hair back into its knot at the base of her neck. Without speaking they strolled over to the side of the house for a moment to look over the fell, so beautiful in the sunlight and stretching up to the blue top which divided them from Teesdale, blue and hazy.

Karen placed a hand over her stomach, almost unconsciously. She was accepted as a widow now

277

in the dale, there had been no comment from the people they met in the little Chapel on Sunday. Already she felt part of the life at Low Rigg. Things could be worse, she mused.

'Well,' said Gran who had followed her out, 'this won't buy the bairn a new dress.' They laughed together. This time the old saying had a literal meaning.

Slowly they walked back, luxuriating in the warm sunny day, reluctant to begin the next round of chores. The sound of a car coming up the lane made them turn, glad of the excuse to stay outside a little longer. Cars were rare in the dale where even horses and carts were infrequent.

A wild hope was rising in Karen's breast. Perhaps it was Patrick, perhaps he was coming to say it was all a mistake, he loved her and was perfectly free to marry her? The fantasy brought the colour up in her cheeks and she lifted her head and gazed at the bend in the track to where they would first see the car. Then it was there. It chugged heavily into the yard and came to a halt a few yards away from them. Karen's heart leapt as she saw the tall, broad-shouldered man climb out of the driving seat. He was wearing a cap pulled over his brow and goggles over his eyes and for a moment her love made her see Patrick's face under them. She watched as he pulled off the cap and goggles and loosened the scarf around his neck, her breath caught in her throat.

'Hallo, Karen,' said Robert, and a crushing weight fell on her and she went limp under it.

'How are you, Mrs Rain?' asked Robert, taking off his driving gloves and holding out his hand.

'Grand, thanks,' Gran answered.

Karen put out a hand to the wall to steady herself. She couldn't believe that neither of them had noticed how close she had come to fainting only a second before. She bent her head and stared at the flagged step of the door. Vaguely, she could hear the angry honking of the gander and Gran shooing him away.

'You don't look too well, Karen.'

Robert had indeed noticed how white she was. He took her arm. With a great effort of will, she looked up at him and smiled.

'I'm all right, thank you, Robert.'

'Howay in, now, you'd better sit down, Karen,' counselled Gran. 'We'll have another cup of tea with Doctor Richardson, anyroad.'

There was speculation in Gran's eyes, Karen saw, as the old lady glanced from Robert to her granddaughter and back again to Robert.

He said no more, though he kept giving Karen concerned glances as they sat at the table drinking tea. And as soon as they'd finished he suggested they go for a spin in the car.

'You too, of course, Mrs Rain,' he said, 'if you can spare the time, that is?'

'I cannot. But you can take Karen if you like, it will do her good.'

'If you're sure, Gran,' Karen said doubtfully, 'but I think I'd rather go for a walk than a ride, Robert.' In truth, she was worried the car might make her nausea return. A walk would be better.

They walked along the track a little way and cut across the fell to the little wooded ghyll hidden in a fold of the moor. It was a favourite walk of Karen's and she loved the way it suddenly revealed itself as they walked near, by the sparkle of the burn

279

tumbling down the steep, wooded side of the ravine.

'It's beautiful,' commented Robert, looking at the bird cherry which grew in profusion between the outcrops of limestone.

'It is,' agreed Karen. 'I've always loved it here.'

She showed him a rare wild orchid and pointed out the 'cuckoo pint'; they even found wild arum, its purple flower spike shielded by a pale green hood.

'Let's sit awhile,' he said.

Robert took her hand and led her to an outcrop of rock which had been smoothed by the weather to a broad fiat top. He saw her seated and sat down beside her and for a few minutes they stayed in a silence broken only by the murmur of the stream, the 'chack-chack' of the jackdaws as they swooped about the sky, and the strange cry of the peewits circling over their nests.

'Why didn't you tell me, Karen?' asked Robert.

'Tell you?' She was startled. Had Sean said something to him after all? She trembled. 'Tell you about what?'

'The baby.'

She looked up at him quickly. How did he know? The question must have shown in her eyes for he answered it.

'I can see you are pregnant, Karen. Why didn't you tell me when we met in the village? Why did you let me think there was a chance for me? Who is he, Karen? Is he going to marry you?'

'Oh, I'm sorry, Robert, really I am. I couldn't tell you—I didn't want to hurt you. I like you too much for that. But yes, it's true, I am going to have a baby, that's the real reason I have come home.

And no, I am not going to marry the father.'

Robert stood up abruptly and walked to the side of the tiny stream. He picked up a pebble and flung it into the water. Karen watched him dumbly.

'Who was it? The father, I mean.' Robert continued to stare into the water, keeping his back to her. 'Was it a soldier? Has he been killed? Is that what happened, Karen?' Already he was searching for excuses for her behaviour, she thought numbly.

'No, nothing like that.' How could she tell him about it? How to tell him she had fallen in love with a Roman Catholic priest, tell him her lover could not possibly marry her?

Robert turned to face her. 'He left you then. He made you promises and then left you. When he found out about the baby coming, was it?'

'No, no, it wasn't like that,' cried Karen.

'No, it never is. Oh, Karen, don't you think I haven't heard this tale a dozen times before? A girl comes to me and begs me to help her. She always thinks her case is different, she's not like those other girls who get caught.' He sighed. 'And now, with this war, it happens more and more. Tell me who it was and I'll seek him out, make him do the right thing by you.'

His voice was hard and bitter, impersonal almost. Karen held out her hand to him.

'Robert, Robert, leave it alone. I can't tell you who the father is. I can only say that he can never marry me, never.'

'He's married then?'

'No, he's not married. I can't tell you what it is, Robert.' She got to her feet and walked towards him, gazing up into his handsome face, seeing the

281

hurt in his eyes.

'Come on, let's walk a little more. Let's not talk about it,' she said, and he took her arm and helped her up the bank side.

They strolled past the old lead mine workings where so many of Karen's ancestors had toiled. The scars on the earth and the fallen stone of the buildings were faded now; they blended into the landscape as though they had been there as long as the limestone outcrop beside them. Only the song of the skylark disturbed the silence as they walked, Robert keeping a distance of a few feet between them. Eventually he stopped walking and turned completely away from her, gazing out over the moor, straight-backed and still. Karen watched him, biting her lip. She didn't know what to say to him. She felt guilty for causing him such pain, he made her feel morally inadequate. She had not realized his love for her was so strong and she knew she should have done. But after all these years, surely his feelings for her should have weakened?

'Robert?'

Her voice was tremulous, uncertain. His shoulders shook silently. Dear God, she thought, was he *so* upset? Surely there was nothing so special about her that a man like Robert should love her so much? She remembered Sean telling her she had ruined Robert's life; how at the time she had thought that to be an exaggeration.

Robert began walking again and she followed him. They crossed the rough grass to the track which led to Low Rigg and soon they were by the gates of the farm. He paused and she looked up at him anxiously, noting that his face was composed

282

now, the high colour gone. The sun was high in the sky and she could feel the spring warmth of it on her face and he, ever solicitous, drew her under the shade of the rowan tree.

'Karen,' he said, taking her hand in his, 'there is only one solution to this. You must marry me.'

'Marry you?' she echoed him, her eyes widening in surprise, and shook her head. Oh, no, she couldn't marry him, she couldn't do that to him. Robert halted her refusal before even it was spoken.

'You must, Karen. For the sake of the child. I would be a good father to your child, Karen.'

He has a father! she wanted to shout at him. She didn't want any other father for her baby but Patrick.

'Think about it, Karen, don't say no immediately. I know you are thinking of me, how it would affect my life if I married you and a baby came in just a few months. But I have broad shoulders, and the gossip will soon die down.'

Karen felt even more guilty than before. She hadn't even considered the effect such a marriage would have on him, both in his life as a doctor and as a local preacher. All she'd thought about was herself, she wasn't even considering what it would be like for her baby to be labelled a bastard.

'Robert, I don't know what to say,' she whispered.

'Don't say anything now. If we marry we should do it as soon as possible, I know, but another week won't matter. Think about it, Karen, pray to the Lord about it. I know he will put it in your heart to do the right thing. I'll go now, leave you to come to a decision.'

Gran came out of the door of the house, and seeing them standing there by the rowan tree, walked over to them.

'Are you staying for a bite of dinner, Doctor Richardson? We have plenty and you're very welcome. If you don't mind lamb and barley broth, that is.'

Robert dropped Karen's hand and smiled courteously at the older woman. 'It's very kind of you, Mrs Rain, I would have loved to stay. But I'm afraid I have to leave. Work, you know.'

'Well, if you have to go, you have to,' said Gran. 'I'll say goodbye then, lad, it was nice of you to call. I have to work an' all, there's the stock to see to.' She nodded her head and walked back to the house and around the side to the back.

Robert waited until she was out of earshot before turning back to Karen and taking her hand. 'You will think seriously about my offer, won't you? Even if you can't feel for me the way I feel for you, we could be happy together, I know we could, Karen. And then there's the child, think of the child.'

'Please, Robert, don't press me. It's too soon,' begged Karen. 'I can't think properly about anything just now, I need time.'

'But that's it. There just isn't any time, is there? With the child . . .' He broke off what he was saying when he saw the hunted expression on her face. 'No, you're right, I shouldn't press you now, I know I shouldn't. I'll go, but you'll let me come back next week, won't you? Perhaps you'll give me my answer then?'

'Robert, I don't know, I really don't. Everything is such a muddle in my head. Go on, go home,

284

you'll be late for surgery.'

'Yes, I'm sorry. Of course I'll go. Just . . .' He moved closer to her and bent his head and she lifted her face to him, thinking he was going to kiss her on the cheek. But evidently he thought better of it for he turned abruptly to his car. He started the engine with his starting handle and when it fired he climbed into the driving seat before smiling ruefully at her. 'Goodbye, Karen. God keep you safe until I come back.'

She stared after him as the car laboured up the track and disappeared round the bend. Dear God, she agonized, why couldn't I have loved him? Why is everything so complicated? Slowly, she walked back to the house. Gran was in the kitchen boiling up vegetable peelings for the pigs. She looked up as Karen came in and gave her a shrewd glance.

'I knew fine and well that lad has a fondness for you,' she observed. 'It's there for anyone to see.'

'Oh, Gran, don't,' said Karen helplessly. 'Robert is just a good friend, that's all.'

'Aye, I'm sure. But remember, lass, it's hard bringing up a bairn on your own. You could do worse than marry a lad like Robert Richardson. There's many a one has to settle for the one they can get, not the one they want. It usually works out fine in the end.'

Chapter Nineteen

Surely Patrick feels as I do? thought Karen. He could not cut her out of his life, forget about her altogether. He loved her, she knew it in her being.

It was you ran away from him, not he from you, she told herself. You don't want him to come, you know it will ruin his life. Forget, that was what she had to do, forget all about him.

She was standing by the yard gate. Beside her the rowan tree was coming into full leaf. It was summer already, the winds were light and warm. But still she couldn't stop her heart racing every time she heard the familiar rumble of the cart or the roar of an engine on the road at the end of the track.

She couldn't help the aching need within her either, the deep physical ache which sometimes threatened to consume her. She placed her hands on her stomach and concentrated on the baby. At least she had the baby, Patrick's son. Or maybe his daughter, a girl who would look at her with Patrick's clear grey eyes ringed with dark lashes, and that way she would always have something of Patrick with her.

*　　　*　　　*

On Saturday Robert came back to see her and they drove down into Stanhope and on, across the ford over the River Wear and up the steep fell-side to Bollihope Common, the great breadth of moorland which divides Weardale from Teesdale. He stopped the car about halfway between the dales and they sat quietly, looking out over miles and miles of heather and bracken to where the distant horizon lay shrouded in a shimmering mist. Robert had put down the car hood and Karen could feel the sun on her head and neck, pleasantly warm. Sheep baa-ed all around them as

286

they cropped the turf which edged the heather and a curlew cried mournfully close by. They were too near to its nest probably, thought Karen abstractedly, it was worried. Its cry sounded so human, so sad, it brought ready tears to her eyes.

Quickly she looked out over the moor, away from Robert, until the moment passed. A peewit flew low over the ground only a few yards away, trying to draw the intruders away from its nest. It too was worried for its young. And what of her young? She had the baby to think of. She had to provide for it and protect it, even though Patrick was gone from her life. Oh, why had she listened to Sean? Why had she not stayed a little longer at least? She and Patrick were meant to be together. Dear God, she cried silently, give me strength.

'Karen?'

She looked at Robert who was turned sideways in his seat, watching her anxiously. 'If you are sure you want me, I'll marry you, Robert,' she said. 'But I have to be sure you want the baby an' all, you can see that, can't you?'

Robert smiled and the smile lit up his face so that it glowed. He took hold of her hand and lifted it to his lips. His kiss was as soft as thistledown.

'The baby is part of you, isn't it?' he murmured. 'How can I not want your baby?' He drew her to him and held her close, kissing her lips. His arms were strong about her and he smelled cleanly masculine and familiar. She closed her eyes and leaned against him. Oh, it was good to have a man such as Robert to lean on, and she would play her part, she wouldn't let him down, oh no, she would not. She could feel his heartbeat against her breast and he ran his hand up and down her spine. His breathing quickened and suddenly his hand was on her breast, cupping it, and his thumb brushed across the nipple. Abruptly, instinctively, she pulled away from him, as far away as she could get, and huddled against the door of the car. For he was not Patrick.

'Karen? I'm sorry, really I am. I got carried away . . .' Robert's voice trailed into silence. She forced herself to sit up and move into a more natural position beside him, giving him a tremulous smile as she did so.

'Are your breasts sore? I'm sorry, I should have known they would be with the baby. It was just . . . oh, I'm so happy Karen, this is the happiest day of my life. I got carried away, I'm sorry.'

'They are sore,' she said, jumping at the excuse. 'But don't be sorry, Robert, please. You have nothing to be sorry about.'

'Let's go down into Barnard Castle and buy the ring,' he said, reassured. He started the car and they set off across the moor, descending slightly all the way now as they moved closer to Teesdale. 'We'll have to begin planning now, won't we?'

Karen felt herself carried along on his enthusiasm and indeed it was pleasant for her to leave everything to him and relax. But she still had a feeling of guilt, as though she was taking an unfair advantage of his love for her.

'I'll make you a good wife, really I will,' she said impulsively and reached out and put her hand on his arm.

They got to the jeweller's just before closing time and chose a ring.

'I don't want a betrothal ring, please, Robert,' she whispered urgently to him when he began looking at a tray of diamond rings in the window. 'A wedding ring, that's all, please.'

He smiled euphorically. 'Anything you say, my love. I can always buy you a diamond ring later.'

They decided on a plain gold band and the jeweller put it in a box which Robert stowed in his waistcoat pocket.

'We'll call the banns tomorrow,' he said as they drove back up the moor. 'I'll speak to Father tonight. We can be married in three weeks.'

Three weeks! Panic fluttered in Karen, almost closing her throat. 'Maybe we should wait a week or two,' she managed to say.

'Best do it now. Don't worry, dearest, everything will be fine. I will look after you now.'

'But I have no proof that Dave is dead.' Relief swept over Karen. She couldn't get married unless she could prove her first husband was dead, could she?

'I'll telephone Australia House tomorrow,' Robert answered cheerfully. 'I'll ask them to confirm the death in writing, there should not be any trouble.'

They drove across the ford at Stanhope and on up to the farm. As they came into the yard they saw Gran standing in the doorway.

'So you're back,' she called over to them, 'have you had a good time?'

'We have indeed, Mrs Rain, and we have news—' Robert broke off what he was saying as the sound of a cart coming round the bend in the track made them all turn to look.

'The carrier,' said Gran. 'He's late today. Someone with him an' all. Eeh, two visitors in one day, aren't we doing well?'

289

Karen didn't hear her, she was standing stock still, her face frozen.

'Mind the cart, Karen.'

Robert grabbed hold of her arm and pulled her back towards the rowan tree, out of the way. The cart trundled past them and she followed its path, her gaze riveted on the passenger in the front seat.

Not again, she was thinking dully, not again. Her senses must be deceiving her and she couldn't bear it: that the elation should rise in her only to fall flat as a stone when she realized she was mistaken. She had forgotten Robert altogether. All she could see was the stranger in the dark suit, tall, black-haired, slimly built. The cart came to a halt and she watched him climb down and stand quietly beside it, his eyes only for her. She was not mistaken this time.

'Who's this?' said Gran. She looked at the stranger and then at her granddaughter and was taken aback by Karen's expression. She glanced quickly at Robert and away again; his distress showed much too plainly for outsiders to see. He too was watching Karen as she stared at the new arrival. Gran felt desperately sorry for Robert. It had only been a few seconds and the carrier hadn't noticed anything as yet, he was busy fitting a nosebag of oats to his horse.

'Come in, Amos, I have the kettle on the bar and I just baked scones this morning,' she said, hustling the startled carrier into the house despite his protests of work still to be done.

Karen went on staring at Patrick, still unsure if she was seeing aright. I must be dreaming, she thought. Everything seemed to have gone into slow motion. Had the sun gone to her head? She closed her eyes but when she opened them again Patrick was still there, his grey eyes drinking in the sight of her.

'Karen,' he said at last, in a quiet contented sort of tone, as though he had finally found what he was seeking. He crossed the yard slowly, steadily, ignoring the angry hoot of the gander who spread his wings in threatened attack. And then he was standing before Karen, not touching her, just searching her face. The moment seemed to last forever before he broke into her trance by stepping forward and taking her into his arms.

'Patrick,' she breathed, and he held her head in the crook of his arm as they swayed together. She drank in the remembered smell of him and the baby moved in her womb as though in recognition and approval. They gave themselves up to the overwhelming sense of peace and belonging which washed over them.

She had forgotten all about Robert until he took hold of her arm and pulled her away from Patrick. Surprised, still bemused, she looked up at him. 'Robert,' she said with a twinge of sadness, but he seemed remote somehow. She couldn't yet think of anyone but Patrick. 'I'm sorry, Robert.'

'Sorry? Why are you sorry, Karen?'

Patrick was suddenly alert. Though he spoke to her he was staring at Robert. He was still, strangely still, his eyes intent.

'Karen has promised to marry me,' said Robert flatly, still holding her arm. She made an involuntary movement away from him then stopped.

'Robert, please,' she said, but he didn't hear her. All his attention was on Patrick.

291

'She's mine now, she is going to marry me,' Robert said again. His head held high, his shoulders back, he glared at his adversary over his nose. 'You deserted her,' he added.

'I'm here now,' said Patrick.

'Karen?' said Robert, still looking at Patrick. She could feel the tension between the two men. It was so strong she could almost see it.

'Please, Robert,' she said. 'I love him.'

Robert slumped, seeming to fall in on himself. Without another word he got into his car and drove off up the lane, and they waited until the sound of his engine faded along the top road. Then Patrick took her arm and they went into the house together.

* * *

Earlier in the evening Patrick had descended from the train at Old Morton village and began to look for Chapel Row. He had tried to get her address from Annie but in the end had had to go to the hospital. It was Doctor Clarke who had searched the hospital files and found the address for him, but only after weeks of opportuning. Patrick was on the point of leaving for County Durham to look for her on his own account. After all, there couldn't be many mining villages such as the one she had described to him, could there?

'I'm making a mistake, I know,' Doctor Clarke had said as he handed the information over. Patrick thanked him profusely and rushed away, and within two days he had left Essex for the North-East, leaving without any further discussion with his superiors.

The countryside looked quite pleasant in the evening twilight; much to his surprise, not at all what he had expected. He thought it would only take a few minutes to find out where Chapel Row was. This was a small village, after all. The platform of the tiny station was deserted but for the man who took his ticket.

'Is it far to the village?' Patrick asked him, gazing around at the empty fields.

'About ten minutes' walk, sir,' the man answered, looking curiously at him. Strangers were not too common in Old Morton.

Patrick thanked him and set out to walk along the road. His long legs soon covered the distance to the village but when he arrived there he looked around him in perplexity. There was a village green complete with pond and an old stone church with a square tower instead of a spire. On the opposite side of the green to where he stood he could see what looked to be an inn. Perhaps that would be the best place to make enquiries, he thought, and walked over to it.

Inside there was a small group of men clustered around a darts board in the corner and a stoutish man polishing glasses behind the bar. The place had the familiar smell of beer and tobacco of most public houses, but the atmosphere was welcoming in spite of the fug.

'Evening,' said the barman, nodding laconically at him while continuing to polish a glass.

'I'll have a small whisky,' said Patrick, adding hopefully, 'Would you be having the Irish whiskey now?'

'Aye, we would,' said the barman, and produced a bottle of Jamieson's from beneath the bar.

Patrick was surprised. Irish whiskey had been practically unobtainable in Essex yet here it was in a tiny village in the remote north-east of the country.

A darts player detached himself from the group in the corner and came over to him.

'Sure now, and wouldn't you just be knowing your whiskey, sir?' he said admiringly. He was a small, sinewy man with faded red hair and a red freckled face, and his accent was pure Galway.

Patrick smiled at him. It felt extraordinarily pleasant to hear the accent of home after so long.

'Will you be having one with me?' he asked.

'I will, I thank you, sir,' the Galway man said, with some satisfaction. The barman poured out the drinks and they each sipped in appreciation.

'I'm looking for Chapel Row,' said Patrick, putting his glass down on the bar.

'Chapel Row, is it?' The Irishman looked surprised. 'Oh, not in Old Morton there's no Chapel Row. In the pit village there might be, Morton Main, that is.'

Of course, thought Patrick, he should have known.

'Is it far from here?' he asked.

'About two miles it is, sir.'

Patrick pondered on the information. It would be too late now to go there, the evening was too advanced. It would have to wait until morning. Perhaps he could get a bed for the night here. After he finished his drink he would ask the barman.

'Michael, come over here and take your turn,' a darts player called, and the man from Galway left his drink and went back into the darts corner.

294

'Can you put me up for the night?' Patrick asked the barman who shook his head slowly.

'Sorry, we don't let rooms.'

Michael came back to the bar, coughing softly to attract Patrick's attention. 'If it's a room you're after, sir, there's more chance at Weston. That's only a mile away. I'm going that way myself, I could put you on to the right road. I have to go now though, I work on the railway, have to be up at six.'

Weston. Of course, that was where Sean lived. He could stay with Sean for the night. It would give him a chance to try to explain to his friend, tell him why he had to leave the church, make him understand.

Thank you, Michael, I would be grateful for that,' said Patrick. The two Irishmen said their goodnights and went out on to the green, Michael pointing out the road to Weston.

'Would you be having business in Morton Main, sir?' he asked after a while. 'You'll be going to see the manager, maybe?'

'No, just a friend,' said Patrick. They came to a bend which brought the road alongside a railway track. Between the road and the track was a small terrace of cottages. He could just make out the sign 'Railway Terrace'.

'Paddy's Row, the locals call this,' said Michael, noticing Patrick looking at the sign. 'From the time when the men came over from Ireland to build the railway. Ah, but they're all right, they meant nothing by it.' He laid his hand on the gate of the first house.

'I'll be leaving you now, sir. Now, you just go on up the road and you'll come to the church—the

295

Catholic church I'm meaning, sir, it's the only Catholic church hereabouts. Just a bit further on, there's an inn. I know they take in travellers, sir.'

'Thank you for your help, Michael.'

'That's all right, sir. Will I be seeing you at Mass on Sunday?'

'Very likely, very likely,' said Patrick. What else could he say, though he knew it would be very unlikely indeed for him to attend Mass next Sunday.

As he walked up to the church and found the presbytery next to it, Patrick thought about what he was going to say to Sean. Of one thing he was determined: he would not allow his friend to change his mind, not now. Briefly, he considered going to the inn anyway, putting off his meeting with Sean. But that would be no good, he was bound to meet his friend sometime, he might as well get it over with. Marching up to the front door, he rang the bell firmly.

*   *   *

'Good God, man, think what you are doing!' exclaimed Sean angrily.

It was two o'clock in the morning and they had been talking ever since Patrick had arrived.

'I know what I'm doing,' he said doggedly. 'I am going to the woman I love. She is my future now.'

'Damnation is your future if you go ahead with this,' said Sean. 'I know this woman. I tell you, you are not the first man to think himself in love with her. My friend Robert has been hopelessly entangled with her for years. He won't hear a thing against her. Why, man, she—'

'Neither will I hear anything against her,' said Patrick quietly, though a shaft of jealousy ran through him at the mention of another man in connection with Karen.

'I went to see her, Patrick. I thought I had convinced her that she couldn't marry you. Perhaps she will heed me and then where will you be?'

Patrick got to his feet. He felt bone-weary and sick to death of the argument. 'I've made up my mind, Sean,' he said. 'Now, I'm going to bed if I may?'

Sean realized he had to leave it there. 'Well, I'll speak to you again in the morning. Perhaps when you've had some sleep you will be more sensible.'

True to his word, next morning Sean launched a further attack as soon as his housekeeper had served breakfast and left the room.

'Patrick,' he began, trying to keep his tone reasonable, 'you should go back. Nothing good can come of you just upping and leaving as you did. Go back, man, talk to the bishop, ask for further counselling. Don't do this.'

Patrick carefully folded his napkin and put it back in the ring beside his untouched plate.

'I thank you for your hospitality, Sean,' he said, 'but I will be getting on now. I want to get to Morton Main this morning.' Rising to his feet, he went out into the hall and picked up the bag which he had already packed and left by the hall stand. Opening the front door, he turned to say goodbye to Sean who had followed him out of the dining room and was standing, napkin in hand, watching him.

'If you leave the priesthood now, run away
297

without permission, you will forfeit your right to remain a Catholic,' said Sean, desperately, trying to make Patrick see how wrong he felt him to be.

'Goodbye,' said Patrick. 'You see, it doesn't matter, none of it does. I don't even believe in your God, not any more.'

As he walked towards the huge winding wheel he could now see in the near distance, he heard the sound of a motor car coming towards him. Moving to the side of the road, he waited while an Austin Tourer drove past with a tall dark man at the wheel. Robert was on his way to see Karen.

*　　*　　*

'So you're the man who ruined our Karen's life,' said Kezia, glaring pugnaciously at Patrick. 'Proud of yourself, are you?' She stood guard in the doorway of her parents' house, arms folded across her chest.

He sighed. 'I haven't ruined her life. I've come here to get her to marry me, if only she'll have me.'

'Kezia, who is it?' Mam's voice came down the stairs, frail and anxious. Once again she had been ordered to bed for a few days' rest.

'It's nobody we know, Mam, just someone wanting to know the way,' called Kezia. She turned back to Patrick and lowered her voice.

'Will you treat her right if I tell you where she is?'

'I give you my word.'

'Hmm,' said Kezia, evidently thinking little of his word. She went into the room and came back out with a scrap of paper. 'Here it is. If you hurry, you'll catch the ten o'clock train from Morton station. Mind, I'm only giving it to you for our Karen's sake.'

'And I thank you for it,' said Patrick, and without more ado set off, hurrying down the row.

Chapter Twenty

Patrick and Karen sat side by side on the train going down to Bishop Auckland. Patrick was very quiet and Karen glanced up at him often. She wanted to ask him if he had any doubts about what they were doing but she was afraid to in case he said he had.

I don't know him, not really, not what he is thinking or how he feels, she thought desperately. What am I doing, marrying a man I don't know? She stared out of the window, at the tall hedgerows and hills behind. Robert, she mused. She had known him since they were children together attending Sunday School. Why could she not have loved him? What sort of a God did this to people? Was it all just for His amusement?

Blasphemy. She could almost hear her father's voice berating her. I'm sorry, God, she said in her mind. And I'm sorry, Robert, I never meant to hurt you. A pang of compunction shot through her. She had written to him and tried to explain her actions but she was well aware that there was no excuse for the way she had treated him. So far she had not received a reply and she didn't expect one. She moved restlessly and glanced up at Patrick once more. His expression was strained and in her anxiety she promptly forgot all

299

about Robert.

Their wedding day though somehow it didn't feel like one. And the registrar was going to marry them, not the Minister in Chapel, not a proper wedding. She looked down at her bulging stomach, only half-disguised by the cloak she had covered herself with despite the July heat. Desperately she wished Gran had come with them. Surely she could have managed it if she had really wanted to?

'Fred's going to give me a hand with the hay,' Gran had said in a voice which brooked no argument. 'You know as well as I do that July is a bad month to take time off. I can't do as much as I used to neither. I'm glad of Fred Bainbridge, bless his good soul, and take him whenever he can come.' She had turned away and her voice sharpened. 'Anyroad, I don't hold with these Register Office weddings. New-fangled things. We would never have got wed in my day, not without the Minister and the blessing of God.'

She had turned back and seen the stricken look on Karen's face and her tone softened. 'Eeh, lass, take no heed of me, I'm just a daft old woman. I'll be here when you get back. An' at least the bairn won't be born out of wedlock, you can take comfort in that. An' you'll have the certificate to prove it.'

The train slowed down for Etherley station and the woman opposite them got out. They were alone in the carriage now and Patrick took hold of Karen's hand. She was filled with a sudden rush of emotion so that she smiled at him tremulously. Of course he didn't have any doubts, she scolded herself for thinking it. He was here with her now, wasn't he? That was enough for her. They were on

300

their way to be married and the baby would bear the name to which he was entitled.

As the train drew nearer to Auckland, Patrick clutched Karen's hand tighter, his thoughts as confused as hers. This morning he hadn't been able to get the thought of his mother out of his mind. He could picture her face as it would be when she heard of his defection. How hurt she would be, who had been so proud of him once.

It's my life, he thought, mine and Karen's, this is the right thing for us. I couldn't go on living a lie. This is what I want more than anything in the world. He looked down at Karen. Her cheeks were flushed and as she looked back at him her eyes were anxious. He squeezed her hand, feeling protective. This is the right thing for us, he told himself. The train slowed and puffed into the station and came to a halt.

'Bishop Auckland! This is Bishop Auckland,' came the call, and they alighted on the platform, both of them bracing themselves to face Karen's family.

'Well now.' Kezia moved away from Luke to greet them at the barrier. 'Here you are then. We'd best make haste, we've not a lot of time.' She glanced up at the station clock which showed ten minutes to eleven o'clock. Luke stepped forward and hesitantly Karen introduced Patrick to her sister and brother-in-law. Kezia avoided looking directly at Patrick.

Karen looked round the station yard, hoping that her mother and father had come after all. Were they just in the waiting room?

'How's Mam?' she said as they passed the waiting-room window and she saw no sign of her

301

parents. 'I thought . . . I thought they might come.'
She had sent a letter to them and one to Kezia
three weeks before as soon as the wedding
arrangements were made but she hadn't heard
from them.

'You surely didn't think they'd come, our
Karen?' Kezia answered. 'Mam's upset, how did
you think she'd be with such news? And when she
gets upset it makes her badly.'

They walked out of the station yard and along
the road to the Register Office.

'I'm sorry, Kezia.'

'Oh, aye, you're sorry.'

She relented as she saw the look in Karen's eyes.

'Eeh, pet, don't take on. Me mam'll be all right
but naturally it was a shock to her when she got
your letter. She thinks you deceived them about
the babby. And then there was getting married like
this an' all. "Why not in the Chapel?" she asked.
So I had to tell them about him.' She gave a brief
nod in Patrick's direction.

Patrick looked at her keenly. He seemed about
to say something but a glance at Karen made him
change his mind and in the end he made no
comment. Instead, he pulled her hand more firmly
over his arm and she gained some comfort from it.

'I wish you'd given me time to prepare them,
that's all,' continued Kezia. 'By, Da was upset, but
he had to cover up a bit with Mam being poorly.
But I reckon he'll come round if he has a bit of
time—you know Da, he'll forgive you anything.
Anyroad, you'd best not come home till after the
babby is born, then likely they'll make their peace
with you.'

They had reached the Register Office by this

302

time, just as the clock on the Wesleyan Church down Newgate Street struck the hour. They sat in the drab, brown-painted waiting room, all four of them staring at the highly polished linoleum on the floor. The atmosphere was hushed, almost like the anteroom of a court, but thankfully they had not long to wait before a clerk ushered them into the office.

Karen handed over the paper from Australia House which proved she was a widow and the ceremony began. It was brief and very simple, almost impersonal. To Karen it was unreal, she couldn't quite believe in it. But Patrick's voice as he made his responses was firm and sure. In no time at all they were back outside on the pavement, the sun beating down on them.

Luke shook Patrick's hand awkwardly and kissed Karen.

'You be as happy as me and Kezia now,' he said, and Karen's eyes pricked with unshed tears.

'We'd best be getting straight off,' said Kezia briskly. 'I don't want to leave Mam for long, she's having to see to the bairns.'

Karen nodded, she too was aware of work waiting on the farm—work which was too much for Gran even with Fred's help. The place had to feed three of them now, not just Gran herself.

'Let me know how things are with Mam and Da,' Karen said as she kissed her sister at Station Approach. Kezia and Luke were travelling back on the new bus which now ran to Morton Main and the pit villages beyond and they had to go down to the market place to get it.

'We will keep in touch, Kezia, won't we?'

Karen looked suddenly lost and vulnerable as

303

she appealed to her sister. Her face was pinched and her loose cloak clung closely to her in the slight breeze, emphasizing her swollen shape.

'Why aye, Karen, don't be so daft,' said Kezia. 'We're family, aren't we? An' you let us know about the babby an' all. Look after yourself, our Karen. An' you look after her an' all, do you hear me?' This last was directed at Patrick. They were practically the only words Kezia had addressed to him during the morning. He nodded seriously and put an arm around Karen's shoulders as they waved goodbye. Luke and Kezia walked off down Newgate Street and though they were not even touching, for Luke would have felt shame to hold his wife's arm in a public street, yet there was something about them which proclaimed their closeness to each other.

Once they were seated on the train, Karen opened her dolly bag and gazed at the Certificate of Marriage. It was done, there was no going back for Patrick now. She felt as though a hidden burden was lifted from her. She watched his face against the greenery outside the window. His eyes, reflected in the glass, looked calm. She felt strange, the feeling of unreality came back to her. Can I really be married? she asked herself. Wed to a stranger, an Irishman, a *Catholic?* She didn't know him, not really know him, yet here she was, tied to him for life. But at that moment he caught her eye in the window and smiled and her panic left her. It was going to be fine. He loved her and she loved him and that was all that mattered.

*　　　*　　　*

By the time they got back to the farm, the afternoon was almost gone. Patrick lost no time. He changed into an old shirt and trousers and hurried out into the hayfield. After all, Karen told herself, the weather might change tomorrow, then where would they be with the haymaking?

She felt empty, let down somehow, but occupied herself with transferring his things from the tiny attic room he had occupied since he arrived to her room on the floor below. The baby chose that moment to do a quick flip in her womb, making her feel nauseous and dizzy. She sat down on the high bed and closed her eyes. After a moment she opened them and gazed out of the window and saw the two men strewing the hay. She walked over to the window seat and sat down to watch.

There was Fred Bainbridge, a typical Weardale man, gnarled with hard work, economical in his movements, swift and sure. And Patrick, who obviously knew what he was doing. After all, hadn't he been brought up in the west of Ireland? County Clare, Killinaboy, he had said, on a small farm. Though he had told her little else of his family or background. Surely that was farming country?

Patrick was built like an athlete, she mused, though she had to admit that his movements were less sure than Fred's. He often checked with the older man too, as though for reassurance. Karen sat awhile and watched him as he raked the hay, his movements becoming surer as the day wore on. And soon she began to feel better, more content. Oh, yes, she knew why she had done what she had done, she thought. It was because she couldn't help herself, she had been driven by her love.

Pulling herself up by the bedpost, she laboriously made her way down to the kitchen and set about preparing the evening meal. The men, and Gran even, would work until the daylight faded, she knew, in case the weather broke and the crop was spoiled. And that was a disaster to be feared for hay was the only crop on the little farm. It was most important to the holdings on the moor where the winter was long and hard. They could not afford to buy feed. Such a course would be ruinous.

Karen checked the pan on the fire, it was simmering nicely. She was making a special meal, both to mark their wedding day and also because the men would be hungry after the long hours of work.

'Got the ham on to boil, have you?' Gran came in through the scullery. 'I've cut some salad greens. By, I'm fair whacked! Maybe I am getting old. I couldn't do another stroke.'

She plumped down on the rocker with a cushion at her back and watched Karen as she prepared the meal. She felt somehow sorry for her granddaughter even though she was married now. What a difference there would have been if she'd married that nice Doctor Richardson, she thought.

'I hope you've done the right thing, Karen,' she said. 'It's been a right to-do and no mistake. Still, I'll say no more.' She folded her arms and stared at the bubbling pot. Interfering would do no good at all. Not now, with the bairn on the way.

'How did it go then? Everything all right?' she asked belatedly.

'Oh, yes, all right.' Karen gave a wry smile. 'It was a bit quiet, something of a let down, I suppose.

It was good of Kezia and Luke to come.' She paused for a moment before continuing, 'I'd have liked to see Da there though, even if Mam wasn't well enough to come.'

'They'll come round, pet, once the babby's here and the fuss has died down. But Kezia is your sister after all, she did right to go to your wedding. What's done can't be undone, we have to make the best of it. I'll not be having a feud in the family, it's not Christian. If you're happy that's everything.' This string of trite remarks brought a smile even to her own face. She was tired and getting to an age when she realized things would settle down anyway, given time.

'I am happy, Gran. I don't think I could live without him, not now.' With this rare confidence Karen pushed aside her own doubts and fears for the future. Today they were happy, both she and Patrick, of course they were. Restlessly, she went to the door.

'I'll go and lock up the hens, shall I?'

'That's a good girl.' Gran settled herself more comfortably on her chair as the shadows lengthened and the fire began to cast strange shapes on the wall. She closed her eyes and dozed for a while before Karen called her to the table for supper.

*   *   *

Later, in the old double bed under the patchwork quilt, Karen lay in Patrick's arms. He kissed her gently on the lips, cupped her swollen breasts and rounded belly. And then he fell asleep, exhausted. He had not yet grown accustomed to the hard

307

physical labour needed for hay-making and it had drained him utterly, but Karen was content. She savoured the warm masculine feel of him lying beside her, she felt safe and secure as though nothing could touch them here in their own little world. They were hidden away in this remote place, safe from any threatened danger.

'I love you,' she whispered, 'I love you.' And as if responding in his sleep, his arms tightened around her. Patrick had seldom put his feelings into words but the intensity of the way he felt towards Karen was obvious always in the touch of his hands, in his eyes, even somehow in the way he held her now, in his sleep.

The baby moved inside her and she placed one of his hands on her stomach, gently, so as not to waken him. They were together and they would stay together, she, Patrick and the baby. Slowly she drifted off to sleep.

Briefly she dreamed of a horde of men, all dressed in black and all holding out their arms to Patrick, calling to him. She looked into the face of one of them and it was Sean.

'No!' she cried in her dream and woke, hot and sweaty. The bedclothes felt too heavy and she tried to push them away but it wasn't a blanket or quilt that was heavy on her, it was Patrick's arm.

'I'm just not used to sleeping with anyone else,' she whispered and snuggled down under his arm in spite of the heat, going back to sleep immediately.

*   *   *

Next morning broke very cloudy and close. At five o'clock Patrick and Karen were out of bed and snatching a quick breakfast before he went out into the hayfield, the need to get the crop in before the weather broke being imperative. Early as it was, Fred was already there. He had yoked both Galloways to the reaper and was already cutting the hay which was left standing, mowing without a break and not finishing until three o'clock in the afternoon. Then he went back to his own place, leaving Gran and Patrick to rake and strew.

Karen took cold pie and a can of tea out to the field at noon, worrying to herself as she saw Patrick's strained face and blistered hands. He seemed to know the general way of doing things but it was glaringly obvious that he was out of practice.

'I wish I could do more!' she said fretfully as they sat down to eat.

'Well, you can't,' came the flat answer from Patrick, unsmiling, and he looked away from her dismissively.

'There's not much you *can* do is there?' interposed Gran quickly. 'You might as well just settle yourself. Anyroad, you can see to the meals, I'm grateful for that.'

Karen sat down heavily after pulling hay together for a cushion. She brushed the midges away from her face impatiently. The dratted things got everywhere. She watched Patrick. He seemed absorbed in eating, taking swift swallows of the cold, sweet tea, every few moments swatting the flies away from his food. Sensing her eyes on him, he looked up, pausing for a moment. The faraway look left his face and he smiled at her, understanding, and held up the remains of his pie.

'Just what I needed to put new life into me,' he

said, his tone warm and intimate, making her feel better immediately. 'I'm getting the hang of it. We'll get it all in, don't worry.'

'Not if we sit here much longer.' Gran was getting to her feet and brushing crumbs from her apron. Patrick followed suit. Striding over to Karen, he helped her rise. Gran watched for a moment as the young couple were oblivious to her and everything else in their closeness. They were so vulnerable, she thought, there were so many things against them. Then the moment was over and Karen turned back to the house.

'When Fred comes tomorrow the hay from backside rigg can be sledded in,' said Gran, picking up the wooden rake. She was tired. If Patrick had not come she would have had to try to get extra help, not an easy thing at this time of the year, what with the war and all. That was one good thing about the situation, she thought, a man about the place. Patrick would get better at it, he just needed practice.

*   *   *

The following Sunday Karen decided to accompany Gran to Chapel for the evening service. She had not been since Patrick came to the farm, and shrank from seeing the neighbours. But they would know about her marriage by now, there were few secrets in the dale, and they had to be faced sometime.

Patrick sat before the fire in the kitchen, watching her put on her hat. His expression was unreadable. He had not mentioned anything in connection with his own church and Karen felt

310

abysmally ignorant about it, though hesitating to bring it up. When Gran went upstairs to get her Sunday coat she decided that this was as good a time as ever.

'Why don't you go to your own church?' It came out baldly, and she felt embarrassed.

'Leave it now, Karen. I don't want to talk about it at all.'

'But—'

'Leave it alone!' his voice thundered out, stopping Gran in her tracks halfway down the stairs. It was the first time Patrick had spoken in anything but a low tone. Abruptly he got to his feet and brushed past Karen, stalking out of the house and up the field to the fell.

'Fred's waiting for us at the gate.' Gran looked at Karen's troubled face. 'Well, come on, lass, never mind now. You'd better leave it like he says, he'll be better off on his own for a while.'

Karen hesitated but decided there was nothing else she could do so she followed Gran out to join the Bainbridges.

The service in the Chapel and the gathering afterwards passed over quickly enough. Fortuitously the preacher was talking about brotherly love and the congregation came out in a mellow mood.

There was only one searching question and Gran fielded it adroitly.

'Your man not Chapel then?'

The question was innocuous enough but it came from Betty Best, an inquisitive little woman who lived on her own further up the common.

'No, he's Irish,' Gran said quickly, before Karen could answer. 'I was meaning to ask you, Betty,

311

have you got that recipe I wanted for your rowan berry jelly? Yours always tastes better than mine somehow and I've a fine crop of berries coming on.'

Betty flushed with pleasure and began an animated discussion of her recipe. The moment was over. The people near by who had been listening for an answer turned away. So many of the young men had been killed that even in this remote dale there were young widows thinking of remarriage. There were speculative glances at Karen's obvious pregnancy but nothing was said. After all, the baby could just as easily be her dead husband's, Betty confided to her friend after Karen had gone.

Back at the farm Patrick was still missing from the kitchen, though the kettle was simmering on the bar. Karen left her coat and hat on the settee and washed her hands quickly before setting out the cold meat and pickles for supper.

Tidying her hair before the glass on the wall, she carried her outdoor things upstairs to the bedroom. Patrick was sitting on the window seat, gazing out over the shadowy fell.

'Oh, there you are,' he said, his voice quietly normal. 'Is supper ready?'

Despite his mild tone she could see he wanted no questions about his attitude earlier in the evening. Perhaps they would discuss the way things were someday but that time was not yet, she thought sadly. She nodded and busied herself hanging up her cloak and hat, unsure what to think. Tonight was the first time he had raised his voice to her and she hadn't liked it at all. But at least he was calm enough now.

Patrick stood patiently waiting for her, his grey eyes showing no trace of the trouble they had held earlier in the evening. He touched her hand softly and the usual warm feeling ran through her.

'We'll go down then.' He shepherded her out and down the stairs. Gran was pouring tea.

'By, I'm glad we got the hay in,' she said with satisfaction while cutting thick slices of bread and coating them liberally with butter. She chatted on during the meal, taking Patrick at face value, never looking deeper, very matter-of-fact. She was a treasure, was Gran, thought Karen.

The evening passed pleasantly as they relaxed after the week's work and Gran told stories of when she was young and the farm-house was full of brothers and sisters and the fine time they'd had together. And the hard, gruelling work.

'Of course, the dale was busy with lead miners then,' she said, 'and fierce, independent chaps they were an' all. Considered themselves better than "outsiders", Teesdale men and such like.'

Slowly Patrick relaxed further, giving Gran a smile of encouragement when she paused, challenging them to deny some of her wilder stories. Karen was in a happy mood as she climbed into bed where Patrick put his arms around her in spite of the warm night, holding her gently as though she might break.

*   *   *

The last few weeks of Karen's pregnancy went quickly and quietly. Patrick was slowly hardening to the work though he would never be like the other men of their dale. He was not quite so deft

313

and economical in his movements though he was never clumsy or inept. His hands had hardened and no longer blistered so easily but they were still the hands of a 'gentleman' with long tapering fingers and well-shaped nails, even though he came from a working family himself. He tanned, but his skin had not the leathery look of those who had spent all their lives out of doors. Sometimes Karen thought about how deft he had been with the wounded soldiers. The thought brought a niggling doubt, he had been more sure of himself then.

'At least the baby won't starve if your milk fails,' commented Gran to Karen one day. She was admiring the two new milking stools Patrick had made to replace the ancient ones which were falling to bits. In August the red cow had calved and there were now two cows to milk.

'Our baby won't starve,' said Patrick, smiling at his wife. And if hard work counted for anything that was true. He never stinted, mused Karen. He mowed down the nettles in the pasture bottom, carted lime and manure to improve the land in-bye, and sledded down bedding for the moor in readiness for the winter when the stock would be brought in. There was always something to do.

One afternoon Patrick was up on the fell cutting bedding. It was early September and a fair, sunny afternoon, though with a touch of autumn in the wind. Karen fed the hens and afterwards walked over to the rowan tree, bowl in hand, and rested for a moment with her back against the tree, gazing out over the fell. With one hand she rubbed the small of her back, where it ached a little.

It was then she noticed the trap coming up the track. Strange, she thought, it wasn't the carrier's day and she couldn't think of anyone else who could be visiting at this time.

Shading her eyes against the afternoon sun she tried to make out who the visitors were, but couldn't recognize the two men at that distance. Recollecting herself, she turned and went back into the house to tidy up and get rid of the feed bowl. She was back at the door as the trap entered the yard and the first thing which struck her was the clerical dress of the men.

Oh, God, she thought, and her stomach lurched. The baby moved restlessly within her. She stood dumbly as they descended from the trap and walked towards her.

'Good morning. We have come to see Patrick Murphy.'

The older man spoke in the clipped, impersonal tones of a man used to exerting authority.

'He's not here.'

Karen's answer was just as brief as she stood blocking the doorway, arms folded over her bulging apron in instinctive protectiveness. Hearing voices, Gran came out to see who it was at the door and with only one glance at her granddaughter, Karen's agitation was communicated to her and she came and stood four-square beside her.

'What do you want?' She stared with uncompromising hostility at the two men. If this was trouble then Karen was not going to face it on her own, not in her condition.

'We wish to see Patrick Murphy,' the older priest repeated.

'Well, tho' cannit,' Gran replied flatly. 'Ee in't

315

'ere.' Her accent had broadened in her determination to send these men on their way.

'Will he be long away?' This was the younger man and he asked his question of Gran, studiously avoiding looking at Karen.

'Aa wadn't knaa.' Gran felt very strange. This was all in sharp contrast to her usual warm welcome for strangers. But she stood her ground while she could feel her granddaughter trembling beside her.

'Sean, why can't you leave us alone?' pleaded Karen.

The older man's face purpled. *'Father Donelly* is doing his duty,' he snapped.

'Away inside, Karen,' Gran ordered her granddaughter. 'Gan on, bide in the parlour a while.' She gave Karen a little shove and blindly she fled indoors.

'May we wait for him?'

This was Sean, a man who had lived among women such as Jane and thought he knew how to deal with them. In this case he was wrong.

'Nay, that wouldn't be wise of me now, letting you wait here, would it?'

Now that Gran had calmed down a little she was unconsciously returning to a more standard form of English. 'I have my granddaughter to think of.'

'If you could just tell me when he will be back . . .'

But Gran had lost patience. 'This is not a good time, I tellt ye, din't I? If you had eyes in your head, man, you would see this is not a good time. Let the lad be. Let them both be.'

The priests looked at each other, considering their next move.

'Let it lie I tell you, let it lie!' Gran's voice rose and she started to close the door.

Sean put out a hand and held the door open while he said: 'I'm sorry, Mrs Rain. Tell him we'll be in Wolsingham though, will you? I am his friend, the priest over at Weston.'

'Get your hand off my door,' she said, her voice low but full of threat. Sean pulled away and stepped back from the door

'Good morning to you, Mrs Rain,' he said courteously, and the men retreated to the trap. Clucking to the horse, the older man turned it round and they made their way back along the track. Gran stared after them, dismay welling up in her. She'd be blowed if she told Patrick anything of the sort, she fumed silently. Not before the baby was born, anyroad. It would only upset things.

'It's all right, flower, never you mind,' she comforted a woebegone Karen waiting in the parlour. 'They've gone now and it doesn't matter, it makes not a ha'porth of difference.'

'But Patrick . . .'

'He doesn't know they were here and if you've any sense you'll not tell him. It will only upset things.'

Gradually she managed to calm Karen down and presently she began preparations for supper.

'Here's Patrick now.'

Gran saw the tall figure coming into the yard and turned to Karen who was still slumped in the rocking chair by the fire. 'Now, come on, pet, smile. Don't let him see you've been upset. Go on, go and meet him.'

Karen smiled dutifully and, straightening her apron, went to the back door. Crushing down her anxiety, and with her will bolstered by Gran's, she hurried over to the barn where he was unloading the sled.

'Oh, Patrick, I'm so glad to see you.'

She went up to him and hugged him, her smile radiant. A flicker of surprise came into his eyes before he responded to her unspoken appeal and kissed her thoroughly.

'I wasn't so long as all that, was I?' he said teasingly, his brogue endearing him further to her.

She blushed slightly but said nothing, watching him for a while, happy again. No one was going to separate them. They were married, weren't they? She twisted the gold ring round and round on her finger, self-confidence returning. The threat posed by the afternoon's visitors faded and blended with that of the occasional nightmare which still plagued her, frightening at first but unreal in broad daylight.

The evening shadows were lengthening and a cold wind stirred the leaves of the rowan tree as she waited. Patrick paused in his work and put a hand on her shoulder.

'Go on in now, I won't be long. You'll catch a chill if you stay out here, the night's turning cold.'

Obediently Karen nodded and went into the house, happy to do his bidding.

Chapter Twenty-One

'The postman's coming along the lane, Gran,' said Patrick as he came inside to wash his hands for breakfast some days later

'He can have a cup of tea then, I'm just about to make it.'

Gran filled the large, brown teapot and set it on the table, followed by three plates of bacon and eggs. Then she brought another pot for the postman, together with a plate of fresh made singing hinny scones.

'A few letters today, missus,' he said as he propped his bicycle against the wall, and, sure of his welcome, walked through. Gran pulled out a chair for him.

'Would you like some breakfast? Or maybe a singing hinny?'

'No thanks, not today. Just a cup of tea will be fine.' He sat down at the table and put the bundle of letters before her.

'It's getting a bit nippy in the mornings now,' he remarked, and rubbed his hands together before taking a long, appreciative swallow.

'Young Joe Tyndale's missing.'

Jack looked sombre. A man in his fifties, he was often the bearer of bad news to the people of the dale and sometimes it bore him down.

Gran clucked sorrowfully, but Karen didn't hear. She was sitting oblivious to everything but the letter addressed to Patrick which lay on top of the pile. She continued eating mechanically, looking neither at Patrick nor Gran. It seemed to her to be an age before Jack got up from his chair, rubbing his mouth with the back of his hand, thanked them and left. The scrape of Patrick's chair made Karen jump convulsively and she stared up at him. But without a word he rose to his feet, picked up the letter, and strode out of the door.

'What's the matter with him?' Gran had looked up in surprise.

'Oh, nothing, Gran. He just wants to get on,' Karen answered. She couldn't trust herself to say anymore. Patrick never got letters, this was the first, she was thinking—and was filled with foreboding.

'There's a couple here for you.' Gran was looking through the rest of the post. 'And one for me.' She held out two letters.

'Karen?'

'What? Oh, sorry, Gran.' Karen took the letters and stared at the envelopes.

'Must be something up. One from your father and one from Kezia,' Gran commented as Karen opened the letter from Kezia and read it aloud.

Mam's had a bad turn but seems to be pulling round again though she has lost some weight. The rest of us are fine. We had a letter from Joe too, he's doing well.

I forgot to tell you at the wedding but just after you left home a tramp came looking for you. I had my hands full at the time, what with Mam and all, and gave him short shrift, I'm ashamed to say. Anyway, he went off and it was only after he had gone that I realized he only had one arm. Or at least there was something wrong with one arm, he kept his

320

right side away from me.

I've felt guilty about it ever since as I think it might have been your disturbed soldier. I did tell him you were up the dales so he might show up one of these days. Well, that's all, now I've told you about it. Let me know how you are, and about the baby and all.

Karen pondered over the letter for a while. If it was Nick why was he not still under a doctor's care? And surely he had a pension, there was no need for him to tramp? For a short while her attention was diverted from her own worries.

'Your mother has been bad again, I see,' said Gran, who was perusing her own letter short-sightedly. Karen nodded.

'Kezia says she's getting better though.' She opened her letter from Da.

He commented on Mam's health in a similar vein to Kezia, praising God that she was now a little better. Then he came directly to the point.

The Catholic Father from Weston came to see us. [That would cause a minor sensation in the row, thought Karen.] I wouldn't lie. He asked me if I knew where Patrick Murphy was and I told him.

Karen giggled hysterically, causing Gran to look up from her own letter in concern. The giggling turned to tears and Karen felt sick. Abruptly she rose, scraping her chair loudly on the flagstones as she rucked up the mat. Despite her bulk, she ran out of the house across the yard and on up to the rowan tree.

321

Patrick was nowhere to be seen. He had harnessed Jess and gone on up the fell somewhere. Karen closed her eyes and leaned against the trunk of the tree, her breathing fast and shallow and it was not just from the exertion.

Why can't they leave us alone? she thought desperately. Now Patrick would know she had not told him about the visit from the priests. She should have told him . . . Karen leaned over and vomited on the grass.

A sharp pain shot through her, taking her completely by surprise, making her double over. No! Not yet! The baby wasn't due yet. She straightened up slowly, holding her breath. The pain receded, leaving a dull ache through to her back, but her pulse still raced. It was only a few days early, she reckoned swiftly, reassuring herself. Maybe this was a false alarm, but then maybe it was the real thing.

Taking a deep breath, she set off to retrace her steps to the farmhouse. If she could only lie down for a while she would be fine. But she had only gone a little way when it hit her again, the ache intensifying until she doubled up once more. Panting heavily, she schooled herself not to cry out, hanging on so as not to alarm Gran until she was sure it was the baby coming. Until she was sure . . . Dear God, if this wasn't the baby, what was it? Of course she was sure.

At last the wave of pain receded and she realized from her training that she should have sufficient time to reach the kitchen, even her bedroom.

A wry grin played around her lips as the thought crossed her mind that this wasn't at all as she had thought when she had helped other women

322

through it.

'Now keep calm,' she had said, 'there's nothing to worry about.' She would just have to take her own advice. Karen resumed her careful progress to the back door, wary now of the return of the pain.

And return it did, with such swiftness and intensity that it brought her to the ground, scattering loudly clucking hens. She cried aloud despite her resolve, her vision fading, her whole being flooded with pain, becoming the pain. She lay there, moaning, oblivious of anything else. A fog closed in on her, obscuring the sunlight.

'Now then, come on, pet, it's all right.' Gran's voice came through the mists to her, Gran's arms were around her, helping her up, supporting her.

'Not far to go. Howay now, be a good lass, lean on me.'

Karen had little choice but to lean on Gran as she was dragged, half walking, half sliding, into the kitchen and on to the settee. Her vision cleared and the pain receded yet again.

'Why is it coming so fast?' she asked, panicking. How was she going to get into the front room? Patrick hadn't even brought down the bed from upstairs yet. Karen gazed imploringly at Gran. She would know what to do.

'Let's have a look at you then.'

Indeed Gran was calmly efficient. Deftly she manoeuvred Karen into position as the pain took its hold once more.

'All right now, all right, there's nothing to worry about, just do as I say.' Gran was in command and Karen was at her mercy and that of the mysterious forces which had taken hold of her. The pains returned, closer together, almost blending into one

323

long pain which threatened to tear her apart.

'Hang on, lass. Don't push. Breathe, Karen, pant,' said Gran, snatching a clean towel from the brass rail over the fireplace and putting it under her legs. And Karen tried, but the force within her was too great. She half sat, leaning on her elbows, legs drawn up, and in a long, last surge of pain the baby was there. When at last she could think for herself again she was as much exhausted from the shock of the sudden delivery as from the labour. She lay passively as Gran did what had to be done, placing the child in Karen's arms before attending to the afterbirth.

She gazed at her son. His tiny face was puckered, a tuft of black hair stuck incongruously on the very top of his head. He was infinitely precious, a miracle, with a bubble forming at the corner of his mouth.

'By, lass,' said Gran laconically, 'that's only ten minutes from getting you on the settee to the end. A pity it's not always like that.'

'A bit of a shock to the system, though,' Karen said shakily.

'Aye. Well, you lie quiet there, you'll be all right.'

Karen was content to do just that. She lay with her baby in her arms, quietly adoring him.

'There now, I think that's that,' said Gran. She had made Karen clean and comfortable and brought a blanket downstairs to cover her. Now she turned her attention to the baby who was wrapped solely in the clean towel.

'We'll wash His Nibs, I think. It's a good job Patrick brought the water in for the day before he went.' She held out her arms for the baby and Karen gave him up, somewhat reluctantly. Her joy

324

in motherhood and love for the tiny scrap of humanity were the strongest emotions she had ever experienced, even eclipsing her love for Patrick. The worry of the letter he had received that morning seemed suddenly quite unimportant.

She watched anxiously as her grandmother washed and dried the child before dressing him in one of the gowns Karen had ready and wrapping him in a soft shawl she herself had crocheted. Placing a pillow in a drawer from the kitchen press, she laid him on it. That would do for a bed for him until Patrick could bring down the heavy old cradle from the attic. The baby cried a little when he was being handled but settled down when laid in the drawer.

'Eeh, that was a good morning's work. A cup of tea for us both now, I think. You'll have to stay there until Patrick comes in. I don't think I could manage to get you in the front room. I'm not as young as I was, you know. I feel as tired as if I'd had the bairn myself.' Karen managed a weak smile. Gran had shown herself to be as strong and dependable as a woman half her age.

'You all right, pet?' she asked, checking Karen over, straightening the cushion under her head, watching for tell-tale signs of anything wrong.

'Oh, yes, I'm fine, I feel great. Isn't he lovely though, Gran?' Karen was exhilarated.

'Oh, aye, he's lovely. Though why he was in such a hurry to get into the world has me beat. We'll just see if he's as lovely when he cries half the night.'

'Gran!' Karen was shocked at the idea that he would ever be anything but lovely and her grandmother laughed fondly and set about

325

mashing tea. There was nothing else she could do until Patrick came home. Glancing at the clock on the wall, she was surprised to see it was only a quarter to twelve. All over and done with in under two hours. And thank God for it!

Patrick didn't turn up for his dinner and didn't turn up for his tea. Karen slept for most of the afternoon, still on the settee. Gran worked about the yard, feeding the hens and geese, boiling swill for the pigs in the set pot and eventually milking the two cows. Every half hour or so she popped her head around the door to check on Karen and the baby. But a niggling doubt was worrying her. Where was Patrick?

Stolidly she worked on, finishing the chores before going back to the house to start the evening meal. Karen was awake, fresh and rosy-cheeked, sitting up against the cushions nursing her baby. Her hair curled in profusion round her shoulders and the light in her eyes made her beautiful, the anxiety of the morning evidently completely forgotten.

'Was I asleep when Patrick came in?' She looked up happily. 'He should have wakened me, Gran. I feel so fit, there's nothing the matter with me. Working in the barn, is he?'

The old lady looked at her, not quite knowing what to say. Surely Patrick hadn't just up and gone? The thought had only just occurred to her.

'He has been back, hasn't he, Gran?' Alarm was creeping into Karen's voice.

'Now, don't go getting yourself in a state. You'll only upset the little 'un. He'll be back before long, just wait and see. He must have gone on up the fell, that's all.'

326

Gran took the baby and started to change his nappy, cooing to him as she did so. All Karen's attention turned to the child as he was undressed, anxiously checking yet again that he was complete in every detail, no blemishes, no extra toes. She had already assured herself of his perfection but an extra look did no harm.

It was into this scene of two women absorbed in a baby that Patrick walked a few minutes later. They had not even heard him unload the sled or turn Jess out into the field. As he walked in, the unhappiness which Karen thought she glimpsed in his face gave way to amazement and he halted in the doorway.

'The supper's not ready yet. Your son took up a bit of our time,' Gran said prosaically. She carried on dressing the child and put him in Karen's arms, instinctively leaving the room and the moment to the young couple.

'But . . . how did you manage?' Patrick found his tongue at last. 'What about the midwife? Who went for her?' He crossed swiftly over to the settee and took Karen's hand. 'Are you all right?' His last question was a little belated, he realized, but she didn't seem to notice. She looked rosily beautiful lying there, her velvety brown eyes tender and proud.

'I'm sorry I wasn't here, I am so.'

'It was all right. Gran was the midwife and she managed splendidly. And, yes, I'm fine. What do you think of your son?' For so far Patrick had not looked at the baby. Now he did, holding down the shawl which overshadowed the baby's face with the tip of a finger.

'He's very red, isn't he?' he asked, looking

327

anxiously at the tiny bundle. 'Do you think I should be going for the doctor? Just to be making sure?'

'No, no, there's no need to fetch the doctor out all this way tonight,' Gran said before Karen could answer, as she came back into the room with fresh water for the kettle. She stirred the fire and settled the kettle on it before continuing, 'He can check tomorrow if you like, but they are both well, I promise you. There's nothing a doctor can do, he's an unnecessary expense. But please yourself. Now, what you have to do is bring the bed down into the front room and help Karen into it so she can be quiet for a while. Oh, and the cradle from the attic. By the time you've done that, supper will be ready.'

Gran was beaming. She tried hard to be matter-of-fact in issuing her instructions to hide the delight and relief which had washed over her when Patrick walked in. As he rushed out of the room to do her bidding, her eyes met her granddaughter's in mutual understanding. He was back. Gran had not been slow in picking up Karen's feelings of vulnerability, her insecurity.

Soon Karen was ensconced in the front room with the cradle beside the bed, deliriously happy. Patrick hovered around, unwilling to let them out of his sight even for supper, which he ate in the kitchen in record time so that he could go back to them.

'I think it's time you settled down, Karen, you've had enough for today,' Gran said at last, beginning to feel concerned at the excitement on her granddaughter's face. She looked meaningfully at Patrick who jumped up from his seat on the end of

328

the bed.

'Oh, yes, to be sure now, you must get some sleep, my love. We may be disturbed by the baby during the night. You must get some rest.' He bent to kiss her and she settled down obediently. The letter was forgotten, she thought drowsily, Patrick was so delighted with his son all other thoughts were pushed out of his mind.

'Well, there's nothing surer than that you're in for disturbed nights now for a while,' said Gran. She smiled as Patrick went into the kitchen. Then she picked up the lamp, leaving only the soft light of a candle for illumination, and followed him.

Karen snuggled down under the enormous patchwork quilt, the events of the day going round and round in her head. She had been so miserable at the breakfast table yet here she was at the end of the day feeling so happy and elated she thought she would burst. Then she fell asleep suddenly, as suddenly as the baby in the cradle beside her.

*   *   *

Patrick went outside, finishing up a few evening chores in the yard, bringing in extra water, checking on the hen house—he had seen signs of foxes about that morning. The night was turning frosty, a hazy ring surrounding the moon. It would be colder before morning.

He walked over to the gate by the rowan tree and looked out over the fell. Nearby he could hear the sheep baa-ing softly as they settled down. He thought about the letter he had received in the morning post.

It was from his father in Ireland. As he saw the

329

handwriting on the envelope, he had been filled with a sense of guilt—not so much for leaving the Church, but for the way he had let down his mother and father. But there was a feeling of resentment too. They had brought up a large family, all married now with families of their own, but it was only Patrick who had been expected to enter the seminary. From childhood it had been taken for granted that he would work to become a priest.

Patrick thought about the letter he had written to his parents, only to tear up. His reasons for leaving the priesthood were so confused in his own mind that the task of explaining them was impossible. He pondered on them now with a sad melancholy. The rage he had felt at the suffering he saw among the wounded, the suicide of the young, blind soldier at Greenfields. He thought about what it must have been like to realize you had to live in a sightless world, how the boy must have felt as he found his way down to the river, what his thoughts must have been. Sighing, Patrick closed the hen house door and secured it against foxes. If there was a God, why would he allow such things? And why would he allow such a thing as the powerful attraction Patrick had felt for Karen, his love for her growing stronger every day when he was forbidden such a feeling? That crisis in his faith his parents would never understand.

He finished his work and walked to the gate. Leaning on the rowan tree, he looked out over the dark dale and listened to the silence broken only by the rustling of night creatures and the chirping of grasshoppers.

The letter from Ireland had been bitter to say the least.

> Your mother will never be able to hold her head up in Killinaboy or Corofin again. And you didn't even tell us yourself, you dirty rotten coward. To run off after an English hussy, a Protestant . . .

Patrick could hear his mother speaking through his father's words. She was the strong one of the two, the more forceful. But he suspected that the last line came from his father alone: 'Let us know how you are, son. Don't just disappear.'

Patrick sighed and turned back to the house. He had spent the day on the fell going over everything in his mind. He was committed to Karen and the boy, his life was here now, on the Durham moors.

But he had to face up to the grief he had brought to his family back home in Ireland, had to write to his father and mother.

When he came into the front room, tip-toeing in case he woke his wife and child, and lay down beside Karen, she turned to him and snuggled up to him but did not waken until the first cry of the child in the early hours brought both of them instantly awake and reaching for him. And Patrick, who had lain awake until then, fell asleep along with his family when the child had been attended to and placed back in his cradle.

*   *   *

They decided to name the boy Brian Patrick. Karen herself went to register the birth when the

331

baby was three weeks old for the travelling registrar was visiting Stanhope.

There was a chill in the air as she halted the trap in the marketplace in Stanhope and already she could see that leaves were turning colour and falling from the beech trees. Summer was almost over, she mused, winter lay ahead. But it would be a cosy winter for them at Low Rigg Farm, for Patrick had brought coal from the station at Stanhope and cut peat on the moor and brought it in, under the guidance of Fred Bainbridge. They would be happy and safe away from the world in their house on the fell. Soon they would be snowed in, perhaps.

'The name of the baby?'

Karen hesitated as the registrar asked the question. She would have liked to call him Patrick Joseph in honour of her brother, but she had gone along with Patrick's wishes in the end, though Brian sounded strange to her at first. In the warmth of her happiness and in the reassurance of Patrick's love for both her and Brian, which she saw in his every action now, she had quickly recovered her strength.

'Brian Patrick,' she said firmly.

Patrick had not mentioned 'The Letter', as she privately thought of it, and Karen was content to let it lie. He went about the work of the farm with renewed energy, his silent periods, when she had felt shut away from him, becoming fewer and fewer until they had all but disappeared. His face was sunny, he was becoming hardened to the work, and his absorption in his little family dominated his life.

There was still bunting in the streets as Karen

332

came out of the office for it was not long after Armistice Day. There had been great celebrations in their corner of the dale and thanksgiving services in the little Chapel. Yet the war seemed all unreal to Karen, something from another life. This valley in Weardale was remote from the happenings of the outer world.

Walking along to the post office, she posted her letters to Morton Main, one for her parents and one for Kezia.

'I ought to go and see them,' she murmured to herself. 'Make my peace.' But she was reluctant to leave the farm or do anything which might alter the mood of the old place, break the spell as it were. She would wait a while, she decided, and crossed over to the trap with Polly waiting patiently between the shafts.

Anyway, she excused herself, Gran wasn't too good lately, she always seemed to be tired. Karen often walked into the kitchen to find her dozing in the rocking chair, even in the middle of the day. Gran would jump up and begin doing something busily but Karen was not fooled. It wouldn't be a good idea to leave her alone at present.

*   *   *

Within only a few weeks, the snow which was already covering the tops began to blanket the moor and high valleys, making travelling foolhardy in any case. They were tucked into their own little world and Karen was content to remain there. Then the first serious argument, appearing insoluble at the time, loomed large in their lives.

Karen began to talk about having Brian baptized

in the Chapel.

'I don't want him baptized,' Patrick said, softly enough.

This had never occurred to her. That a child should go unbaptized was a scandal and she opposed it with all the strength of her Non-Conformist background. It certainly wasn't going to happen to her beloved Brian. He would be baptized, he would.

'He will be baptized in the Chapel and by our own Minister.'

'He will not.' Patrick was equally adamant and uncompromising. Karen gazed at him. Most of the time he was easy-going, falling in with her wishes about everyday things. Now she was finding his will to be as strong as her own. A thought occurred to her.

'Do you want him baptized in your own church then? Take him down to Wolsingham? But you don't even go there yourself.'

The words 'And you a priest' hung on the tip of her tongue but remained unspoken.

'No, I don't want him baptized.' Patrick's tone was final. As far as he was concerned the discussion was at an end.

Karen went over to the cradle where Brian had begun to cry loudly at the unexpected sound of voices raised in anger. She picked him up and hugged him, staring at Patrick who was showing a steely will she hadn't seen before in him. Even if he himself had lost his faith, what did it matter if she had Brian baptized? He whimpered then cried in earnest, stirring restlessly in her tight clasp. She hushed him automatically, her face flushed, still staring at Patrick. He stood silently, staring back at her, his eyes hard.

'Good God deliver us!' Gran came in the door from the yard where she had been feeding the hens. 'What's the matter with the babby? Give him here to me.' She took the child, holding him against her shoulder and clucking softly. Sitting down on the rocker before the fire she rocked him gently until his sobs quietened to an occasional hiccup and at last he fell asleep on her shoulder. Gran took no further notice of Patrick or Karen, focusing all her attention on Brian. She had a rare talent for making herself practically invisible when she thought they needed some privacy.

Meanwhile the young couple stood like statues, Karen moving only to give the child up to Gran, until at last Patrick turned wordlessly and stalked out of the door and on up the fell. Only then did the tension leave Karen and she sank down on the settee. Mechanically she adjusted her hair, pinning it back into its bun, and wiped her face with her handkerchief and blew her nose.

Gran watched her over the downy black tuft of Brian's hair. Best not say anything, she thought with great forbearance, they would sort it out. All couples had their problems at first, but there was no getting away from the fact that these two had got off to a particularly bad start even though this was the first time she had heard them row. So she sat rocking the child and staring into the fire. Eventually Karen stood up and went out to the scullery where she could be heard clattering and banging a bucket about against the flagstones as she scrubbed the floor. She was trying to calm herself with hard physical work.

When Patrick came in to supper they spoke

calmly enough to each other about the ordinary everyday things of the farm but they were avoiding each other's eyes.

When the snow abated and it was safe to take the boy to the Chapel, Karen had him christened there by the Minister. It was a quiet ceremony before the Sunday Service and she said nothing to Patrick about it. Brian's baptismal certificate she hid in her dressing-table drawer.

Slowly the immense attraction they had for one another overcame everything else, drawing them together as closely as before. Their passion was undiminished and the secret delights of the marriage bed through the cold winter nights were yet only part of the deepening love which enveloped them both. The sound of Patrick's step in the yard brought a lightening to Karen's heart, a feeling echoed in his eyes when he saw her waiting for him. And Brian throve and Karen thought this was the happiest winter of her life. Sometimes she would look at her baby and words from the New Testament would run through her mind: 'This is my beloved Son, in whom I am well pleased.' And she couldn't think it was blasphemy.

Chapter Twenty-Two

'Hey, missus, you haven't got a cup of tea in the pot, have you?'

The woman who had been washing the front windows of the cottage jumped at the sound of the man's voice. She hadn't noticed anyone coming up the lane when she'd started the job. The lane led

336

up from the main road into Hexham but not many people turned up it unless they had business at the farm further up.

'By, you made me jump,' she said now, looking the man at her garden gate up and down. A poor sight he was an' all, she thought, thin and scrawny, his hair down to the collar of his scruffy suit jacket and what looked like a week's growth of stubble on his chin. He stooped over the gate, one hand held behind his back and the other holding on to the gatepost.

Mrs Timms wrung out the wash-leather in her hands as she looked at him, feeling a bit apprehensive. She was on her own in the row of four cottages, the men were at work on the farm and the women had gone into Hexham for it was market day.

'Come on, missus, just a cup of tea.'

Nick asked again, without much hope. The last few months had taught him that women and even some men felt threatened by such as him and resented his presence if they had men-folk away at the war. For he couldn't bear for anyone to see his hand had gone. He usually managed to hide the stump so that people thought he was whole.

'Aye, all right then,' Mrs Timms said reluctantly. After all, it was her Christian duty. And God knows, she thought, he didn't look like he could be a threat to her. A puff of wind would blow him over.

'You can come in and sit on the bench,' she said, indicating a garden seat under the window.

'Thanks, missus.'

Nick carefully inserted his stump into his frayed jacket pocket, making sure she didn't see what he was doing, before opening the gate and walking up the path. This made him look lop-sided and Mrs Timms showed her puzzlement. But she said nothing, merely going into the house and fetching an old enamel mug from the pantry, filling it with tea from the pot standing as usual on the hearth. She added a good dollop of sweetened, condensed milk and stirred it vigorously. As an afterthought she buttered a fresh-baked scone and took that out too. The lad looked like he could do with something in his belly. She smiled as she handed it over to him, feeling pleased at her magnanimity. She felt a bit more pleasantly disposed towards him now she was feeding him, despite the rank stink of him as she came near.

'Eeh, thanks, missus.' Nick took the mug of tea and put it down on the bench before taking the scone.

'Something wrong with your hand?' she asked.

Nick shoved the stump further down behind the rags he kept in the pocket for bulk. He shook his head vigorously and chewed on the scone. His mouth was dry but he had to get rid of the scone before he could drink.

Mrs Timms looked at him, her lips pursed. Well, if he didn't want to talk, she certainly didn't. Anyway, the smell from him was getting stronger. She backed away and carried on washing the windows, rubbing angrily at the panes. Idle good for nothing, why wasn't he away at the war anyway? she thought. Her good mood had evaporated swiftly and she was sorry now she had let him into the garden. Well, she'd stay out here washing windows till he'd gone and make sure nothing of hers went with him.

Nick finished the tea and put the mug down on the bench.

'By, that was grand,' he said fervently and looked up at Mrs Timms hopefully.

'You haven't got a tab about the place, have you, missus?'

She exploded. 'No, I have not got a cigarette,' she said, her voice rising. 'What do you think it is?' She picked up the mug and faced him, quivering with rage.

'You've had your tea, now get off the place or I'll call my man.'

Nick sighed and got to his feet. This happened so often he was getting used to it.

'Thanks, missus, anyhow,' he said and trudged off, down the lane and on to the road to Hexham. Maybe he would get something to do there. The spectre of the workhouse was looming larger as the summer faded and the nights grew colder. What's more, he had left his greatcoat in the barn of the last farm he'd stayed at.

Nick had returned to the farm where he had worked before the war, the farm which had taken him on as an orphanage lad. He had been there four years before the war. Surely that counted for something? he had thought. He had always been a good worker, he had worked hard all his life. But that had not counted in his favour, not now he was short of an arm.

'You can sleep in the barn tonight,' the farmer had said to him. 'But there's no work. Why, lad, what good is a one-armed man on a farm? I ask you, man, I'm not running a blooming charity.'

The farmer spoke in a reasonable tone, putting to Nick the unfeasibility of a farm worker with one

339

hand. Besides, the war would be over soon and there would be plenty of men after work—two-handed, able-bodied men.

Nick thought about it without bitterness next morning as he took the Tynedale road out of Hexham. He was feeling stronger this morning, it was a fine September day and his belly was filled. A kindly stall-holder at the market had given him a couple of stale pies and he had saved one for his breakfast. He set out along the road swinging both arms, for there was no one to see the stump. He felt behind his ear for the dog-end of cigarette which he had been saving from the night before. He'd found a penny in the street at Hexham and bought a packet of five Woodbines. But he had learned to ration cigarettes out carefully if he was lucky enough to be able to buy any.

As often happened his thoughts returned to Karen as he walked. He hadn't managed to find her yet, but he was going to give it another try today . . . surely if he walked the dales long enough somebody would have heard of Sister Knight? The longer he searched unsuccessfully for her, the more his obsession with her deepened. If only he could find her, ran his muddled thoughts, everything would be all right.

* * *

A few days before Christmas, Patrick was out bringing in sheep from the low fell to the home pasture. Though the cover of snow was light, the wind was sweeping over the top, stinging his face so that he buried his chin in his muffler and thrust his hands deep into his pockets. It was so cold. He

340

just couldn't get used to how bitterly cold the weather was in Weardale. They had storms enough in County Clare, God knows, he thought, but this icy cold and frozen snow which came down on the high fell were something different.

He had acquired a young border collie bitch, Flossie, from Fred Bainbridge together with a few tips on how to handle her. He was trying to get into the way of using her and now he watched her, racing on ahead of him. She didn't seem to mind the cold, she didn't even seem to feel it. Patrick climbed higher, against the wind, until at last he could turn and get a good overall view of the fell in his search for strays. Flossie had disappeared, he realized, and he scanned the moor for her.

'Wheeee,' he whistled, and when this had no effect, called, 'Flossie! Here, Flossie.'

A movement caught his eye and he turned to look. It was the bitch, she was running towards what looked like a bundle of old clothes. He hadn't noticed it before, greyish-black it was and huddled against an outcrop of limestone, not all that much different from the outcrops on his father's farm back home in Ireland.

He stared hard at the bundle. He must have passed it on his way up, he thought, cursing his own lack of observation, something essential on the moor as he should have learned by now. It must have been hidden by the rock, he reckoned. It puzzled him somehow. It did not look at all like one of the little black-faced ewes of the dale. It was too big. After a quick glance round for anything else unusual, he went to investigate.

Huddled close to a sheep which was still alive but caught between two stones was the figure of a

341

lad, very still, slight and pitiful in threadbare and ragged clothes. Flossie was standing over him, wagging her tail and barking excitedly.

'Quiet, girl,' he said and she subsided, sitting back on the frozen ground and watching him. As Patrick knelt and turned the boy over to see his face, he gave a start of recognition. It was Nick Harvey. The stump of the boy's right arm pointed grotesquely into the air and it was blue with cold.

He was alive, Patrick realized. As he moved him a groan escaped the boy and his eyes flickered open. But he was cold, very cold, his face icy, Patrick found as he took off his own glove and felt the skin. It was probably only the warmth from the trapped sheep which had kept him alive. Patrick laid him gently down again and freed the ewe, which, after a few faltering steps, accompanied by plaintive bleating, ran down to join the flock. But the young man was unable to walk, his strength gone. His eyes barely flickered open and closed again with no sign of recognition. Patrick had perforce to sling him over his shoulder and carry him down over the steep, rough ground and on, back to the farm. The ewes had to be left where they were for a while. Flossie danced along beside him, pleased and excited with herself.

Once on more level ground Patrick found he could manage quite well, his burden was not so heavy. What was Private Harvey doing out on the inhospitable moor in this weather, and in such poor condition? Patrick wondered about it as he neared the farm, walking slower now as his burden seemed to grow heavier, every breath he took feeling like a knife in his chest. The night when he had helped Karen and Doctor Clarke with Nick

342

came back to him vividly. He remembered her compassion for the young and maimed soldiers, her skill and knowledge of her job. She had given it all up for him. Up until now Patrick had not thought of that, he had thought only of the sacrifices he himself had made, and suddenly he was humbled.

He came to the track and paused for a moment to get his breath back, drawing deep, painful gulps of air into his lungs. He leaned Nick against the boundary wall and had a good look at him. The boy was pitifully thin and only semi-conscious but it was the hectic flush on his cheeks which worried Patrick the most. There was no time to lose in getting him indoors. Whistling Flossie to heel, he hoisted Nick on to his shoulder again and strode out for home.

'Goodness to gracious, what on earth have you got there?' Gran was startled into asking as Patrick brushed past her in the doorway to the kitchen and went straight to the settee. He laid Nick down on the cushions and pulled the settee closer to the fire. Gran had followed him in, still holding the bucket filled with a bran mash she had been taking to the horses.

She quickly sized up the situation, though, and wasting no more words began to strip the sodden clothes off Nick, sending Patrick for blankets to wrap him in. She set milk to warm in the small iron pan, then raised Nick with one arm and tried to get him to take some. This did not prove so difficult for as soon as he realized what it was, he grabbed the cup with his good left hand and drank thirstily.

'Poor lad,' said Gran. 'Was he out on the fell, Patrick? It's a wonder he's alive. As it is he looks

343

set for pneumonia. You'll have to go for the doctor. Go on, you can leave the sheep till later.'

'Where's Karen? Can you manage him on your own? Will I go and find her first?'

'No, no. She's just gone down the ghyll for some holly and tree ivy. She won't be long, it's nearly time for Brian's feed so she's sure to be back soon. Hadaway with you, I'll manage fine.'

With a quick glance at his son, who was sleeping peacefully in his cradle by the fire, Patrick went out and caught Jess to ride her into Stanhope for the doctor.

*   *   *

'I'm back, Gran. Did the bairn wake up?' Karen called through from the scullery. 'I've got a nice bit of berried holly, plenty of berries on it this year.' She poked her head around the door when Gran didn't answer immediately, her expression enquiring.

'Gran? Who's that?'

'He's a tramp. A poor lad Patrick found on the fell. And just as well he did, he wouldn't have lasted much longer in this weather. Patrick's gone into Stanhope for Doctor Oliver.' Gran turned from her task of washing Nick. With the heat from the range the smell from the lad was getting to be overpowering.

'Nick!'

Horrified, Karen stared at the prone figure in disbelief.

'You know him?'

'He was a patient of mine, Gran. He was in the hospital in Essex where I was during the war. What

344

on earth is he doing here? Oh, it's my fault, I'm sure it is, he was looking for me.' Karen was stricken with remorse. 'He was looking for me, Kezia told me he was, said he had been to Morton Main. And I was too much taken up with my own affairs to think about it any more.' Karen came closer and looked down at Nick. His eyes were closed now, his breathing harsh and laboured. She became business-like at once.

'What do you think, Gran?'

'Underfeeding and the cold, I should think. Maybe pneumonia.' Gran stood back and let Karen examine him. She felt his head. It was burning hot in sharp contrast to his frozen hand. As she touched him his eyes opened and he saw her.

'Sister,' he breathed, looking directly at her, his gaze clearing. He smiled fleetingly, rational for a moment, before lapsing into delirium, babbling on.

'I think we'd better keep him here on the settee, for the present at least. It is the warmest place in the house. His pulse is weak but not too erratic.' Karen tucked the wrist she was holding back under the blankets.

'Well, we'll see what Doctor Oliver has to say. Patrick shouldn't be long. Meanwhile we can only keep him warm.' She stood up and moved over to the cradle, pushing a tendril of hair away from her face, A tiny fist was beginning to wave in the air accompanied by hungry cries. Brian was getting impatient for his meal.

Patrick was back with the doctor quite soon. He was in luck that he had found him at home and not on a visit to an outlying farm. The thick-set little man hurried into the kitchen and went straight

345

over to the patient with only a brief nod to Gran and Karen. Without more ado he set about his examination. After a few minutes he replaced the blankets carefully over Nick and rose to his feet.

'There is some congestion there. And of course he is in very poor physical shape. He'll need careful nursing if we are to avoid pneumonia.' Doctor Oliver turned his keen gaze on Karen. 'Who is he?

Do you know him? I can arrange to have him taken down to the cottage hospital, if you like?'

'No, Doctor, not unless you think it is absolutely necessary. I think he has had enough of hospitals. I do know him, I nursed him when he lost his arm in the war. He has no family. I don't know what he was doing wandering around on the fell, I thought he was in Durham City. That's where he came from originally. He was supposed to be still having treatment for shell-shock.'

'Well, if you give me his full name and rank in the army, I'll try to get hold of his records. Then we'll see what we can do. It's shameful to see someone who has served his country in a war coming to this.' Doctor Oliver paused and gazed quizzically at her. 'If you are sure you want to look after him, of course it would be the ideal solution for him. But are you sure? Have you thought of what it will entail? He will have to be poulticed six-hourly and watched around the clock.'

'Thank you, Doctor, I'm sure I can manage.'

'Well, I'll leave you a sedative for him in case you need it. I must say you look fit and well, both you and the baby.'

Doctor Oliver bent over the cradle, casting a critical eye over Brian. Karen picked him up and held him against her shoulder, the better to show him to the doctor. Brian blinked sleepily, a bubble of milk escaping the corner of his mouth. His cheeks were rosy with sleep.

'So long as you can manage. Don't worry, I won't send you a bill for him anyway.' Doctor Oliver smiled. 'Baby certainly looks the picture of health.' He drew on his thick leather gloves and turned for the door, nodding to Patrick and Gran courteously. 'I'll be back tomorrow, weather permitting. I have to visit old Mrs Tyndal down the lonnen so I can easily call in. Well, a very goodnight to you all.' With a little wave, he went out to his trap.

Patrick was anxious. 'Do you think you can manage?' he asked Karen after the doctor had gone. 'Where will we put him? It's no good putting him upstairs, it's too cold, and anyway the spare room hasn't been prepared. I don't want you to do too much, Karen, he would be better in a hospital.'

'Of course we can manage,' Gran cut in. 'We can leave him there on the settee for tonight and you can put the camp bed up in the front room as soon as the doctor says it's all right to move him. I can help. Karen won't have to do it all.'

Gran looked thoughtful. 'You know, when my father was alive we always had a tramp for Christmas dinner, no matter how hard up we were. They got exactly the same to eat as we did though when they were particularly smelly they had to eat in the barn. They expected that, though. But I thought it was a bit hard when I was a bairn.' She looked at Nick who had obviously brought back the old days to her. 'Aye, well, better be getting on,' she said, going upstairs for more blankets.

347

The three of them took it in turns to sit with Nick that first night though Patrick insisted that Gran should do no more than a couple of hours. At intervals when he was awake they tried to get him to eat a little of Gran's nourishing broth and each time he was able to take a little more.

Next morning when Karen came down to relieve Patrick so that he could go out to see to the stock she found the patient much improved. He was awake, sitting propped up on the cushions, and Patrick was dozing in the rocking chair.

Poor Patrick. She would have to wake him soon but she would give him a little while longer, she decided. Nick was looking at her with wondering eyes and she smiled at him.

'It is you, Sister,' he blurted out. 'I thought I had been dreaming.'

'Oh, it's me all right,' she laughed, 'but how on earth did you find me? No, don't answer that, save your strength. I'm going to change your poultice now and then I want you to take some gruel. It's nice and milky. We'll save the explanations for when you are better.'

Karen took the linseed poultice out of the oven where it was keeping hot and set about applying it to her patient's chest over a layer of flannel. She put another layer of flannel over the poultice to help retain heat and finally helped Nick put on a clean nightshirt of Patrick's.

Patrick had woken during this exchange and was sitting watching her deft movements as she made Nick comfortable. He saw the worshipful expression in Nick's eyes whenever he looked at Karen and he was disturbed. A tiny flicker of jealousy stirred within him. Then, with a rueful

348

smile, he changed into his work garb and went out to see to the animals. He had no right to resent Nick, none at all, he told himself. If Karen realized it she would never understand, but would think him a fool.

It was a cold, crisp morning so he brought in more wood and coal to replenish the fire and went down to the spring for water for the house. The man who travelled the dale to kill and dress the pigs was coming today so plenty of water would be needed.

The pig designated for slaughter was the very one which had caused the upset on that summer's day which now seemed so long ago, before he came to the farm. His tail was still bent from his encounter with the gander. Patrick had heard the story often from Karen and Gran and thought about it now as he filled the set-pot in the yard and raked and laid the fire beneath it, ready to light directly after breakfast, deliberately trying not to think of Nick and his devotion to Karen.

'Howay in now, breakfast is on the table,' she called from the back door, shivering in the cold air as she pulled her shawl around her shoulders before going thankfully back inside. Patrick followed closely. They settled down to their usual bacon and eggs, though Nick had a coddled egg which he managed very well. Afterwards Karen sat on the rocker before the fire with Brian, drawing her shawl modestly over her breast as a screen when she began to feed the baby.

Nick lay quietly, quite unable to believe his luck, still unsure of the reality of it all. If this was a dream he had no intention of waking up. The horrors of his days and nights spent on the open fell at the mercy of the bitter wind and driving snow were still vivid in his mind.

By the time Christmas finally arrived, he was well enough to sit up in the chair by the fire for most of the day. He knew this was entirely due to the nursing care he got from Karen, with the help of Gran and Patrick, and he worshipped them for it. Doctor Oliver had not yet received his records from Durham but was content to let him stay at the farm where his health, both mental and physical, was improving every day.

Just as well, Karen opined, for the alternative was depressing. 'Without loving care he would probably end up in an institution,' she commented to Patrick. 'Winterton Mental Hospital, very likely.'

How could I have been jealous of the poor boy? Patrick asked himself, feeling guilty, especially when Nick told how he had lived on handouts all the way from Hexham. 'I'll write to Durham and see he gets his pension,' Patrick said to Karen. 'It's not much but he has a right to it.'

Chapter Twenty-Three

'A good morning to you, Jack,' said Patrick. 'And a Merry Christmas to you and yours.' He had got into the habit of walking up the lane to meet the postman and glancing through the letters before taking them into the house.

'Merry Christmas,' Jack echoed. 'A better one than last year, eh? Thanks be to God that the war is over. There'll be no more bad news coming from

350

France, eh? Let's hope that was the last war. What is it they say now? The war to end all wars. May 1919 be the start of better times.'

'Indeed,' agreed Patrick. 'Are you coming in for a bite of something now, a drink maybe?'

'Not today, thanks, I want to get home. The wife's got a grand dinner waiting and I promised I'd be back by twelve. You know what it's like though, always a lot of cards on Christmas Day.'

He handed over the post and went on his way. There were ten cards for Low Rigg Farm and Patrick took them in with him when he went in for breakfast. Karen was stuffing the goose ready for the oven and the atmosphere in the kitchen was warm and cheerful. The fresh spicy smell of Gran's ginger parkin and sweet mincemeat pies permeated the room. Nick was sitting with one foot on the cradle, rocking gently and crooning softly to the baby. His face expressed his adoration of Brian. Already he was showing some benefit from his new life. His eyes were calmer and the fear which had long lurked in them had vanished.

'The wind's getting up,' said Patrick as he sat down at the table. 'There'll surely be a gale tonight.'

'Oh, dear.' Karen frowned. 'I hope it isn't too bad. We said we would go to the concert and supper at Chapel tonight.' She noted the swift look of disapproval on Patrick's face and continued quickly, 'That is, if you will look after Brian? We are getting a lift with Fred Bainbridge. Nick will be here, of course.'

'I'll see to the babby,' he said, ever eager to help.

'Brian will be fine with the both of us,' said Patrick. Today was not the day to start any sort of argument. Best leave things for a while, he thought. Nodding across at Nick he said, 'I don't think I'll be doing much in the way of baby-minding though.'

Karen changed the subject. 'There's a card from Annie, look, I'm glad I sent her one. Oh, and see, an embroidered one from Joe. Isn't it beautiful?' She arranged them alongside the one from Morton Main on the high mantel shelf decorated with festive tinsel along its length. Closing one hand over the brass rail hanging under the shelf she leaned against it and stared into the fire, reflecting for a few seconds.

The gale did not prove strong enough to prevent the little party from setting out for the concert. Gran loved these meetings with her friends and neighbours and though in some ways Karen would rather have been at home with Patrick and Brian, she still enjoyed herself hugely.

The Chapel was crowded. The concert was part sacred and there was community singing of carols which rang out lustily over the deserted fell in competition with the roar of the gale.

Afterwards they sat down to a groaning board though hardly anyone could do it justice after the Christmas dinner they had eaten at mid-day. And then they were saying goodbye and wrapping up against the wind for the journey home, calling out to each other as they made their way in separate groups over the lonely fell.

The wind had risen further and Karen and Gran huddled together in the back of Fred's trap behind his family. As they approached the farm entrance with its guardian rowan tree they could see the lighted lamp in the window. Karen felt there was something magical about the darkness and the light, symbol of the love drawing them back to the house.

'Thanks, Fred, we had a fine time,' said Gran, echoed by Karen. 'Merry Christmas, God bless you all.' She stood waving to the trap as it disappeared down the lonnen and Karen waved dutifully too but felt she couldn't wait to get inside to the kitchen, the lovely kitchen where Patrick and Brian sat. She had to make sure they were still there, as though they might vanish from her life if she turned her back. She ran ahead of Gran to the door.

'We're back!' she called, and not even waiting to shed her over-boots ran anxiously into the kitchen.

'So I see.' Patrick looked up from his seat at the table where he had been reading. He smiled to see her bright face flushed with the cold and her hair all over the place where it had been whipped out of her scarf by the wind. Nick too sat up straighter in his chair by the fire, glad to see her back, happy again.

'The baby's asleep,' he murmured softly, wanting to show that he had been watching Brian. Karen gave him a special smile and walked over to the cradle, looking down at tiny sleeping Brian, his face rosy and his long, dark lashes fanning out on to his cheeks. Love surged through her, love for all three of them.

'By, you were in a hurry, Karen.'

Gran had followed her into the house but had taken off her outdoor things before entering the kitchen.

'What a wild night,' she went on. 'Never mind, I see you have the kettle on the bar. We'll have

353

some cocoa before we turn in, eh?' She bustled about with cups and milk and sugar and soon they were drinking contentedly.

Gran chatted happily about the concert. She felt more alive now the farmhouse was full of family for the first time in years, it was just like the old days. Her face was animated as she talked but the warmth had made Karen sleepy and it was not long before she and Patrick took up the child and went off to bed.

Magic, she thought, as she drifted off to sleep in Patrick's arms, that's what today has been, magic. Maybe Patrick had grown used to her going to Chapel. He had looked black for a moment before she went but hadn't said anything. Nothing was going to spoil their happiness, nothing, she told herself firmly. But still, she would have liked to cast a spell over them all so that they could remain as they were forever. For her feeling of insecurity was not really banished, not yet.

*   *   *

'I'm worried about Gran,' Karen said to Patrick one day, a day which was even colder than the one before. Snow was piled high in the lonnen. They were cut off from their neighbours and had been for days.

'I know what you mean,' he answered. 'She doesn't look well. The cold's too much for her, I think.'

'This winter is dragging on longer than usual,' mused Karen. The cold seemed to diminish Gran somehow. She had complained that morning that it was the worst winter ever and she thought she

354

would never be warm again. Karen watched her in concern as she huddled by the fire. It just wasn't like Gran to complain, the winter must really be getting her down. 'I'll see to the hens,' she said, and the frightening thing was, Gran didn't demur. Yet Karen felt safe when they were cut off by the weather. She still dreamed of faceless men dressed in black clerical garb, and woke up in a sweat of fear. In some ways she dreaded the coming of the spring.

She was in the barn one day, watching Nick awkwardly forking hay to the two cows and the ponies which had been brought into shelter as the weather looked like it was blowing up for a blizzard. She had only paused for a moment, but Nick was whistling a tune as he worked, *Bobby Shafto* it was, and she joined in and sang a verse enjoying the warmth radiating from the animals.

> *Bobby Shafto's gone awa',*
> *Combing down his yellow hair,*
> *He'll be mine forever mair,*
> *Bonny Bobby Shafto.*

Nick grinned in delight. 'We could have a sing-song the night, Sister,' he said eagerly. 'I remember in the Home we had sing-songs. By, it was grand.'

Karen laughed. 'We could do, Nick,' she began when the door opened and Patrick came in, a flurry of snow behind him. 'Oh, you're home early!' she exclaimed, smiling.

He scowled, looking from her to Nick and back again. 'What are you doing in here?' he asked abruptly. 'Where's Brian, who's looking after him?'

355

'He's asleep,' answered Karen. 'Gran's in the house with him, I thought she would be better off in the warm.' She was perplexed. Something was obviously bothering Patrick. She saw him looking hard at Nick and a suspicion came to her. But surely not . . . Patrick couldn't be jealous of Nick?

'Come into the house, Patrick, and have a proper warm,' she said. 'Nick, I'll have tea ready by the time you've finished in here.'

'Thanks, Sister.'

'You should call my wife "missus",' said Patrick, and Nick flushed.

Karen bit her lip and forebore to say anything about his attitude until they had crossed the yard and entered the scullery. But as they shed their outer clothes, she said quietly, 'Nick is just a lad, Patrick, don't be too hard on him.'

'A lad with a man's feelings for a woman, that's what he is. You shouldn't encourage it, Karen. What were you doing in the barn, laughing and singing with him like that?'

'Patrick! You can't think—'

'No? Then why does he follow you about with his dog's eyes? Why is he always ready to jump to do your bidding?'

'Patrick, Patrick, he's an orphan boy. He thinks of me as a substitute mother, that's all. Why, man, he still has the reactions of a bairn. Don't resent Nick, please. He has nowhere else to go.'

They had been speaking softly so that Gran, in the kitchen, wouldn't hear them but she still had sharp ears and now she called through to the scullery.

'What are you two doing loitering in there on a day like this? Have a bit of sense and come into

356

the warm.'

'Coming,' said Karen. She stared up into Patrick's face but could read little there except a faint hostility. 'Nick's only nineteen,' she whispered. 'He must think of me as an old woman.'

Patrick grunted and turned away, walking into the kitchen in front of her. She watched his back and sighed. Maybe she should feel flattered that he was jealous, she thought, but in reality it just made life uncomfortable for the three of them. Nick would feel the atmosphere and it would upset him. It's all in Patrick's imagination, she told herself, he'll get over it. But if it comes to it, I'll not let him send Nick away, it's not fair on him.

As it happened, Patrick didn't say any more about Nick. Perhaps he's realized he was being silly, Karen thought, and sighed. She herself was beginning to realize that her husband had faults just like anyone else, he was only human after all.

When Nick came in he held a wary look in his eyes when he looked at Patrick and he called Karen 'missus', as commanded. Karen felt a small surge of anger and almost told Nick to call her Karen, but refrained from saying anything. Perhaps she had been independent too long, she thought. It was only after she was in bed, snuggled against Patrick's back, that she remembered they had not had that sing-song after all.

Chapter Twenty-Four

'Will you come with me to see my parents?' Karen asked Patrick one evening as they prepared for bed. She had been steeling herself to ask him all day, building herself up to it for weeks, and at last she had managed it.

'Oh, Karen, I don't know,' he answered. He was sitting on the edge of the bed, taking off his socks. He paused, gazing down at the socks, his face troubled.

'We have to take Brian to see them, Patrick, it's only right,' she urged. 'There was the excuse of the weather before, but now the snow's going—'

Patrick rolled the socks into a ball and threw them on to a chair. 'We'll go then,' he said calmly, surprising her by his easy acceptance. 'When do you think?'

'Saturday? I can write to them, let them know we're coming.'

'If you like,' he said, climbing into bed. 'Now for the love of God, woman, come to bed. I'm dead on my feet.'

Karen hurried to do his bidding. Indeed he did look tired, lines of exhaustion circling his eyes. She turned to him and he took her in his arms and kissed her brow. But then she felt his arms slacken and saw he was fast asleep.

It's my fault, Karen thought, worry nagging her. The farm can't keep us all. If it had been capable of supporting a family without any outside work to supplement the income, Gran's sons would not have had to go away to work in the coalfield. The small-holdings had been created for lead miners, that was the trouble, and now there was no lead mining in the dale and very little limestone quarrying. And Nick's pension, which had only just come through, was small and barely paid for his board. If Brian was older she could get nursing work in Stanhope, but she couldn't leave him yet. It was a thought for the future, though. She lay awake, listening to the rhythmic breathing of Patrick and the occasional tiny snort from Brian in his cot at the foot of the bed. He was just recovering from a cold. Now they had decided to go to Morton Main, she began to feel apprehensive about the meeting with her father and mother. And once she began to feel a little low, her mind running relentlessly on and on over her money worries. She'd had to dip into her meagre savings for the last month's grocery bill from the store. If she carried on doing that the savings wouldn't last long.

These last three weeks, Patrick had worked at the lime burning kilns with John Bainbridge, Fred's son. This was the usual work for the men of the dale in the winter and spring and Patrick had worked from dawn till long after the early dusk, carting coke from Stanhope with Polly harnessed to the old cart. He found it hard.

Karen tried to think of other ways to make extra money, anything. But the small farm on the fell was only fifty-two acres, with allotment of four cows and thirty-six sheep allowed to graze the moor. And even this allotment had not been kept up when Gran was on her own. Now it had to be built up and it cost money to do that. And there was the rent. That was £52 a year.

Oh, Lord, she thought, why do things always look black in the small hours? Deliberately she decided to count her blessings rather than her worries.

Spring was coming, wasn't it? And Patrick would become used to the hard work, he was a fit and healthy man, wasn't he? And there was Nick. Though he only had one arm, he was still useful on the farm, especially when Patrick was away working, and a grand help to her with the animals. And she had Patrick and Brian, wasn't any hardship worth that?

On cue, Brian hiccuped and woke up, and she slipped out of bed and picked him up, offering him her breast. He grabbed the nipple hungrily and sucked away and she was thankful that his cold didn't seem to be bothering him. His nose must be free for breathing if he could suck so lustily. The quiet contentment which suckling the baby always gave her settled on her mind. She finished feeding him and laid him down in his cradle again, rocking it gently for a few minutes until he fell asleep. Then she climbed back into bed, her mood lighter, and snuggling up to Patrick, fell asleep.

* * *

'By, it's good to be alive,' Karen exclaimed. 'Aren't the flowers grand?'

'They are indeed,' said Patrick. They were walking along the lane to the road where they would meet the bus for Stanhope. Karen had Brian in her arms and Patrick carried a basket of fresh eggs and butter which Gran had insisted on sending for the family in Morton Main.

360

'I wish you could have come with me,' Karen had said to her, but Gran had shaken her head.

'Nay, lass, I'm all right here, with Nick to help me with the animals. Somebody has to stay to see to them. No, it's best you go and make your peace with your da. The sooner you go the better for everybody.'

But Karen wasn't thinking of the meeting with her parents, not yet. It was enough to savour the day and the rare outing from the work of the farm. The harsh sharpness of the moorland air which caught at the breath during the long winter months had softened to an invigorating tang which was almost intoxicating. The very air was optimistic in the spring, she mused, especially now that awful war was over. She shifted Brian on to her other arm. He was growing, she thought happily, getting quite a weight.

*　　　*　　　*

'You're here then,' said Kezia. 'I've been watching for you. I thought you might like to have a cup of tea with us before you see Da.'

Patrick frowned and Karen said swiftly, 'There's no need for that, is there? I wrote to them an' all, they're expecting us.'

'Please yourself,' said Kezia tartly. 'I just thought you might want to catch your breath, like.'

'We'll go straight in if you don't mind, Kezia,' said Karen. 'We'll see you later, will we?'

'Mebbe. Luke's in fore shift and he'll be in for his dinner, and there's the lads'll be coming in for theirs. They're at the Sunshine Corner at Chapel. And little Meg's fretful.'

361

'Oh. I hope she's not sickening for anything?'

Karen clutched little Brian closer to her and Kezia noticed and smiled in understanding.

'Nay, lass,' she said. 'It's her teeth. She's cutting a double tooth.' A child wailed in the house behind her and Kezia glanced over her shoulder. 'I'll have to go in and see to her. Don't worry, Karen, it'll be all right with Mam and Da, you'll see.'

Patrick had said nothing at all during the short exchange between the sisters. His face was impassive; he could have been just an interested bystander.

Karen knocked at the door of number two then felt like an idiot. Why on earth had she done that? Pressing down the thumbpiece of the sneck latch, she opened the door and went in, followed by Patrick.

Mam and Da were in the kitchen, sitting on either side of the fireplace. The room was spotless, not a thing out of place, and Da had on his Sunday suit while Mam was in her good woollen dress. Karen could have cried. There they were, arrayed as for company. Was she not their daughter any more?

Da got to his feet and went to them. Gravely he kissed Karen on the cheek and, hesitating only a moment, held out his hand to Patrick.

'Now then, Karen, Patrick,' he said.

'Hallo, Da,' she said. 'We've brought your grandson to see you both.'

'And not before time,' he answered. 'It's long past when we should have made our peace with each other and I pray the Lord will forgive us for it.' He pulled the blanket away from Brian's face and gazed at the sleeping baby. 'He's more like his da than you, our Karen,' he observed, his tone lighter now he had said his piece.

'Eeh, Karen, let's have a look.'

Mam had risen and Da stood aside for her to look at Brian.

'Nay, I don't know, lad,' she said. 'He does have a look of our Joe when he was a bairn.' She looked up at Karen and smiled. 'Hello, pet,' she said softly.

Karen put her free arm around the frail shoulders and kissed her. Rachel's cheek was wet with tears.

'Come and sit down, Mam,' she said gently. 'You can hold the bairn while I take off my coat.'

'I was going to mash some tea—' her mother began.

'I'll do it in a minute,' Karen insisted.

She covered her rush of emotion by busying herself with the kettle and teapot. The best teaset was already out on the embroidered linen cloth which covered the bare boards of the table. Mam sat crooning to the baby and Brian woke up and stared solemnly up at her, with Patrick's black-fringed eyes.

Patrick . . . oh, she hadn't even introduced him properly! Karen suddenly remembered that he hadn't even met her parents before today. She had brought him in to the house and almost forgotten he was there.

'Da,' she said, turning to begin a belated introduction, 'Da—'

But her father was pulling out a seat for Patrick.

'I'll take your coat,' he said courteously, and waited while Patrick put the basket of eggs and butter on the table and took off his coat. Da took

363

it over to the hook behind the door and then turned sternly to the younger man, his tone changing.

'So you are my daughter's man,' he said. 'Are you treating her right? You don't stop her from going to Chapel, do you? And you a Catholic, I mean.'

'I don't stop her,' said Patrick.

'Aye, well, I had to ask you. There's those Irish up at Paddy's Row, spend half their time in the pub at Morton. You drink strong liquor, do you?'

'Da!' cried Karen. 'No, he doesn't. Don't question Patrick like—'

'Let the lad answer for himself,' said Da quietly. 'I just want to know what sort of a man he is.'

'I don't drink,' said Patrick, glancing at Karen's distressed face. And he thought of the last time he had had a drink. It was with a man from Paddy's Row, he remembered.

Da opened his mouth to continue the catechism.

'Thomas,' said Rachel Knight quietly, 'leave the lad alone.'

'But he's a Catholic, born and bred,' said Da. 'I have to make sure he won't force our Karen. And then there's the bairn, an' all.'

'I won't,' said Patrick. His voice was still reasonable but his eyes had gone hard and Karen felt a twinge of foreboding. 'I am not a practising Catholic.'

Da was struck dumb. He sat down at the table, unsure what to make of this.

'We'll have our tea now,' said Mam, and Karen brought the food out of the pantry and poured cups of tea in a lengthening silence broken only by her father's intoning of the Grace.

Karen took Brian into the front room to feed

364

and change him. All the while she sat on the hard, prickly seat of the horsehair settee and strained her ears to catch any signs of normal conversation from the kitchen. She could hear her mother's voice, offering Patrick an extra buttered teacake, and his courteous acceptance. But she couldn't hear her father at all. She thought of how he had questioned Patrick. He hadn't mentioned anything about his being a priest; the fact that he was a Catholic was more important to him. The baby finished his meal and she buttoned up her dress and put him against her shoulder to bring up the wind. And then the door opened and she looked up eagerly. Kezia's presence would help, she thought. If she brought in the children everyone would relax.

But it wasn't Kezia, it was a man, a tall, dark, sun-tanned man, still in a khaki uniform with a sergeant's stripes and wearing a bush hat.

'Hello, our Karen,' he said. 'I didn't expect to find you here, I was coming up to see you tomorrow.'

'Joe!' she cried. 'Oh, Joe.' Still holding the baby, she jumped to her feet and rushed to him and he opened his arms to her and hugged her and her baby to him.

Suddenly the room was filled with family. There was Mam crying over her son and holding on to his arm as though she would never let him go. And Da was patting him on the back and beaming with delight. And Kezia came running in with little Meg in her arms and Tommy and Young Luke by her side, closely followed by her husband, fresh bathed after his night in the pit and with his trousers pulled hastily over his nightshirt. Everyone was

365

laughing and talking and asking how long Joe could stay and no one noticed Patrick at first as he stood in the doorway from the kitchen and watched.

'Howay, lad, don't be shy. Come on in and meet your brother-in-law. Joe, this is our Karen's man.'

It was Da who had been the first to remember Patrick and he had gone to the door and taken hold of his arm and drawn him in to the family group.

Joe, who had taken Brian from Karen and was holding him easily in his arms, admiring him, looked at Patrick and nodded his head slightly. But he smiled and Karen knew he liked what he saw.

'Hello there,' he said at last, giving Patrick his free hand. 'So you're the fellow who's taken on our Karen, are you? Aye, well, no doubt you'll make her a good man and look after this little chap.'

Karen's heart swelled. Everything was all right, Patrick was accepted into the family. She smiled gratefully at Joe. It was his coming home which had worked the miracle, she thought. Dear Joe, all her life he had helped her over difficult times, even when he had been all that way away in Australia.

'We sail next Saturday,' he was saying, his arm around his mother's shoulders and Kezia's children gazing up at him with round, wonder-filled eyes.

'So soon?' said Mam, her smile dimming for an instant.

He kissed her lightly. 'I'll be back though, Mam, don't fret. I won't forget you.'

'I should think not indeed,' said Kezia tartly, and they all laughed.

Reluctantly, Karen and Patrick prepared to leave. They had to be back to help with the evening chores. The whole family walked with them to the bus stop at the end of the rows, just outside the gates of the pit yard.

'Try and get down to see us a bit more often, pet,' said Mam, kissing Karen goodbye. 'I know it's not that easy, what with your gran and the farm, but we do love to see you. And give my love to Gran, will you? Maybe this summer I'll be well enough to get up to see her.'

'I will,' promised Karen.

Joe, who had been carrying Brian, handed him over to her as the bus came round the corner with a grinding of gears and Karen and Patrick climbed aboard and sat down. To a chorus of goodbyes from the others and a 'chin-chin' from Joe, they were off, the longed for yet dreaded visit over.

Karen's eyes met Patrick's and they smiled at each other in mutual understanding. They had made their peace with Karen's parents, or at least they were reconciled, and Karen felt as though a cloud was lifted from her mind. The bus wound its way through the pit villages to Bishop Auckland where they would change for Weardale. It was as they descended from it that they met Robert walking along the pavement, his medical bag in his hand.

'Hello, Karen,' he said quietly, stopping short and politely lifting his hat. She moved the sleeping Brian to a more comfortable position on her arm as she looked up at him. Beside her she could feel the change in Patrick, a tension in him.

'Robert,' she said. 'It's nice to see you.' Looking up at him she saw there were fine lines around his eyes and mouth, a bleak look in his eyes as he glanced at the sleeping baby and then at Patrick. There was a small silence. She wanted to tell him she was sorry, for him to tell her it didn't matter, he was getting on with his life, she hadn't hurt him really. But as he looked gravely down at her, she faltered, there was nothing to say. In the end it was Patrick who took her arm in a proprietorial gesture.

'We have to go, Karen,' he said, and drew her away.

*   *   *

'There's influenza in Stanhope. Spanish, they reckon,' said Jack, and Karen felt a surge of apprehension.

The postman began to bring daily reports of the folk laid low with the new plague and eventually of the deaths which it brought in its wake. And then, almost inevitably, it made an unwelcome visit to Low Rigg Farm.

It happened one day when Patrick was out on the fell seeking a lost ewe. It was lambing time and Nick and Karen were busy among the sheep in the pasture. Gran had been persuaded to stay in the warmth of the kitchen to look after Brian and prepare a hot meal, for the weather had taken a turn for the worse as so often happened in April. It was very cold with an east wind promising snow.

'Well, we found her. Or I should say Flossie did,' Patrick announced as he returned with the ewe and her lamb and turned them into the fold.

'A good strong lamb too,' Karen answered, and smiled in satisfaction. 'That's twenty so far. Not

368

bad if we can manage to keep them all.'

'Are you done?' Patrick was hungry, it had been a long day. 'I wonder what there is for supper?'

'You'll be getting fat,' laughed Karen as Nick came up behind them. Linking her arm through Patrick's, they all walked leisurely back to the farmhouse.

Foreboding struck all three as they turned into the yard. Something was wrong. No smoke curled from the chimney, no delicious cooking smells emanated from the house. They quickened their steps and eventually broke into a run as they heard fretful cries from the kitchen. Brian was awake and obviously nobody was attending to his needs. Karen was the first to burst through the door.

'Gran? Gran?' she called anxiously, but there was no reply. Going into the kitchen, she gazed anxiously around but couldn't see her grandmother at first. Quickly she ran over to the cradle and picked up the red-faced, sobbing baby, checking him fearfully. But the only thing wrong with him seemed to be that he was decidedly damp and chilly. His sobs lessened as he felt his mother's arms around him and Karen looked about her as Patrick and Nick came in. The fire was out and the air was cold and dank. Where on earth was Gran?

'Gran!'

Patrick had seen her first, lying on the flagged floor, half-hidden by the dresser. Carefully he picked her up and laid her on the settee, chafing her hands which were blue with cold. She must have been lying on the cold stones for some time, they realized, to get as thoroughly chilled as she had done. Karen handed the baby to Nick who rocked him gently in his one arm to still his

369

protests.

She felt Gran's fluctuating pulse and burning brow and immediately took charge, issuing directions to the two men.

'Get some firewood and light the fire, Patrick. And you, Nick, go and get the blankets from her bed.'

'What about the bairn?' he said, perplexed.

'Oh, give me the baby.'

Deftly she whipped a nappy which had been airing from the brass line under the mantle shelf and made the child comfortable. Then, despite his protests, she put him back in his cradle, fastening him in with the strap. Brian was getting to the age when he could sit up and maybe climb out.

Soon the fire was blazing up the chimney and giving off a cheering heat which quickly warmed the kitchen. Karen filled the stone bottles with hot water as soon as the kettle boiled and placed them around Gran, who was flushed and delirious and breathing heavily.

Meanwhile, Patrick had harnessed Polly to the trap and rushed away for the doctor. But Doctor Oliver was already out on calls and it was not until the early morning that he arrived at Low Rigg Farm, looking grey and exhausted. He shook his head as soon as he saw the old lady, who looked somehow diminished as she lay propped up by the pillows which Karen had arranged behind her in an effort to help her breathing.

'Careful nursing, that's all you can give her,' the doctor said to Karen. 'She is in good hands at least which is more than can be said for some of them. But, you know, Mrs Rain's a good age now. You must be prepared for the worst.'

Gran was buried in the little churchyard in the dale the following week. It was pneumonia which had complicated her illness, a particularly virulent type, and the end was swift and inevitable. But still Karen was devastated. With all her experience of nursing she should have been able to save her, she agonized. What had she done wrong?

'Nothing,' said Patrick. 'You did all you could for her, Karen.'

The interment followed a moving service in the Chapel attended by few mourners, for the dale was stricken with the new plague and most people who were still well were attending to their own sick or dying. Karen stood with Patrick's arm around her as Gran was lowered into the grave, and her shoulders shook with sobs. Keenly, she felt the absence of friends and neighbours. Even the Bainbridges were absent for Mrs Bainbridge was also down with the 'flu. But worst of all there was no one from Morton Main. None of the family could come to the funeral. The plague was taking its toll there also and Mam was one of its first victims. She was gravely ill.

Patrick and Karen went back to the farm afterwards. He put away the trap and turned Polly out into the pasture and Karen went into the kitchen to start the dinner. For the first time since she could remember there was no proper funeral tea, no one had come back with them to eat and reminisce about the departed. 'Giving her a good send-off', as Gran would have said.

'There's a telegram on the table,' said Nick,

looking at Karen with red-rimmed, anxious eyes and the nervous tic pulsing away in his face. Everything which affected her affected him also, she thought numbly, but there was no comfort left in her to give him.

When Patrick came in she was sitting holding the sheet of yellow paper in her hand, the telegram which told of the death of her mother from the same plague.

'Nick, take Brian out a while, will you?' he asked, and Nick picked up the baby without a word and went out into the yard.

Patrick took the paper from Karen's hand and read the few stark words then he lifted her up in his arms and held her tight.

'It was too much for her worn-out heart, I should think,' said Karen, her voice expressionless. 'Poor Mam, poor Mam. And Da . . . Patrick, what will Da do now?'

But he had no answer for her. All he could do was hold her and comfort her.

*   *   *

Karen and Patrick took Brian and travelled down for the day of her mother's funeral, leaving Nick in charge of the farm. Karen was quiet and sad throughout the journey, full of wild regrets because she had not made time to take the baby to see Mam again before she died. Patrick too was quiet, his concern for her pain showing in his attentiveness to her.

Coming into the old village of Morton, he was struck by the difference between it and its newer neighbour of Morton Main. The last time he was

372

here he had been too concerned with meeting Karen's parents to notice so much. The stone cottages had been built for agricultural labourers long ago, he surmised, they were far from being palaces but each had a front garden bright with flowers in sharp contrast to the mean rows of the pit village. But even here the towering slag heap and winding house could be seen overshadowing everything. He wrinkled his nose at the strong smell coming from the coke works and evident even this far away. He glanced at Karen but she seemed unaware of it. She held the baby to her, a set look on her face, as she started to walk down the road to Morton Main.

'I'll take Brian,' Patrick said gently, holding out his arms for the baby.

'No, no. Men don't carry babies here,' Karen said, and smiled briefly at him before the closed expression returned to her face. 'It's all right, love, I can manage him fine.'

They walked in silence for a while until they turned into the rows. The windows of Chapel Row all had their curtains drawn as a mark of respect for the dead woman in their midst. An all-pervading dust permeated the air, but the windows and doorsteps were shining clean, obviously scrubbed that morning. The street was quiet, the children all at school and most of the men on shift at the pit, the rest in bed after night shift.

Kezia opened the door to them, nodding coolly to Patrick and kissing Karen briefly on the cheek.

'She's in here.' Kezia nodded towards the coffin in the front room and led them over to it ceremoniously. 'I'll be in the kitchen,' she went on, and slipped away.

Karen gazed down at her mother, tears welling in her eyes.

'Come away now,' said Patrick quietly. 'Come away into the kitchen. A cup of tea is what you need just now.'

He led her away into the warm kitchen where Da was sitting in his hard chair by the fire. He seemed dazed, overwhelmed by his loss, Karen saw, and she kissed him and murmured softly, her own grief submerged in his.

After a moment or two she showed him the baby.

'Here's Brian, Da, look how he's grown.'

But he was taking little notice of anything, he didn't look at Brian.

Karen glanced at Kezia who was busy making sandwiches and tea, and Kezia caught her glance and gave her a direct stare in return.

'Pity you didn't bring the baby to see them more often before this happened,' she said. Kezia was bitter, Karen realized.

'Well, the weather. And Gran . . .' she began lamely.

Kezia's expression showed she thought the faltering words poor excuse but she simply tossed her head and held her tongue.

'I'll help you with that,' said Karen. She gave the baby to Patrick and, picking up a knife, started to butter bread. The sisters stood side by side at the table working on the sandwiches and eventually Kezia spoke.

'I'm sorry, Karen, real sorry. I know you had Gran an' all. I felt terrible when we couldn't get up to the funeral, but what with Mam and young Meg both having the 'flu, well . . .'

374

'I know,' said Karen. 'How's Meg now, then?'

'Better, thank God,' sighed Kezia, pausing and closing her eyes for a second. 'She's awful poor-looking, though.'

The door opened and both sisters paused and looked up, knives poised in the air.

'Jemima!'

Everyone turned to look at the thin, middle-aged woman who stood in the doorway.

'Yes, it's me,' she said. 'Did you think I wouldn't come to my own mother's funeral?'

Jemima walked up to her father and kissed his cheek and he half-rose from his chair to greet her, his face crumpling.

'Jemima, oh, Jemima,' he breathed, and hugged her to him.

'Are you on your own?' asked Kezia, glancing through the middle door which led from the front room.

'I am,' said Jemima, offering no further explanation.

Karen and Kezia looked at each other, Kezia raising her eyebrows.

'I sent her a telegram,' she whispered to Karen, 'but I didn't even know if she was still at the same address. She's not been back for years.'

But any questions they had for Jemima had to wait as neighbours and friends began to file into the little house to pay their respects to the family before the funeral and there was no chance of further private conversation.

Everyone but for the men on shift followed the coffin to the Chapel on the end of the row. Mr Richardson, a Supernumary Minister now, his hair sparse and white and his figure frail, led them into the Chapel intoning the words of the funeral service in a high, quavering voice: 'Man born of woman has but a short time to live.' The family filed in and took the front pew, Karen sitting between Patrick and Kezia.

'We are here to celebrate the life and mourn the death of Rachel, a much loved member of our Society and a faithful handmaiden of the Lord,' said Mr Richardson. Amen to that, thought Karen, oh yes.

They sang 'Abide With Me', the sound swelling in the packed Chapel, and 'The Lord's My Shepherd', to the tune so loved by Durham miners, *Crimond*. The old Minister gave a glowing account of Mam's life, her fortitude in the face of ill-health, her love for her God and her family. And Karen, looking across at Da, saw how he was comforted by the words, and made proud. And then the service was over and they were thanking the Minister by the door of the Chapel, and for the first time, Karen noticed that Robert was there, standing by his father, offering words of comfort to Da and Jemima and Kezia. And then he was holding his hand out for hers and taking it in his cool, firm grip.

'I am so sorry, Karen,' he said, his own eyes reflecting her pain. 'I did my best for her, but you know the condition of her heart.'

Of course, thought Karen, Kezia had told her Robert was the panel doctor now, looking after the miners and their families. He was a good man, he could have had a high flying career as a surgeon. 'Thank you, I'm sure you did,' she answered, and then they were following the coffin to the churchyard in Morton village where Mam was to

376

be buried, and afterwards they returned to the cottage for the obligatory funeral tea.

Patrick was very quiet and stayed near Karen, watchful. People cast curious glances at him, the stranger among them, but he was oblivious to them, his eyes only for her unhappiness. But it was her own folk Karen needed this day.

'We can't stay long, we must get back to the farm,' she said to Kezia as they met in the little off-shoot pantry to fetch cakes and biscuits. Jemima, of course, took no part in serving the meal. She was sitting by Da and eating heartily.

'No, of course not.' Kezia was still a little formal with her as she bustled back out with laden plates. Karen watched her for a moment, troubled. She felt guilty herself because she had not made the time to visit her parents more. Kezia was right, she thought miserably. She should have found the time somehow.

'We have to go, Da.' Laying her hand on his shoulder, Karen kissed his cheek but he only nodded dumbly and looked back at Jemima. Karen was reminded of the parable of the prodigal son, or in this case, daughter. Sighing she looked at Patrick, unable to think of what to say, what comfort she could give.

'Yes, yes, that's it. The journey that is.' Patrick came to her aid with quick concern, finding her coat and hat, helping her on with them.

'You're going already?' said Jemima. 'I thought we would have a talk.'

'Sorry, I must. The animals, you know.'

Jemima sniffed and turned away. Karen gazed at her back. Jemima never changed, she thought. Kezia went with them to the door.

377

'I'm sorry if I was sharp with you, our Karen,' she said. 'I know it wasn't easy for you to get down. And look at Jemima, she hasn't been here for years.'

'I'll be back a bit sooner than that,' promised Karen, and hugged Kezia.

They did not linger, for indeed it was true that they couldn't leave Nick for too long even though he was good with the stock despite his handicap. Sadly they walked up to the bus stop to await the bus to Old Morton village.

On the train back to Stanhope they were silent, each of them lost in thought. Karen gazed at the sleeping baby, symbol of the future. She looked out of the window at the fields which were bright with the green grass of early summer. This was the time for a fresh start, she told herself firmly. But her mind was full of scenes of her childhood and an aching regret for things she should have said to her mother, or perhaps have left unsaid.

*   *   *

Patrick held on to his own thoughts. He was remembering the rickets he had seen in the children of the mining village, the worn faces of the adults. He felt ill from the smell of the coke works and had been unable to eat anything at the funeral tea. His own childhood had been poor but at least the air had been fit to breathe. Thank God they were living on the moor, breathing clean, fresh air, no matter how hard the life, he thought. Seeing Karen among her family at such a time had made him look at her with new eyes, giving him renewed respect for her strength of purpose in getting away from the mining community, making her own way and yet still maintaining close bonds with her family. And he thought again of his own parents. He would write to them before it was too late, he had put it off long enough. And surely, after all this time, his mother would have forgiven him?

'Here we are.' Karen broke into his thoughts as the train drew into Stanhope. She was wrapping the shawl closely round Brian against the cold wind which was blowing down from the tops and sweeping through the valley.

He watched the curve of her cheek as she bent over the baby. Mother and child seemed vulnerable somehow tonight. He felt a surge of protectiveness sweep over him. Tenderly he helped her down from the train. They were both shivering in the strong wind.

'Soon be home,' he said, and realized the farm really did feel more like home to him after the pit village.

Chapter Twenty-Five

Life on the farm without Gran seemed strange to Karen and the feeling lasted for month after month. She would come into the kitchen and look around for the familiar figure, and each time the feeling of loss which overcame her as she remembered was just as strong. They had applied to the Church Commissioners for the tenancy to pass to them and one morning, Patrick came into the kitchen with the letter in his hand.

'We've got it then,' he commented.

Karen looked around her in satisfaction. She had always loved this place but since she and Patrick had come to live here she loved it more. They could work for a better future now, she thought. He had found work in the kilns in May. It was hard labouring and poorly paid, but it was work. He helped fill the small wagons with coke and limestone which then ran on the railed wagon-way to the kiln where they were tipped. It took two full days to load it up to the top, another two days to burn through. Only then could the lime be shovelled out at the bottom.

Karen worried about him. She worried about him all the time, even now as he sat down to his breakfast before going to work. It was morning, he hadn't even started yet, and he still looked tired.

He had come in white from the lime the night before and had, as usual, to sluice himself down in the scullery. His clothes were thick with the dust and Karen dashed them against the wall in the yard to get rid of it, just as she had dashed her father's clothes when she had lived in Morton Main, to get rid of the coal dust. Oh, yes, she worried about him. She was aware that he found the work hard, not being raised to it. Even when the lime was washed off, he looked white and strained. He did not complain, though almost every night he fell asleep in his chair the moment he sat down.

Nevertheless, Karen was happy and content with her life. Sometimes love for Patrick and their baby would bubble up in her and she would think, it can't last, with a little pang of foreboding. But she pushed it away, the thought. Of course it would

380

last, why shouldn't it? The feel of Patrick's hand on her breast was still enough to make her pulse leap in ecstasy, just as it had in the beginning, and she felt his need for her was still as intense as it had ever been.

She rushed to the door and picked up Brian who was climbing over the step in search of his beloved Nick.

'Howay, my lad, you stay here and eat your breakfast,' she said as she put him in his high chair. Brian's mouth turned down and he prepared to wail for Nick.

'Nick's coming, he's coming now,' Patrick put in swiftly. Karen looked at him, wondering if he was jealous of Brian's affection for Nick, but he was smiling indulgently at the boy.

'Aren't you a big strong lad, then?' he said, picking Brian up and swinging him in the air, and Brian's pout turned to a delighted grin.

He was growing strong and healthy, Karen thought happily. Now he could walk, he would toddle after Nick on his sturdy little legs whenever he got the chance. He was devoted to Nick and Nick was devoted to him. Brian showed no fear of the animals in the yard, waving his arms imperiously at them if they were in his way or chattering to them unintelligibly. Consequently they were friendly towards him, even the gander and his harem, now grown to six.

Karen went out to the gate to call Nick in from the pasture. It was one of those days when she could see clearly over to the far horizon, the sweep of the fells around her filled with the bleating of sheep. A blossom from the rowan tree above her drifted down and landed on her shoe. She looked idly at it. The tree had been covered with blossom this year, there would be a good crop of rowan berries.

'Rowan tree and red thread, Put the witches to their speed.' Idly she quoted the old Weardale saying. Leaning against the trunk, she called to Nick who was busy at the other end of the pasture, checking Polly's hooves. He lifted his head and called back, and she waved and straightened up and walked slowly back to the kitchen. For the first time since the deaths of her mother and grandmother, Karen felt a lightening of the sadness within her.

'Mammy, Mammy,' cried Brian from his high chair by the table, his chubby face smeared with honey. Patrick looked up from his breakfast and smiled and somehow he didn't look so tired and strained, just happy. And Karen felt her own love for them welling up in her and filling her world.

Chapter Twenty-Six

Karen walked along the lane to meet Patrick, Brian trotting solemnly by her side. At two and three-quarters he was the quiet one of her two children. Eighteen-month-old Jennie clung to her skirts, stumbling a little but independent, insisting on walking herself.

Patrick was bring home the two little pigs which would be fattened throughout the year. It was the spring of 1921, fine and dry, the birds were singing, fresh grass pushing strongly through the ground. Karen was completely absorbed in her family, exulting in the warmth of the day and the sun on her back. She even gave a little skip as she walked along.

'Clap your hands for Daddy coming down the waggon way, a pocket full of money and a cartload of hay,' she sang to Jennie, and caught her up in her arms and swung her over her head. The little girl crowed with delight. She sang along merrily, completely out of tune and making up the words as she went along.

'But he's bringing piggies, not hay, Mammy.' Brian had stopped to face her. 'And this is the lane, not the waggon way.' He had a literal frame of mind, and knew the waggon way was up by the kiln.

'Oh, Brian, it's a nursery rhyme,' Karen laughed helplessly as she stooped and gathered him into her arms with Jennie, hugging them both. He wriggled to be free.

'Don't, Mammy, don't! Let me down. I'm a big boy now,' he cried.

'Oh, yes, I forgot,' she answered, and put him back on to his feet.

'Daddy! Daddy!' Jennie had caught sight of Patrick as he came out of the dip in the lane. Amid great excitement and exclamations over the piglets, even Brian broke into little hops and skips while grinning from ear to ear.

'Let me hold one,' he begged. 'I can hold one.'

'Me, me!' cried Jennie.

'Not now,' decreed their father. 'Later, when they've settle down.

'Please, Daddy?' pleaded Brian, but Patrick shook his head and reluctantly they made their way back to the farm.

'Nick, Nick.'

The little girl struggled from Karen's arms and ran to him, her excitement bubbling as she stumbled to him on fat little legs. Nick caught her up with his good arm, pleasure shining from him.

'What is it, flower?' he laughed at her. 'Piggies, is it?'

'Piglets. It's piglets.' This was Brian who had given up baby talk.

'Let's see then.' Nick turned to Patrick, becoming businesslike, holding the child easily on one hip. He cast a critical look over the squealing animals as they were turned into the pen. He still did not trust Patrick's judgement entirely, not in farming matters, though Patrick protested he had been born and raised on a farm.

'It was not a dales farm, though, not like these round here, was it?' Nick had pointed out.

'Not much different,' Patrick had argued, but Nick had been disbelieving about that. After all, the farm where Patrick had been born was in a different country altogether, wasn't it?

In this case, however, he could find no fault with the piglets.

'Not bad little 'uns,' he pronounced, and Patrick grinned at Karen. She smiled back at him, remembering the little outbursts of jealousy he had once shown towards Nick. Now at least the two men seemed friendly enough.

'Tea then, eh?'

Karen's smile embraced them all as she went into the kitchen and put on the kettle. It was baking day and the loaves were spread on the steel fender to rise. The room was warm from the fire needed to heat the warm air oven, and the stotty cake, a flat bread cake baked on the bottom shelf of the oven, was now ready to come out to eat with the tea. It smelt heavenly. Taking the oven cloth from the brass line, Karen deftly slid the cake out on to the table to cool while she waited for the kettle to boil. Testing the oven with her hand, she filled it with the waiting loaves.

'Don't touch,' she said as she looked round and saw Brian reaching for the cake. 'It's hot. I'll give you some in a minute.' She smiled fondly at his blush. Brian hated to be scolded. Patrick and Nick came in with Jennie and they sat around the table eating great chunks of the hot bread smothered in butter and treacle.

'We might do well with them,' observed Nick, meaning the piglets.

'Aye, we might,' drawled Patrick, imitating Nick's accent and winking at Karen.

These had been good years for them since the war, she reflected. They were making a modest living and the children were growing up strong and healthy. Nick still helped out on the farm, rarely leaving it. She glanced at him, wondering whether to broach the subject of wages with him once again. She no longer took board money from him but he refused any payment for his work, saying his small pension was enough for him. After a moment's thought, she decided to wait. She would ask Patrick to try.

All in all things were working out well, thought Karen as she looked round the table. Patrick, though brought up in the country, was not what anyone would call a handyman. His mind was often on other things, he didn't seem to notice when small repairs needed doing around the place.

Nick, despite his handicap, was more practical; he would suggest repairs and improvements when he saw the need for them.

Karen counted her blessings, thinking of the news from Morton Main, contained in her last letter from Kezia a few weeks before. That had been a very different story. The post-war boom in coal production was waning, the outlook was unsure. Young Luke would soon reach his thirteenth birthday and would leave school to join his father at the pit.

Kezia's tone had been defensive as she wrote this last. The extra money was needed at home and Luke would reach the standard and pass the examination so he could leave school, Karen thought about it with sadness. Luke was a bright boy. In another world he would have gone to university perhaps but here he would sit the exam which would allow him to leave school, the one which showed he could read and write and do arithmetic and didn't need any more schooling.

'Something wrong?' Patrick said softly as he noticed the faraway expression on her face.

'No, no.' Karen smiled intimately at him, her brown eyes tender. 'I was just thinking how lucky we are.'

For a moment they shared the precious communion of minds while the children laughed and talked to Nick in the background. They were brought rudely back to the present by a loud knocking on the door. They hadn't heard a cart or trap coming into the yard. Who could it be?

'I'll go.' Brian jumped up, excitement lighting his eyes. He loved visitors, they were usually people of the dale and he knew them all.

Karen rose too, pleasantly anticipating a chat with a neighbour and laughing at the boy as he rushed through to the scullery. She followed him leisurely, glad that there was new baking to offer whoever it was. Brian stood on tiptoe to reach the latch and she let him stretch to do it himself. But when the door swung open at last his excited words of greeting were cut short. These visitors were strangers. Brian backed away shyly to his mother's skirts and stood there, peeping round her. Karen stared in sudden shock. Unable to speak for a moment, she held on to the door with one hand while with the other she pulled Brian close in to her protectively.

'Is Patrick Murphy at home?'

The question was bald, unaccompanied by a greeting. The speaker was the priest who had come to the farm a couple of years earlier, the friend of Robert Richardson's. Sean, that was his name. He was with another priest, a stranger to Karen, but she had not forgotten Sean. She gazed past him at a man and woman in their early sixties, an ordinary enough looking couple but it was the man's face which filled Karen with foreboding. She knew this was Patrick's father. It could be no one else, the likeness was so striking. Though shorter than Patrick and careworn, he had the same black-fringed grey eyes, the same build and bone structure.

Mother and child stared at the visitors, unmoving. Brian, ever sensitive to his mother's feelings, stood up as straight as he could and reached for her hand to comfort her. He looked up at her for guidance on what to do.

The woman looked hard at the boy out of blue

387

eyes which registered no sort of greeting.

'Mother.'

Patrick loomed in the doorway behind Karen, his eyes on the woman. He came past his wife and embraced the plump little woman who promptly burst into tears and threw her arms around him. And Karen started forward as though to hold him and then stopped herself.

'Patrick. Oh, Patrick,' said the woman, her voice fraught with emotion.

'Come away in now, Mother,' he said gently. His arm was still around her but his eyes were on his father. He led the way into the kitchen and Sean and the other priest followed without a glance at Karen or the boy. She wanted to shout at them to stop. No, they couldn't come into her house, her life . . .

Jennie was sitting on Nick's knee, giggling as she tried to stuff bread and treacle into his mouth. Treacle was smeared over her face and hands and all down her pinafore and Nick's chin. He glanced up, laughing, but one look at the visitors made him hurriedly stand up.

'Here's the bairn, Karen,' he muttered, and handed the child to her mother, backing away out of the door, murmuring something about getting back to work.

'Karen, these are my parents. And Father Donelly you know of course,' Patrick said stiffly while Jennie set up a screaming protest at the departure of her beloved Nick.

'Mother, Father, my wife, Karen.'

She acknowledged the introduction with a nod of the head and a 'How do you do?' The priest and Mr Murphy glanced at her and away again, their

388

reply inaudible. Mrs Murphy looked straight through her.

'Take the children into the front room, Karen.'

Patrick saw her stricken face and attempted protest but he ignored it. She wanted to hear everything, felt her life depended on it. How could he dismiss her like this? Her face burned.

'It's all right now, don't take on so.'

His tone was reassuring. 'We can't hear ourselves speak now, can we? Not with Jennie's carrying on so.' Comforted only a little, she held the crying Jennie against one hip and took hold of Brian's hand. Silently she left the room. Jennie protested loudly and struggled to get down from her mother's restricting arms, succeeding eventually as Karen closed the door of the front room after them.

She stared out of the window at the rolling moor, beautiful in the sunlight. The children stood solemnly beside her, Jennie quiet now as though sensing her deep foreboding and disturbed by it. They clung to her skirts with only an occasional sniff from Jennie. Those people in the kitchen were the children's grandparents, she thought dully. She ought to be offering them hospitality, showing off the children to them. They should be proud of such fine, healthy bairns. But they had hardly glanced at Brian or Jennie, had ignored them. And the woman had looked at Karen as though she was the Whore of Babylon. She smarted under the implied insult, felt sullied and dirty.

Voices came from the kitchen. She could hear them but not what they were saying. Suddenly she could stand it no more. She wasn't going to wait

389

here like some servant waiting to be called into the presence of the mistress. She snatched up Jennie and turned to the front door.

'Come on, Brian, we'll go for a walk. Let's go down to the ghyllie and see if we can find some wild flowers. We'll pick a big bunch, shall we? Then we can put them in a vase on the table.'

Wrenching open the rarely used front door, she strode off down the garden path and out on to the lonnen which led to the fold in the fell which hid the little wooded ghyll and its sparkling burn. Brian's face cleared as he trotted after her. A cool breeze had sprung up, buffeting them as they walked along and bringing roses to their cheeks, but as they came to the shelter of the little valley the sun was warm on their heads once again.

Spring flowers bloomed in profusion and the children soon recovered their spirits, laughing and playing among the bushes and bringing wild flowers to Karen to show what they had found. She exclaimed over celandines and wood violets, dandelions and daisies. But her mind was really far away and her actions mechanical. She sat down on an outcrop of limestone, watching them play, and her smile slipped a little.

'Mam, who are those people, Mam?'

Brian was standing before her, anxiously twisting the flowers in his hands. He always sensed when she was unhappy and he felt his own little world threatened. She gazed at his small, solemn face and chided herself for letting her distress show. Forcing herself to smile, she hugged him to her. But what could she say? 'It was your grandmother and grandfather?' How could she tell the children that their grandparents didn't want to know them,

390

didn't even acknowledge them?

'People your daddy knows, that's all. Nobody important.'

She heard the words as though they were said by someone else, not herself. 'Nobody important,' she repeated and knew it was true. They were not important to her, that couple, and neither was Sean, Patrick's one-time friend, not unless they all changed their attitude. Only her little family was important and if outsiders, even grandparents, thought they could separate them, then they would find they had a fight on their hands.

All at once she stood up, a new look of determination on her face. Brushing down her skirts and pushing back escaped tendrils of hair into their restraining pin in a characteristic gesture, she scooped up Jennie once more.

'Howay, pet, we're going home now.' She smiled at Brian's upturned gaze. 'Home to see Daddy and Nick. And you can feed the little pigs, Brian, would you like that?' His face cleared and he broke into a trot to keep up with her purposeful stride.

'Piggies,' cried Jennie in delight. She had forgotten the piggies and now remembered them, rosy face alight. She clutched her bedraggled flowers to her.

'Pretty, Mam?' She looked doubtfully at the crumpled blooms.

'Pretty flowers, yes. We'll put them in a vase, pet,' Karen agreed. 'We'll put them on the table when we have our tea, won't that be nice?' Jennie was satisfied and skipped along beside her mother.

As they walked into the garden Karen hesitated for a moment only. Should she slip in the front?

No, she decided, she would walk round to the back of the house and confront them. This was her home and they were not going to make her feel an interloper in her own house, of that she was determined.

The unmistakable smell of burning bread was the first thing to greet her as she opened the scullery door. Good Lord, she had forgotten all about the bread! Housewifely instincts to the fore, she rushed through to the kitchen, hardly noticing the group at the table, but they looked up and their talk stilled as she entered. Dumping Jennie in Patrick's lap, she rushed over to the oven and reached for a cloth from the rail.

'Couldn't you smell the bread burning?' she said sharply to him, her tightly strung nerves making her vent her frustration. Then her headlong rush came to an abrupt halt. The bread had been taken out of the oven and ranged on the fender. The crusts were burnt, it was true, but most of the bread was salvageable. She stared at it intently, trying to collect herself before turning to face them, feeling rather foolish.

'Daddy! Mammy says I can feed the piggies.' Brian's voice sounded excited and happy as he pulled at Patrick's hand. Jennie was gurgling as she held out her flowers for his inspection. They sounded so normal that Karen found the courage to turn.

The older couple were staring at this picture of the young father with his children, their expressions mixed. Patrick himself was momentarily absorbed by them, love and pride shining from his eyes as he talked to them about the piglets. Karen's heart lightened as though a great weight had been lifted from it. Surely he would never leave them? She dragged her gaze away and forced herself to look at his parents.

'Won't you stay and have some tea?' she heard herself saying, though she could hardly believe her ears.

Patrick's mother stared at her with no attempt to conceal her hostility.

'I took out the bread,' she said, and looked pointedly at the burnt crusts of the loaves on the fender. On top of everything else, Karen immediately felt like a careless housewife though she told herself she was being stupid. She looked at Patrick who seemed uncomfortable. He bent over Jennie to cover up his embarrassment. Sean glanced at the children and stood up, his face unsmiling.

'We'd better be on our way, I think.'

Patrick looked at his father and mother, appealing for understanding. 'Have some tea at least.'

The older man took a step towards his son and grandchildren but was brought up short by his wife's unrelenting voice.

'Michael.'

A stubborn look came into Mr Murphy's eyes.

'We will stay and have some tea,' he said. 'This is my son's house and we will behave in it with decency.' Surprisingly his wife didn't argue and even the priests sat down again. Karen mashed the tea from the kettle singing on the hob and buttered scones from the morning's baking. They sat silently as she poured out tea and handed round the plate of scones.

'You talk funny, just like my daddy,' said Brian.

'Do you want to come and see our piglets?' He was standing by his grandfather's chair, looking up at him earnestly.

'Brian—' Karen began, but she was interrupted.

'I would that,' Mr Murphy said emphatically, ignoring his wife's fierce frown. He drained his cup and took Brian's hand.

'You'll have to show me the way now.'

'I'm coming, I'm coming,' shouted Jennie, and Mr Murphy held out a hand to her too and all three went out into the farmyard, watched by everyone else in the room. Then Mrs Murphy looked down at Patrick's hands significantly.

'Will you just look at your hands, Patrick,' she said mournfully, causing Karen and the priests to look at them too. Patrick quickly put them down on his lap but not before Karen saw how work-stained and calloused they were, something she hadn't really noticed for a long time. That, after all, was how men's hands always got if they were farmers. Certainly they were not the well-cared for hands which she remembered from their first meeting. Even the long fingers were scarred and stained, with one or two of the nails broken down to the quick.

'There's nothing the matter with my hands, Mother,' he said defensively.

'They were so nice, it's a terrible shame. Olive oil and sugar, that's what you want on them,' Mrs Murphy said. She was talking across Karen as though she wasn't there.

Karen couldn't help a small smile. Olive oil and sugar had been Gran's favourite recipe for softening and cleaning her hands.

Now she realized, as she watched Patrick's

mother, that there were a lot of similarities between Gran and Mrs Murphy. They were the same type of woman, country bred and worn by a lifetime of work. Karen began to feel a little softer towards Mrs Murphy. After all she had had her dreams of Patrick as a priest shattered, it must have been an awful shock to her.

'Have another scone, Mrs Murphy,' she said, holding out the plate. Mrs Murphy ignored her.

'It's time we were going,' she said to Patrick. 'I can't talk to you any longer, I'm so upset. Will you be calling your father?'

'But he won't be . . .'

'I have to get back in any case,' the older priest said quietly and his words were echoed by Sean.

'Yes, of course, Father.' Patrick looked at the priest in understanding. He had seemed uncomfortable for most of the visit, unlike Sean who had been as unbending as ever. But his colleague had said very little, and would obviously be glad to get away from this awkward situation. No doubt he thought he had done his duty in bringing the old couple up to see their errant son.

'Will I see you again, Mother?' asked Patrick as the party prepared to leave.

'If it be the will of God,' she answered. 'We're not getting any younger, and with James in London and you here we've only Daniel to comfort us in our old age.'

'Brigid, come away now.' Mr Murphy stepped forward and took her arm to lead her out of the door. Patrick followed them and kissed them both. His mother clung to him suddenly, all her fire gone now. She began to cry, tears running unchecked down her face.

'Mother, Mother,' said Patrick, his own voice breaking.

'Come away now,' Mr Murphy repeated, putting an arm around his wife's shoulders and they went out to the trap.

Sean paused in the doorway before he followed them.

'Goodbye, Patrick,' he said, and somehow there was a finality in his tone.

Karen and Patrick stood shoulder to shoulder as the party climbed into the trap and Sean clucked the pony into motion. The leave-taking over, they went out of the gate and past the rowan tree which was showing signs of the bursting buds of spring blossom. Mr Murphy turned and waved. Patrick and Brian waved back. Then away went the trap down the lane and on to the road to Stanhope. They followed it with their eyes until it was out of sight and Karen looked up at Patrick anxiously. She had heard the emotion in his voice as he said his goodbyes to his mother and felt as though a lump of lead was in her own throat, but the expression on Patrick's face was enigmatic.

Karen suddenly realized how stiffly tense she was as her neck began to ache unbearably. Forcing herself to relax she went into the house, not daring to look at Patrick in case she saw signs of regret on his face. He glanced quickly after her and went into the barn. For the next few hours he worked furiously at fetching manure for the vegetable garden and spreading it over the ground which was at last beginning to dry out after the long winter. He worked on and on at various tasks until well after dark, coming in late for supper, white-faced and exhausted. He looked around the kitchen.

'Where are the children?'

'I fed them early and put them to bed, they were both tired. And I thought we could talk.'

'Oh.'

Patrick looked meaningfully at Nick who was sitting at the table, indicating this was no time for a private discussion. Indeed, Patrick's face had a shuttered look which did not invite conversation anyway.

Nick offered a few comments on the work that was needed on the roof of the barn but soon went off to bed himself, feeling the strained atmosphere. He knew that the visitors had upset Karen and was troubled by it.

She sat quietly for a while, not knowing how to broach the subject of his parents' visit, wanting to know what had been said while she was out, whether there had been an argument, whether Patrick had been swayed in his resolve by the appearance of his parents. But she couldn't ask, she couldn't. He ate his supper in silence, seemingly lost in his own thoughts and not aware of her anxiety.

'Patrick.'

At last she gathered enough strength of mind to look him in the face and speak of it.

'Leave it.'

'I can't leave it.'

Patrick looked up and saw the resolution on her face. She was not going to be put off, not until she knew where she stood. He pushed back his chair and brushed past her to the back door where he turned the key in the lock.

'Patrick, I must know.'

'Leave it, I said.' His brow was thunderous but

397

she could take little heed of the warning. As she opened her mouth in repeated protests he left the kitchen.

I'm off to bed,' he called over his shoulder.

Karen was left with her unanswered questions still on her lips.

Mechanically she cleared the table and laid it for breakfast, taking the plates into the scullery and sluicing them in cold water from the bucket into the pig pail. She banked the fire and turned back the clippie mat. Then she sat down in the rocking chair and did her best to bring her emotions under control, willing her heart beat to slow down. At last she extinguished the lamp and took a candle to light her way upstairs.

Would she never be able to feel secure? she wondered. The day had begun so well, on a pinnacle of happiness, but it seemed that every time she was happy something came along to knock her down.

*   *   *

Next morning Patrick was withdrawn and quiet. Soon after breakfast he went into the yard and saddled Polly, riding out without saying where he was going and leaving the yard work to Nick and Karen. He had not asked for a packed meal so Karen assumed he would be back at mid-day. She was still too unsure of herself to ask his plans and watched him go in silence. He hadn't even said goodbye, she thought miserably.

He couldn't be going on the fell because he hadn't taken Flossie so maybe he was going to Wolsingham. The place was beginning to assume frightening proportions to her. Wolsingham was where the Catholic Church was, the priests and the nuns . . .

Karen got through the day, going from one job to another. She fed the hens and collected the eggs. She helped Nick with the sheep and lambs in the home fold. She comforted Flossie, in despair at being left behind by Patrick. But her actions were mechanical, her mind on Patrick, waiting minute by minute for him to come home. Her agony of mind was a physical pain in the pit of her stomach.

The day was again fine and warm with signs of new life all around her, from the young green grass in the pasture to Jess's wobbly filly, born a few days earlier. The fine weather meant the children could play outside while she worked, Brian watching his sister for her. They chattered quietly and Karen watched and listened absently. The time went slowly, unbearably so, yet the sick feeling in her stomach intensified when she realized it was already teatime and there was no sign of Patrick.

Sensitive as usual to her mood, Nick watched her anxiously. His facial tic returned as an outward sign of his disturbance though he said nothing.

It was half-past six when the clip-clop of hooves was heard in the yard. Karen was bathing the children in the tin bath before the fire in the kitchen, for the evenings were still chilly. Her hands stayed as she caught the first faint sound of the horse coming through the gate and she gazed up at the doorway to the scullery though Patrick, if it were indeed him, couldn't possibly get there yet.

A moment later he was there.

'Supper won't be long,' she said to him. 'I

daresay you're famished. It's been a long day, especially if you didn't have anything when you were out.' She had decided she would not mention the visit again, not unless he brought it up first.

Patrick began taking off his outdoor things. 'Yes, I am hungry,' was all he said.

'Sit down, Brian, wait until I'm ready for you,' Karen admonished, and he sat back with a splash which wet the clippie mat.

'Come on, son.' Patrick came over to the fireside and took down the towel hanging on the rail. 'I'll dry you, eh?' He lifted the boy out of the bath and methodically dried and dressed him in his nightshirt. Sitting in the chair opposite Karen, he caught her eye and they smiled in mutual understanding and support.

Together they fed the children and took them up to bed, settling them before coming down to their own supper of home-fed ham and pickles bottled by Karen the previous autumn. She mashed the tea and called in Nick for his supper as though it was just like any other evening in their busy lives. Nick ate heartily, his nervous twitch disappearing for the tension in the house was gone. As soon as he was finished he went back to the home pasture where he was keeping an eye on the lambing. Tactfully, he did not reappear until bedtime.

'I'll fix the roof of the barn tomorrow,' Patrick said as he sat down in his chair before the fire.

'Yes,' Karen replied, and began to clear away the supper things. 'It's time it was done.'

'Well, I'll do it tomorrow.'

'Good,' she said and took the dirty dishes into the scullery. She hummed happily to herself as she worked. Patrick had volunteered no information as to where he had been all day and she didn't ask him. It was enough for her that he was back.

Chapter Twenty-Seven

'Another grand day,' said Karen as she laid the table for breakfast. 'If we don't get some rain soon the hay crop will be short.' She looked out of the window at a cloudless sky. The sun shone warmly and only a slight breeze was blowing down the valley.

'No point in worrying about that, is there?' Patrick answered. 'I think I'll go up to the moss, cut some peat today. I'm not needed at the kilns.'

'A good idea. It's good, hot fuel for the baking, and less coal to haul from the depot at Stanhope.'

Patrick was soon striding over the fell, his peat cutter over his shoulder and his long legs eating up the distance. Once there, he cut peat steadily and put it to dry out in the summer sun. The job reminded him of his home in County Clare, though here on the high moor the peat layer was somewhat thicker than he had known in Ireland. Still, the work was familiar, pleasantly so. He remembered going out with his father and doing just this same work. Every half hour or so he would pause and wipe his brow and lean on his cutter, gazing round at the heather-covered moor with the tiny patches of green around the smallholdings. Even the limestone was similar to the rock he remembered in Clare, he mused.

As the sun climbed to its highest point in the sky he dropped his peat cutter and went over to a limestone outcrop where he had left his jacket and 'bait', as Karen called it. He smiled softly as he thought of it, how he had teased her about it.

'I'm not a fish,' he had laughed. 'Bait is for fish, isn't it?'

Karen had bridled. 'In Durham, it's sandwiches for your dinner.'

Opening the battered tin box, Patrick sat down on a flat piece of stone and started to eat the cheese and home-made pickle sandwiches she had made for him, relishing the food after the hard work and the feeling of ease in his legs as he stretched them out before him. His thoughts wandered back to his childhood at home as had happened so often since his parents' visit.

'Cill Inine Baoith.' He said the old Irish name for his birthplace aloud, and sighed as he felt a sudden longing to see the old place again. To walk up the narrow track away from the village to his father's tiny farm, to step through the door and be met by the smell of new soda bread baking on the griddle, or even the all-pervasive smell of paraffin oil from the lamp hanging down from the rafters. And to see his father sitting by the side of the fire with his pipe smoke drifting up the chimney, and Daniel, his brother, and the friends from his younger days . . .

Patrick rose to his feet abruptly and went back to the laborious cutting and stacking of the peat. He couldn't go back, how could he? He must be the scandal of the place. They wouldn't have stopped talking about his defection even now. That was if his mother hadn't managed to keep it a dark, shameful secret. He worked on until a crick in his back made it imperative that he straighten and

402

lean backwards to ease it. He looked out over the high moor, as Karen called it, but somehow the day seemed not so bright as it had done earlier. It was overshadowed even though there was not a cloud in the sky.

*   *   *

Patrick was still up on the moor when a letter arrived from Morton Main. From Kezia, Karen saw by the handwriting, and was pleased. There had been no letter for a month and she'd been beginning to be concerned about it. Nick was having his mid-morning break and the children were with him so she took the letter out into the sunshine and sat down under the rowan tree, her back supported by the trunk.

The miners were locked out, Kezia said. Well, of course, Karen knew that. They had been locked out since May when they'd refused to agree to new terms in an attempt to protect the wages and conditions which had been hard won in the war. And which the mine owners were now determined to change back to what they were in pre-war days. Kezia and her family were in dire straits, as were the rest of the mining community.

You know I wouldn't ask, but if you could take the children, Karen, just until things get better? Little Meg isn't very strong and then there's Tommy. He was on the slag heap with Young Luke and a few of their friends. They were gleaning bits of coal for the fire—the coal house is bare by now. An official saw the bairns and chased them off. God knows why,

403

it's only waste, rubbishy stuff on the tip anyroad. Well, the bairns scattered, and Luke and Tommy ran back over the old tip. You know they've been told not to go near it, there's been a fire smouldering away under the surface for years . . .

'Dear God,' breathed Karen, almost fearing to read on. In her imagination she could see the old tip with some of the stones burnt red and sometimes tiny puffs of smoke coming from holes in the ground. Shaking her head to rid herself of the image of a little boy falling through to what would seem like the flames of Hell, she forced herself to continue.

Anyroad, Tommy went through the crust with one leg. He was lucky Luke was nearby to pull him out, but as it is he's got some nasty burns. Doctor Richardson treated his leg. I'm telling you, that man's an angel, Karen, he was so good with the bairn. But Tommy does need building up and I thought of you and the farm. At least he'd get a fresh egg there sometimes.

Of course Kezia knew she could rely on Karen, there was hardly any need to ask. In times like these any relations who were in a position to help were expected to do so to the limits of their ability. It had been so for generations. Karen didn't even consider waiting to ask Patrick but immediately sent a letter back to Kezia, walking up to the box on the main road to post it.

When Patrick came in that evening, she showed him Kezia's letter.

404

'I sent a reply off this morning, telling her to send the bairns.'

'But Karen—' Patrick started to protest, to say that they were having enough trouble seeing to their own while trying to save a bit for the bad times. But he stopped as Karen lifted a determined face to him. For the first time, she looked hard at him, as though he were a stranger.

'What?'

'Nothing, we'll manage,' he answered, backing down as he so often did nowadays. Perhaps he could get some extra work, helping on one of the larger farms nearer to Stanhope?

'If we're hard up, maybe I could get part-time nursing,' she said.

'No!' said Patrick. 'You have the children to see to, that's your work. And if there are Kezia's little ones—'

'Nick will be glad to help with the bairns.'

Patrick strode over to where she was standing and grabbed her by the upper arms. 'I said no,' he said quietly. 'And, by God, I meant it.'

Karen looked up at him and opened her mouth to protest but something in his gaze stopped her. They looked at one another for a few minutes then Patrick dropped his hands and she turned away to see to the stew cooking on the fire.

*　　　*　　　*

Karen's heart ached when she saw Kezia's children descend from the train at Stanhope. Patrick and she had driven down with the trap to meet them.

Luke got down first then helped the youngest, Meg, on to the platform. She was a little stick of a girl with bent legs denoting rickets. Tommy at ten was more sturdy. The vital years of his growth had been during the war when the miners were in work, but he climbed down painfully and Karen's heart felt full when she saw his bandaged leg. Tommy had the soft intelligent eyes of his grandmother and aunt and smiled excitedly at Karen despite his injury, for he thought it a great adventure to be going to live on a farm. Young Luke took hold of Meg's hand and with Tommy limping beside them they came to meet Karen.

'Hallo, there,' cried Patrick, for he could see how overcome Karen was and jumped in to cover up. 'Now won't you all be having a fine time taking a holiday on the farm with your Uncle Patrick and Auntie Karen and your cousins?'

He lifted them up to the bench seat on the trap without waiting for an answer, then swung their box up between their feet. Even Luke's tired eyes glowed with excitement, though only for a minute. Patrick walked the pony up the hill from the station. Tommy was looking round, interested in everything he saw, but Luke had a closed expression on his face. He sat holding on to Meg and staring straight ahead.

He had not wanted to come. He felt himself almost a working man and big enough to show solidarity with his father and grandfather in their struggle with the mine owners.

'You must go. You can help on the farm and maybe even get some outside work,' his mother had exhorted him as she packed the box. 'And you can see to Tommy and Meg, make sure they are not a nuisance to your Auntie Karen and Uncle Patrick.'

So now they were in Weardale, going up the fell with Patrick driving the trap and Brian sitting beside them, tongue-tied in the presence of these older cousins. The ride itself was a novelty for them. Karen watched them eyeing Polly. The only ponies they saw nowadays were the old ones from the pit when they were brought to bank, too old to work, she thought, remembering how she had loved to see them when she was small and had saved a crust from her tea to hold out with trembling fingers, just in case the large teeth nipped. But they were always gentle, stretching their necks forward to take the bread delicately in soft, slobbery lips. They were blind at first in the sunlight, then drunk with the freedom of galloping around the field behind the slag heap. How she had loved to see the sturdy little pit ponies enjoying the light and air and fresh grass.

That was how the children were at first, quiet except for Meg weeping for home and her mother. She clung to Luke who tried roughly to comfort her. In the beginning she would not take any comfort from Karen at all, resenting her for not being her mother, but gradually her hostility lessened. After a few days they roamed about the moor, free and wild and delighting in the space and pure air, even Tommy, whose leg was healing fast now.

'Do you want to see the fairy caves?' asked Brian one day. He had already shown them the hidden ghyllie with its myriad delights and desperately wanted to impress them further.

'Fairy caves?' Luke scoffed at the very idea, but he was grinning indulgently. 'Oh, go on then.'

So Brian took them to the caves under a

limestone outcrop and showed them where the little people feasted and danced as they had done ever since humankind came to these hills.

'Where are they then, the little people?' asked Tommy, looking round. 'I don't see any fairies.'

'We're not supposed to see them,' Brian hastened to inform him. 'If they think we've seen them they'll take us away to live with them and we won't see Mammy again. That's why we can't go inside.'

Luke laughed, bringing sudden doubt about the tale to Brian.

'It's true, it's true,' he insisted stubbornly, despite his doubts. He had never doubted the story before, had learned it from the children in Sunday School and they told it as fact not fiction.

'You'll find out when you go to Sunday School,' he said to Luke. 'Then you'll know.'

But Luke only laughed again and turned away.

However, Meg and Tommy were thrilled by the story though it was scary. Meg kept her eyes shut firmly when they were near the caves and clung to Luke's hand. Even Tommy kept his eyes averted, just in case, though he professed not to believe it when he saw that his brother did not.

Luke helped with the hay-making, showing himself to be a willing and adaptable worker even at his age for he was quick to learn and steady. The hay crop was ready by the middle of July which was something of a record for the dale, but because of the drought it was scanty. It was lovely green hay which went further than usual, however, so they were satisfied.

So the long days were occupied from dawn to dusk with Patrick rising at three o'clock to cut hay or dry peat or do the hundred and one jobs which needed the strength of a man and one with two hands. He had got a job as well and had to go off every weekday with Polly and the cart, transporting stones for the council and working on the roads which criss-crossed the fells.

This work was available now as the council improved communications in the dales by having the roads made up. Patrick took advantage of the presence of Luke to earn outside cash but the hard work and long hours took their toll. He began to look fine drawn and pale under his tan, coming in exhausted in the evenings to fall asleep over supper.

Karen worried about him incessantly, he was so quiet. His hands bore new callouses from working with the stone and he was developing a slight stoop as though he had trouble with his back. But when she asked about it he denied it. When she went to the Co-operative Store in Stanhope for the groceries, she drew twelve and sixpence from her dividend book and bought him a good, wide leather belt. She offered it to him the next morning, and he put it on without comment.

Eventually as the moors were once more clothed in their cloak of purple heather the burden of farmwork eased. The children were fit and brown and even Meg's little legs seemed straighter since she had been having a regular supply of good, fresh milk.

The miners had to capitulate in July and go back to work for less money. Eventually a letter arrived from Kezia asking for Luke to return home. Tommy and Meg were to stay until the end of August: 'Just until we get back on our feet'.

Luke hated going back, notwithstanding his reluctance to come to the farm in the first place, for he had grown to love the dale.

Karen watched him sympathetically as she took him down to the station at Stanhope. He sat quietly in the trap, face averted, while the other children, who were only there for the ride, laughed and chatted, happy to be having the outing.

'Be careful with the eggs, Luke,' Karen said gently to him as she handed over a covered basket containing butter as well. Luke took it wordlessly, unable to speak in case he broke down and spoilt his manly facade.

When he climbed on the train Meg realized he was actually going without her and set up a loud wailing so that Karen had to catch her up and hold her.

'Hush love, there's a pet,' Karen rocked the little girl to her, whereupon Jennie lifted her arms and joined in the crying, jealous of Meg. It was in this pandemonium that the train pulled out of the station, Luke's set face retreating from the little group.

Karen couldn't stop herself from thinking about him. He was destined for the pit, just as most of the men in her family had been, generation following generation. But Luke had loved the outdoor life, just as his great-grandmother had done. He'd loved the high moor. But it was no good thinking about that.

Driving back to the farm in the brilliant morning sunshine, Karen felt her spirits lift in tune with the buzz of the bees busy in the heather and the butterflies fluttering above it. High overhead a curlew called and the children called back. They

410

had recovered their high spirits and even Meg began to smile as Low Rigg Farm came into view in the fold in the track, the rowan tree in all its summer glory standing sentinel at the gate.

'Home again,' said Karen, and lifted Jennie and Meg down from the trap. But Tommy jumped and Brian followed suit, not to be beaten. Meg grinned proudly at him as he kept his balance on the cobbles. Nick poked his head round the barn door, wiping his hand on his sacking apron.

'Nick! Nick!' Jennie was as delighted to see him as usual. She still loved him with an uncritical devotion. There was no Patrick though, he was working on the roads. Sighing, Karen turned into the scullery and lit the fire under the copper. She had filled it before she went out for the washing was to start. There was plenty of work to occupy her mind.

*   *   *

At the end of August Karen decided she would take Tommy and Meg back to Morton Main herself so that she could see Da and Kezia and assure herself that they were all right. There had been no further letter from Kezia since the brief note saying Luke had arrived home safely and Karen found her thoughts returning to them all the time.

Accordingly she baked pies the day before and left them for Patrick and Nick to eat cold. The four children went with her, happy and excited and quite unnaturally clean. Patrick drove them to the station.

'We'll be back by nine.' She smiled up into his

411

eyes but knew better than to expect a kiss such as he gave the children. She would have liked some sign of affection but knew him well enough now to understand that outward displays embarrassed him, the more so as they grew older. So, contenting herself with the smile, she took the basket of farm eggs and butter in one hand and lifted Jennie with the other.

Was it her imagination, she wondered wistfully, or was Patrick growing away from her? But that was a thought she couldn't bear so she turned to the children. They were clambering eagerly on to the seats in the carriage and waving to Patrick in great excitement while Karen settled down in a corner with Jennie on her knee. There was quite a difficult time ahead with a change of train at Bishop Auckland but there was a bus nowadays which ran from Morton village to Morton Main, making the last part of the journey easier, for which she was thankful.

The day was very warm and the children were hot and tired by the time they got to the village. The heat shimmered by the roadside where tar had run, sticky and black. Karen got down from the bus at the Chapel stop and stood Jennie on her feet while she helped Meg and Brian. And then Kezia was there, laughing and crying and hugging her children to her. Karen stood back and watched the happy reunion.

'Thank you, Karen,' Kezia said simply, looking at her sister. It was all she said but it was enough. Karen knew all rifts were healed. They walked together down the row with the children all talking at once, interrupting each other as they told of the wonders of life on the farm.

'Da's finished at the pit,' Kezia said quietly, bitterly. 'They reckoned he was one of the ring leaders, a trouble maker.'

Karen stopped walking for a moment in shock at this description of Da, that stern law-abiding man. How humiliated he must be.

'He'll have to get out of the house, of course. He can come in with us for now, then maybe he will be able to rent a cottage over at Morton.'

Of course, Karen thought, the house belonged to the colliery.

'Can you manage?' She gazed at Kezia anxiously. She could have Da at Low Rigg Farm but at sixty-three years old he wouldn't want to move far from his beloved Chapel.

'He'll be all right.'

Kezia saw the uncertainty on Karen's face and understood.

'He's better here. Da was never one for the dale, that was Mam. Anyway, he'll get his pension in a few years.'

'Not till he's seventy,' Karen reminded her. A few years can be a long time, she thought as they all went into Kezia's kitchen. Da was sitting by the range, quietly staring at the fire. He seemed shrunken somehow, not himself at all, and Karen felt her heart drop at the sight of him. But his smile was warm enough, especially when he saw little Meg and Tommy. Brian hung back. He hardly knew his grandfather, Karen realized guiltily.

'How are you, lass? And that man of yours?' Da kissed her gravely on the cheek and surveyed her closely.

'We're fine, Da. Patrick an' all.'

He seemed satisfied with what he saw for he turned his attention to her children.

'By, she's a bonny lass you've got there, mind. And the lad's growing fast, isn't he? Howay then, Brian, let's have a look at you.' Da became hearty when he spoke to the children. He'd changed a lot, thought Karen, losing his job had diminished him. And of course he would still be feeling Mam's death . . . A lump grew in Karen's throat and threatened to choke her. To cover up she talked to him in a straightforward manner, helping him in his pretence that there was nothing wrong, and after a while the urge to cry receded and the emotional moment passed. The lunch was of salad culled from the allotment accompanied by Kezia's new bread and some of the farm butter. The children ate heartily, made hungry by their early start.

'Howay then, troops. We'll away and see what's on offer at the shop,' said Da when the meal was finished, and to whoops of joy he took the children up the street to Lizzie's, the corner shop, and spent some of his precious pennies on sherbet dabs and black bullets. Soon even Brian and Jennie were competing for his attention, completely won over.

'Granda, Granda, look at me, me!'

'No, me!'

Their loud cries rang down the row intermingled with the gruff tones of Da. Karen marvelled at the difference between the relaxed, smiling man he was with her children and the stern father she had known as a child. The children were working their magic and taking his mind off his troubles, at least that was something.

The afternoon flew by with 'Do you remembers' and up to date news of the village, and soon it was time to wash hands and faces for the return home. Jennie and Brian protested loudly but to no avail. The train back to Stanhope had to be caught at Bishop Auckland so they must adhere to a time-table.

Karen's heart was lighter. Despite the poverty of the community the people were cheerfully indomitable and she felt as one with them. Kezia and Father, Tommy and Meg, came to the bus stop with them to set them off on the early-evening bus.

In the little town, Karen carried the sound asleep Jennie to the station with Brian hanging on to her skirts with one hand while he sucked the thumb of the other. She was tired and her arms ached as she joined the straggle of people climbing the hill leading to the station, thinking only of collapsing into a seat on the train to take the weight off her legs.

It was then that she saw a familiar form in the crowd in front of her and her head jerked back in shock. Her stomach plummeted and turned into a hard, aching knot and her mouth went dry and sour-tasting. She closed her eyes tightly and stood still.

'Mam? Mammy?'

Brian was tugging at her skirt with his face upturned in anxious enquiry. She opened her eyes. There was no sign of him now, the man who was so like . . .

Imagination, that's what it had been. Why should it suddenly play such a trick on her? She hadn't seen him for years. It must have been something to do with being so tired.

The whistle of the train set her off walking rapidly uphill again, with Brian having to trot to keep up with her.

'Mammy!' His protest penetrated at last and she slowed her pace.

'Come on, pet, we'll have to hurry, the train's coming,' she said. Quickly she handed over her ticket and headed for the platform. The train was standing still, with little puffs of steam coming from the engine. Half afraid of what she might see, she gave only a short glance up the platform. Was that him getting in at the other end of the train? No!

Karen bundled Brian into a compartment and followed with Jennie. Looking neither to left nor right she went straight to the first vacant seats. She sat there, not lifting her head until the train arrived at Stanhope. Jennie slept on and Brian leaned against her, tired and quiet and as ever receptive to her moods. Her lovely day had darkened and her mind was filled with formless fears she shrank from naming.

Yet in the end those fears seemed groundless for they had reached Stanhope without seeing anyone she knew. The evening sun brightened and love threatened to spill over as she saw Patrick outside the station, wafting patiently beside Polly. He smiled in mild embarrassment when she kissed him exuberantly, unable to hide her feelings, then he turned to the children to hide that embarrassment.

They drove home past the avenue of limes which cast long shadows as the sun was going down, they passed the old church and went on into open country. As they climbed the fell the heather was deeply purple and splendid, fading into a blue haze on the top of the moor.

Chapter Twenty-Eight

The winter closed in once more. The moor became wild and white, cutting people off from one another, obliterating roads and tracks so only the snow poles standing on the roadside denoted its outline. And yet, even though winter meant the living was hard and every morning there was ice to break on the bucket of water which Nick had brought in the night before, it was still Karen's favourite season, the time when she felt safest. No one from the outside world could get at them.

Work on the roads came to a halt so there was no money coming in and Patrick and Nick spent long hours tramping the low fell, bringing in sheep nearer to home, digging sheep out of drifts, carrying hay to sheep, lifting sheep back on to their feet when they fell over and were unable to regain their footing. Patrick even dreamed about sheep: sheep with foot rot, sheep falling down crags or trapped between outcrops of limestone. The world revolved around sheep. So he was glad of the change when the weather at last allowed some respite and they could spread manure and lime the moorland around the pasture in an attempt to wrest it from the heather.

The short days were hard for Karen too; she had to see to the farmyard stock and the children. But the children were growing up strong and healthy

417

and she was happy.

One Sunday she decided to take them to Sunday School. They hadn't been there for a few weeks because of the snow and both Brian and Jennie liked Sunday School. She sat in the caretaker's tiny kitchen and drank tea while she waited for them, chatting idly with the caretaker's wife who was busy preparing the dinner. It was a pleasant little interlude in the week. The caretaker's cottage adjoined the schoolroom and she could hear the children reciting prayers in unison. Listening hard, she picked out Jennie's piping voice among them.

The children began to sing an old song, 'Jesus Bids Us Shine', and she sang along with them under her breath while the caretaker's wife was busy in the pantry: 'You in your small corner, and I in mine.' She liked that; it expressed just how she felt.

Afterwards they walked home through the slush and snow, and by the time they got back their feet were damp and frozen and their noses and chins were red and stinging in the wind.

'Patrick!'

Karen hurried into the kitchen calling for him as she went to the fire with Jennie who by this time was fractious and crying, for the fire had burned low and needed mending and Patrick usually had a good fire going for them when they got back. But there was no sign of him now and she was puzzled.

She blazed up the fire and warmed milk in a saucepan and still Patrick didn't come in. Leaving Brian and Jennie sipping their milk, she went out into the yard where Nick was just coming out of the stable.

'Have you seen Patrick?' she asked him anxiously.

Nick sniffed and rubbed his nose with the back of his hand.

'He went out just after you did, missus. Said he was going to the village,' he answered. Lately he had taken to being more formal with Karen, calling her 'missus' again, and she wondered if Patrick had been getting on at him as he had when Nick first appeared.

At Karen's frown, he hastened to add, 'Well, there was nothing for him to do, was there, missus?'

'No. I just wondered where he was, that's all. Thank you, Nick.' Karen went back to the children but a tiny nagging question was pushing into her thoughts. Patrick had been quieter than usual these past weeks, perhaps a little withdrawn. Was he unhappy?

When he came home, around two o'clock, she questioned him with her eyes but he offered no explanation as to where he had been. He sat down at the table and she brought his meal from the oven where it had been keeping hot. His manner forebade enquiry and as she bent over the table she caught a strong smell of whisky.

'Oh!' she exclaimed, visibly shaken.

'What is it?' Patrick said coldly. He looked up at her unsmilingly, challenging her to comment.

'Nothing.' Karen collected herself quickly and turned back to the fire. She put a hand up to the brass rail, leaning on it, and gazed into the glowing turves. Deliberately she closed her mind to her suspicions though she didn't even know what it was she suspected, she told herself angrily.

'Good God, woman, do I have to tell you everywhere I go?' demanded Patrick, unappeased.

' "Thou shalt not take the name of the Lord thy God in vain",' quoted Brian primly. He had been learning the Ten Commandments at school.

Patrick exploded. 'Get to bed!' he shouted at the boy, and Brian fled, his lower lip trembling.

'Don't shout at him,' said Karen, turning to face Patrick.

'You're turning him into a bloody little hypocrite,' he snapped. 'He has to learn not to speak to his father like that.'

Jennie was staring at them, her eyes wide and troubled, so Karen bit her tongue and turned back to her contemplation of the fire. And after a while Patrick seemed to regret his outburst for he went upstairs to Brian and brought him down again. The boy's face was tear-stained but he brightened when his father sat with the two children on the settee and told them stories of Ireland. He told them of the merrows, or *morhuads,* which were sometimes to be seen on the wild coast of Clare, and Karen listened too. He spoke so infrequently of the land of his birth.

'The men have green teeth and green hair,' he told them, 'but the women are lovely except that they have the tails of fishes.'

'Mermaids! You mean mermaids,' interjected Brian.

'No, that I don't,' said Patrick. 'I mean merrows, though maybe the English would call them mermaids.'

Karen smiled as she brought out the flour and yeast to make bread while she listened to the story of Jack Dogherty who looked for them and eventually saw one and followed him beneath the waves to the country of the merrows beneath the sea where he fell in love with a lady merrow.

'What's the sea like, Daddy?' asked Brian plaintively. 'I've never seen the sea.'

'Oh, but you will, when you go on the Sunday School trip to Redcar,' put in Karen. And somehow, the mention of Sunday School seemed to mar Patrick's mood again and he stood up abruptly.

'I have work to do,' he said, and went out to the barn.

Jennie started to cry fretfully. She wanted to hear more stories, so Karen told them how they would go to Redcar and see the sea for themselves. And maybe, if they were very lucky, they would see a mermaid.

When the snow barricaded them in again Karen was happier. She felt safe, her fears silly to her now. And Patrick was snow-bound too, he had to stay on the farm. After a while, she forgot about his little outings. She even forgot about the man she'd thought she had seen in Bishop Auckland.

*   *   *

'There's a man in the lane, Mam! He wants to see you, he gave me a penny to run and tell you!'

Brian's eyes were bright and sparkling, he was bursting with the importance of the message he had to give. He clutched his penny tightly in his fist then held it out for her to see.

'A man? Why doesn't he come here then?' Karen's surprised question turned into an admonishment. 'You shouldn't have taken his penny, Brian. I've told you that you must not take money from anyone.'

He was crestfallen. He hadn't thought of that. Not many pennies came his way and when they did he usually had to share them with Jennie.

'But, Mam, he said I was doing him a favour.'

'Why doesn't he come up to the house?' she repeated, mystified.

'I don't know. He said he wanted to see you in the lane. "Tell her it's Dave, he said . . ." ' Brian stopped abruptly, startled by his mother's exclamation.

'Dave? You're sure he said Dave?' In her anxiety and shock she bent down on one knee and took hold of Brian by the arms, speaking harshly and urgently. He began to cry, sure now he had done something wrong. But what? Karen forced herself to moderate her voice, to keep it under control. She was being stupid, there were hundreds of Daves in the world. Loads and loads of Daves, and anyway, her Dave was dead. Someone was playing a game, on and on ran her chaotic thoughts.

'All right, son, you can keep your penny to buy sweets when the travelling shop comes around. As long as you share them with Jennie, mind. Now go and have your tea. Nick's in the kitchen and there's some strawberry jam.'

Brian's face brightened as he saw things were not so bad after all. He skipped into the house to tell Nick and Jennie about the penny.

Karen stood straight, squaring her shoulders and smoothing down her apron, forcing herself to be sensible. Dave was dead, she told herself, hadn't Joe told her he was dead? And Joe wouldn't have told her that if it wasn't true. These last few years had been more settled for her and Patrick; his periods of withdrawal had lessened, he was as any other husband and father. Their coming together in bed had become more relaxed and natural and a source of quiet joy. A sense of fulfilment and security marked her life. She had begun to put on weight and was supremely happy. It was 1924 and they had been married for six years.

Now she looked out through the gate at the lane. All she had to do was walk past the rowan tree and along the track to the bend and she would find all her silly fears were without foundation. She had had a letter from Joe only last month, and if Dave had been alive and there had been a mistake he would have known and warned her. It was someone else. It had to be someone else.

Yet still she stood rooted with dread that somehow Dave was not dead but had come back. The memory of the man she had seen at Bishop Auckland station a couple of years ago came back to her and she shivered.

'Will I go and see who it is, missus?' Karen hadn't heard Nick coming up behind her. He had got the tale from Brian and was gazing at her anxiously. When she was disturbed so was he, even after all these years.

'No, you stay with Brian and Jennie,' Karen decided as she looked back at him. 'It's all right, Nick. Really, I'll be fine. I'll just walk up to the bend.' She put her hand on his arm in reassurance; it wasn't right that he should be disturbed.

'Just watch the bairns for me.'

'Aye, I will. You know I will.'

Karen nodded her thanks and resolutely stepped out of the gate, trying to convey confidence. Nick watched until her slight figure turned round the bend in the track then went in reluctantly to watch the children. At three and a half Jennie was full of mischief and not to be trusted for long on her own. But his instincts were to go with Karen. He was disturbed by some nebulous, unknown threat.

*   *   *

Karen approached the dip in the lane with a thumping heart even while she was telling herself that this must be some other man, for Dave was dead. Dead at Gallipoli as Joe had told her, so how could it be him in the lane? She walked on, her whole being focussed on seeing *the man.* At last she realized she was on the last stretch of the rutted track before the road and it was deserted. She stared down it, sure she must be wilfully not seeing anyone.

Hardly daring to hope, she went to the end and looked up and down the winding moorland road. There was no one there, not a soul, only the faint sound of a motor bike further along. The relief was shattering. It had been her imagination, Brian had mixed up a message, that was all. She almost danced back to the yard, her spirits bubbling.

Just before the gate she stopped abruptly. Someone had given Brian a penny. What was a strange man doing giving the boy a penny? Her forehead puckered as she leaned against the sturdy trunk of the rowan tree. She would make sure he was accompanied in his walks to and from the bus which now ran along the end of the lane. It could have been a neighbour, she thought, someone they knew, though she couldn't bring to mind a Dave living nearby and she knew everyone in the dale. But that must be it, Dave was a common name, perhaps he was visiting someone.

Her brow cleared and she went back into the kitchen smiling, deliberately putting the puzzling incident out of her mind. As she seemed to be doing so often these days. Nick's face lightened when he saw her and he moved to the door to meet her.

'I'll just get on now then, missus,' was all he said, but he stepped out jauntily into the yard.

Karen soon became busy with the evening meal and seeing to the children and didn't mention the episode to Brian who seemed to have forgotten about the man.

Patrick came in and if she seemed unusually quiet he didn't notice. He had been sledding firewood from the plantation of trees further along the fell and was tired for it was hard work hauling over the uneven ground. But it was necessary to prepare for the long winter ahead; they couldn't afford to buy a great deal of coal and there was only so much peat he could cut and dry on the high moor.

'I buried a dead ewe on the fell,' he volunteered, 'liver fluke.'

Karen compressed her lips but said nothing as she placed his plate of stew and dumplings before him. Liver fluke was a problem with the flock, something they had to watch out for.

'The weather's on the turn, there's a coolness in the wind,' he observed.

'Yes, it'll soon be winter again.'

Karen sat down at the table and poured herself a cup of tea. She considered whether to share her

425

fears with him but after all, what were they? Fanciful imaginings. Sighing she went over to the oven and brought over his barley milk pudding which had been keeping warm for him.

Brian and Jennie were sitting close together on the settee reading, or rather Brian was reading a story to Jennie. Karen looked at them with pride. Brian was only five and a good reader already. Both of them looked healthy and happy in their nightclothes, with shiny hair and rosy, plump cheeks.

'Nearly time for bed,' she reminded them.

'I'll just finish this, Mam, can I?' Brian asked as he looked up with pleading dark eyes.

'All right. Then off you go. I'll come up later.'

'Are we going to Stanhope Show on Saturday?'

Karen stared at Patrick, startled. He was smiling at them across the table. It wasn't like him to suggest an outing. Most of the time he was quite reluctant to leave the farm, apart from those times he went off on his own and they were growing fewer as time went on.

'Oh, can we?' she exclaimed, the prospect of a little holiday brightening her eyes and colour suffusing her cheeks. She had become used to taking the children out on her own and it was lovely to think of Patrick coming too. Nick would stay at home, he would be happier here, she thought, and he could see to the stock. Though his nerves were so much better now, he still got worked up in crowds so he would rather stay and keep an eye on the place.

Karen forgot her fears in her pleasure at Patrick's suggestion. She cleared away and prepared for bed in a light-hearted mood.

426

*　　　　*　　　　*

Saturday came cloudy but dry and Karen packed a
picnic and dressed the children in jerseys for there
was a chill wind blowing over the fell. As the trap
took the road leading down into Stanhope,
however, they were more sheltered and the sun
came out, gleaming through the scudding clouds
and promising well for the afternoon.

Brian sat beside his father in the front seat while
Karen and Jennie sat in the back. Jennie laughed
in delight as they rode briskly over the ford with
the water tinkling and gleaming in the sun and
Polly's hooves splashing it up in sparkling sprays.
She leaned out over the side of the trap so that
Karen had to catch hold of her around the waist to
hold her.

'Careful,' she warned. 'You'll get wet. You don't
want to have to go home before we get there, do
you?'

At last they came to the show field and all
climbed down on to the grass. Jennie stood staring
round at all the bustle with her thumb in her
mouth, suddenly shy.

'I'll take the trap over to park,' said Patrick.
'You've got everything now?' Karen nodded.

The family was dressed in their Sunday best,
Karen in a new shorter length cotton dress she had
made for herself from a pattern in *Woman's
Weekly*. It was dark blue with white daisies, cut
straight and with a belt around the hips. She had
got the material in the remnant sale at the Co-op
Store and Jennie's dress was made from the same
material but her skirt was full and gathered and

427

the little girl's plump dimpled knees showed brown and sturdy beneath it. Her jersey was blue too and now Karen took it off and folded it into her basket as the day had grown warm. Jennie suffered her attentions impatiently, eyes round with excitement as she looked at the crowds and tents and animals.

'Give me your jersey, son.'

'Can we see the sheep dog trials, Mam?' Brian asked as he struggled out of his jersey. He had recently acquired a puppy and was sure he could train it to be an absolute miracle worker, much better than his father's Floss.

'If you wait, we'll see everything,' promised Karen.

The show field was crowded with farmers and their families all dressed up for the holiday. Before long, Brian saw a school friend and begged to be allowed to go round with him so Karen arranged a meeting place by the tea-tent.

'Mind, don't get lost. And watch what you're doing,' said Patrick.

Karen and he were interested in the livestock, casting now experienced eyes over the pigs and rams and cattle. They inspected the new machinery, a little wistfully. Maybe they could invest in some one day. And of course there were the produce and flower tents for their critical scrutiny.

'We might be able to afford a motor bike next year, Karen. With a side-car. I've been looking at an Enfield. It would be as useful to us as anything else, living up on the moor. Think of the time I could save. And we could take the children out more often.'

Patrick questioned Karen with his eyes. In

money matters he always deferred to her judgement. She realized he had been thinking about it for a while and gave it her consideration.

'We'll see, eh? If everything goes as well as it has done lately we should be able to afford it. It will be lovely to have days out.' She watched Jennie playing on the grass, her dress already showing less than fresh and a smudge of dirt across her cheek and nose.

'We'll see,' she repeated, and Patrick was satisfied.

'Having a good time, Karen?'

She looked round and saw Mr Bainbridge, her neighbour, with Mrs Bainbridge beside him. They stood for a short while and chatted and soon it was time to eat the picnic they had brought with them. They met Brian and his friend by the tea-tent and bought the children dandelion and burdock pop and tea for themselves and ate their meal on one of the wooden benches outside.

After tea they took the children up to the marketplace for a ride on the roundabouts.

'Having a good time?' asked Patrick softly as they walked along behind. 'Grand,' said Karen.

They stood close together as the children climbed on to the roundabout and handed over their pennies. They shared a glance of amusement as they watched the glee on Jennie's face as the roundabout began to turn. Brian wore a look of solemn concentration but the little girl waved and laughed every time she came round.

'Hallo, Karen.'

The well-remembered voice, low though it was, sounded like a thunderclap in her ear. The blood left her face, leaving her eyes black and staring.

Slowly, she swung to face him and stared mutely at the smirking, freckled face under thinning, sandy hair. He was older, coarser, his nose red and cheeks covered in broken veins, eyes set in a network of wrinkles. But it was definitely Dave. Dave Mitchell, not a ghost, not dead at Gallipoli. Suddenly the world was dissolving around her and she would have fallen but for Patrick who caught her as she swayed and led her to a bench. She bent her head to her knees and struggled to regain full consciousness.

When at last Karen raised her head, Patrick was bending over her with a cup of water he'd got from a nearby cottage and the children were standing close together, watching anxiously, thumbs anchored firmly in their mouths. The mechanical music from the hurdy-gurdy churned round and round in her head.

The sun had gone in and the day was suddenly chilly. Karen shivered uncontrollably and tried to stand up, despite Patrick's protestations.

'Will you lie still, Karen, for the love of God?' he said anxiously, but she took no heed. She had to know if *he* was there or if it had all been some horrible nightmare.

Fearfully she cast a quick glance around. Sure enough, there he was, she saw, her heart beating painfully in her breast. He was standing a few yards away, waiting, saying nothing. Lifting her chin, she stared straight at him and Patrick stood aside, bewildered. Then, moved by something in her face, he went to the children and put his hands on their shoulders.

'Why aren't you dead?' The idiotic question came flatly from Karen's lips almost of its own

430

volition. 'Joe said you were dead.'

She stared at Dave and her voice began to rise hysterically.

'No, no, it's not true!' she cried, and Patrick moved a step towards her.

'Karen?' he said. 'What is it?'

'Sorry to disappoint you, dearest,' Dave said at last, and grinned with sly amusement. Patrick's head jerked at the endearment and his hands tightened on Jennie, causing her to wriggle in protest.

'Karen? Who is this man?' he asked.

Dave grinned. 'Tell him who I am, Karen. Go on, tell him.' He was enjoying himself; malice shone from his eyes.

She dragged her eyes away from him and looked at Patrick, but she was dumb, misery swamping her.

'I tell you what, my love,' Dave said softly with mock consideration, 'you've had a shock. Maybe you'd better go home now and I'll come up about nine o'clock. Then we can have a canny little talk, eh?'

Karen stared at him, hardly hearing what he was saying.

'Tell me what this is all about, Karen.'

It was Patrick. He took hold of her arms and swung her round to face him. 'Karen, tell me!'

She looked up into the grey eyes. 'It's Dave,' she whispered.

'But Dave who?' Patrick shook her gently. 'Come on, Karen, I need to know.'

'Dave. My husband. My first husband, I mean . . . I thought he was dead.' She dropped her eyes before the shock and anger in Patrick's, gazed

431

at his waistcoat button, a few inches before her face.

'Very much alive, my dear,' interposed Dave, and the amusement in his voice was barely controlled. 'Now don't you think you should do as I say? People are beginning to stare.'

Patrick glanced round. It was true, people were starting to show an interest in the drama being played out on the square. He glared icily at Dave before turning back to Karen.

'He's right. Come on now, we'll go home. Can you manage to walk back to the trap? Come on, I'll help you. Brian, Jennie, come on now, Mam's tired, we're going home now.'

Subdued, the children followed obediently as Patrick supported Karen on his arm and they walked down to where the trap was parked. Once, he glanced back and Dave Mitchell was still standing there, legs astride and hands on hips, laughing.

Patrick collected Polly from the field where she was tethered and yoked her up while Karen stood dumbly by, the children hanging on to her skirts. He lifted them into the trap and helped Karen up too, and still no word was spoken. Geeing up the pony, he set off across the ford over the River Wear and even the water seemed different somehow. It still splashed up high on either side of the wheels but it was dull and grey and not even Jennie bothered to look.

In no time at all they were on their way back to Low Rigg Farm with their lovely day in ruins. They rode home in silence, the children huddled against Karen, tired and sleepy. Though they didn't understand, they felt as though something

432

momentous was going on and they felt threatened.

Oh God, prayed Karen silently, her eyes tight closed, let this not be happening. Tell me it's a nightmare.

What was the penalty for bigamy? If she went to prison what would happen to the bairns? To Patrick? To Nick? Why had this happened? If the papers got hold of it, what would it do to Patrick?

But they couldn't, they wouldn't send her to prison. Hadn't she a paper from Australia House? Oh, it was all too confusing, she couldn't think straight.

So ran her chaotic thoughts. She knew now why she had not felt safe all these years, it was because the safety was a sham, unreal and in her heart she had always known it.

Patrick was quiet. Either he was remarkably patient or he was biding his time until they were on their own. Quietly he saw to the pony and put the trap away in the barn. Nick started to ask questions about the show but Patrick's answers were short and terse. Nick was puzzled and inclined to be curious, but when he saw the emotion on Karen's face he quickly backed away and went into the stables.

Nick was still there, having refused to go in to the house for the evening meal, when Dave came riding into the yard at nine o'clock that evening.

'I'm not hungry, pet,' Nick had told Brian when the boy was sent to fetch him. 'I'll just bide a while.'

But he started forward from his hiding place when he heard the motor bike coming down the lane and into the yard. When he saw the stranger he thought better of it and returned to his stable.

He sat on a pile of straw in the furthest corner, miserable without knowing why. The twitch at the corner of his mouth reappeared, out of control.

Chapter Twenty-Nine

Dave parked his motor bike and walked up to the farmhouse door, knocking loudly. It was opened by Patrick who led the visitor through to the kitchen without speaking. Karen was sitting at the table waiting as she had done since putting the children to bed. Her mind had quietened in the intervening hours so that at least she was able to think more clearly. And what she thought was that Dave wanted something from them. If he had known where she was, why hadn't he got in touch sooner? He could surely have found her any time if he had put his mind to it.

The way he had gone about engineering a meeting, his attitude when they'd met, these things made her think he was after something. And what he was after was money, she thought bitterly. Well, he was going to be sadly disappointed—they had none. She tried to think of other possibilities but could not. Her mind ranged frantically over what he might do. Oh, why hadn't she had him declared dead as soon as he had been missing seven years?

'Sit down,' Patrick was saying as he indicated a chair opposite Karen for Dave. He himself took one beside her.

'Now, I understand you were once married to my wife and deserted her?' He took her hand and squeezed it and Karen gave him a grateful glance.

434

Patrick sounded calm and assured, as though he was in command of the situation. He would stand up for her, she thought, and a surge of love for him rose in her.

'Was married? Am married more like!'

Dave sat back in his chair and grinned. Patrick opened his mouth to retort but stopped as Karen began to speak.

'What do you want, Dave?' She had found her voice at last. 'You've come here for something. And it's not because you want me back, I'm sure of that. So, what do you want?'

'No, no, of course I haven't come to claim you back, what do you take me for? I wouldn't break up a happy family. You know the last thing I'd want is to hurt you or your bairns. But you must understand my position, your poor husband, who only emigrated to make a better life for us both. And what did you do? You upped and married someone else when my back was turned. Oh, yes, my mother, God rest her soul, told me all about it. Broke her heart, it did. I went to see her just before she died.'

Karen gasped at the enormity of this distortion. 'Your mother hated me, you know she did!'

'Nay, she didn't, it was just the natural feeling of a mother for the woman who took her son, that's all. She didn't hate you.'

'And it was eight years after you left before I married again, I hadn't heard from you in all that time, you deserted me fifteen years ago. And then Joe said you were killed at Gallipoli.'

Patrick, hearing the tremor in Karen's voice, intervened, tightening his grip on her hand to calm her.

'Enough of this,' he said. 'Just tell us what you want then get out.' His face was harsh as granite, eyes glittering as he glared at Dave, but Dave only smiled in return.

'Well now, it's like this,' he said easily, 'I made a mistake in coming back to England, I know that now, and I fancy going to Canada. England's finished. The trouble is, it takes money to get to Canada. I can hardly apply for an assisted passage, can I? And besides, I can't go with nothing in my pocket, now can I? I'm in a bit of a hurry an' all, you see.' He spread his palms in a mock appeal which met with a marked lack of response.

'We have no money,' Karen said flatly.

'Oh, come on now, just think, with me out of the country your secret will be safe. A proud woman like you, you know you wouldn't like it if all your neighbours were whispering about you. You can carry on as before with no one to bother you.' He chuckled. 'Carry on, that's a good one.' He eyed Patrick's set face and his obviously growing anger and added hastily, 'Only fifty pounds. Surely you can raise fifty pounds? I'm sure I could sell my story to a newspaper for that. Maybe the *News of the World* or the *Pictorial.*'

There was an astounded silence as the implications of the last remark sunk in.

'Patrick,' Karen said at last, her voice full of despair. He rose to his full height, appearing even taller in his anger.

'Get out of my sight! You son of Satan, get out of my sight. I warn you, I won't be responsible for my actions if you don't.'

'Righto, righto, I'm going,' Dave said hastily, and the grin slid from his face as he went to the door.

436

But his expression turned ugly as soon as he got out of range of Patrick and his eyes were suffused with red.

'I'll be back though. I was going to give you until the end of next month but if you want to play nasty . . . next Saturday in Stanhope market place, one o'clock sharp. Fifty pounds, or you'll be reading all about it in the newspapers.'

He went out through the door but turned back to add, 'And don't think I don't know all about you being a priest. It's surprising how a thing like that gets about, you know. A nice scandal that'll make, eh? I bet I could get a bob or two from the Irish papers for that one. A priest in a nice little love nest up here on the fell, safely away from the troubles an' all. Did you think you were hidden away? A priest with two little bas . . .' But here he broke off suddenly and beat a hasty retreat as Patrick lunged at him.

'Don't!' Karen rose to her feet and caught hold of Patrick. 'Let him go. You'll only make things worse.'

He shook her off but the slight delay was enough for Dave to reach his motor bike. After a couple of false starts it roared into life with a noise which sent the chickens squawking in the hen house and Flossie barking in a frenzy.

'One o'clock,' he called again, pulling on his leather helmet, then he was off, churning up clouds of dust behind him as he disappeared down the dark lane.

Patrick and Karen stared after him until the roar of the engine faded into the distance. Neither of them had quite realized the reality of the situation they now found themselves in.

It was the sound of Jennie crying which brought Karen out of a near trance and she turned back to the house without looking at Patrick. She couldn't look at him, not yet. Couldn't bear to see the condemnation there might be in his eyes.

'I'll see to the bairn,' she muttered, and fled upstairs to Jennie who was screaming with fright after being wakened by the noise of the engine.

'There, there, pet, it was only a noisy old motor bike,' Karen soothed, and picked up the child and sat on the bed, rocking Jennie against her breast till the gentle calming motion subdued her own wild thoughts along with Jennie's sobs. After a few minutes her own heartbeat slowed down and the child too became quiet except for an occasional hiccup. Her eyes closed and the long lashes beaded with tears swept her cheeks. Her thumb was once more firmly in her mouth. Abstractedly Karen thought she would never break her of the habit of sucking her thumb, not at this rate.

Carefully she tucked the bedclothes round Jennie and checked Brian in the other bed. He had turned over in his sleep but had not woken.

Karen tip-toed from the room and went downstairs to put the milk pan on for cocoa. Nervously she rattled cups and saucers and put out biscuits she had made the day before. How happy she had been then, making food for the picnic at Stanhope Show, anticipating the fun they would have today. How different from how she felt now. Well, it didn't help to think like that, she told herself, and took the pan from the fire to fill the cups.

Patrick was sitting by the fire, staring at the flames, saying nothing, seeming remote. Nick came in and quietly drank his cocoa after refusing anything to eat with it.

'But you've had no supper,' Karen protested. He only shook his head and went off to bed with a brief 'Goodnight.' Karen sat down opposite Patrick with her cup in her hands. They sat for a while in silence. Karen was the first to speak.

'How will we manage?' They had to get the money together somehow, she thought desperately.

'How much have we saved?' countered Patrick, for Karen was the one who attended to such things despite her helpless question.

'Fourteen pounds and fifteen shillings.'

It might as well have been nothing, it just wasn't enough. Sighing, she took the cups into the scullery to rinse. When she came back Patrick was still in the same position before the fire.

'I'm going to bed now. I can't think straight, I'm so tired,' she said dully.

He nodded then asked abruptly, 'Why didn't you tell me about Dave?'

'I . . .' Karen bit her lip. She felt as low as could be and terribly culpable. What could she say?

'There was nothing to tell. I thought he was dead.'

Patrick nodded again and turned back to the fire. Karen looked at him helplessly. He had known she was married before, but her first marriage had not been a subject for discussion. Karen had wanted to put it out of her mind altogether and she had been so sure she was a widow. Now she felt guilty, and worse, as though she had done something which had turned Patrick against her, he was so remote.

'Well, as I said, I'm going to bed. Are you coming?'

'Later.'

Karen shivered in the early-autumn chill and as she undressed and climbed into the large double bed, she felt bone weary. Sunday tomorrow, she realized. Could she face Chapel? Her mind shied away from the thought. She wished Patrick would come up. They needed to comfort each other. She felt she wouldn't sleep a wink, her body ached for him. How could he, with his sensitive nature, face being plastered all over the newspapers? A lapsed priest and a bigamous woman. She could see the headlines written out before her as she lay with her eyes closed. And her father, what would it do to him? He'd had so many body blows lately. Fresh anguish filled her mind as she remembered her father.

Downstairs, Patrick stood before the fire, his hand clasping the brass rail which hung from the high mantel shelf, his head leaning on his arm. I'm tired, he thought, tired to death. But it wasn't a physical weariness which had overwhelmed him despite the harsh, grinding nature of the work that had been his lot since his marriage to Karen. Marriage, he thought bitterly. Why, it was not even a real marriage, not even a civil marriage, and certainly not a marriage recognized by his church or his God.

His God. Oh, he had tried to deny his beliefs, he had even managed to convince himself that there was no God. Or he thought he had, but rather he had fooled himself, he realized now. He had tried so hard to believe he was living the life he wanted to live, a normal life, and hadn't he two beautiful children to prove it? Children being brought up in the Methodist faith, a voice in his mind said

440

darkly, but he pushed that aside. And Karen, yes, he had her. These last few years he had seen the anxious look leave the back of her eyes. Poor girl, she thought she had won. Until this happened.

Was it a judgement from Heaven? His mother would say so, oh yes she would, and feel vindicated in saying it. God is not mocked, she would say. And Sean, stern man of the church, unmoving and immovable in his views of right and wrong. Sean, a saint of a man and recognized as such by the Church for wasn't he a bishop now?

Patrick felt a great longing to talk to Sean, his friend and mentor. Sean saw things so clearly, he would sort out the muddle in Patrick's mind. For it was a muddle, one unholy mess. He dropped his hand from the rail and shivered. The fire had died and the kitchen was cold. But he could not face going to Karen's bed, not now. He hesitated a moment then took his overcoat and went to the settee in the sitting room.

* * *

The morning dawned cold and grey. Before Karen opened her eyes she sensed the emptiness of his side of the bed. Where was he? Oh, God, her mind cried, and it was a prayer not a blasphemy, had Patrick gone?

Scrambling into her clothes without bothering to wash, she hurried downstairs. The kitchen fire was out, the room bitterly cold. Where was he? Where was he? Panic invaded her mind. He'd left her, he had! She rushed out into the yard, into a falling drizzle of rain. No sign of him there nor in the barn or the stable. It was only five-thirty, she had

441

taken note of the wall clock in the kitchen, he couldn't have gone, he couldn't. Half demented she ran back into the house and along the passage to the sitting room and there he was, lying on the settee, his overcoat over him. Relief flooded her whole being, making her giddy. Thank God! Thank you, God! she breathed, sagging against the door jamb.

Her legs were weak as she returned to the kitchen without disturbing him and sank on to a chair, her head throbbing. After a while she rose and raked out the ashes and relaid the fire with twigs and cinders and a few lumps of coal. She soon had a fire going so she could boil the kettle.

Drinking her tea, she faced up to her main fear, her ever-present fear, the fear that had dogged her for so long: that Patrick would leave her and the children.

After all, in the eyes of his church they were not married at all, and now, after yesterday, they were not even married according to the law. Her mind jumped to the problem of Dave. If Patrick meant to stay then he could get work on the roads, that would keep them. They would have to sell stock, though. But would Dave keep his promise, would he go to Canada? Whether or not, they had to take his word that he would, they had no choice.

Patrick came through from the front room looking drawn and tired. Impulsively she reached up and kissed him and they held each other briefly. She could still feel the strong emotional bond between them, surely he did too? She considered whether to ask him why he had slept on the settee but couldn't bring herself to say the words.

'We'll manage, pet,' she said instead, speaking

442

softly to him as to one of the children. She poured him out a cup of tea from the pot keeping warm on the hob. It was hot and strong.

'I've been thinking.' Patrick took a long swallow of the hot, sweet liquid. 'I sat up so late last night going over it in my mind, I thought I'd just get a couple of hours on the front room couch. I needed to be by myself, to think.'

Karen nodded, trying to show understanding, though in truth she did not understand. Why couldn't he think in their bed?

'We'll have to sell Jess and her foal,' Patrick continued, 'it's the only way. We can manage with Polly for now, at least until the filly's broken in.' This was Polly's foal, a strong two-year old.

Karen felt a pang of regret for Jess, such a gentle mare. And Brian had had plans to break in the colt for riding. Nick would help him, he had insisted.

'I can help round up the sheep if I have a pony,' he had urged Patrick. Now he would have to be disappointed.

'I can go over to Jack Tarn's place tomorrow, maybe,' Patrick said now. 'Then we can sell one of the cows if need be.'

'That means a lot less butter to sell during the year.'

'I don't see what else we can do,' he answered, and Karen knew he was right. Restlessly, she got to her feet and began to tidy up the kitchen. She folded the towels hanging on the brass rail and took away the cups to wash in the scullery. Anything to take her mind off her worries.

Nick was surprised when Patrick told him they had to sell the pony and her foal.

443

'But why?' he said. 'We don't need the money that bad, do we?'

'We just have to, that's all,' said Patrick.

It had something to do with 'that chap', Nick decided. He pondered over it, foreboding clouding his mind. As usual, anything which troubled Karen troubled him and he knew this was big trouble, he knew it instinctively.

Chapter Thirty

Jack Tarn was coming at two o'clock on Tuesday afternoon and Patrick walked up the fell to catch Jess so she could be viewed by the dealer. The autumn was turning cold and wet and he hunched his chin inside his collar and thrust his hands in his pockets as he bent forward against the wind to climb the uneven ground. His eyes watered and he paused for a moment, turning his back on the wind as he took his handkerchief out and wiped them. Sourly, he gazed down on the water-sodden fell, the heather dull and bent now the purple blooms were gone and the bracken brown and dead-looking. It suited his mood. His depression was almost total and he longed for a drink. A man needed a drink to keep him going, make life bearable, though Karen didn't think so. He thought of her as he continued his climb to where he could see Jess and her foal grazing on a section he and Nick had cleared two or three years before. Damned hard work it had been, too, back-breaking work, not fit for a man.

And Karen now, why had she let him think her

first husband was dead? And what was he doing here, on this God-forsaken moor where icy blasts raged over the heather for the better part of the year?

He came to a dip in the fell and startled a group of curlews with their long curved beaks plunged into the mud on the bottom as they grubbed for food. They lifted into the air, flapping their wings reproachfully and crying mournfully. He stood still, remembering seeing curlews feeding like that in small pockets of bog on the Burren. A lifetime ago, it seemed now.

Patrick shook his head. He was thinking too much about the past. It did no good, nothing would bring it back.

*　　　*　　　*

'Ten pounds for the mare and foal,' Jack said after a sharp appraisal of the animals.

'I thought fifteen,' said Patrick.

Jack sighed. 'Well, I tell you, eleven pounds ten. That's my final offer. Things is hard right now.'

Even so, thought Karen indignantly, the price was pretty disgusting. But they had to sell. How was it dealers always knew when the need to sell was desperate?

'Take it or leave it,' Jack prompted them, and after a glance at Karen, Patrick reluctantly held out his hand and Jack slapped it. So the sale was agreed.

The red cow brought twenty-nine pounds at the auction mart in Stanhope so one way and another they had raised the money though it left them with little more than ten pounds of their savings.

I'll take it to him, Patrick. It will be better if I take it,' Karen begged. 'This is all because of me and I'd best see to it.'

'No, I'll do it,' he demurred. 'It's a man's job.'

'But I know him better than you . . .' She didn't notice Patrick's pained look at this, too intent on getting him to agree to her meeting Dave. 'I can talk to him, show him that we won't be able to raise any more. Nick can go with me, I'll be all right with him.'

Patrick felt the now familiar surge of irritation as she spoke of taking Nick instead of him but he said nothing. What was the use? So reluctantly he agreed and at midday on the following Saturday, Karen, accompanied by Nick, set out for Stanhope. Nick had been unsure at first about going into the town; he was happier on the farm. But when he understood that he was there for Karen's protection he went readily enough. Though he was puzzled. He wasn't sure what he was supposed to be protecting her from.

Karen was simply thankful that Patrick stayed at home with the children, fearing another confrontation between him and Dave.

He was lounging against the wall at the side of the market square; she saw him immediately they came round the bend. She pulled up alongside him and handed the reins to Nick.

'You stay and hold Polly, please,' she said, but Nick wasn't too sure about that.

'I'll tie the reins and come with you.' He had seen Dave too and knew at once that he was the threat to Karen. Nick was determined to protect her whatever happened.

'I'll come with you,' he insisted stubbornly.

446

'No,' Karen said firmly, 'I'll be all right. Please stay.'

Reluctantly he sank back on to the seat, glaring at Dave menacingly, ready to spring out if he was needed. Karen climbed down from the trap and walked over to the wall with her bag, holding the precious bundle of fivers clutched in her hand.

'You've got the money?' An avaricious gleam came into Dave's eyes as he straightened up and held out his hand.

'I've got it. But first I have to be sure you'll go to Canada. There'll be no more money forthcoming, I'm telling you. It's a poor little farm and we've had to sell stock to raise this. You've got to prove you are really going.'

'Well now, my love,' Dave grinned at her, 'how am I going to do that? You're just going to have to take my word for it, aren't you?' He laughed at the expression of fury on her face. 'I'm going! Don't worry. I'll be glad to shake the dust of England off my feet.'

Karen still hesitated. She looked hard at him, wondering if she could trust him. His grin disappeared and his stance became threatening.

'Howay now! Give me the money or else . . .'

Nick stood up quickly at this, ready to jump off the trap into the street. He still didn't know what was going on as he was just out of earshot but recognized the threat all right. As Polly moved restlessly with him, Karen glanced quickly over and waved to him to stay where he was.

'No,' she called, 'I'm all right.' She held out the money to Dave. 'Here it is. Now go. I never want to see your face again.'

'Don't be like that.' Dave's grin reappeared. 'Of

course I'll go. I said I would, didn't I?' He counted the notes carefully and stuffed them in his waistcoat pocket, his good humour restored.

'Aren't you going to wish me luck, Karen?'

She gave him a bleak stare, disdaining to answer. With a mocking laugh he touched his forehead and strode off down the street, whistling cheerfully.

Karen watched him disappearing around the corner to the station. Had they really seen the last of him? she wondered. She couldn't stop the hope rising despite her distrust of him. Oh, if only he would go to Canada then things might turn out all right, she thought. Please let him go to Canada.

'Karen.'

Nick had tied up the horse and walked over to her.

'Howay, Karen, let's gan yam.'

He took hold of her elbow hesitantly. He was deeply troubled and it showed by the twitching in his face and the way he had lapsed into his native dialect. Karen felt a stab of compunction. She had no right to involve him in this, she had not. She forced herself to smile at him.

'Yes, Nick, we'll go home.'

They climbed into the trap and turned Polly round to take the road back to Low Rigg Farm.

'Who was it, missus?' Nick asked suddenly as they pulled out on to the moorland road. He looked sideways at Karen, seeing the hesitation on her face as she prepared to answer him. 'Eeh, you don't have to tell me, it's none of my business, like.'

'Oh, Nick, it's not that,' she said helplessly. But she couldn't bring herself to tell him the truth. 'He's someone I used to know. I owed him

448

something.' After a moment she added lamely, 'He's gone now, gone to Canada, we'll see no more of him.'

Nick said nothing to this, simply stared at the road ahead. Karen watched his face. What did he really think? she wondered. Well, no matter, Dave had gone now and they would all just have to get on with living, trying to make up their position to what it was before he came. And that would take a lot of doing, she thought dismally. It meant Patrick working long hours on the roads. And she would have to use less eggs and butter for the family. She could sell them in Stanhope perhaps, to bring in extra cash.

They reached the farm and Karen climbed wearily down. Patrick came out of the stable, his eyes anxiously questioning. She shook her head. 'There was no trouble. He's gone now, Patrick.'

*   *   *

There was a little aching void in Karen, troubling her like a broken tooth. It grew larger as time went on and she couldn't leave it alone but kept probing it with her mind.

It was Patrick. He was different somehow. Oh, he was civil enough and hard-working as ever. He rarely lost his temper as he had sometimes done before. He was soft-spoken most of the time, even when she herself spoke sharply. And she spoke sharply often these days, both to him and the children. He was good to them and they loved him though they seemed to love Nick almost as much. But there was often a remote look in his eyes, a look which set aside the closeness they used to

449

enjoy, the two of them.

Karen found it difficult to bring up the subject of their coming together in the closeness of the double bed; she couldn't discuss sex. She found it impossible, his remoteness inhibiting her. Not that he left her bed, apart from that night following the Stanhope Show, but more often than not he simply turned his back when she was aching for the comfort of his love-making. Not that sex was gone altogether from their lives. Patrick was a lusty man, or had been until September. But on the few occasions when they came together in bed nowadays he seemed driven to it. It was not as it had been, thought Karen. Here it was January and things had been this way since September.

It was 1925, she thought wearily as she broke the ice in the bucket of water in the scullery one morning. Her thoughts matched the cold white dawn, so cold her fingers had stuck to the iron handle on the back door, causing a slight freeze burn.

At least they had heard no more from Dave so maybe he really had gone to Canada, she thought as she sucked her finger. She filled the kettle and went into the kitchen where the newly kindled fire was blazing up the chimney.

Patrick had managed to get work on the road the council was building over the top of the moor, the snow was slight so far and the road-building went ahead as long as the weather allowed. It was hard labouring work and he needed a good breakfast before meeting the waggon which took him and the others to work.

Karen sucked her sore finger again pensively. Patrick and Nick came in to wash their hands

450

before breakfast. The children were still in bed. Both of them had feverish colds and needed a little extra coddling.

'Beauty calved all right, a strong white heifer.' Patrick volunteered the information as he sat down to his porridge which would be followed by bacon and eggs. He had to have a good breakfast so as to last the day, even if Karen herself made do with porridge.

'Thank God,' she said, smiling at him. She poured tea for him and Nick. 'Maybe I'll have time to paint that sheep rack you made later on.'

They fell into silence as they ate breakfast. The warmth from the range was beginning to fill the room and what with the smell of the bacon there was an air of snug comfort to it, contrasting with the cold outside. Patrick glanced at the wall clock and with a reluctant sigh took a last drink of tea and put on his outdoor clothes. As he moved to the door Karen followed.

'We'll be all right now, Patrick?' He noticed her hesitation as she looked up at him, and patted her arm.

'Don't worry so, Karen. Yes, we'll be all right now.'

Waving to Nick, he went out. Nick coughed, scraping his chair back as he rose.

'Well, missus,' he asked, 'shall I clean out the pigs and byre then?' He knew he could do the work in whatever order he liked, he was steady and could be relied upon despite his disability, but he always deferred to Karen.

'Right, Nick.'

Karen rose too. Time to check on Brian and Jennie. They were awake and peevish, Jennie

451

sobbing as Karen went into the bedroom while Brian was looking flushed and defiant. The reason for the trouble could be seen clutched tightly to his chest. It was a precious story book he had received as a Christmas present.

Jennie held out her arms to Karen, her lower lip trembling.

'He hit me! Brian smacked me,' she wailed.

Karen took her in her arms. 'Why did you do that, Brian?' she asked over the head of her daughter.

'She wrote on my book.' Brian's voice was accusing as he held out the book, sadly covered in scribble. He was an early reader, encouraged by his father. His most prized possessions were his books, he couldn't get enough of them and he hated Jennie to touch them. Consequently, she always tried to get hold of one.

'Still, you shouldn't smack her, she's smaller than you,' Karen admonished. 'And you, Jennie, shouldn't write on Brian's book.' The guilty Jennie sobbed even louder, hiding her face in Karen's pinafore.

'Come on now, never mind, just don't do it again. I'm sure we'll be able to rub it off, Brian . . .' Karen was interrupted by the sound of Nick shouting up the staircase.

'Missus! Karen, come down a minute, will you?'

'What is it, Nick?' She tried to put Jennie down on the bed but the child clung to her tightly, renewing her sobs. 'I can't come down just yet,' she called back and returned her attention to the little girl who was at last becoming quieter. Karen wiped her face with a large, soft handkerchief. Jennie's nose was sore and inflamed and red with her cold.

'It's that man, missus. Asleep in the stable.'

Nick's quiet voice was yet loud in her ears. He had come upstairs and was standing close behind her, startling her before she took in the import of his words.

'Nick, you made me jump!' Her arms tightened round Jennie convulsively. 'What man? What man do you mean?'

Nick stood in the bedroom doorway, miserable and uncomfortable. He shifted from foot to stockinged foot for he had left his boots in the hall. 'You know, Karen, *that* man.'

She stared at him in disbelief. It couldn't be! He couldn't mean Dave. Brian and Jennie were quiet too. All three stared at Nick. At last Karen moved, putting down the child and standing up, automatically pushing a stray tendril of hair behind her ear.

'Be good now, pets,' she said mechanically to the children, 'I won't be long.' She turned to Nick. 'Stay in the house until I'm back, will you?'

He nodded mutely, his eyes unhappy as she walked down the stairs and out to the stable. She could see he was longing to go with her but he wouldn't leave the children, not when she'd asked him not to.

Karen stood in the stable doorway staring at Dave. He was sitting on a pile of the dried brown bracken so laboriously sledded down from the fell by Patrick.

'Aren't you going to offer me some breakfast?'

He was looking up at her confidently, the bad penny which always turned up, she thought numbly. She didn't hear what he said, her mind too busy coping with the realization of all her

453

nightmares of the last few months.

The scene swayed before her. She put out a hand to the door post to steady herself. Dave stood up, brushing bits of bracken from his trousers and straightening his jacket.

'Did you hear me, Karen?' He had lost his mocking tone, his voice was sharp.

'What?' She was still staring, dazed.

'I said, how about a spot of breakfast for a hungry man? Now I know you wouldn't turn anyone away hungry, not even me.' He walked indolently over to her.

'What are you doing here? Why aren't you in Canada?' At last Karen trusted herself to speak.

'Well now, I'm not in Canada as you can see and at the moment I'm hungry, so will you get me something to eat when I ask you to?' He smiled unpleasantly. 'We'll go into the house, eh? Bit nippy out here.'

She swayed as Dave brushed past her and strode into the house, heading for the kitchen fire where he stood with his back to the heat, his feet apart, his hands in his pockets. He sniffed appreciatively at the appetizing smell of ham and eggs still hanging in the room.

'By, something smells good. I reckon I'll have some of that.'

Karen had followed him in, her mind seething incoherently. To steady herself as much as anything she set to with the frying pan and cooked him ham and eggs. Dave sat down at the table and looked around appraisingly.

'Nice and comfortable you are here, Karen,' he remarked smugly, ignoring her lack of response.

Nick came downstairs and stood beside her as

she worked. He kept his eyes on Dave, his face twitching, the stump of his right arm moving spasmodically.

'Who's this then?' Dave stared back at him. 'Don't tell me you've got two fancy men?' He laughed a taunting laugh, and Nick was goaded.

He stepped forward, growling in his throat, fist doubled up.

'Nick!'

Karen put out a hand to him, holding him back. 'It's all right, Nick. Look, why don't you get on with the yard work? Really, it's all right.'

He looked at her doubtfully. 'I'd better stay, missus,' he said simply.

'No, really, everything's fine. Just get on with the work, there's plenty to do and we want a private talk.'

Reluctantly, and with many glances behind him, Nick went out into the yard, but reappeared at the window at intervals, peering in anxiously.

Karen put the plate before Dave and sat down.

'Righto, now tell me what it is this time,' she said, her voice hard and flat.

Dave picked up his knife and fork and began eating. 'Well, it's like this, see.' The words sounded thick through his full mouth. 'I had a bit of bad luck. I was going to Canada, honest, but I reckoned I could save a bit of money by making my own way to Liverpool and then maybe sign on as a deck-hand on a ship. Leave enough money for a good start, see?' He beamed across the table at Karen, obviously expecting her to appreciate what good thinking this was. She stared back at him uncompromisingly.

'Yes?' she prompted. He looked down at his

plate, his smile disappearing.

'Yes, well, to cut a long story short, I fell in with some travelling folk and ended up with nowt. "Well, Dave," I said to myself, "Karen will help you out. You can be sure of Karen." ' His grin reappeared wolfishly as he licked his lips and folded his arms confidently and leaned back in his chair.

'I can't,' she said flatly. 'We have nothing. You can see we have nothing.'

'Come on now, I can't see any such thing.'

Dave sat forward and leaned his arms on the table. His expression became ugly and his voice softer.

'I can see that there is good food on the table and sheep in the fold. I can see your fancy man has a job. Don't you tell me you have nothing because it's a bloody lie! And I'm telling you now, I want some of it. Or else.'

'Or else what? What can you do?' Karen's voice rose.

'I can get you into plenty of bother, my lass. I could still make a bob or two if I told it to the papers. Then what would your holier than thou father have to say? And where would the Irish feller be and all? What would happen to your bastard bairns if you had to go to gaol?' Dave stood up triumphant, pleased with the reaction he saw in Karen's horrified face.

She was white and staring, fascinated as a rabbit by a stoat. She gripped the table with both hands until the knuckles gleamed white through red, chapped skin. She was bereft of speech, her mind a black, swirling mist. There was a sound behind her, a low, animal sound.

'Call the loony off, Karen.'

Dave was looking over her shoulder. For a moment she sat still, frozen into position, before his voice penetrated her confusion. She turned slowly in her chair.

Nick was standing in the doorway with a hayfork in his hand. His face was a bright, angry red, eyes suffused with hatred as he glared at Dave. Alarm galvanized Karen into action.

'No! Nick, no!'

Karen flung herself at him and caught hold of his good arm. Earnestly she stared into his face, willing him to look at her, keeping herself between him and Dave.

'It's all right, Nick, it's all right. Look, he hasn't hurt me. Nick, come on now, we'll go outside, eh?'

She tugged at the hay fork in his hand and after an agonizing moment he looked down at her and his resistance melted and his grip slackened. The wild look left his eyes and he merely looked bewildered.

'Karen?'

'Yes, Nick. Howay now, we'll go outside, get some fresh air.'

He allowed her to lead him out to the yard and across to the stable where she propped the fork against the wall.

'Come on, Nick,' she forced herself to say briskly. 'There's work to be done. Will you feed the hens for me?'

'But missus . . .'

'No, really, Nick, I do want you to get on with the work and I'll have to get back to the bairns. You'll do it for me then?'

He looked doubtfully at her and back to the

457

scullery door.

'There's him, though,' he said uncertainly.

'No, he's going now. Listen, there's the motor bike starting up,' said Karen. And it was. From round the corner came the 'thrum, thrum' of the engine.

Nick nodded, his face clearing. Thankfully Karen hurried back to the house. Jennie could be heard crying fretfully from the bedroom.

'Mammy! Mammy!'

Karen rushed into the kitchen and if it hadn't been for his dirty plate and mug she would have thought it had all been a nasty nightmare and Dave had never been. She hurried upstairs to comfort her daughter.

'There now, flower. The kitchen's warm now, we'll go down and you can dress by the fire. Come on, Brian, you too.' She took the little girl in her arms and hugged her.

It was only when she was back by the fire pulling on Jennie's dress that she happened to glance up at the wall-clock to check the time. Or rather she glanced at the bare patch on the wall where the clock had hung for so long.

Dave must have taken it, she realized in shock. But how had he managed to take such a bulky thing on the motor bike? A thought struck her. Had he taken anything else? She put Jennie aside for a moment and reached up to the mantel shelf for the ornament where she kept her savings. There had been eleven pounds there. Not a lot really, but it represented the hard work and thrift of the last few months. And it was gone.

Chapter Thirty-One

Patrick sat in the bar of the Quarryman's Arms, a glass of whiskey on the table before him. He shifted uncomfortably. He was still in his working clothes and the warmth from the fire in the bar combined with the dust embedded in his trousers and made them sticky. He gazed morosely at the whiskey before him. Threepence it had cost and already he was feeling guilty about it. They could ill afford the money. Lifting the glass, he took a tiny swallow and the liquid burnt a fiery path over his tongue and throat. Ah, he thought, placing the glass carefully back on the table, but it warmed the belly too. A man was entitled to something after a hard day's work.

'Good evening, Patrick.'

He looked up from his contemplation of the glass of whiskey as the door opened and Sean came in.

'Sean!' he said, pleasure lighting his face. 'It's good to see you. What brings you up here?'

'I came to see you, Patrick.'

'But how did you know I'd be here?' he asked, mystified.

'No mystery really, I saw you come in. I was visiting in Wolsingham and thought I'd come up here and try to see you. And as I got off the bus, there you were. Will you be having another drink now, Patrick?'

He half-rose from his seat. 'Let me get them,' he began, fingering the change in his pocket and wondering if he had enough.

'No, I will,' said Sean quickly, and Patrick was glad to let him.

He turned to the barman who was taking a great interest in the two Irishmen. Patrick he had seen before but the parson was new to him. The only other man in the pub was a quarryman, sitting in the corner and morosely drinking ale.

Sean came back to the table with the whiskies and sat down opposite Patrick.

'Well,' he said, 'however you found me, it's great to see you, so it is. We can talk of old times at Maynooth, it's just what I'm needing. My workmates are all right, but I haven't much in common with them. And you look grand, Sean. You'll have to excuse me, sitting here in my dirt like this. I've just come away from my work.'

'I know, I heard you were working on the roads.' Sean lifted his glass. 'Good health to you, Patrick.'

'And you, Sean,' he echoed.

Sean looked his friend over keenly. He hadn't seen him for a while and concern showed in his eyes. Patrick moved uncomfortably, pulling his scarred and work-roughened hands down on to his lap. He was acutely conscious of his dirt-encrusted clothes and the smell of coal tar and sweat which clung to him.

'What are you doing to yourself?' Sean asked softly. 'You, with your brain and education. For the love of God, man, why are you doing this heavy labouring work?'

'We have to live,' said Patrick. 'How else can we manage if I don't work?'

'But you look terrible, man, ten years older than you are. If you can't earn enough with the farm, why don't you get work in the towns? An educated

460

man like you, surely you could find something—office work or something?'

Patrick drained his first glass and picked up the second. He didn't answer Sean, how could he? How could he tell him that the reason he was so poverty-stricken was because they had been blackmailed by Karen's real husband? All the pleasure which he had felt when Sean came into the bar evaporated. They couldn't talk naturally, he thought, they were too far apart now. Draining the glass, he rose to his feet.

'I have to get back, Karen will be waiting supper.'

'But Patrick—'

Sean too stood and put a hand on Patrick's arm. He looked down at it. The skin was white and soft and the nails well cared for. Against his grimy sleeve it pointed up the difference between them, the gap which was growing wider.

'I have to go,' he said.

'I'll see you again,' said Sean. 'I can come over more often. We can meet in Wolsingham.' He followed Patrick out of the bar.

'Funny blokes,' said the barman to the quarryman as he set a pint of ale before him. 'Irish, I think.'

'Aye,' agreed the quarryman.

'Patrick,' Sean said earnestly, 'listen to me, man. I've left you alone all these years, thinking you would come to your senses. Look, I'm not here as a representative of the Church, I'm here as a friend, Patrick. Someone has to make you see—'

'I'm going now, Sean,' he said. 'I've got the pony and trap, can I take you anywhere?'

He walked over the road to where Polly, still in

461

the traces of the cart, was grazing the sparse January grass on the verge.

'No, I can catch the bus, I'm dining at Wolsingham tonight,' Sean answered, defeated. 'You get along home now, you look ready for your bed.'

Patrick held out his hand to his friend. 'It was good of you to come, Sean.' Then he climbed up on to the cart and took the reins.

'I'll see you soon then,' called Sean as Patrick turned the pony round and headed for the road up to Low Rigg Farm. He turned up his collar against the bitter January wind and sank his chin into his muffler. He felt tired to death and the whiskey in his stomach burned, making him hiccup and the taste in his mouth was sour.

* * *

All day long, Karen had thought about how she was going to tell Patrick that Dave had returned. She felt utterly defeated, sure that there was no hope for the future. There was only poverty and worry for her and Patrick and the children. Even Nick was suffering.

She considered the effect that Dave was having on Nick. His carefully balanced peace of mind, so hard won during these years with them after the disastrous effects of the war, was disintegrating before her eyes. She didn't know what to do for him, couldn't send him away. If he left the farm he would crack up altogether. But if he stayed at Low Rigg Farm and there was more trouble with Dave, he would crack up also.

Restlessly, she walked out to the gate of the

farmyard, and looked over to the home pasture where Nick was spreading hay for the pregnant ewes. He saw her coming and straightened up to see what she wanted and she saw his facial twitch was getting worse. He held a bundle of hay in his good hand, balancing it with the stump of his forearm which was wrapped in grimy rags against the cold.

'Are you wanting something, missus?'

'No, no, Nick, I just thought I'd see if you needed any help,' she said lamely.

'Nay, I'm about finished,' he answered.

She nodded, forcing herself to smile as though everything was normal and walked back to the gate. Pausing at the rowan tree, she suddenly thought of the old rhyme:

Rowan tree and red thread,
Put the witches to their speed.

She put a hand out to the trunk of the tree and looked up into the bare, windswept branches. If only it were true, she thought, she'd cover the tree in red thread. For if ever there was an evil witch, it was David Mitchell, a true son of Satan. Sighing, she walked back indoors.

Karen gave the children their meal and put them to bed. It was a while before she got them settled for Jennie was still a little feverish and fretful, but at last she was able to come downstairs where Nick had just come in from the pasture.

'Patrick not back yet?' she asked, and Nick shook his head.

'Something must have kept him,' she said, and began to set the table for the evening meal.

463

How was she going to tell him? she wondered. Her mind revolved round and round the problem of Dave, fruitlessly, for she could see no solution. Every time she looked up her eyes were drawn to the bare patch on the wall where the clock had hung. It was so glaring.

Patrick came in and Karen dished out the food, not even noticing the smell of the whiskey on his breath. Though he was even quieter than usual and looked drawn and tired, he was hungry and paid attention only to the food. She watched him, hardly touching her own and Nick only picked at his.

At last Patrick pushed back his plate and relaxed in his chair.

'That was good, Karen, I was ready for it,' he said. For the first time he looked at her properly and his tone changed.

'What's the matter?' As he looked at her his attention was drawn to the bare patch on the wall and he sat up straight with surprise.

'Where's the clock?'

'Dave came,' said Karen, but she was unable to go on. Across the table, Nick put down his knife and fork with a clatter and stared at his plate. Suddenly he pushed back his chair so that it fell over backwards and rushed for the stairs.

'I'm going to bed,' he said, and fled.

'Nick!'

Karen's concern for him overcame her need to tell Patrick. She berated herself for being so thoughtless as to bring up the subject of Dave's visit in front of Nick. She went to the bottom of the stairs but he was already closing his bedroom door.

464

'Tell me what has happened, Karen, tell me,' said Patrick, catching hold of her arm. 'What happened when Dave came?'

'Oh, Patrick, he's not going to leave us alone,' she said, allowing herself to be drawn back into the kitchen. 'I don't know what to do. He took the clock of all things and the money out of the ornament.

He's going to leave us with nothing at all. And then there's Nick . . . It's not fair on him, all this trouble, it'll send him over the edge. None of this is his fault but he's so upset about it, I'm frightened for him.'

'I'll go up to him,' decided Patrick. 'I'll talk to him, tell him not to worry. Dave can't really hurt us.'

If only that were true, Karen thought miserably after Patrick went into Nick's bedroom. Please God, she prayed silently. Please make Dave leave us alone. Let him be satisfied with what he's had from us, make him go away to Canada.

Patrick was still in with Nick. She couldn't hear anything from the bedroom, even when she went upstairs to check on the children. They were both sleeping but restlessly, as though they knew something was wrong. The strained atmosphere was affecting them all, she thought. Oh God, let this nightmare end.

Karen filled the kettle and settled it on the glowing coals. When it boiled she filled the stone hot water bottles and took them upstairs and put them in the big bed in their room. She considered filling one for Nick and using that as an excuse to interrupt the men, find out what Patrick was saying to him, but in the end she changed her mind.

At last she heard a bedroom door open and close upstairs and Patrick came down. Anxiously, she looked up at him.

'He's all right, Karen,' was all he said. 'Now, let's away to our bed, I have to be up at five in the morning.'

She wanted to protest, to know all that Patrick had said to Nick, but she held her tongue. Wearily, she followed him up to bed and when he turned away from her after a chaste peck on the cheek, she thought nothing of it. Exhausted, she fell asleep immediately she put her head on the pillow.

*   *   *

The weather closed in and for a month there was snow almost every day, accompanied by high winds which formed it into mountainous drifts which blocked the lane and obscured the normal landmarks of the fell. Work on the roads was put off until spring and the family at Low Rigg Farm had to live on what they had. Karen was by now well used to this happening, so she had a good store of flour and pulses in, besides a side of bacon from the Christmas killed pig. The eggs were few at this time of year and the butter sparse since the remaining cow had dried up, but they eked out what remained with pork fat.

At least it meant that Dave couldn't come to harass them, Karen thought thankfully. The snow had been an answer to her prayers.

The work was still hard, even though Patrick was home and could do his share. To venture out even into the yard entailed wrapping up as warmly as possible against the bitter wind which flung

466

particles of ice and snow into their faces as soon as the door was opened. Patrick and Nick took to wearing large woollen scarves over their caps and tied round their necks, and Karen made Nick a sheepskin cover for his stump which tied securely around the upper arm and kept the forearm snug and safe from frostbite.

The menace represented by Dave Mitchell faded into the background as the weeks went by. Karen even allowed herself to hope that he had gone from their lives altogether.

'Do you think he has gone?' she asked Patrick one day. There had been a slight thaw and pale sunshine sparkled on the frosty snow on the roof of the barn, and in the yard below slush was threatening to become a quagmire.

Patrick didn't need to ask who she meant, Dave was never far from his thoughts either.

'I don't know, Karen,' he replied, sounding slightly impatient. What on earth was the use of supposing anything? He pulled on his high boots over his fisherman's knit socks and struggled into his worn overcoat. Sometimes he thought it took more energy to get dressed these days than it did actually to do the work.

'I'll have to clear the yard before it becomes a swamp,' he remarked to Karen, and trudged through the slush to get a shovel from the barn.

*   *   *

The slight thaw continued and Fred Bainbridge brought his tractor up the lonnen and cleared a track through the remaining snow. Karen invited him in for a cup of tea and a piece of lardy cake.

'I'm sorry, there's no butter but there's plenty of rhubarb jam,' she said humbly, feeling ashamed that she had no more to offer.

'Never you mind, missus, I'm fond of a bit of rhubarb jam, I am,' he replied. But when he had finished his lardy cake and rose to go, he paused.

'I can let you have a bit of butter, if you like,' he said. 'Have both your cows dried up, like?'

Karen blushed. 'We had to let the red cow go, Fred,' she said. He looked hard at her but said no more. Next morning, his son arrived and handed over a pound of butter.

'The postman's coming down the lane,' he said as he came in. 'I'll wait for him and save him a journey down to our place.'

It was the first time the post had got through for a while and Karen felt a little surge of pleasure. There was probably a letter from Morton Main, from Kezia; she could just do with reading a chatty letter, it would cheer her up.

Fred's son walked out to meet the postman then went on his way, waving cheerily to Karen as he went. She pushed the kettle back on the fire so she could freshen the tea and offer the postman a cup. She hummed a little tune to herself as she went back to the door to greet him, putting out a hand for the letters which he was holding.

'Aren't you coming in for a cup?' she asked as he half-turned to go. She didn't look down at the pile of letters, she could open them later.

'I'll not stay, thank you, missus,' he replied. 'I have a lot to get out today, what with being held up by the snow an' all. I'll be getting on my way.'

'Goodbye, then,' she said and closed the door after him. She would take five minutes before the

468

men came in from the low fell for their breakfast. Brian and Jennie were playing quietly on a clippie mat under the table, they were playing house. Sitting down in the rocking chair before the fire, she looked at the bundle of letters. Yes, the top one was from Kezia and there was one from Annie. Dear Annie. She still wrote twice or thrice a year, giving all her news of Greenfields, and Karen wrote back telling her about her own family. There was a letter from the Chapel steward about a members' meeting and underneath there was another in a man's hand. Dave's hand.

Karen jumped to her feet, hardly realizing she was doing it, and the letters went skidding over the flagged floor of the kitchen, dropped from her suddenly nerveless hands. All except for one, the letter from Dave.

'Is something the matter, Mammy?'

Brian crawled out from under the table. He had picked up the other letters and was holding them out to her. Karen didn't hear him, she was still staring at the envelope covered with Dave's crabbed handwriting.

'Mammy?'

Karen looked down at her son. After a moment she took the letters from him and put them on the table. Slowly she sat down again and opened the envelope.

Just to let you know I'll be up to see you on the thirteenth. I'll expect you to have a little present for me when I get there. D.

The thirteenth, that was tomorrow. How was she supposed to get any money together by tomorrow?

How was she supposed to get any money together at all? Patrick had no pay from the road making, the weather had been too bad. And there was nothing else to sell. All they had was the stock and how could they sell that? They wouldn't be able to live at all if they did.

'Mammy, I'm hungry,' Jennie said plaintively. With a start, Karen glanced up at the bare patch on the wall. She just couldn't get out of the habit of looking for the clock. There was no other clock in the house but she realized it must be nearing noon; it was past time she had the dinner ready. Fortunately, she had a pan of mutton stew all ready to warm up. She raked the glowing coals to the middle of the fire and added lumps of peat to the sides. Soon she was able to place the pan on the coals to heat up the stew.

'Go and call in Daddy and Nick,' she told Brian, and he obediently went out to the barn.

I won't say anything to Patrick, she decided. Not yet, not until I have to. Patrick intends to be out tomorrow, he is fetching lime to spread on the near fell. I'll just have to tell Dave I can't give him any more money, and he can do what he likes. We have to make a stand.

Chapter Thirty-Two

Dave crouched down in the shepherd's hut high on the moor above Low Rigg Farm. He shivered and shook with the cold. There was a makeshift fireplace in one corner but he daren't light a fire in the daylight for fear someone saw the smoke. The night before he had had to; he would have frozen to death else. He thought of the warm kitchen down on the farm. There would be hot food there an' all. And Karen, by, she was a corker when she was angry. Fair gave a man ideas.

He smiled as he thought of the note he had sent the day before yesterday. That would have shaken them up a bit down there. It had just been a joke really, he'd had much richer pickings in mind, him and his mate Jacko. They had been watching a house in Jesmond, a posh house in a posh area. And the best thing was the house belonged to a jeweller, a good jeweller an' all, with a shop in Northumberland Street. He was bound to have plenty of money stashed away in that house, not to mention other things, Jacko had said. So what did he want with the few coppers that poverty-stricken bitch he was married to could scrape together? No, it had just been a joke at the time.

Dave blew on his hands. God, he thought, he'd have frostbite before long if he didn't make a move. A hell of a joke, he told himself savagely, it was all in earnest now. Karen represented the only way out he had left. No one would think of looking for him on these Godforsaken fells. No one in their right mind would be here in this weather.

Everything had gone wrong, everything that could happen did. The jeweller had come home and changed into his evening suit, as he had done last Friday and the Friday before that, and the chauffeur had brought the Rolls round to the front door for him as he did every Friday evening and the jeweller had gone out.

That was their chance, said Jacko when they were planning it all. The staff were all in the back of the house having their own bit of a do and they could get in the front, up the ivy, and in at the bedroom window, for the house was hidden from the road by trees.

I might have known it would all go wrong, Dave thought grimly. He'd got up the ivy all right and had the bedroom window open in no time. A case of practice makes perfect. But Jacko, the bloody fool, had slipped and done something to his leg and the butler had come out to see what the noise was and there was such a commotion as he'd never heard in his life. Of course, he'd come down the ivy a bit sharpish, like, and the old feller had set up such a hollering and screaming he'd had to bash him with his jemmy before he could get away on his bike.

And here he was on this bloody awful fell, frozen half to death, and wherever Jacko was it served him bloody well right, that's all.

Funny about that note he'd sent Karen, though. Dave even smiled as he thought of it. Maybe she had managed to scrape something together, he'd just away down there and see. Best leave the bike hidden away in here, though, the polis would likely be looking for a man on a motor bike. He'd take it careful, creep down the fell and across the road and down the lonnen. It wasn't more than a couple of miles.

*   *   *

'By, you look grand today, lass.'

Karen started and the cup she had been drying fell from her hands with a crash but she didn't even notice. She was watching Dave as he walked

472

past her into the kitchen and over to the fire. She followed him as he held out his hands to the blaze, watching him as he stripped off his top coat and muffler and dropped them on the floor before leaning forward to the heat.

'Bloody hell, that hurts,' he said, wincing as it reached his frozen hands and the blood began to return to them. Steam began to rise from him and a rank, sour smell started to fill the room. He wasn't usually so scruffy, she thought dully. He looked like Nick had done when he had been sleeping out on the fell. Bits of dried bracken were stuck to his trousers and sheep droppings had fallen from him all over her clean floor.

'What do you want?' Karen asked at last. 'Whatever it is, you won't find it here. We have nothing, Dave, you've seen to that. We'll be lucky to last out the winter.'

He turned and faced her. 'Nay, lass,' he said, 'I only want a place to stay for a few days. For the minute, anyroad. I need food and a bed, that's what I need. And who else would I come to but my lawful wedded wife?'

'You're not staying here!' she cried. 'Get out, get away from us. Leave us alone, I'm telling you.'

'Oh, but I am staying here,' he said softly. He sniffed, leaning towards the oven where Karen had a dish of panhacklety cooking for the midday dinner.

'Mind, that smells great,' he went on, opening the oven door and peering in at the bacon and onions and potatoes bubbling in the pot. 'Ready to eat, is it?'

'I told you, you're not staying here, neither are you eating our dinner. Get out, I said, and I meant it. I'm not giving in to you any more, do what you like.'

Dave smiled and Karen's hatred intensified. She felt like clawing the smirk from his face. Her hands clenched at her sides and the nails dug into her palms as she imagined them digging into his eyes.

'Don't talk daft, Karen,' he said easily, and walked over to the stone jar on the dresser and took out a heel of bread. He took it to the still open oven and dipped it in the gravy, pulling a lump of bacon on to it. Turning again, he grinned at her.

'I'll just have this to be going on with,' he said, and bit hugely into the bread. As gravy and bacon fat ran down his chin he wiped it away with the back of his hand and licked his hand with his tongue.

'An' very nice it is, an' all,' he pronounced judiciously.

A low growl from the doorway made him turn and he paused in his wolfing of the food.

'Keep that loony away from me, Karen,' he snarled. 'And see the hay gripe's locked away an' all.'

She moved swiftly to Nick's side. She'd thought she'd made sure he would be working away from the house and yard. Oh, she hadn't wanted him to see Dave. She put a restraining hand on his arm.

'It's all right, Nick, howay outside. There's work to be done in the barn.'

But he stood unmoving, glaring at Dave. Suddenly he lunged across the room, his one fist bunched ready to strike and his stump flailing wildly.

'Nick!' screamed Karen, but Dave laughed

474

derisively. With one blow he knocked Nick across the room to bang sickeningly against the wall. In two strides, Dave was there beside him, kicking him as he lay.

'Go for me, would you?' he snarled. 'Howay then, get up, have another go. It's not the same without a hay gripe in your hand, is it, though?'

Karen flung herself on Nick, protecting him from Dave's cruel boots, taking a kick on her own shoulder as she did so.

'Leave him alone, don't touch him!' she shouted, and Dave stood back, rubbing his knuckles.

'Aw, he's not worth it, the crazy sod,' he laughed.

'Get out, go on, get out! You could have murdered the lad.'

'Aye,' said Dave equably. The fight seemed to have improved his mood. 'If I'd had me jemmy, I might have done an' all.' He walked over to where his top coat lay in a heap on the floor, picked it up and put it on. Casually, he wandered into the pantry and looked around.

'Mind, lass, you weren't joking when you said you had nowt. A bit of cheese and a couple of pig's trotters, is that all you have in the house? Aye, well, they'll have to do.'

He took the tea towel from the brass rail and wrapped the food in it while Karen watched him helplessly.

'Right, I'm off,' he said, and she breathed a sigh of relief. At least he was going before Patrick got back with the children.

'And don't come back or I'm telling you, I'll lay you in with the bobbies.'

'Will you, then?' Dave's face darkened as he moved towards her and Karen cursed her unbridled tongue.

Dave laughed as she shrank back towards Nick who groaned and moved suddenly.

'There you are, he's all right. It'd take more than a few kicks to dent that thick head.'

Karen fell on to her knees beside Nick and lifted his head. There was an ugly gash on his temple where he had fallen against the wall and his lip was swollen and bruised. But he was coming round. He moaned now and struggled to sit up.

'Come on, lad, I'll help you,' she whispered to him. Putting her arms around him, she helped him to his feet and on to the settee in the corner. He sat there, feeling his head gingerly.

'I'll get some water and bathe it,' said Karen. 'Lie down now, Nick, do.' She was worried sick as she saw his face so white and strained and the twitch disfiguring it horribly. Vaguely she realized that Dave had gone but it was attending to Nick which was most important now. Had he fractured his skull? In any case, he needed a doctor.

She brought water from the pail in the scullery and took it into the kitchen to add hot from the kettle. And Nick rushed past her and was gone out of the open door and away up the fell, running as if the hounds of hell were after him.

'Nick!' she cried. 'Nick!' Banging the dish down on the table so that the water slopped all over it, she ran out after him just in time to see him disappearing.

'Karen, for God's sake, what's the matter? Where's Nick gone?'

It was Patrick, the children trailing after him. He caught hold of Karen's arm as, clad only in her dress and pinafore, she started to run after Nick.

476

She collapsed into his arms.

'Oh, Patrick, Patrick, he's run off and he's hurt! Dave came back and he hurt him. He threw Nick against the wall and hurt his head. I think he may have a fractured skull, or concussion at least.'

'Karen, quiet now, quiet,' said Patrick, holding her tight in his arms. 'You're frightening the children. Come inside and tell me properly.'

At the mention of the children, she raised her head and looked at them. Jennie was starting to wail in fright and Brian was staring at her, his eyes round and anxious in his white face. With a great effort of will she composed herself, forcing herself to calmness.

'Come along now, inside,' Patrick said to them and they went in, he with his arm still around Karen, followed by the stiff little figure of Brian and a wailing Jennie bringing up the rear.

'Brian, Jennie, go and wash your hands for your dinner,' said Patrick, and obediently they divested themselves of their outdoor things and trooped into the scullery.

Karen took out the panhacklety and filled plates for the children. When they were sitting at the table eating she and Patrick went into the front room, out of earshot.

'He came back,' Karen said, quieter now, 'and Nick went for him, and he knocked Nick out.'

'Where's Dave now?'

'I don't know, he went off when I was attending to Nick. I told him we had nothing left.' She looked up into Patrick's grey eyes, not so clear now as they had been, no, they were cloudy with trouble. 'He won't come back, I'm sure of it,' she lied as a vague plan began to form in her mind. 'I

477

told him I would tell the police, he won't chance that. I'm sorry, Patrick, I am, it's all my fault.'

'Don't say that, Karen. If it's anybody's fault it's mine, I shouldn't have let it come to this.' He touched her cheek softly with his fingertips. 'I'll bring Nick back, Karen, don't worry. He can't be so bad, not judging by the way I saw him run anyhow. I'll bring him back and then I'll decide what I'm going to do about Dave Mitchell.'

'At least have some dinner first, Patrick.'

'Yes, I'd better. The weather's on the turn again, there'll be a frost tonight.'

They went into the kitchen and Karen ladled out the meal. Patrick ate quickly, pushing the food down. He would need it if he was going out on the fell. The children were big-eyed and quiet, watching their parents solemnly.

Karen went with Patrick to the door. The sky was darkening already and ice was forming on the slush in the yard. Oh God, she prayed, please let Nick be all right. Please, God.

'Remember this, Karen,' said Patrick, as they stood in the doorway. 'I'll bring Nick back and we are going to face up to this. But whatever happens, remember I love you and the children, even if . . .'

'Even if what?'

Karen stared at him. What did he mean? His words had summoned up that old fear that he would leave, and could she blame him if he did?

'Nothing. I meant nothing.'

He went to the back door and Karen watched from the scullery window as he called Flossie from her kennel. He searched the farm buildings, just in case Nick had returned and was hiding.

'Nick! Nick!' he called but there was no answer

478

but for the hoot of a barn owl as he disturbed its daytime slumber. After a reassuring wave to Karen, he went out on to the track, his lantern already lit against the gathering gloom. She watched the point of light until it disappeared into a fold in the fell and then she went back to the children.

* * *

The afternoon dragged on and on. Karen fed the stock and locked up the hens as the dark deepened into night. She gave the children their supper and put them to bed and sat down to wait.

It would be best if Dave came before Patrick got back. It was for her to deal with her former husband, it was her mess, it was up to her to clear it up. She felt alone, very much alone. Restlessly, she stoked up the fire, boiled water for the hot water bottles. She went upstairs and checked on the children who were sound asleep. That was one good thing, they were good sleepers. They would probably sleep straight through the night and whatever happened during it. She watched them for a moment or two, Brian curled up into a tight little ball and Jennie lying on her back with her thumb firmly anchored in her mouth.

Downstairs, Karen got out the mat frame. She would work on the proddy mat. It would take her mind off things, keep her mind and body occupied. She tipped the coloured strips of woollen cloth out of the bag and picked up her prodder. There was a red flower in the middle of the pattern and she began working on it, stabbing the strip through the harn backing with the prodder. Stab, catch, stab,

479

catch. Catching her finger with too sharp a stab, she sucked it briefly then carried on.

How long she sat there she didn't know. One hour? Two hours? Three? No, it must be longer. She had completely filled in the first flower and was halfway through the second. Karen felt confused. She wanted Patrick to find Nick and bring him home; they might both freeze out there on the moor unless they had found a place to shelter. But if Dave would only come first she could . . . she could . . . But her mind baulked at the thought of what she could do to stop him.

Abruptly, she got to her feet and went to the kitchen drawer where she took out the gully, the large knife which had last been used to cut up a slaughtered pig. She stared at it for a long time before she put it back and closed the drawer. How could she even think of doing such a thing? Restlessly, she went back to the mat frame.

Where was Patrick? And Nick? Was he lying out on the moor in this bitter weather, was he freezing to death? Well, this situation had come about because of her and she *was* going to do something about it. Wild plans formed in her mind. She would bring in the hayfork and do for Dave herself. No, she couldn't, not when the children were lying asleep upstairs, she couldn't. Suppose one of them did wake up?

A distant roar impinged on her consciousness and as it gradually became louder she jumped up from her chair, upsetting the mat frame so that it fell to the floor with a crash, spilling strips of red on the flagstones, dark as blood in the light from the lamp.

Dave. It was Dave's motor bike, it had to be. Oh,

now he was actually coming, what could she do? It was stupid of her to think she could do anything to him herself. No, all she could do would be to tell the police as she had threatened him she would. Getting to her feet, she rushed to the back door and pushed the thick wooden bar into the slots on either side of it. It was the first time the bar had been used that she could remember and it was a little proud, she had to force it in. But at last it was securely in place and she turned and leaned her back against it.

Closing her eyes tightly she listened, hypnotized by the sound of the engine as it came nearer and nearer.

Chapter Thirty-Three

Dave waited until dark before bringing his bike down from the fell, just in case the local bobbies had heard anything about his exploits of the night before. He had to walk down to the road with it. The snow was frozen solid with only the tips of the heather showing through and he found himself slipping and sliding down, falling every so often, once with his motor bike on top of him. By the time he got to the road he was feeling murderous, cursing and swearing at Jacko and the snow and everyone who had brought him to this pass. At last he reached the road and paused for a few minutes to get his breath. In spite of the intense cold he was sweating and breathless from his exertions.

He wasn't going to stay there, he decided, not in this Godforsaken hole. No, it would just be till the heat was off. Karen and her fancy man would have to find the money for him to get away. His old idea of going to Canada returned to him. He'd do it this time, he said to himself, he would do it. And those two would find the money for him all right. Even if they had to sell the whole damn' place, stock an' all, they would pay for him to get to Canada.

His thoughts were interrupted as he heard someone calling in the distance. He paused and turned his face to the bitter wind. The sound came again.

'Nick! Nick, where are you? For the love of God, come on home now.'

It was the Irish fancy man looking for the loony. Good, that meant Karen was on her own at the farm. Dave grinned to himself as he climbed on to his motor bike. He'd make life so bloody impossible for them they'd be glad to do anything to see the back of him. And maybe, while he had her on her own, he would shaft her one, just to remind her what a real man was like. There was no bloody half-wit there to interrupt him. Evidently he hadn't the sense to come in off the moor and out of the storm. He pressed his foot down on the starter and the engine spluttered into life. Settling himself on the seat, Dave roared off down the road to where the track turned off for Low Rigg Farm. He grinned again as he saw the light from the house, pleased with the feeling of power he had over the lives of the folk who lived there: he'd make them dance before he left them alone, he chuckled. But first there was Karen. He felt a pleasurable stirring in his loins at the thought of what he would do in the next half hour.

He didn't see the patch of ice by the gate; it was

hidden in the shadow of the rowan tree. All he saw was the open gate and the light of the house beyond. Without realizing it, he relaxed, his grip loosening on the handlebars. Then it happened. A figure flitted across the yard, outlined by the light from the window, and his attention was diverted for a brief second. And the front wheel of the motor bike skidded sideways, almost unseating him. But his reactions were swift. His grip tightened and he leaned forward, trying to steer the bike into the skid. But it seemed alive and to be fighting against him. He struggled to maintain control as it slipped and slid over the ice, but in that split second he knew it was too strong for him. It slid over and into the frozen bankside and his mouth opened in a scream as he went flying into the air, head first into the trunk of the rowan tree.

*   *   *

Inside the house, Karen listened to the approaching motor bike and then the screech of brakes. And the scream . . . it didn't sound like a man's voice, it was so high and penetrating, then it was cut off abruptly by a dull thud. She paused for a moment, unbelieving, before she realized that there had been a crash. Faintly, she could hear the throb of the idling engine, the only sound now.

Collecting herself, she tried to remove the bar from the door but it was stuck quite fast and she had to fetch a hammer to knock it up and out of the wooden slots. At last it came free and she opened the door and flung it wide. A pool of light shone out over the yard, making the ice sparkle and lighting up the snowflakes which were beginning to fall. And the motor bike, lying on its side, with the front wheel still spinning. There was no sign of Dave, where was he? She peered beyond the pool of light, vainly trying to see into the gloom beyond. Dear God, she thought, lifting a hand to her neck, where were the men? A moment ago she had been hoping Patrick wouldn't come home just yet, but now she prayed that he or Nick would appear.

'Don't come out, missus, it's too cold. I can see to things here.'

Karen jumped at the sound of Nick's voice. It was almost an instant answer to her prayer. 'What . . . What happened? Where is he, Nick, have you seen Dave?'

'There's been an accident. He crashed into the rowan tree. No doubt he's burning in Hell already.' Nick nodded towards the tree and Karen fetched the lamp from the kitchen and walked carefully over to the gate. As she neared it, she saw the body lying at the foot of the tree, the head turned at a very unlikely angle.

'You shouldn't have come out, missus, I told you I could see to it,' said Nick. He had followed her to the gate and was standing watching her with a look of concern which was only for her, not the body on the ground. She stared at him. Had he cracked up altogether? But no, he seemed perfectly calm and in control of himself.

'Well, we can't leave him out here,' she said at last. 'Come on, Nick, we must put him in the barn.' For the moment her mind could think no further than that.

'Righto, missus.'

Between them they managed to lug the body

484

away from the tree and across the yard to the barn, stopping once or twice to get a better grip on it. It felt incredibly heavy to Karen even though Nick took it by the shoulders, tucking his stump under one armpit and so taking most of the weight. But at last they had it inside and simply dumped it there, closing the door on it and dropping the bar into place outside to make sure. Though what she was making sure of, Karen didn't know. Dave was certainly not going to try to get out. He was never going to bother them again, she thought dully, but somehow the thought brought her no comfort. Her emotions were dead. She walked across to the gate where she had left the lamp and took it back into the kitchen, Nick following.

The warmth of the fire began to thaw not only her body but her frozen thoughts too. Her mind began working again. Perhaps it was just as well that Patrick wasn't here. If he was up the fell, the snowfall would be heavier. He would probably have to take shelter in one of the shepherd's huts up there.

'Did you see Patrick when you were out?' she asked Nick.

'No, I didn't. Did he go up the fell? But surely all the sheep are inbye, aren't they?'

'He didn't go looking for sheep, he went looking for—Oh, never mind. He'll be all right.'

Karen gazed at Nick. She was rapidly making plans, plans which would get rid of any threat from Dave for good. If she reported his accident to the police, they would want to know what he was doing there, there would be a chance something of their story would get out and it would kill Patrick if that happened. The chances were that he had already

485

taken shelter in a shepherd's hut, he wouldn't be back tonight. The snow was falling too thickly and it would be worse up on the fell. If Nick would help her, she could take the body away from the farm and no one would ever know Dave had been there.

'Will you help me, Nick?'

He never hesitated though he had no idea as yet what she was going to ask of him. 'Aye, I will, missus. What do you want me to do?' He had sat down and unlaced his boots ready to take them off but now he did them up again and got to his feet.

'We can put him down the old lead mine shaft, him and his bike. We can, can't we?'

Nick considered for a moment before answering. 'We can,' he said slowly at last. 'If we put him on the hay cart. The little hand-pulled one will take the load, I reckon. Right then, I'll go and get it out.' He didn't even question the wisdom of doing it, she marvelled for a second. But there was no time to think about that. She went to the bottom of the stairs and listened. The children were quiet, fast asleep.

'Come on then, it's not far,' she said as she re-entered the kitchen but Nick was already outside, bringing the handcart from the stable and opening the barn door. She ran after him and took the storm lantern from the wall just inside. She didn't look at the body as she helped Nick heave it on to the cart.

'I'll pull the cart and you push the bike, missus,' he said, very businesslike. He set off in the thickening snow, through the gate and up to the old waggon way. After a second's hesitation she followed, puffing hard as she struggled with the motor bike up the gradient after him. It was easier on the waggon way, at least it was level and led directly to the old mine shaft. But when she got there, she began to tremble.

The snow had abated and a frosty moon appeared from behind a cloud and illuminated the black hole of the shaft. Karen looked about her. Moonlight was shining on the broken windows of the building where generations of lead miners had bunked during the working week, huddled together for warmth and only going back to their steadings on the moor at the week's end. She shivered, fancying the eyes of long dead men looking down on her, condemning her.

'I can't do it,' she said, her teeth chattering together so that her words came out in a stutter. Her chest heaved, each breath seeming to tear at her lungs, so out of breath was she with the effort of pushing the heavy motor bike.

'Aye, you can, missus,' said Nick calmly. 'Howay now, it's nearly done.' He wheeled the handcart to the edge of the shaft and turned it round, easily tipping its burden off. Karen listened numbly to the splash which came seconds later. She stood holding the bike until he took it from her and pushed it down the shaft after the body.

'There now, it's done,' he said. 'Let's get back inside before we catch our deaths.'

Fool, Karen told herself. There was no one there, no one but themselves, there hadn't been anyone there for a generation or more. She took a few steps away and then turned back.

'Just a minute, Nick,' she said. Bowing her head, she stood for a moment in silence and he, seeing what she was doing, doffed his cap and followed suit. She prayed to God for forgiveness of all her sins and murmured the 23rd Psalm while Nick stood beside her, silently respectful.

The journey back to the farm was difficult, the snow coming down so thickly again it was hard to see the way. Their earlier tracks were already obliterated. But they made it at last and Nick took the handcart back to the stable. Karen went inside and stood before the fire, staring into the flames. Had they done the right thing? Already she was regretting it, but it was too late now. All she could do was pray they would never be found out.

Pray? She had no right to pray, she told herself, not after this night's work. Mechanically she took the kettle and filled it from the bucket in the scullery. A slight sound made her look towards the staircase. Were the children awake? Had they heard something after all? She hurried upstairs to see. Both Brian and Jennie were fast asleep, Jennie with her thumb stuck firmly in her mouth.

Coming back down she saw Nick was inside and the kettle beginning to sing. There was congealed blood on his forehead.

'Sit down,' she said, surprised to hear her voice was back to normal. 'Let me look at your head.'

'Nay, it's all right,' he demurred, but nevertheless he suffered her to wash his brow and bandage on an antiseptic pad. Then she made hot, sweet tea for them both. Nick sat rocking himself in the chair, back and forth, back and forth. She watched him, her own nerves at screaming point. It took all of her will power to hold herself together. Gradually, the warmth of the fire seeped into them.

'Patrick . . . he must never know,' she said after a while.

Nick looked up in surprise. 'Why no, missus, of course not. I doubt he couldn't live with it, him being as he is. He'd have to confess and then we'd all be in bother.'

Karen stared at him. Of course he was right. But she somehow had not realized Nick had read Patrick's character so well. And he seemed so calm, though his face was pale beneath the bandage on his brow. There was no sign of his nervous tic.

'I'll go up to bed now, missus,' he said, putting his mug down on the table. 'By, I'm tired, I am. I'll see you in the morning then.' Nodding to her, he left the kitchen.

Karen waited until the sounds from his bedroom quietened then went upstairs and checked again on the children. She tucked the quilt under Jennie's chin and placed a hand on her brow. The skin was pleasantly warm to the touch. She took a candle and waved it from the window for a moment or two and then went through to the front of the house and did the same. If Patrick saw it and was close enough he might come back tonight. But she wasn't worried about him, he would be all right. She undressed and washed her face and hands in the wash basin in their room before climbing into bed.

She was weary to the bone. Tomorrow was time enough to consider the events of the night and what she had done and any regrets she had. For now she had to try to sleep. She would need all her reserves of energy, both mental and physical, tomorrow and in the days to come.

489

Chapter Thirty-Four

A bright light was shining on Karen's closed eyelids, dragging her from sleep. Groaning, she turned over on to her back and flung an arm across her eyes to shut out the light.

'Mammy?'

Karen opened her eyes to see Jennie standing by the side of the bed, shivering slightly in the cold. 'Jennie,' she said wearily, 'come into bed before you freeze to death. I've told you not to get up until I have the fire going, haven't I?'

Jennie scrambled into the bed and burrowed down by her mother. 'But I'm hungry, and Brian says he will take me out sledging after breakfast. Can I go, Mammy, can I? I'm not poorly any more, honest.'

'We'll see.'

Karen closed her eyes again, filled with a great lassitude and longing to go back to sleep.

'Where's Daddy, Mammy? Has he got up already?' Jennie persisted, and memories of the night before came flooding back to Karen, and with them worry and apprehension. She jumped out of bed and crossed to the window to open the curtains, blinking as the dazzling light intensified. The sun shone on a wide expanse of snow which stretched as far as she could see, only the top of the hedge and the rowan tree showing above it. Well, she thought, at least there can't possibly be any tracks left from last night. No one will be able to tell what happened. Unless there are marks on the rowan tree . . .

490

Hastily, Karen pulled on her clothes and tied one of Kezia's thick woollen shawls round her shoulders. She would have to trudge through the snow to the gate and see. With a last look through the window she ran downstairs, first admonishing Jennie to stay where she was until she was called.

'Morning, missus.' Nick was sitting before an already lit fire, pulling on his boots. I'd better clear a path to the gate before breakfast,' he said calmly. 'There's been a foot or two of snow during the night. Still, I don't think it'll stay long.'

Karen watched him as he went to the door and out into the yard. In a moment she heard the scrape of his shovel as he began clearing a path. There had been not a sign of his nervous tic or any hesitation in his speech; he was back where he had been before Dave came. Why, it was almost as if Dave had never been. The thought gave her a curious sort of comfort and she got on with making the breakfast and when it was ready called the children to the table before following Nick out into the yard. He had already reached the gate and was standing, leaning on his shovel, regarding the rowan tree. She walked over to him, fearing what she might see.

There was nothing, no bloodstain, no bits of hair stuck to it. Just a small piece of bark missing, the wood underneath showing pale against the brilliance of the snow.

'That'll soon cover, missus,' said Nick, nodding his head in satisfaction. 'By, I'm famished, I've properly worked up an appetite digging that snow. I'll just see to the horses and then I'll be in for me breakfast.'

Of course, thought Karen as she went in, Nick

had become used to violent death during the war. She herself had become used to death, but not like this. Suddenly she began to shake. Her head swam, her pulse raced. Somehow, she found a chair and sat down, lowering her head between her knees, and after a while it cleared. Reaction, she thought dully, reaction, secondary shock. But knowing what it was didn't make it any easier. She had to pull herself together. She couldn't let Patrick see her like this, he would want to know why and he must never know, never. She made herself swallow a cup of hot, sweet tea and willed her tight, aching muscles into relaxing. After a while, her pulse slowed and she began to feel better.

Shortly after, Patrick returned. 'Nick back then?' he asked. 'I might have saved myself the trouble of going after him. Never mind, I found a warm enough billet in that shepherd's hut. I think someone had been there recently, there were signs.'

'Were there?' said Karen, thinking of Dave. Had he hidden out there before coming down to Low Rigg last night? Best not to think of Dave. No, she had to hold on to normality. 'Yes, Nick came back during the night. It was good of you to go looking for him in that weather though, Patrick, I'm grateful to you. Thank the dear Lord the snow has stopped now. Well, come by the fire, you must be frozen.' She turned to the stove and busied herself with the porridge, keeping her face averted from him. Oh, why had she been such a fool as to hide the body? Dead, he couldn't hurt them.

No, but the truth would have come out if he'd been found at Low Rigg, another part of her brain reasoned. No one would find him, no one went

492

near the old mine these days. She was safe.

Nick came in and she served the porridge. The children giggled together on the mat before the fire and the men ate steadily, fuelling themselves for the day's work ahead.

'No sign of Dave then?' Patrick asked after Nick went out to the cowshed.

'No, thank the Lord. I think he must have gone to Canada. He won't come back. Even he must have realized there was no more money to be had from us.' Karen kept her eyes on the dishes she was stacking as she spoke.

The policeman came a few days later. Karen wasn't even thinking of Dave, he was gone and he was never coming back. That was it, she told herself. But when Constable Peart came to the farm she was startled into wary alertness.

'Morning Mr Murphy, Mrs Murphy,' he said. 'I'm doing a round of the dale. A bit belated really what with the weather. It's an enquiry from Newcastle. It seems there was an attempted burglary at Jesmond and during the course of it a man was injured and has since died. One of the burglars was caught but the other got away on a motor bike and was seen heading this way. About a week ago that was. Have you seen any strangers about?'

'No, no one,' said Karen, rather too quickly.

'Oh, but you remember, Karen. I said I thought someone had been using the shepherd's hut on the high moor.'

The constable sighed. 'I'll have to have a look up there now the snow has eased. But he's likely long gone now. And if he's been up there hiding out, I don't think we'll find him alive. Ten to one he's

493

laid out on the moor somewhere, likely under a drift, frozen to death. That would save the tax payer paying the hangman an' all.'

'Do you think it was Dave?' asked Patrick after Constable Peart had gone.

'Probably. But in any case, I don't think we need worry about him any longer. If he's not dead, the police will get him. He won't dare come back here. He's probably gone to Canada, that's where he meant to go. We have to get on with our own lives, Patrick.'

And hope to God no one goes down the old shaft, she thought silently. Though if they did, how could anything be traced back to the occupants of Low Rigg Farm?

*   *   *

'We might have to buy in some feed, hay at least,' said Nick one morning. 'If the spring doesn't come soon anyroad.'

Karen bit her lip. The winter was dragging slowly on, one of the hardest and longest she could remember, and the stocks of animal feed were becoming lower and lower as were the supplies of flour and sugar and other staples they needed for themselves. She glanced at the bowl on the kitchen table. It held only three eggs. The hens had almost given up laying altogether and Karen was hard put to scrape the meals together. It didn't matter that the carrier wasn't managing to reach them through the drifted snow, they had no money to buy anything with and she was determined not to run up a bill on his 'slate', not unless it was an absolute necessity.

Dave had taken just too much, she thought bitterly. He deserved the end he got. Going into the pantry, she scooped flour from the bin into the bread-making bowl and brought it out. There was no yeast, so she went back for the box of Lingford's Baking Powder. She would have to make soda scones.

Patrick, who was sitting by the fire, pulled a face. 'I'm not fond of your soda bread,' he said. 'It's not like my mother's at all, it isn't.'

Karen's temper flared. 'If you were that fond of your mother's bread maybe you shouldn't have left Ireland,' she said tersely.

'I only said—'

'Yes, I heard what you said. Why don't you do something useful instead of complaining? Like taking the pony and going down into Stanhope to the store and bringing back some yeast?'

Patrick looked hurt. 'I would have offered but I thought we didn't have the money,' he said mildly. 'Leave the bread, there's half a loaf left and some porridge oats, we'll manage till tomorrow. I'll go down first thing, how's that? I can't go today, I promised Fred Bainbridge I'd help him mend the boundary fence.'

Karen stared down at the packet of baking powder in her hand, then she took it back to the pantry. Coming back into the kitchen she saw Patrick was lacing his boots, ready to go out.

'It's no good, Patrick, we'll have to get money from somewhere,' she said flatly.

'But where? You know there's no work on the road this weather.'

'I can work. I could get work down at the hospital.'

495

Patrick finished tying his boots and rose to his feet, his face hard and unsmiling. 'You will not,' he said and walked out of the house before she had a chance to argue. Karen stared after him, regretting the way she had spoken to him earlier. It wasn't his fault there was no work, she reminded herself. And it wasn't his fault Dave had come back and taken their meagre savings. She had hurt him, she knew. Oh, why couldn't she guard her tongue? Sighing, she went out into the yard and along to the hen house. The hens were to feed whether they laid or not. And at least things could only improve with the coming of spring.

Chapter Thirty-Five

Next morning, Patrick was withdrawn and quiet. Soon after breakfast he went into the yard and saddled Polly. Karen followed him.

'Where are you going?' she asked.

Patrick climbed on to the pony before replying. 'You wanted some yeast, didn't you? Well, that's where I'm going.'

'Patrick, about me going back to nursing—'

'No.'

He turned the pony and headed out of the gate. Karen watched him go in silence. The day was fine and the icy tang had gone from the wind. Behind her, water dripped from the roof of the house and as Polly trotted along she was kicking up clumps of mud. Patrick would be back at midday for something to eat, Karen told herself. As she went back into the house she remembered he hadn't even said goodbye. In the kennel by the back door, Floss whimpered, miserable because he had gone without her.

'Never mind, Floss,' she said. 'I know how you feel.'

Was he just going for the yeast or was he going to Wolsingham? Wolsingham loomed large and frightening in her mind. It was where the Catholic Church was, and priests and nuns and maybe Sean . . .

Karen got through the day going from one job to another. She fed the hens and collected the eggs. They had responded to the break in the weather and there were a few more eggs, God be praised. She helped Nick with the sheep and the lambs in the home fold. She comforted Floss, still in despair at being left behind by Patrick. She fed the children and Nick when it was dinnertime and Patrick did not come home. Her actions became mechanical, her mind on Patrick. She was waiting minute by minute for him to come home; her ears ached with the strain of listening for him above the chatter of the children.

The afternoon continued warm and Brian and Jennie played outside while she worked, Brian keeping an eye on his sister. They came running up to her and showed her where the crocuses were poking up above the slushy flower beds, purple and gold. Birds began to sing above their heads and at the bottom of the garden two robins pecked at each other furiously until one gave in and flew away. The victor preened himself busily and poked in the mud for worms.

The sick feeling in Karen's stomach intensified and she realized it was already teatime and there

497

was no sign of Patrick. She boiled eggs for the children and Nick and cut up the last of the loaf. When Patrick did come home she would have to begin baking at once if they were to have bread for tomorrow. In any case, she ought to make some of the despised soda scones for supper. She brought the makings from the pantry and began, trying to think of nothing but the task in hand.

It was half-past six when the clip-clop of hooves was heard in the yard. Karen was bathing the children in the tin bath before the fire in the kitchen. She had lifted Jennie out and was drying her on her lap but her hands stilled as she caught the first faint sound of the horse coming through the gate and she gazed up at the doorway to the scullery, though she told herself Patrick couldn't possibly appear there yet.

'Look at me, Mammy.'

Brian was sitting in the bath making bubbles with his hands and squeezing the slippery soap until it shot out against the side of the bath with a satisfying thud. Jennie began to cry, competing for her mother's attention, and automatically Karen wrapped the towel round her and cuddled her and Jennie quietened.

Then Patrick was there, filling the doorway and looking across the room at her, swaying a little on his feet. Even across the room, Karen could smell the whiskey on his breath. Where had he got the money for whiskey? He had only twopence for the yeast when he went out.

Her attention was distracted when Brian stood up in the water with the soap clutched in his hands and a wide grin splitting his face.

'Daddy! Daddy, look,' he shouted, and squeezed

498

the soap. It flew across the room to whack Patrick on the chest and bounce to the floor where it slid under the table, leaving a slippery trail.

'Brian!' snapped Karen and the boy's lower lip stuck out, quivering. 'Now don't start crying. Here, take the towel and dry yourself.' She pulled a towel from the brass line underneath the mantel shelf and gave it to him.

'Never mind, son,' said Patrick, his words slurring into each other.

'I'll get it for you.' He squatted down on his hunkers and reached under the table for the soap and promptly fell over, sprawling on the floor. Brian stared, forgetting his feelings were hurt.

'Come on, Brian,' said Karen. 'I want you dry and in your nightshirt and up the stairs in five minutes, do you hear me?'

'There's no clock, how can I tell when it's five minutes?' asked Brian. But he stepped out of the bath after glancing at his mother's set face and hurriedly dried himself and pulled on his nightshirt. Patrick had raised himself to his hands and knees and was crawling backwards from under the table. He got to his feet, his face red with the exertion, and sat down heavily on the settee. He and Karen still had not exchanged a word.

She took the children off to bed and hurried them through their prayers then came down and began clearing away. She emptied the bath water and hung the bath up on the scullery wall and put the towels over the rail to dry. Patrick was sitting watching her sombrely and she realized he was not so drunk as not to know what was going on.

'Well,' she said. 'Have you got the yeast? A fine time of the day this is to have to start baking

499

bread.' She turned away from him, biting her lip, knowing she sounded shrewish but unable to help herself. Oh, why couldn't they be happy now that the biggest threat had gone from their lives?

'I forgot to get the yeast,' he admitted.

Karen whirled on him. 'You forgot? How could you forget?'

'I've been working, a day's casual at the station. If I hadn't gone as soon as I heard I would have missed it,' he defended himself. 'I'm sorry about the yeast, Karen, but I'll go back tomorrow, we'll have soda bread till then.'

'The carrier will be here tomorrow, there'll be no excuse for you going down the pub again,' she said. 'Well, let's see the money you earned today, there's nothing else to pay the carrier.'

Patrick fumbled in his waistcoat pocket and brought out five pennies and placed them carefully on the table. He looked at them for a moment and then searched through the rest of his pockets. In his trousers he found a halfpenny and solemnly added it to the pennies.

'Is that all?' asked Karen. She stared at the coppers, despair making her voice harsh. 'You must have some more, how much did they pay you?'

'I had to have a bite of dinner, didn't I?'

'A bite of dinner? A bite of dinner? You've been in the Moor Hen, that's where you've been, supping whiskey, do you think I can't smell it on you? You're drunk, man, and me without a shilling to buy in supplies. Patrick, Patrick, how could you do it?'

'Shut your mouth, woman!' Rising to his feet he glared at her. 'Sit down and shut up.'

Karen stood her ground. Angry tears started to her eyes and she brushed them away impatiently. 'I won't shut up, why should I? What's the matter with you, Patrick? Just when we have a chance to start again after all the trouble, you go off drinking. By, it's a good job Gran isn't here to see you coming in drunk, I can tell you. When I think—'

Whatever Karen was going to say she thought was knocked out of her head as Patrick lifted his hand to her and slapped her so hard she fell across the table and the jug of water toppled on to its side and the water ran off on to the flags beneath. She lay there for a few seconds, half on and half off the table, more stunned by the fact that he had hit her than by the actual blow, before sinking on a chair. Unbelieving, she put a hand up to her face which was still stinging from the slap. She moved the hand round to the side of her head where it had hit the water jug and felt the bump rising under her hair. And then she looked up at Patrick and they stared at each other as though they were strangers.

'Maybe that will shut you up,' he said. 'It's about time I showed you who's master in this house.'

Karen watched, in something of a daze, as he walked out of the room to the stairs, stumbling only once against the door frame. After a moment she rose and looked critically in the over-mantel mirror. Her face was red down the left side but she thought it wouldn't bruise. She let her hair down and brushed it to that side, wincing as the bristles caught the bump on her head. Then she sat down in the rocking chair, laid her head back on the cushion and closed her eyes.

'Are you all right, missus?'

Nick's voice startled Karen and she jumped to her feet, feeling dizzy. He was standing right next to her and he put out his good hand to steady her. 'Eeh, I'm sorry, missus, I didn't mean—'

'It's nothing, I was just dreaming. I couldn't think who it was for a minute,' she said, putting a hand up to her face. But Nick didn't notice, he was looking at the water on the floor and the turned over jug on the table.

'Something knocked the jug over?' he asked.

'Yes, I did, I was going to wipe it up . . .' She picked it up and went into the scullery and refilled it from the pail. 'I'll just wipe up the mess and then I'll make your cocoa.'

'Patrick gone to bed then?'

Her hand stilled momentarily as she reached for the floor cloth. 'Yes. Yes, he has. He was tired, he's had a day's labouring in Stanhope.'

'What's that mark on your face?' Nick asked suddenly.

'Nothing, it's nothing. I . . . I started to clean up before but I banged my face on the side of the table.'

She mopped up the water and made him a cup of cocoa, holding her head down and allowing her hair to fall forward and shield her face. But Nick had accepted her explanation and said no more. When he had drunk his cocoa he too went to bed.

Karen sat for a while before the fire, trying to sort out her chaotic thoughts, not wanting to go up to the bedroom and get into the bed she shared with Patrick. But weariness overcame her and she drifted off into sleep, heavy and dreamless.

It was the cold which woke her. The fire had dropped down to a white ash, and the lamp had gone out. The air in the kitchen was icy and she was shivering uncontrollably. She reached up to the mantel shelf and felt for the candlestick and matches. Soon the small flame lit up the blackness and she crept upstairs.

Patrick was asleep, lying on his back in the middle of the bed, snoring gently. There was still a smell of whiskey about him, hanging stale and sickly on the air. Karen undressed and pulled on her flannel nightgown, snuffing the candle before climbing in beside him, careful not to touch him with her cold flesh, hoping she would not disturb him. She couldn't bear to talk to him, not yet, not until the morning at least. He grunted and turned over on his side away from her and she held her breath but after a few seconds his rhythmic breathing recommenced. Gradually, her shaking limbs stilled and the warmth of the bed crept through her. She lay quietly, her mind going over the events of the evening.

No man had ever slapped her before, not even Dave at his nastiest, not even her father. Oh, Da had kept a leather strap with two tails in the kitchen drawer all through her childhood and that of her sisters and brother. But she couldn't remember that he had ever used it, not even on Joe at his naughtiest.

Of course, it was the drink that made Patrick do it, she told herself, and was reminded of the sermons she had heard her father preach about the evils of the demon drink. But that didn't make it any easier to bear, oh no, it didn't. But Patrick drank because he felt trapped into poverty, that was it. If they had just a little more money he wouldn't need the whiskey, he would be happy with her and the bairns, they could get back to the way they had been in the years before Dave came back.

I could work, she thought. I am a trained nurse, I could get work in Stanhope. I could even be a district nurse, the dale could do with its own district nurse. Then we wouldn't be dependent on Patrick getting work on the roads or burning lime. He's not fit for such hard labour, that's the trouble. I will see about it tomorrow, I will.

'I'm going down to Stanhope to see about getting some nursing work,' Karen said at breakfast. They were sitting round the table eating soda bread spread with a thin smear of butter and a good dollop of treacle.

She had waited until Nick went out to see to the hens before saying it. Patrick sat opposite her, steadily eating and Jennie was licking the treacle off her bread. Brian gazed at her over his cup, looking worried.

'What about us? Who'll make our tea?' he asked.

Karen smiled. 'Don't worry, pet, you'll still get your tea.'

Patrick put down his piece of bread and looked fully at her for the first time that morning. He had already been gone when she woke, and when he came in for the meal with Nick he had said nothing to her.

'You're doing nothing of the kind,' he said now calmly, not raising his voice at all. 'Your work is here, looking after the children.'

'We need the money, Patrick.'

He pushed back his chair and stalked to the door before turning back to her.

'You can put the idea out of your head, Karen. I'm telling you so and you can just make up your mind to it. Now, I'm going out to the sheep, I'll be back at dinnertime.'

Karen watched him go through the scullery window, his tall figure passing out through the gate and round the path by the rowan tree to the sheep fold, and her face was set. He could say what he liked, she thought. If she once had a job and was bringing in a little each week, he would realise that it was for the best.

Turning back to the children, she said, 'Come on, Jennie, I'll wash your face. We're going to take Brian to school and then we're going to see Granda.'

Chapter Thirty-Six

Karen travelled to Bishop Auckland on the bus. It was cheaper than the train though the journey was longer. The basket of eggs she had at first intended to give to Kezia, she managed to sell to a small grocery store in Stanhope. She regretted having nothing to take for her sister but she needed the one and sixpence she was paid for the eggs for fares.

Bishop Auckland marketplace was quiet for all it was eleven in the morning. There were few customers about. She took Jennie's hand and crossed over to the bus for Morton Main, stepping round piles of dirty, melting snow and lifting the little girl high over puddles, making a game of it. Karen's own feet were wet and cold even crossing

505

the few yards between the buses for the soles of her boots were well past the time they should have gone to the cobblers to be renewed.

The bus was empty but for the driver and conductor; evidently no one wanted to go out to the villages.

'Nice break in the weather,' commented the conductor as he took her penny ha'penny and gave Jennie the ticket. Karen nodded agreement.

'You're not very busy today,' she observed, for something to say.

'Aye, well, it's Tuesday. Things are different on Thursdays when the market's going. Not much like, not now half the pits are idle or working part-time.'

As they wended their way round the small pit villages, most of them with the winding gear in the pit yards still and quiet and the coke ovens cold, Karen was struck with guilt. She hadn't realized just how bad things were, she had been so full of her own problems. She hadn't even brought the eggs. Perhaps she could have done with only selling half of them, then she would have had some to give to Kezia who surely must need it judging by the poverty she saw all around. Everything and everybody, from the apathetic children playing in the streets to the men sitting on their hunkers on the corners, watching idly as the bus went by, told the same story. No work, no money. And Morton Main was no different, she noted as the bus drove up to Chapel Row. Except that the pit wheel was turning. At least Morton Main colliery was working.

'Luke's at work, thank the Lord. Three-day week but better than nothing,' said Kezia after the sisters had greeted each other and Kezia had exclaimed at how fast Jennie was growing. Her own children were in school. 'There's no work for young Luke though.' She sighed and lowered her voice. 'He's talking about going away, tramping round the country looking for work. Some of his friends are going and I'm worried to death. Don't say anything to Da though. He's not well.'

Da was sitting hunched over the fire and Karen was shocked by his appearance. He seemed to have sunk in on himself somehow, his broad shoulders shrivelled and his face grey and lined. His mouth hung permanently open with the effort of drawing breath. It was miner's lung, Karen recognized his disease immediately. Poor man, she thought, even as she smiled and went forward to kiss him on the cheek.

'Hallo, Da,' she said brightly. 'I've brought Jennie to see you.' 'By, it's grand to see you both an' all,' he said, his words breathy and laboured through the mucus which bubbled up into his throat. 'But mebbe you should have waited till the weather got a bit warmer before venturing all this way.'

'We came on the bus, Da, it was no trouble,' replied Karen. She watched him covertly as Kezia filled the kettle for tea and buttered lardy cakes. There was an air of defeat about him even worse than the last time she had seen him and her heart ached. It was Jennie who brought a little life back to his eyes. She went up to him and laid her hand on his arm.

'Granda, are we going to Lizzie's shop for a sherbet dab?' she asked.

'Jennie! I've told you it's rude to ask for things.

507

And Granda hasn't got the money to spare to buy sherbet dabs,' Karen admonished. But he was fishing in his waistcoat pocket with two fingers. Bringing out a penny, he held it up.

'Nay, lass,' he said. 'The day hasn't come yet when I couldn't buy my grandbairns a bit of a treat.'

'That's his baccy money,' said Kezia after he and Jennie went off hand in hand to the shop. 'He'll do without his smoke now until pension day, but don't let on I told you.'

Karen drank her tea, oversweet because it had condensed milk in it as it was cheaper than fresh. The sisters chatted about this and that and then Karen came to her main reason for coming to Morton Main.

'Is Robert Richardson still the doctor?'

Kezia looked surprised. 'Why, yes, he is. And a godsend he is an' all. He's grand with the bairns, never grumbles when he's called out during the night. Not like that last doctor we had. Do you remember when he told Mam to go to the West Coast for a holiday? No idea, that man, no idea at all what it was like for pit folk, even though he lived among them. Now Doctor Richardson—well, let's just say Africa's loss was our gain.'

'Would you mind if I just slipped along to see him? I mean, give an eye to Jennie for me, I won't be long.'

'There's nothing the matter, is there?' Kezia looked keenly at her.

'No, no, nothing like that,' said Karen. 'I'll tell you later. I thought I might catch him still in his surgery just now.'

As she had judged, Robert was still in his

508

surgery. There was only one patient left to go to him and Jimmy the dispenser was busy filling up bottles of 'tonic' from a large demi-john in his tiny cubicle off the waiting room. He poked his head round the door and surveyed Karen.

'You're a bit late for surgery, aren't you?' he asked testily. 'Mebbe you'd better come back at six the night. The doctor's got enough on now, it's time he was out on his rounds.'

'I'm not here as a patient,' she said.

The dispenser came fully out of his cubicle, medicine bottle in one hand and funnel in the other. 'Then what . . .' he began when the surgery door opened and the patient came out, followed closely by Robert.

'Jimmy,' he began to say when he saw Karen and abruptly stopped speaking.

'Hallo, Robert.'

The words fell into a small silence broken only by the ring of the patient's hob-nailed boots as he walked out of the waiting room and down the yard.

Jimmy looked curiously from her to Robert who was standing perfectly still, his face expressionless. 'I've got the list for the rounds,' the dispenser said.

Robert moved then, standing aside to usher Karen into the consulting room. 'Just hold on to it for the moment, please, Jimmy,' he said and Karen walked in front of him. He closed the door behind them both. 'Sit down,' he commanded and she took the chair placed by his desk for patients and he sat down at his desk.

'What can I do for you?' he asked formally.

'Nothing . . . I mean, I'm not here to consult you professionally.'

'Then why are you here?'

509

Karen stared at his handsome face, noting the slight lines round his mouth and on his brow. His hair was grey at the temples, the once clear-cut line of his jaw softened. Robert looked his age and more, she thought abstractedly. How old was he? Forty? He lifted an eyebrow, waiting for her to answer and she pulled her thoughts together.

'How are you, Robert? Kezia has told me how good you are to the folk here, how everyone likes you—'

He sat forward in his chair with a look of impatience. 'I'm sure you haven't come here to make small talk, Karen.'

'No. No, you're right. I have to ask you a favour.'

She looked down at her hands, clasped tightly in her lap. He sounded so bitter. Which of course he had every right to be, she told herself. But somehow, she hadn't thought of that. Oh, she had known she had hurt him but she had tried to explain when she wrote to him. He hadn't replied to her letter, she remembered now. But it was so long ago, seven years, surely he had got over her by now?

'A favour.'

'Yes. I want to nurse in Stanhope, maybe become a district nurse. But I need a reference and I thought—'

'You thought, there's Robert, good old Robert. He'll do anything for me. All I have to do is beckon and he'll come running. Even after seven years.'

'Robert! No, it's not like that, not at all.'

'Isn't it?' He rose to his feet and turned to look out of the window, his fists clenched at his sides. 'And what about the great Irish lover? Can he not support you and your children now? Or have you grown tired of him? After all, seven years is a long time with one man.'

Karen was on her feet now, shaken and angry that he should talk to her as he was doing. 'How can you say that, Robert!' She walked round the desk until she was before him, looking up at his face which was suffused with rage.

'I can say it, Karen. Oh, yes, I can say it. Did you think you could do what you liked with me and I would take it, like a puppy dog? I was going to marry you, Karen, even though you were carrying another man's child. You agreed, then when the priest came looking for you, you went to him without a thought for me or my feelings. You acted like a whore. In fact, you are worse than a prostitute. You use men. You used me.'

Karen couldn't believe what he was saying. She lifted a hand and caught hold of his arm. 'Robert, Robert, I'm sorry I hurt you, I really am. I didn't mean to, really I didn't. Please, Robert, forgive me. It was a bad time for me what with the baby coming.'

'So you thought, well, there's good old Robert, he'll look after me.'

'I didn't! I never meant . . . I didn't know Patrick . . .'

'Was coming back to you? Well, I knew I was second best but I didn't expect to be thrown over when I wasn't needed any more.'

'Forgive me, please forgive me,' she pleaded, clutching his arm.

He shook himself free and stepped back from her. 'There you go. You think all you have to do is look at me with those great, brown eyes and—' He

511

broke off what he was saying as a knock came on the door. For a moment he stood there, his mouth working, and the knock came again.

'Yes? What is it?' Robert said at last.

'It's Jimmy. Is everything all right, Doctor? Only there's a long list for your round this morning and it's nearly dinner-time.'

'Yes, all right, I'm coming. I've finished here.'

Robert turned to the desk, taking no further notice of Karen. He picked up his black bag and put in his stethoscope and snapped it briskly shut.

'I'm sorry I bothered you, I'll go now,' said Karen. He lifted his head and stared at the wall above her head. She walked to the door, holding on to her dignity as far as she was able. She paused with her hand on the doorknob.

'Goodbye, Robert,' she said and opened the door and walked past the dispenser who was watching her curiously. She went out of the waiting room and down the yard where the men usually waited their turn during surgery hours, squatting on their hunkers and drawing deeply on their cigarettes. Thank goodness there was no one there now, she thought. Going along to Chapel Row, her cheeks were aflame with mortification though when she got into the house and Kezia commented on her high colour, she blamed it on the wind.

'Still a wild north-easter blowing out there,' she said. At least she had not much time to spare before starting on her journey home, not if she was to be back before Brian.

On the bus going back up the dale, she sat slumped in her seat not listening to Jennie's chatter, and in the end the little girl dropped off to sleep with the motion from the bus and Karen had to half carry her to the butchers for something for tea and then to the connecting bus going up the moor, Jennie fretful and crying. Karen was filled with misery and self-loathing. Robert was right, she thought, all the men in her life had turned away from her and it had to be something in her, not them. She would never understand men, never.

Except for Joe, her brother. Suddenly she missed him as acutely as she had done the first time he had gone to Australia. She could talk to Joe, she told herself as she built up the fire and put the kettle on to boil and bathed the children and put them to bed. But Joe had a life of his own in Australia, he was married now and according to his last letter doing very well for himself. It was silly to yearn for Joe, she was unlikely to see him again.

Nick came in and she made supper for him, boiled cow's heel she had bought in Stanhope between buses, but she couldn't eat herself. The lardy cake she had eaten at Kezia's that morning still lay heavy on her stomach, making her feel queasy. Nick was quiet, eating his meal and going out to the barn again soon after for there were two sickly lambs to nurse. There was no sign of Patrick until much later in the evening. He came in once again smelling of whiskey and the smell made her gag so that she rushed out into the yard without speaking to him.

Leaning against the wall of the house, she drew in great gulps of air, trying to force her system back to normal through strength of will alone. After a while the cold seeped through her body and she had to go back inside.

Patrick was sitting by the fire undoing his boots. He glanced up at her and said, 'Don't start now.'

513

Karen bit her lip. She was weary to death, she couldn't have started an argument now if she wanted to. And she didn't want to, she just wanted to go to bed and curl up into a ball and drop into unconsciousness and sleep for a week.

'I'll get your dinner,' she said and Patrick didn't notice how pale she was, how she trembled, because he didn't look at her. He ate the jellied cow's heel she put before him and went back to his seat by the fire where he sat, staring into the flames.

It was the following week when the letter came from Robert. Just a brief, formal note saying he hoped the enclosed reference was suitable for her purpose.

Chapter Thirty-Seven

'I'm sure you are a very good and experienced nurse,' said Matron. She looked across the desk at Karen, her shrewd eyes taking in the younger woman's neat blue dress which came down modestly over her knees in spite of the current fashion for shorter skirts. 'Doctor Richardson seems to think highly of your abilities. But we don't usually take on married women, especially ones with children. They have too many home commitments and sometimes these have to come first, naturally. I'm sorry, Mrs Murphy, I would like to help you but—'

'I would take anything.' Karen was anxious enough to interrupt, something to which hospital Matrons were not accustomed. But Karen was past caring about hospital etiquette. After all her hopes, she could see her chances of a nursing job disappearing. 'My children are not a problem, Brian is at school and Jennie soon will be. And . . . and I have help at home, someone to look after them if they are ill.' If Matron thought she meant female help, well, why disillusion her? Nick was good with the children and Patrick was there most of the time.

'I would have to ask my Board, and to be honest I think it would be a waste of time. I'm sorry, Mrs Murphy, I'm afraid I have to say no. It's a pity, I need an experienced nurse but there it is.'

Karen rose to her feet, disappointment rising in her throat like bile. 'Thank you, Matron. I understand of course,' she said and turned for the door.

'Have you considered private nursing?' Matron's question stopped her in her tracks. Private nursing? Surely a private nurse had to live in the patient's house, at their beck and call both day and night? But nevertheless she sat down again.

'Private nursing?'

Matron leafed through the papers on her desk until she found the one she wanted. 'I've had a letter from Mr Whitfield at the Manor. He needs a relief nurse for his wife who suffers from rheumatoid arthritis. Just one afternoon and evening per week and alternate Thursdays. The household used to manage between them when the regular nurse was off-duty but now he feels they need a trained nurse at all times. What do you think? I will recommend you if you think you can do it.'

Karen didn't hesitate. 'Oh, yes, Matron, I can do

it. Thank you very much.'

*   *   *

Picking up Brian from school and travelling back up the dale with him on the bus, Karen was filled with trepidation. She had the job, starting from the following Thursday, and she would be paid seven and sixpence a week. Seven and sixpence for twenty hours work! It was magnificent, a life-saver. But would Patrick think so? Yes, he would, she told herself, once he realized what a difference it made to their standard of living. She murmured in admiration at the picture of Floss rounding up sheep which Brian had crayoned and replied to his chatter absentmindedly, her thoughts still full of how courteous Mr Whitfield had been and of the large, low-ceilinged rooms at the Manor, full of polished oak and cavernous fireplaces. And of Mrs Whitfield, lying in a huge bed barely able to move of her own volition. It would be pleasant working there, she thought. With just the one patient she would be able to give her best.

After leaving the bus, Brian ran on ahead down the lane, eager to show Nick the picture he had done of Floss. Karen followed more slowly, trying to marshal her arguments for taking the job. She would confront Patrick with the news at once, she decided. He was taking the flock out on to the low fell this afternoon now that the snow had gone. She would give the children their tea and then go up to meet him and tell him in the privacy of the open fell. Changing into her rubber boots, for the ground was boggy after the melting of the snow, she covered her dress with the decrepit old

516

macintosh she wore for her outside chores in wet weather and set off. At least the daylight hours were lengthening, she thought, there was plenty of time before dark.

It was Floss who saw her first, as she closed the last gate and began to climb on the open ground. The dog came rushing down to her, tail wagging and tongue lolling, her whole body showing her delight in seeing Karen. Patrick was more circumspect. He plodded down the bankside, his face unsmiling.

'Floss! Here, Floss, heel!'

The dog's tail dropped and she slunk back to her master, grovelling behind him when she got there. Karen stopped walking and waited for Patrick, her heart thumping. He questioned her with a look. It was a long time since she had come to meet him like this.

'Hallo, Patrick,' she said as he reached her and she fell into step beside him. She tried to think of the openings she had rehearsed but her mind just went blank so she came out with the news baldly.

'I've got work, Patrick.'

He went on walking, not even turning his head to look at her, and she hurried after him.

'It's just part-time, private nursing at the Manor in Stanhope. Only one full day and one half-day.'

He had reached the gate by now and stopped walking. As he turned to face her she saw his grim expression. His eyes seemed to have changed colour to a slatey grey and there was a thin, white line round his mouth.

'You took a job after I told you not to?'

Karen flinched. His words were mild enough and he didn't raise his voice at all but his tone cut her with its venom. 'Patrick, it's for the best, you'll see it is. I'll have seven and sixpence a week, for only twenty hours. Think what we can do with the money. And Nick will watch out for Jennie, and Brian's at school. We need to build up our reserves, Patrick, you know we do. Even if you get work on the roads again this summer, we need every penny we can get.'

'We will manage. You can go back to Stanhope today and tell them you've changed your mind, you can't do it.'

'I can, Patrick, I can. You'll see, we'll manage fine—'

'If you don't tell them, I will go myself and tell them for you.'

Karen bridled. 'Oh no you won't! You have no right to do that. I'm going to at least try to do this job, even if it only lasts a few months. But I'm going to do it, Patrick. Mind what I say, I am.'

'I tell you, you will not!'

'And I say I will!'

They stood face to face, their voices rising until Karen was practically shrieking out her defiance. 'I am a trained nurse, it's lunacy not to take advantage of the fact when we are so hard up. It will be ages before we get any return on the farm and Nick has just his pension. And you, what are you trained for?'

'Shut your mouth, woman, or by Jesus I'll shut it for you! It's for me to go out to work, not you.'

He towered over her, his hand raised, but she was too furious to back down now.

'Go on, hit me, that's all you're good for. You're trained for nothing, nothing useful at all. Why, Nick with his one hand is more use—'

518

She stopped, appalled at what she had said. Stepping back, she stared up at him, expecting him to knock her down and knowing she deserved it if he did. 'I'm sorry, I didn't mean it.'

Patrick lowered his hand and smiled a bitter smile. 'No, you're right. What good am I? I'm not man enough to support my family, my wife has to go out to work because I'm not trained for anything. Nothing except one thing. Perhaps I'd be better off going back to that—if they'll have me, that is.' He strode off down the bankside at such a pace that he rapidly put a distance between them.

Karen stared after him. Oh, God, dear God, tell me I didn't say those things to him, she prayed, closing her eyes tightly and lifting her face to the darkening sky. A slight rain had begun to fall, icy spring rain which numbed her cheekbones and mingled with her tears. His last words repeated themselves in her ears. He was going to leave her. Her worst nightmares had come true and she had done it all herself.

But no, it would be all right. All she had to do was run after him, catch up with him, convince him that she hadn't meant what she had said, she had been off her head. She loved him, he loved her, of course he did. She began to run, slipping and sliding on the wet grass, falling down on her hands and knees and struggling back to her feet.

'Patrick!' she shrieked. 'Patrick! Come back, I didn't mean it, I didn't! I love you, Patrick.' She sobbed out the words, gasping and crying as she ran. In the end, she was barely breathing them for her breath had gone altogether, taken by the effort of running across the uneven ground, falling over ruts made by the melting snow and trodden into jagged heaps by the sheep. A pain in her side intensified and she doubled up, falling to the ground, but after a few minutes of desperately trying to catch her breath she started again. Patrick was long out of sight by now. As she neared the farm there was no sign of him. There was only Nick, followed by the children, coming out of the hen house, locking the hens in for the night, Brian importantly sliding the wooden bar into its slots and looking to him for approval.

'Missus?' Nick saw her distress as she opened the gate to the yard and stumbled across to them.

'Where's Patrick? Has he gone? He hasn't gone, has he, Nick?'

'Nay, missus, I don't know. He's in the house, isn't he? By, you're in a state, just look at you, covered in clarts. Has something happened, is somebody chasing you?' He snatched the bar from the door of the hen house and strode over, gazing behind her up the fell, holding the piece of wood like a club. Brian ran to his mother, taking her hand and gazing up into her tear-streaked face in alarm.

'You're crying. What for, Mam? Why are you crying?' he asked. He looked at the mud on her skirt and the old mackintosh. 'Did you fall down, Mam?'

Jennie, still standing by the hen house, put her thumb into her mouth and stared fearfully. 'Mam, I'm frightened,' she wailed.

With a great effort of will, Karen tried to speak normally to calm the children. She seized on the excuse provided by Brian.

'It's all right, no, there's no one after me, no one at all. I just tripped up on the fell and hurt my

520

knee. It's nothing, I'm all right now. It knocked the wind out of me, that's all. Now go and help Nick while I speak to your daddy.'

She bent down and kissed Brian's forehead and scooped Jennie up and hugged her. The little girl stopped crying.

'Is there baked potatoes for supper?' she asked, her fright of the minute before forgotten. 'Can I have butter on mine? I like butter better than cheese, Mam. Can I have butter?'

'Yes, you can. Now be a good girl and go with Nick.'

Nick looked searchingly at Karen, aware that there was more to her distraught appearance, but he said nothing, merely taking the little girl's hand and leading the way to the stable.

'Howay, Brian,' he said. 'You can help me with the pony. And Jennie can look for eggs in the corners. I'm sure one of the hens is laying away, she's looking broody.'

'Thank the Lord for Nick,' breathed Karen as she sped into the house and took off her mackintosh and rubber boots in the scullery. 'Patrick? Patrick, are you there?' she called as she went through to the kitchen, but the room was empty, the fire in the grate burned down to white ash and black cinders. She ran up the stairs and searched every room, even the attic, not believing that he had gone. Downstairs, she looked in the cupboard under the stairs and in the pantry, not even considering how foolish her searching was. Why should he be hiding?

In the end, she returned to the kitchen and sat down by the table, burying her head in her hands. After a while, she got to her feet and mended the

521

fire with bits of twig and, when she had them ablaze, piled on pieces of coal from the dwindling store. She propped the metal blazer on the top bar and opened the back door so there was a draught and soon had the fire hot enough to boil the kettle and warm the oven for the potatoes. Then she washed the mud from her face and arms and changed her skirt, putting it before the fire to dry.

She would brush off the worst of the mud tomorrow, she decided. Strangely, her wild grief had subsided. All she felt now was a numb weariness.

She made the supper and fed the children and put them to bed. Nick came in and she forced herself to eat a baked potato filled with cheese and drink a mug of tea. Nick finished his off quickly.

'He's gone off to the pub again, has he?' he ventured once. Karen nodded, her mouth full of potato which refused to go down her throat. She took a long swallow of tea and at last the potato went down. Sitting back in her chair, she held the mug in both hands, staring into the brown liquid.

'Well,' said Nick, 'I half-promised Mr Bainbridge I'd go with him to the men's meeting at Chapel.'

Karen looked up, slightly surprised. Nick rarely went out in the evenings. 'Oh? Yes, well, you'd better be going then.'

Left on her own in the kitchen, she went over the row with Patrick, bitterly regretting her sharp tongue. Why on earth had she said what she did? Why couldn't she have kept quiet? And why, oh why, couldn't Patrick see that what she was doing was for them all? She sipped at her tea, feeling indescribably desolate.

Restlessly, she took the mat frame and began

sorting through the bag of coloured clippings but she couldn't settle to it. Giving it up, she put it away again and walked out into the dark yard, making her way over the cobbles to where she could see the rowan tree outlined against the sky. She stood for a few minutes, looking up the lane, but there was no bobbing lantern showing Patrick was coming home, only the blackness of the night. She shivered. There was a touch of frost in the air though it was coming up to summer. An early night, she thought, that's what I need. Going back inside she went up to bed, lying stiff and unsleeping hour after hour. Every little sound from the night outside she thought was Patrick coming home. But there was no clip-clop of hooves, no whinny from the foal as its mother came home. After Nick came in there was only the hooting of an owl in the ghyll.

*   *   *

Patrick came home in the middle of the day when she was on her own in the kitchen. Brian was at school and Nick was repairing a gap in the drystone wall by the far field and had taken Jennie with him.

A surge of such gladness ran through Karen when Patrick came in that she couldn't move for a moment. Then she flung herself at him, wrapping her arms round his neck, laughing and crying into his rough coat.

'Oh, Patrick, I thought you weren't coming back,' she sobbed. 'I'm sorry, really I'm sorry, I won't take the job, I won't—'

'Karen.'

523

Patrick took hold of her arms and drew them down and held her away from him. At first she couldn't see his face properly through her tears. She dashed a hand across her eyes impatiently and then she looked at him and she knew.

'Sit down, Karen. Come on, sit down, we have to talk.'

'Talk? Yes, of course we'll talk,' she said. Blindly she went to the settee and sat down and he sat in the rocking chair facing her.

'I want you to understand that I will always love you,' he said. 'You and the children.'

'Yes, of course. Oh, and Patrick, I love you, I love you. Don't be angry. I know I've made mistakes but—'

'Don't go on, Karen, it's no use. I have to go back.'

'Back? Back where? Ireland, do you mean? Your . . . your Church?' Her heart thudded as she said it. This wasn't happening, no, it wasn't.

'Ireland, yes, and my Church. If they will have me.'

'No! No, you can't. Not after all we've been through, what I did—'

'What you did, Karen? What do you mean?'

'Nothing, I didn't mean anything.' She gazed at her hands which were twisting and twining her apron round and round and straightening it out, then round and round again, as though they had a life of their own. She didn't even see them.

'You only did what a woman in love will do, Karen. Oh, it's not your fault, any of this, it's mine. I know that now. My mistakes, my sin.'

'Are you saying that the children were mistakes, the results of sin? How can you, Patrick, how can

524

you? They love you, you know they do. How can you leave them, for God's sake, man! And why now? You haven't been to church for years. What changed you Patrick?'

'I have changed, Karen, that's what matters. I'm sorry. I didn't mean to spring it on you like this but I've made up my mind.'

'You've made up your mind? I see.' She jumped to her feet and walked to the window and back, her every movement filled with agitation. 'What about me? What about the children? Well, you can't go off like that, I won't let you. Patrick, you can't, do you hear me? I'll go to see the bishop, I'll tell him—'

'Sit down, Karen, let's talk this over calmly.' He thought fleetingly of Sean. She didn't know yet that he was now the bishop.

'Talk it over calmly? You're proposing to desert your family and you want me to talk about it calmly?' Karen was screaming by now, her whole body shaking with passion. Panic filled her mind, preventing any logical thought.

'Please, Karen, please. I won't leave you with nothing. I'll be able to send you money . . .'

'Money? Do you think that's all there is to this? You've had enough of playing at families, now you can leave us and all you need to do is give us money? For the love of God, Patrick, think again.'

He didn't answer, just looked at her helplessly. Karen drew in a sharp breath and turned away. She had to gain control of herself, she couldn't think straight, she had to think. She wasn't going to give up the fight now, not now. Oh, God, please God, I have to keep him, he is my life, she prayed under her breath. What can I do? No answer came

525

from on high, nothing. It was up to her entirely. Her mind raced.

Patrick was a sensual man, how could he go back to an arid, celibate existence? That was the way, oh yes indeed, if she couldn't move him with words she surely could with her body. Behind her, Patrick was silent but she was intensely aware of him. He hadn't moved.

Slowly she took off her apron and loosed the top buttons of her dress. She touched her face, peering at it in the window. Was it blotchy, ugly? She pulled tendrils of hair down over her temples and brow and then he spoke.

'Karen?'

Taking a deep breath she turned back to him. He watched her as she moved towards him until she was standing so close to him she could feel his breath on her neck. He gave a startled movement but she stayed him with a hand to his shoulder and then the back of his head. She brought his face nearer to hers and he did not resist and she was gazing into his eyes and the invitation in her own was open and explicit. She murmured throatily as desire swept through her veins, a desire heightened by her emotional turmoil. Catching his hand she brought it to the open V of her dress, to the swell of her breast.

His thumb brushed against her nipple and his hand tightened on the soft flesh and he drew her even closer with his free arm. Karen lifted her lips to his. Exultantly she strained herself against him. She had won, oh, he couldn't resist her. He loved her as much as she loved him, it was going to be all right.

Next moment he had caught hold of her arms

and put her away from him. 'No, Karen, it's no use,' he said calmly, and it was his very calmness which got through to her. She couldn't believe it. For a moment she stood there shaking, breathing unevenly. And then she looked at him and his face was that of a stranger. Suddenly she slumped, all the fight drained out of her. She had lived with him for almost eight years and she had been as close to him as one human being could get to another and now he was a stranger to her. She couldn't get through to him, he was implacable. Her humiliation was total.

'Be reasonable, Karen, please,' he said now, his tone cool, almost impersonal. She couldn't believe it. 'You know we haven't been getting on lately. It's my fault, I know. I've tried, I have really tried, but I should not have married. You are a strong woman, Karen, you will be all right. You should have married your Robert, I see that now. And it's true what you say—I'm no good on the farm, you have me to rights there. Look, I'll give you the address of my relatives in London, I'll go there first. And Sean says—'

Karen's head shot up. 'You've been seeing Sean?' It felt like the ultimate betrayal.

Patrick nodded. 'I have,' he admitted.

Her heart beat painfully. Sean, his brother priest, he had always been against her. And now he had won. She sat down before the fire, staring into the flames, defeat bitter as bile in her throat.

Patrick gazed at her, wishing he could help her, knowing he could not. He thought back to his last meeting with Sean. His friend had been so understanding, reminding him of the years they had spent in the seminary, of the hopes and ambitions they had had. And Sean had fulfilled his early promise. Look at him now, a bishop.

'We will pray together, Patrick, you and I. God will reveal his plans for you,' he had said, and knelt with him before the altar. A peace beyond understanding came over Patrick there, a peace which was still with him. A peace which was carrying him through this scene with Karen. He looked at her as she sat dejectedly by the fire. How he had loved her, beyond all reason. But he had to go.

'Your main duty is to God and the Church,' Sean had insisted. 'You pledged your life to his service, he will not let you go.'

'But Karen, the children . . .'

'They will be looked after,' Sean had said. 'She is a strong woman, you have said yourself she is, she will get over this.' Wisely he said nothing against Karen, not then. Patrick was so close to coming back into the fold.

Patrick brought his thoughts back to the present. 'I won't go until summer, Karen. I won't leave until I'm sure you will be all right,' he said, breaking into her bitter reverie. It was enough to shake her out of it.

Rising to her feet, she turned to face him. 'No, go as soon as you like. Go now. Why wait for the weather? There's lambing in the spring and haytime in the summer. There isn't a good time. If you want to go, you'd best be ganning.' Unconsciously she slipped back into the idiom of her own people as at last she found her pride.

I'm tired, she thought, utterly defeated. And she had to face up to it. Just when she thought everything would work out her worst nightmare had returned, and this time for real. Patrick had been reclaimed by his first love.

'You can bring Young Luke in to help you,' said Patrick. 'It will be fine, you'll see.'

'Oh, yes, fine.'

She gazed at him. He had obviously thought it all out. How long had he been planning this? she asked herself. But she would not ask him. Already she was feeling detached from him. Tomorrow or the day after that she would mourn for him, but now her mind could take no more. Turning her back on him without another word, she went into the scullery, pulled on her boots and took her mackintosh. She walked out and along to the ghyll and sat down on a limestone outcrop, staring at the swollen stream, peaty from melted snow off the high moor. Please let him be gone before I go back, she prayed. She couldn't bear to see that final act.

After a while she began to notice the tiny signs of spring: the celandines pushing through the new grass, the scent of wild garlic which hung on the air. Soon the curlews would come crying over the fell, their courting song rising and falling as they danced on the wing. Faintly, she heard the hourly bus go by on the top road. It was time to go back to the farm.

Walking along, she saw Nick and Jennie in the distance. They would be wanting their dinner, it was time already. By the gate, she gazed up into the branches of the rowan tree. The buds were swelling and tiny bits of green showed at the tips. She leaned her hand against the trunk. It was solid and hard. The mark where the bark had been chipped off that night was damp and brown; the raw newness of it had soon faded.

Forgetting the need to prepare dinner, she leaned against the trunk and gazed out over the moor, her mind already working, planning what to do. We will be fine, she vowed to herself. I'll see that we will. I have a job now, haven't I? Like the rowan tree, I'll be here, standing foursquare to the wind, no matter what happens. Resolutely she walked to meet the children and took them by the hand, one on either side of her. They chatted excitedly about their day and she listened absent-mindedly as they crossed the yard and went into the house.

It wasn't easy, oh no, it wasn't easy at all. Sometimes she wondered at herself, how she had stood by the rowan tree the day that Patrick went, thinking fine thoughts of how she would manage without him, fooling herself.

She wondered one day as she walked across the yard and out by the gate, her nurse's case in her hand for she was on her way to work. She didn't look at the tree but stared blindly up the lane, concentrating on putting one foot before the other on the path, for the pain was as a knife slicing inside her today. She tried to turn her mind to the patient she was going to see. It was Mrs Gilbey, a housewife who had contracted polio last summer and was now a paraplegic, paralyzed from the waist down and confined to a wheelchair. Mrs Gilbey, with her three young children and a husband with a fondness for ale.

How much better off she was than Mrs Gilbey, she told herself, but it didn't help cut down her misery, it didn't help at all. Maybe she was being punished for Dave. That was it, his unquiet spirit

530

could be hanging over the farm, she didn't know. Such superstition, the Church would say disapprovingly—Robert would say it was not Christian, an echo from pagan times.

Karen's muddled thoughts ran on unchecked until she climbed down from the bus at the entrance to the Gilbeys' farm. Then, miraculously, her nurse's training took over and she pinned a cheery smile on her face. She attended to her patient's pressure points and replaced her urine catheter, chatting all the time of the gossip in the dale to the news-starved woman. But at the back of Karen's mind hovered the black cloud of despair, waiting to take over altogether should she let down her guard.

Chapter Thirty-Eight

Karen sat on the bus going down the dale, staring unseeingly out of the window at the sun-dappled hedges and hills. The bus stopped at Frosterley and a crowd of women got on. They were on their way to Bishop Auckland market. The bus was filling and a stout red-faced housewife carrying an enormous basket sat down beside Karen, jostling her with the basket.

'Eeh, I'm sorry, missus,' she said. 'Can't this bus be murder on market day? I tried to get the nine o'clock but what with the milking and getting the bairns off to school—'

She broke off as she realized that Karen was ignoring her completely. Offended, she sniffed loudly and pursed her lips. Stuck-up bitch, she thought, who did she think she was? Just sitting there, couldn't even acknowledge a body when she was talking perfectly civilly to her an' all. The woman glanced at her neighbour across the aisle, wondering if she had seen her humiliation. But no, she hadn't noticed.

Karen was oblivious to everything on the bus. It was three months now since Patrick had gone. Patrick. The name seared through her mind and she closed her eyes against the pain for a moment. For all her determination, in spite of all the times she had told herself she could manage without him, the pain of losing him was always there in her mind, even when she was working. And she worked all the time. There was the pressing need to try to close him out, fill her mind with other things. How long could she bear it?

Karen shook her head, trying to rid it of her pain. She turned to gaze into the bus and the woman beside her glanced haughtily at her but when she saw the haunted agony in Karen's eyes haughtiness slipped into concern.

'Are you feeling badly, missus?' she asked. 'Is something the matter?'

This time the question penetrated Karen's mind and she looked at the woman.

'I'm sorry, did you say something?'

'I was just asking if you felt poorly, like,' the woman said loudly, forgiving, for wasn't it obvious that Karen was deaf?

She winced. Why on earth was her neighbour shouting? 'I'm fine, thank you,' she answered and turned her eyes back to the window. The bus was pulling into Bishop Auckland marketplace. She would have to hurry to catch the connection to

532

Morton Main. Pleased to have something to do which stopped her mind dwelling on Patrick, she pushed her way to the door and waited impatiently for the bus to stop.

The marketplace was fairly busy this Thursday morning. Not so bustling as when the mines were working fully though, except round the stall at the end near the entrance to the bishop's palace which sold second-hand clothing. There, women were turning over the piles of collarless shirts and suits with shiny elbows and knees. Two women were arguing over a child's dress, pink and frilled artificial silk.

'I'll give you two shillings, I can't afford half a crown,' the younger one was saying. 'Come on, man, would you have my bairn go on the Sunday School anniversary without a nice dress?'

'Two and threepence,' the stallholder answered stolidly, glancing absent-mindedly after Karen. She passed on to where the fish-wives from Shields were calling their wares.

'Caller herring! Lovely fresh cod!'

She bought a pound of herring and waited impatiently for the fish-wife to wrap the fish up with her red-raw hands, chapped and scarred from the fish pickling. The Morton Main bus was in. Karen paid her twopence and ran for it. At least she had something to take with her to Kezia. She had forgotten altogether to bring the basket of eggs she had intended for her.

'Why, Karen pet, it's grand to see you,' Kezia exclaimed, scrambling up from her kneeling mat before the range, black-lead brush in hand for she had been busy buffing up the shiny black fronts of the oven and boiler. 'Why didn't you write and tell me you were coming? I'd have had the place nice for you.'

The sisters gave each other quick pecks on the cheek though their beaming smiles belied the meagreness of their embrace. Kezia's smile became anxious however as she noted the deep shadows under Karen's eyes and the hollows in her cheeks. She knew that Patrick had left her, of course. Karen had written her a short note, saying so. But there had been no emotion in the letter and her sister had insisted that she was all right, everything was fine. And Kezia had been busy with the problems of Luke working only three days a week and Young Luke not at all, and had taken her at her word. Karen was not fine, she could see that now, feel it in the nervous energy which pulsed from her.

'Come on, sit down, lass,' she said. 'I'll make a pot of tea. I have some new bread and some of last year's bramble jelly left, you look as though you could do with something, you're nothing but skin and bone.'

Karen put her parcel of fish on the table. 'I brought you some caller herring from the market, Kezia. But don't bother about me, I'm not hungry.'

'Rubbish,' she said quickly, 'you have to eat. Thanks for the fish anyroad. I'll soon have them cleaned and fried. It'll be a nice treat for Luke and the bairns when they get in. Luke's on fore shift, you know, he won't be long.' She cleaned and washed the fish and rolled them in oatmeal ready to fry, all the while keeping up a conversation about nothing in particular, just trying to bring Karen out of herself.

'How's Father?' she asked, rather belatedly

534

thought Kezia. Well, at least the news of Da's new job would brighten her up a little.

'I was going to write to you, Karen. Da's working, isn't that grand?'

'Working? Do you mean they took him back on at the pit?' Karen was all attention now, her own trouble forgotten for the minute.

'No, you know they won't do that, not after the lockout. No, he's working for Doctor Richardson, what do you think of that?'

'Robert? He's working for Robert? But what does he do?'

'Oh, all sorts. You know old Mr Clary, he used to collect the panel money for Doctor Brown? Well, he carried it on for Doctor Richardson but now he's retired and Robert came and asked Da would he like the job? Mind, we were flabbergasted, I can tell you. But Da, he perked up straight away. "I will, Doctor," he said. "I will, and God bless you for it." '

' "Not at all," said Robert, "you'll be doing me a favour. I need a trustworthy man and you being a fellow lay preacher I thought of you. What's more I've known you all my life, why you're just the man for the job." '

'But surely that's just a two-day job?' put in Karen.

'No,' said Kezia, over the sizzling noise from the frying herring. 'He works in the surgery too, making up the medicines and such. Why, according to the doctor he's his right hand man, making up bottles and answering the telephone. Doctor Richardson says he saves him no end of time. Oh, Karen, you should see Da now! He's so much better. Why, he looks twenty years younger.

535

I was worried he might think it a cissy job for a miner but he's taken to it grand.'

Dear Robert, thought Karen, he was a real Christian, so kind. What man, treated by a woman as he had been by her, would even have talked to her or her family again? Yet he had given her a reference, he had given her father work. He had loved her, and if he had done so half as much as she had loved Patrick, he must have gone through the same agony she was going through now. The thought made her wretched. She turned away so that Kezia shouldn't see the tears threatening to fall. Luckily, she was distracted as the children came in from school, closely followed by Luke, black from the pit, and Young Luke who was proudly carrying four eggs.

'Well, isn't that something?' exclaimed Kezia. 'Look now, Karen. Luke built a hen house down the garden. He raised the hens from chicks and we thought he was never going to get any eggs but here they are at last.'

'They're a bit small, I know. Mebbe the hens will do better when they are older,' said Young Luke. 'Hallo, Aunt Karen.' He showed her the eggs, she being the farmer in the family. 'What do you think?' He looked down at her anxiously, a thin, gangly lad, his face pink from these days spent out of the pit and in the sun.

'Lovely,' said Karen. 'I bet your mam will be glad of them. You like working with animals, don't you, Luke?'

'Oh, aye, I do. I was thinking, I might be able to get a nanny goat. I could tether it along the line, then we'd have our own milk.'

'There's no money for a goat, lad,' his father said

536

flatly, and Young Luke flushed, the enthusiasm dying from his eyes.

Kezia was serving the fish and Karen was busy for a while, cutting bread and handing slices to Meg and Tom.

'Da won't be in today, he's having his at the doctor's house,' said Kezia.

For a while, the talking ended, everyone tucking into the meal with a will. But when they had finished, Karen brought up the real reason for her visit. After all, she reasoned, it was best approached while the family was all together.

'I have the offer of a full-time job at the hospital,' she said, leaning back in her chair. 'I could do with the money, and I'd like to take it. Trouble is, there's so much work on the farm.' As she spoke, she watched Young Luke who was suddenly all attention, looking at her with steady, expectant eyes.

'There'll be no trouble in getting help in these times, surely?' commented Kezia.

'No. But I can't afford much more than a lad's keep, not yet anyway. I was thinking, Young Luke—'

'Mam?' He didn't have to put his request for permission into words, it was there, shining from his eyes.

Kezia looked at his father, who nodded. 'What about the hens though?' she asked.

'Tom will see to them, won't you, Tom?'

'Will I get an egg every day if I do?' he asked, and Karen was hard put not to smile.

'You'll do as you're told, whether or none,' his father put in sternly. 'Now get away back to school and watch Meg crosses the road safely. Don't you go running off leaving her, do you hear?'

When the children had left for school, Meg protesting loudly that she didn't need anyone to see her across the road, wasn't she a big girl now. Karen looked at Young Luke who was sitting still, his hands clasped together and resting on the table, as though in prayer.

'The lad was a great help when he was with us before,' she said. 'A born farmer, he is.' In spite of the blue-grained scars on his hands, the marks of a pitman, she thought as she gazed at the tightly clenched fingers. Why, there was even one on his forehead, standing out against the pink-white skin.

'The lad can go with you,' said Luke. 'It's better than him having to go to Australia like your Joe. At least we'll see him from time to time. Now, what about my bath, Kezia? I'm ready for my bed.'

It was as Karen and Young Luke were going off for the bus to Bishop Auckland, Luke carrying his straw box and dressed in his best suit and cap and Kezia walking beside them, telling him to behave himself and work hard and write home every week, that a car drew up beside them.

'Now then, you weren't going off without seeing your father, were you, Karen?'

All three of them stopped and watched as Da climbed out of the passenger seat of the Sunbeam coupe and kissed Karen lightly on the forehead. She couldn't believe the change in him, he looked so well, and as Kezia had said, twenty years younger.

'Granda, Granda, I'm going to work on the farm!' cried Luke excitedly, dropping his box on the pavement and quite forgetting he was almost a grown-up.

'Are you now?' Da answered, looking keenly at Karen's shadowed face. 'By the look of your aunt here, it's time she had someone she could rely on.'

Karen looked up at him quickly. Kezia must have told him about Patrick's desertion, of course. Did he blame her for not holding him?

Her father was strictly against broken marriages, separation or divorce. This was her second, too, the thought ran through her mind. But Da's face held only concern for her.

'Hello, Karen.'

The sound of Robert's voice made her look beyond her father to where Robert was just getting out from behind the driving wheel. He walked round the car and took her hand.

'Robert,' she said. 'How are you?'

'Well,' he answered gravely. 'I was just dropping Mr Knight off so he can have a break before the six o'clock surgery. Sarah is seeing to any calls for me. I'm on my way to the town, I have a patient in the cottage hospital. Perhaps I can give you a lift?'

'Well, we were catching the bus . . .' she began to say. Looking up at him, she was shocked to see the band of white which ran through the centre of his dark hair. Had he had it when she asked him for a reference? She was ashamed to find she couldn't remember. He was standing quietly, waiting for her to go on, politely, almost impersonally, as though she was a stranger. And she was a stranger, of course she was. Or had been these last few years since Patrick.

Robert saw the sudden shaft of pain in her eyes as she thought of Patrick. He stepped back and dropped her hand, though he hadn't an idea what had caused it. 'Of course, go on the bus by all

539

means.'

'Oh, no, we will be delighted to ride with you, won't we, Luke?' she cried. 'Luke is coming to live with us,' she went on rapidly. 'He is going to work on the farm.'

'Well then, climb in the back, Luke, and I'll hand you your box,' said Robert. The family said their goodbyes and soon they were on their way, Luke still young enough to be thrilled to be riding in the doctor's Sunbeam, grinning and waving as they passed a group of young unemployed miners, lounging about on the corner of the Chapel wall.

'How are the children? And Patrick, of course?'

The question sent a tremor of shock through Karen. How could Robert be so cruel as to ask such a thing? Could he possibly not know what it did to her? She looked sideways at him with a feeling of outrage but he was gazing ahead at the road, his expression bland and unknowing. He hadn't heard of her trouble, she realized, and found herself wondering that he had not.

'The children are well,' she replied, her voice low.

'And Patrick?'

Karen cleared her throat. 'He . . . he has left,' she muttered.

Momentarily, the car slowed, then Robert recovered himself and kept up a steady thirty until he reached the marketplace where the bus for Weardale was standing in. He stopped the car and turned a concerned face to her.

'Tell me about it,' he said quietly.

'I'm surprised you haven't heard, you being so friendly with Father Donelly,' she said bitterly. 'Patrick has left us, he's gone back to his church.'

540

'I haven't seen Sean since he was made a bishop. I'm sorry, Karen, really I am. If there is anything I can do . . .'

She turned away and opened the car door. 'Come on, Luke,' she said. 'We'll have to hurry or the bus will go without us.'

Robert understood. He too got out of the car and helped Luke with his box. 'Go on, hold the bus for your aunt,' he said, and turned back to Karen. 'I know it's too painful for you to talk about yet.'

'Oh, I'm all right, Robert, don't worry about me. Did I tell you I am working full-time now? I am going on the district as soon as I can and with Luke to help Nick on the farm—well, as I said, we'll be fine.' She smiled brilliantly at him and rushed for the bus, leaving him looking after her. He even took a step after her, his arms lifted, yearning to take her into his arms before the thronged marketplace and comfort her. But they dropped to his side and he walked back to the car. Now was not the time. He would not make the same mistake twice.

*   *   *

Luke was all Karen had hoped for on the farm. He and Nick worked closely together, much more so than Nick and Patrick had ever done. Karen was thinking about it as she came out of the house one morning and got into her little car, an Austin 7 she had bought second-hand for £15 when she started her new career as a district nurse. Nick called over to her as he led Polly out of the stable, her breath blowing white on the frosty air.

'Mind, missus,' he called. 'Be careful on that top

541

road today. It's awful steep and bound to be icy.'

'I will, Nick, I will. What are you up to today?'

'Luke and me are bringing the sheep down inbye, there might be snow the night,' he replied.

'Well, if Brian's in there hanging round Luke as usual, maybe you'll tell him if he doesn't come now, he'll have to walk up for the bus to school.'

Jennie was already climbing into the back seat of the car. Karen smiled softly at her. She had to be careful with Jennie; the child was too anxious to please somehow, and clung to her mother since Patrick had left. Jennie sat quietly as Karen waited for Brian, her thoughts roaming back over the dream she'd had during the night. It was a recurring dream, one she'd had over and over again, but at least the intervals between were getting longer.

In her dream, she was always in Patrick's arms and they were about to make love and she could feel her body responding eagerly to him. Or sometimes they were in the kitchen and the children were in bed and they were sitting before the fire, holding hands in the lamplight, enveloped in love and security. And just when she was feeling so secure in his love she woke from the dream. At first the feeling of euphoria hung on for seconds, even minutes, but always reality broke in and desolation swept over her.

Karen moved restlessly behind the wheel. She must stop thinking about it. She hadn't thought about it for weeks, but the dream had come back as she had known it would. Looking over to the stable, she saw Brian just emerging.

'Hurry up, Brian,' she called sharply. 'Do you want to be late for school?'

542

'But, Mam, there's half an hour yet,' the boy said reasonably as he slid into his seat. She twisted in hers and looked him over.

'You haven't got yourself dirty, have you? Show me your hands.'

'They are clean, Mam,' Brian protested but held them out obediently.

'Well,' said Karen, 'don't keep me waiting again, I have to get to work.' She hated herself for being sharp with him, it wasn't his fault she had such bad dreams. And his father's desertion had affected him badly. He had grown nervous and quiet, and when Luke came to the farm spent all his time with his cousin, keeping out of the house as much as possible. Sometimes Karen wondered if he blamed her for what had happened.

She started the car and edged out of the yard and up the track to the road. Tonight she would make a special effort. Perhaps if she got home early she would have time to make something special for the children's tea. And on Saturday it was the Sunday School Christmas party, she would take them down herself. Jennie would like that.

She dropped the children at the school gates where Miss Harvey the headmistress saw her and came over to her.

'I've been wanting a word with you, Mrs Murphy.' Karen made a move to get out of the car but the headmistress waved her back. 'No, there's no need to come in, I know you are a busy woman nowadays. Everyone is talking about the good you are doing in the dale. We should have had a district nurse years ago. Anyway, what I wanted to ask you was, is it all right if I put Brian in for a scholarship to Wolsingham Grammar School?

543

He's far and away the brightest pupil I've got, though Jennie won't be long before she catches her brother up.'

Karen flushed with pleasure. 'Of course it's all right, I'd be delighted,' she said. 'Jennie too, when her time comes.'

'That's the attitude I like to see in parents,' declared Miss Harvey. 'You know, some of these farmers don't see the advantages of an education, not when the boys are to follow them on the farm. But I always say, an education is an investment in life.'

'Yes, Miss Harvey, how right you are. But I know you will excuse me? I have to be at the doctor's surgery in five minutes and the roads being as they are . . .'

'Of course, Mrs Murphy, mind how you go now,' said the headmistress, and stepped back from the kerb. Karen drove off, her mind lighter than it had been for many a month, for once all thoughts of Patrick banished.

Chapter Thirty-Nine

Robert sat at his desk, leaning back in his worn leather chair, his long legs stretched out before him. Surgery was over at last and he could relax for the first time that day. Subdued sounds from the cubby hole in the corner of the room reminded him that his assistant was likely to be just as tired as he was and glad to go home.

'You can get off now, Mr Knight.'

'Yes, Doctor, thank you. I'm just emptying the

Mist Expectorant demijohn into bottles, ready for tomorrow. Then it can go to be refilled. It seems that everyone has a cough this bitter weather.'

Mr Knight came round the corner of the screen which served as a door to the cubby hole and took his coat from the stand and put it on. As he knotted his white scarf round his neck and buttoned the coat over it, Robert was struck afresh by his likeness to his daughter Karen. The same shape to the head, though the father had the typical miner's haircut, clipped close with only a fringe at the front to show when he put on his cap, as he was doing now, pulling it out of his pocket and jamming it down on his head.

'I'll say goodnight then, Doctor. I'll come early in the morning, there'll likely be a surgery full.'

'Yes, it's good of you, Mr Knight.'

For all their relationship of employer and employee, Robert never presumed to address the older man without his proper title. It was on the tip of his tongue to ask about Karen, how she was, had the family heard from her today, but he held back. After all, he had asked after her yesterday, and only a few days before that. Mr Knight would begin to wonder, if he wasn't wondering already.

Robert clasped his hands behind his head after the older man had gone, enjoying the chance to think and dream now he was alone. Karen . . . it had always been Karen for him, ever since he had rescued her from Dave Mitchell when they were at Sunday School together. Even then, he had planned to be a medical missionary, promising himself that as soon as he was qualified he would ask her to go with him.

He shifted position slightly as he remembered

545

the despair he had felt when he discovered she had already married Dave, and he had missed his chance. And his stay in the mission field had been cut short in any case when he had been hit with illness and had to come home. He smiled wryly. 'Man supposes, God disposes.' It had been a favourite saying of his father.

There had been the time he had thought she would marry him, alone and pregnant as she had been. He had been sure he could make her love him. And he might have done, but the priest had come looking for her and that had ended his dreams once again.

Robert sat up straight in his chair and gathered his papers together. This time, please God, it would be different. He would be careful, he wouldn't rush her, he would wait until the pain she was suffering (and he knew well the pain she must be suffering, hadn't he gone through it all his life?) had lessened. Karen was doing well on the district, the people liked her and she was a good and efficient nurse. He was friendly with his colleague in Stanhope and had had good reports of her, both from her time in the hospital and as a district nurse.

'Dinner's almost ready, Doctor.' His housekeeper put her head round the door.

'I'm just coming, Sarah,' he replied. Rising to his feet, he turned off the lights and went through the door which communicated with the house. As he went, he was humming softly to himself.

* * *

Karen drove into the farmyard and switched off

546

the engine of her little car. She sat quietly for a few moments, her thoughts ranging over the year since Luke had come to the farm. Looking round, she noted how tidy the yard was, and how the hens were already shut up for the night for there had been reports of foxes in the area.

Rays from the setting sun streamed across the yard and the August air was redolent of the cut hay which Nick and Luke had been stacking in the barn. From inside, she could hear the voices of the children and the deeper tones of Luke. He was a young man now, she thought, and a more capable farmer than she had ever been. And, on the Chapel outing to Saltburn she had seen him hand in hand with his fellow Sunday School teacher, Elsie, Fred Bainbridge's granddaughter.

Karen was tired, it had been a trying day. There had been a spate of motor bike accidents in the dale recently, boys and young men with broken ankles and sometimes worse, and after they came out of hospital it was her duty to see to any after care which was needed. She had just returned from a visit to Tom Grainger, where she had dressed the deep gash in his leg. Tom worked a farm further down the dale. He had been proud of his new tractor until he tried to travel on ground which was much too uneven for it and it had overturned. Luckily, he was thrown clear. There were reports of tractors turning over and trapping men underneath and killing them. As it was, Tom had only a slight concussion and the gash in his leg where he had caught it on a sharp rock. Karen smiled as she thought of him as he was this afternoon. She had caught him in the hay field.

'I'm not working, Sister,' he had protested. 'Just

lending a hand, that's all. What's a man to do at hay time?' Grinning sheepishly, he had limped back to the house with her so she could attend to his wound.

'You have to rest the leg,' Karen had said. 'If you pull the gash open it will only take longer to heal. Then what will you do in the winter when you can't go up the fell after sheep?'

She was brought out of her reverie as the house door opened.

'Mother, are you coming in to supper?' It was Jennie standing there, slim and tall for her age, and serious. 'It's all ready, Nick and me did it.'

'Nick and I,' Karen corrected her automatically as she got out of the car. 'Yes, I'm coming now.'

After supper, Luke changed into his good suit and put on a collar and tie. He'd had a shave too, Karen noticed, his chin was all pink and shiny from the razor. His hair was slicked back from his forehead and gleaming with an oil which smelled strongly of bay rum.

'Our Luke's going with Elsie Bainbridge,' said Brian. 'Mind, Luke, if that smell doesn't put her off, nothing will.'

'Hush now, Brian, and get on with your homework,' said Karen. 'You going for a walk, Luke? Well, enjoy yourself, you've earned it.'

After he had gone off down the lonnen towards the Bainbridge place, Karen was washing up the dishes when there was the sound of a car coming into the yard. All the family looked up in surprise. No visitors were expected, the people of the dale were usually too tired during hay-making to pay visits.

'I'll go,' said Brian, and had the back door open

even before whoever it was could knock. When the two men came in, both so tall that they had to stoop to enter and then seemed to fill the kitchen, Karen couldn't believe her eyes.

'Joe!' she cried. 'Joe!' And collapsed into her brother's outstretched arms while Brian and Jennie looked on in bewilderment.

'How are you, Sis?' he asked. 'I've come to see what you've been up to all this time. Robert here was kind enough to run me up.'

She gazed up into his face and he grinned down at her, his teeth white against the deep brown of his tan. A confident, mature face, but nevertheless she could see her little brother's eyes twinkling back at her. 'Oh, Joe,' she said, half between a laugh and a cry, 'what are you doing here?'

'I had to come to London on business, so I took a few days to come up and see you all. And here I am, large as life.'

'On business?'

Joe's grin grew wider. 'That's right, gold mining business. You never thought your little Joe would become a globe-trotting businessman, did you?'

'Mam,' said Jennie, tugging on Karen's skirts, 'is this Uncle Joe from Australia?'

Joe laughed as he bent down and swung the young girl in the air and waltzed her round the room. 'I am, I am, and who are you, may I ask? You can't be baby Jennie. No, of course you're not, you're far too tall and beautiful.' And Jennie was suddenly a tiny girl again, blushing and giggling.

Karen turned to Robert. 'I'm so sorry,' she said, 'I didn't mean to ignore you but in the excitement of seeing Joe . . . Well, how are you? It was so good of you to bring him all the way up here.'

549

'Actually, I wanted to see you in any case,' he answered. 'So when Joe said he wanted to come, I thought it was a good time.'

She glanced at her brother who had sat down on the settee, with Brian on one side of him and Jennie on the other. He was telling them tall stories of the size of the kangaroos and encounters with Aborigines and the children were listening, spellbound. 'Come into the sitting room,' she said to Robert. 'We can't hear ourselves speak in here. Would you like some tea?'

'No thanks, I have to get back.'

'Well . . .' Leading the way into the front room, Karen was suddenly conscious of him as a man, a strongly attractive man, and the feeling was such a shock to her she almost stumbled over the edge of the rug and he put out a swift hand to take her arm.

'Steady.'

Karen bent her head to the table lamp, lifting the glass and fumbling for the box of matches to light it. She was glad of the dusk and took her time in lighting the match, trying to get her confused feelings under control. What was happening to her? She loved Patrick, there was no other man in the world for her, how could she possibly be so drawn towards another man and that man Robert? Why, she had known him all her life. Her fingers trembled and she dropped the match.

'Here, let me,' he said, and took the matches from her. The touch of his fingers made her pull back in confusion. He lit the lamp and soft light glowed on her face and wide dark eyes. He drew in his breath sharply.

'Karen . . .' he began and turned away abruptly,

clenching his hands. I must not rush it, he told himself, I must not.

'Yes, Robert?'

'I . . . I wonder if you would be interested in moving, changing your job?'

'Changing my job?'

She was standing perfectly still, gazing up at him as though she had never seen him before. He glanced away, he had to if he was to keep his voice calm and neutral. 'Yes. I need a good nurse, Karen, the village needs a good nurse. You know what it is—no one wants to come to a dirty old mining village to work when there are so many other places.' He swallowed hard and stepped towards her, his resolve weakening as it always did with Karen. 'Remember how I dreamed of us working together on the mission field in Africa, Karen? Well, we're older now. I know there is as much good work to be done right here, by both of us. Can't you see it, Karen?'

He took hold of her hands and drew her to him. She was enveloped in a warm, magnetic haze. Her will to resist gone, she lifted her face for his kiss.

'Mam! Mam! Uncle Joe says . . . Mam!' Whatever Uncle Joe said was forgotten as Brian saw his mother spring apart from Doctor Richardson, just a moment too late for he had seen them wrapped in each other's arms. And so had Joe. He was in the doorway behind Brian and he was grinning widely.

'Sorry we disturbed you,' he said. But Karen had regained her senses. She couldn't believe she had almost kissed Robert, couldn't believe how she had felt as he'd held her. Now she felt only shocked and confused. Gathering her wits together, she

551

brushed past them all and went into the kitchen. She hardly heard as Robert said his goodbyes.

'Goodbye, Robert,' she said coolly, gazing at a point somewhere over his shoulder.

'You'll think about it?' he asked.

'I will, but I'm afraid the answer will be no. I'm sorry.'

Joe looked on, mystified, as Robert went out. He waited until the sound of Robert's car died away in the distance before turning to Karen, his eyes full of questions.

'Let it be, Joe, let it be,' she said quickly with a warning glance at the children, and he subsided. But later, when the children were in bed, he would not be put off.

'What's it all about, Sis?'

Karen gazed at him, her little brother Joe. When they had been children they had always told each other everything. 'You know about Patrick?'

He nodded. 'I know he has deserted you. But that doesn't mean your life is over, Karen. Now Robert—'

'I can't love anyone else, I can't even think of it, Joe! I'll never marry again, I won't.'

'Well, that wasn't the impression I got when I barged in on you and Robert earlier.'

Karen looked down at her hands and slowly the tears came and increased to a torrent. With them the story poured out too, the whole story, nothing held back, not even the final horror, the death of Dave and how, incredibly, she had found the strength to put him down the mineshaft. Gradually the tears stopped and she gazed at Joe anxiously. Would he be horrified and shocked, would he think he should go to the police?

Joe got to his feet and strode to the window, looking out at the dark of the yard and the outline of the rowan tree, black against the paler sky. He was silent for a while and she desperately wanted to know what he was thinking but was afraid to ask.

'Karen, I'm so sorry, pet,' he said. 'It was me told you Dave was dead, wasn't it? Mind, what that rotten sod has to answer for, may he rot in hell!'

'Joe!' Even in her emotional state, Karen was shocked to hear him swear.

'Well, I'm right, aren't I? And the priest, how could he do that to you?'

'Patrick is a good man,' she said sharply.

'Oh, yes, I'm sure. So good that he deserted—'

'He did what he thought was right.'

'Yes, of course. How many times has that been used as an excuse for ruining people's lives, I wonder? Oh, Karen, why could you not have had Robert? Years ago I knew he loved you. He's a good honest man who still loves you too, you know he does.'

It was her turn to rise to her feet in agitation. 'I can't marry Robert, I'll only ruin his life, can't you see that, Joe? Now come on, let's forget about it all. Here you are, home from the other side of the world, we only have a short time together and you haven't said a word about how you are getting on.'

'I'm doing fine, never better. And we're not going to forget about it, I'm going to sort you out if it's the last thing I do! Good Lord, Karen, you're not going to let the past rule your life, are you? Anyone with half an eye could see how Robert feels about you, and after what I saw tonight, I believe you feel the same way about him. Put the

553

rest behind you, woman, show some sense!'

She gazed at him. All this time she had carried her woes around with her, a black burden deep inside of her. Ever since Patrick left, or before even. Grief had become a companion, a friend almost: she allowed her mind to probe for it, but it was different now. Oh, perhaps it would never leave her altogether but it had faded as her love for Patrick had faded, she realized. Joe was right and he had forced her to see it. And now there was a dawning hope, a feeling of release.

There was a footstep in the yard and the door opened. Luke came in and Karen watched as he greeted his uncle. She saw he was almost as tall as Joe and equally as strong. She had no reason to worry about the farm either, she thought. Luke was running it now, he had a right to it. He would bring Elsie here one day and the old holding would flourish again with a new family.

'I'll run you back to Morton Main tomorrow, Joe,' she said. 'I have to go anyway, I have to see a man about a job.'

'You mean—' he began, and grinned all over his face. 'There now, our Karen, now you're talking a bit of sense!'

*   *   *

The spring morning was crisp and fresh as Karen drove out of the yard and into the lane. Stopping the car, she got out and closed the gate for there were a couple of young pigs rooting about by the barn and a pet lamb cropping grass under the hedge. Karen stood for a moment, looking at the old farmstead. She was doing the right thing, oh

554

yes, she was. It was better by far to move away from the place, time for a new start.

The sun shone on the rowan tree, lighting up the new blossom, and she reached up and picked a spray and stuck it in her buttonhole before walking back to the car. 'You're not changing your mind, Sis?' asked Joe, and she shook her head as she slipped the car into gear and set off on the journey to Morton Main and Robert. Dropping Joe off at Kezia's front door, she went on to the surgery, her heart beating painfully as she entered the waiting room.

Fool! she told herself sternly, halting for a moment before knocking on Robert's door. After all, it was a job she was seeing him about today, that was all. She wasn't committing her whole life to him, was she? No, it was just a matter of her career, that was all. Perhaps he had changed his mind, perhaps he didn't want her any more. Perhaps—oh God, what was the matter with her? Resolutely she lifted her hand and tapped on the door and opened it without waiting for his 'Come in'.

Robert lifted his head from the case notes he was studying, smiling professionally as he did so. In that split second she saw how careworn he looked, the tiny lines between his brows and under his eyes. And then he saw it was Karen and his smile opened up into such a radiant welcome all her doubts were dissolved.

'Karen,' he said. 'It's you.' Rising to his feet he came round the desk and took her hands in his. And it was enough. It was true, she thought, there was plenty of time, there was all the time in the world for them.

Epilogue

The item was tucked away in the middle pages of the *Northern Echo*. Doctor Brian Richardson would have missed it altogether if the name Low Rigg Farm had not caught his eye as he glanced through the paper over breakfast.

'Skeleton found in old mineshaft', he read. 'Farmer Luke Nesbitt found more than he bargained for when he set out to search for his lost dog, a border terrier named Gyp. Somehow Gyp had survived a fall into the old shaft, a relic of lead-mining days, quite close to Mr Nesbitt's farm. The dog had fallen on what looked like a heap of old clothes but when Mr Nesbitt climbed down the shaft to bring up Gyp, he found a motor bike and the skeleton of a man. There was no indication of how the body got into the shaft. Police think he had been dead for forty years or more.'

Brian scratched his head, trying to think back forty years. They had been living on the farm then; it was before his mother had moved to work in Morton Main. He could only have been six or seven at the time. But he could remember some things though his memories were scrappy. He remembered Nick, how he and Jennie had loved him, dead now these twenty years. And he remembered a man who came on a motor bike, oh, he did, he had had nightmares about him. Even after the man stopped coming, every time he heard a motor bike he had been filled with fear for he knew his mother was afraid of that man. In fact, he remembered him better than he did his own father.

Rising to his feet, Brian moved over to the bay window of his house and looked out over the miners' rows of Morton Main. He tried to remember what his father had looked like but though he could picture him sitting in the rocking chair by the fire, he couldn't picture his face. He hadn't even thought about his father for years. The last time had been when he visited a patient in Weston and the powerful smell of whiskey on the man's breath brought back a dim image of Patrick Murphy.

'Morning.'

Brian turned from the window and smiled at his father, his true father, the man he had looked up to all his life. The man who, after he had married Brian's mother in 1930, had adopted Brian and his sister Jennie. The man who had helped him through Medical School and taken him into his practice afterwards, the man he would always love and revere.

'Good morning, Father,' he said. 'Come on in, there's fresh tea in the pot if you want a cup?'

'Thanks, I could use one,' said Robert. 'I've been for a walk. Just up to the cemetery, you know, and there's a chill wind up there. Winter's coming on, I suppose.'

Brian poured tea into the cup which was ready and waiting on the table. Robert dropped in most mornings since Karen had died last year. He was lonely since he'd retired and Jennie had married and gone to live in Yorkshire. And besides, he liked to discuss the practice with Brian, liked to keep abreast of what was happening in medicine today.

'Any news in the *Echo?* asked the older man as he sipped his tea.

'Nothing much,' said Brian. 'Now, Father, I've been meaning to have a word with you about John Fletcher's emphysema. It's not responding as it should and I'd like your opinion . . .'

The two doctors were soon in an animated discussion which went on until Helen, Brian's wife, came back from driving the children to school and reminded him it was time for surgery.

'You're coming tonight for dinner, don't forget,' said Brian as he rose from the table. Absently he picked up the paper and folded it and tucked it under his arm as he went out. Best not to upset the old man with a news item which might only bring back unhappy memories.